SAVING NOAH - DISCREET COVER

SHANDI BOYES

Edited by
MOUNTAINS WANTED PUBLISHING
Illustrated by
SSB DESIGNS

@ Shandi Boyes

No part of this book may be reproduced or transmitted in any form or by any means, electronic or mechanical, including photocopying, recording or by any information storage and retrieval system, without written permission from the author.

This is a work of fiction. Any names or characters, businesses or places, events or incidents, are fictitious. Any resemblance to actual persons, living or dead, or actual events is purely coincidental.

Editing: Mountains Wanted Publishing
Cover: SSB Designs
Photograph: Cadwallader Photography

On paper, Noah Taylor appears to have the perfect life: good looks, a gifted voice, and a multi-platinum record deal in the works.
In reality, expectations exceed actualities, and disappointments are constant.

Everyone he's ever cared about has left him, so what happens when he attracts a girl who sees through the shield others can't? He fights the pull; he tells himself no—but sometimes fate can't wake you from one nightmare without first trapping you in another.

With love on his side, can Noah survive the next devastating event in his life? Or will he discover no amount of dreaming will help him escape his reality?

You will laugh and you will cry, but the story of Noah Taylor will stay with you forever.

Saving Noah is a heart-clutching, ugly-cry rockstar romance that will break your heart before slowly piecing it back together. It is a standalone with no cliffhangers and a guaranteed HEA! Tissues are recommended.

Saving Noah was originally published as two books, Perception of Life and Reality of Life. They have been extensively re-written, re-edited and re-covered.

Saving Noah had me feeling EVERY emotion. A roller coaster ride of epic proportions full of ups and downs. Beautifully brutal!
   — Elizabeth W, Amazon Reviewer

I loved this story with all the laughter, ugly crying for a good half hour and the sweet resolution and coming together! The steamy scenes make you wish you were his Emily.
   — Anne Young Cronister, Amazon reviewer

Saving Noah was a riveting read touching on all the realities of grief including the pain and depression hidden by so many people when experiencing tragedy. The amazing strength of Noah and Emily's romance as it evolves and what they endure brings out so many emotions it is worth having a box of tissues as you embark on this emotional journey with them.
   — Mandy R, Amazon Reviewer.

Play List

- *Dancing On My Own* — Calum Scott
- *Like I'm Gonna Lose You* — Meghan Trainor & John Legend
- *Jar of Hearts* — Christina Perri
- *Little Did You Know* — Alex & Sierra
- *Lost Boy* — Ruth B
- *Always* — Bon Jovi
- *Under Your Scars* — Godsmack
- *I Can't Fall in Love Without You* — Zara Larsson
- *Angel* — Sarah McLachlan
- *Jealous* — Labrinth
- *Lips Of An Angel* — Hinder
- *You Are The Reason* — Calum Scott
- *Someone You Loved* — Lewis Capaldi

Dedication

My one and only,
our four little gentlemen,
and one little lady.

WANT TO STAY IN TOUCH?

Facebook: facebook.com/authorshandi

Instagram: instagram.com/authorshandi

Email: authorshandi@gmail.com

Reader's Group: bit.ly/ShandiBookBabes

Website: authorshandi.com

Newsletter: https://www.subscribepage.com/AuthorShandi

ALSO BY SHANDI BOYES

** Denotes Standalone Books*

<u>Perception Series</u>

<u>Saving Noah</u> *

<u>Fighting Jacob</u> *

<u>Taming Nick</u> *

<u>Redeeming Slater</u> *

<u>Saving Emily</u>

<u>Wrapped Up with Rise Up</u>

<u>Protecting Nicole</u> *

<u>Enigma</u>

<u>Enigma</u>

<u>Unraveling an Enigma</u>

<u>Enigma The Mystery Unmasked</u>

<u>Enigma: The Final Chapter</u>

<u>Beneath The Secrets</u>

<u>Beneath The Sheets</u>

<u>Spy Thy Neighbor</u> *

<u>The Opposite Effect</u> *

<u>I Married a Mob Boss</u> *

<u>Second Shot</u> *

<u>The Way We Are</u>

<u>The Way We Were</u>

<u>Sugar and Spice</u> *

Lady In Waiting

Man in Queue

Couple on Hold

Enigma: The Wedding

Silent Vigilante

Hushed Guardian

Quiet Protector

Enigma: An Isaac Retelling

Twisted Lies *

Bound Series

Chains

Links

Bound

Restrain

The Misfits *

Nanny Dispute *

Russian Mob Chronicles

Nikolai: A Mafia Prince Romance

Nikolai: Taking Back What's Mine

Nikolai: What's Left of Me

Nikolai: Mine to Protect

Asher: My Russian Revenge *

Nikolai: Through the Devil's Eyes

Trey *

The Italian Cartel

Dimitri

Roxanne

Reign

Mafia Ties (Novella)

Maddox

Demi

Ox

Rocco *

Clover *

Smith *

RomCom Standalones

Just Playin' *

Ain't Happenin' *

The Drop Zone *

Very Unlikely *

False Start *

Short Stories - Newsletter Downloads

Christmas Trio *

Falling For A Stranger *

One Night Only Series

Hotshot Boss *

Hotshot Neighbor *

The Bobrov Bratva Series

Wicked Intentions *

Sinful Intentions *

Devious Intentions *

Deadly Intentions *

<u>Coming Soon</u>

Protecting Nicole (November 23)

CHAPTER 1

NOAH

Do you believe in love at first sight? No, me either. If you knew my best friend Jacob, you'd understand why I'm skeptical. Sure, you could meet a girl you find cute, hot, or sexy as hell. You may even develop a severe case of lust, but love? Come on!

Despite my belief that insta-love doesn't exist, I'm being forced to endure Jacob's fifth love connection in the past six months.

No, you didn't hear me wrong.

In just the past six months, Jacob has thought he's been in love five times. Don't get me wrong, Jacob is a great guy—he's been my friend since the sixth grade and has been there for me in more ways than I deserve the past four years—but the instant the varnish fades on his shiny new relationships, he hits the brake and starts fucking running.

Being the third wheel tonight hasn't been too bad. Jacob's current love interest, Lola, is a waitress at Mavericks Bar. Mavs is a standard dime-a-dozen establishment that's seen better days. Mercifully, its rundown condition hasn't deterred the locals. It's a favorite of theirs almost every night of the week. If the guarantee of the coldest beverages in town doesn't entice them back, the live band its owner, Ollie, schedules each night will keep the cobwebs from spreading from its rusty wrought-iron ceiling to its cracked wooden barstools.

My group Rise Up recently scored the coveted Friday night spot after spending two years playing the dreaded Tuesday night schedule. Our gig doesn't pay well, but we're supplied with unlimited beer and are approved to perform two original songs a night.

My band has what it takes to make it big; we just need more exposure. If playing for peanuts at our local bar gives us that, then that's what we'll do. Once the right person hears our music, they'll sign us to a big, lucrative contract. It's that easy.

Unfortunately, it's taking a lot fucking longer than we initially thought.

My eyes lift from the hideous floral sofa I'm sitting on when Lola giggles. "Seriously, Jacob." She slaps him on the chest, her hit playful.

Even though he looks out of place in this cozy living room, things appear to be going well for Jacob tonight. He's the size of a bear—I don't mean the cuddly type. It's lucky he isn't hairy, or he would have been shot, gutted, and mounted in a hunter's gaming room by now.

His six-foot-five height is made out of pure muscle—muscle that requires him to sweat it out a minimum of three hours a day in the gym. Anything that takes that much effort isn't something I'd commit to; that's asking too much. I've never committed to anything long-term, except my band, and that isn't set to change anytime soon.

I divert my attention back to Lola so I can scan her curvy frame. She holds all the attributes required to spark an interest from Jacob. He's predictable when it comes to the girls he dates: Barbie dolls with large chests, pretty faces, and air for brains. Lola has honeycomb shoulder-length hair with a few curls in it. Her complexion is creamy and smooth, and she has a nice rack she clearly likes to display. Her Mavs shirt is so clingy, it looks as if she painted it on.

When my hooded gaze strays back to her face, I catch her murderous glare. She's snarling at me, unappreciative that I was ogling her breasts. I give her a cheeky wink. I've been busted, so there's no reason to deny it.

Lola shakes her head, praying it will hide the smile etching onto her mouth. It doesn't. She's as playful as the hand Jacob's trying to sneak up her skirt. Even sitting, Jacob towers over Lola. That's not hard. He has the height advantage in any relationship... unless he's dating a female Bigfoot. They're an attractive couple, but I've learned not to look too far ahead in any relationship Jacob gets caught up in because they never last long.

That's when I step in. I console his broken heart with a handful of beers and a couple of rounds in the boxing ring, then once he has recovered, he embarks on his next romantic endeavor. And thus begins the vicious cycle of Jacob's love life.

I stop inwardly chuckling when Jacob's thick drawl snags my attention. "We better head out. You ready?"

"Sure am."

I jump up, eager to stretch my weary legs. It's been a long night, and the free beer I guzzled down is catching up with me. "Once you break the seal, you can't stop it," was something my dad always said, but there's no way I'll make it the thirty miles home before the seal needs to be cracked, so I may as well crack it now.

"Is it okay if I hit the can before we leave?"

My question steals Lola's attention away from Jacob, who's no longer sneaking a hand up her skirt. He's somehow managed to get Lola straddling his lap without the chair collapsing in a heap beneath them.

"Sure, it's down the hall on the left," Lola replies in between kissing Jacob.

Gagging, I head for the hall, preparing my eyes for the burn of soap. A hearty scrub may be the only way I can remove the image of them dry humping from my memory bank.

Lola's girly giggle jingles in my ears when I enter the hallway. It's the quintessential hallway every middle class family in America has. It's done in a two-tone effect with fancy wood paneling at the bottom and floral wallpaper on the top.

I stop to gawk at some photos halfway down. The pictures reveal Lola has three siblings: two brothers and a sister. Next to the random family snaps is a large family portrait proudly displayed in a gold-leaf frame. This photo appears to have been professionally taken. Everyone is wearing matching outfits, with Lola sitting in the middle. If I had to guess her age, I'd say she's just shy of her teen years.

Even with a mouthful of metal, her smile beams out of her. Tiny freckles adorn her pointed-up nose, and her sun-bleached hair is a shade lighter than its current color. Although she looks different now than she did in this photo, no matter how hard she tried—*and I'm reasonably sure she'd try*—she could never deny it's her.

After suppressing my laughter with a quick swallow, I appraise the portrait with more diligence. Sitting next to Lola is a girl a few years younger. She has the same sun-lightened hair, but her skin isn't creamy like Lola's. She has an enticing olive complexion. Both girl's locks are styled similarly: long, straight bobs with bangs teased up high.

I want to say that's the worst of the travesty.

Unfortunately, it isn't.

Lola's brothers' blond locks are spiked so high they look like they stuck their fingers in a light socket. The portrait screams 90s rock and roll with the four children wearing matching pinstriped overalls.

No longer capable of containing my laughter, my chuckle echoes down the hall. I feel its shudder down my arm when my hand delves into my pocket to yank out my phone. I want proof of my newly discovered treasure so I can tease Jacob about it later tonight. He thought he hit the jackpot with Lola. This photo may change his mind.

My hand freezes halfway out my pocket when a singsong voice questions, "Is there something funny about my family?"

Busted—again!

While turning to face the voice, I strive to wipe the amused expression off my face. My jaw drops when my gaze meets a pair of stunning brown eyes staring at me. The young beauty's exotic eyes are complemented by the same upturned nose Lola has, but her lips are fuller and plumper. Unlike Lola's creamy complexion, this brunette has flawless olive skin. She's petite, but the Red Devils football jersey she's wearing as a dress reveals she has curves in all the right places.

When she notices me drinking in her long, tanned legs, she crosses them before giving me a curious smirk. I reward her unsure smile with a frisky wink. She doesn't respond to my tease as Lola did. She's not frightened, more curious than anything.

After closing the gap between us, I offer her my hand to shake. "Noah."

She snubs my gesture, but it does little to dampen the excitement zapping down my spine. Although she's acting unaffected by my presence, her dazzling eyes give away her true feelings. She likes what she sees just as much as I do.

She seems a couple of years younger than Lola and much more timid, but she's the first girl in a long time to spark an interest out of me, and no, I don't just mean for a one-night stand.

Ignoring the awkwardness thickening the air, I attempt to ignite a conversation. "I was looking for the bathroom?"

When she glances past my shoulder, I drink in the rest of her features. Her long, shiny locks sit just above the small of her back, and her face is radiant and fresh even without an ounce of makeup. It's unusual to meet a girl without a face full of makeup these days, but when you have natural beauty like this girl does, why cover it up with chemical-filled enhancements?

Her high cheekbones grow even more alluring when a hue of pink creeps across them. I'm about to ask what has caused her roused expression, but her question takes care of my inquisitiveness. "Are you Lola's current squeeze?"

"No," I emphasize with a chuckle.

Lola is beautiful, but she isn't my type. If I had a type, she'd have long brunette hair and pouty lips on a beautiful makeup-free face.

"I'm here with my friend Jacob; he's dropping Lola home from work."

After her eyes float up from the floor, I gaze into them. I don't know what she sees reflecting back at her, but her lips part and her cheekbones rise before a breathtakingly beautiful smile morphs onto her face.

Holy shit-cakes!

I thought this girl was beautiful, but she just turned into an absolute stunner. I don't know whether she needed braces like Lola, but she has perfectly straight teeth, and when she smiles, her eyes shine like diamonds.

As the heat bouncing between us triples, she points to the door opposite her room. With how dense the sexual chemistry is electrifying the air, I expect her to say something more profound than she does. "It's the door on the right."

Confused, I crank my neck in the direction she's pointing. There's a brass sign of a boy peeing into a tin cup tacked to the partially opened door. Just behind the door is a porcelain toilet.

I inwardly chuckle when reality dawns. She's giving me directions to the bathroom, not her bedroom as my perverted mine was hoping.

Happy to end our conversation before I showcase more of my stupidity, I nudge up my chin in thanks before pivoting on my heels. My steps to the bathroom halt mid-stride when she whispers, "I'm Emily. It was a pleasure to meet you, Noah."

She steals my chance to reply, "The pleasure was all mine," by slipping behind her rapidly closing door.

I stare at the white-washed wood for several long minutes, intrigued as to why such a beautiful girl would be so shy. She's comfortable enough in her own skin to approach a stranger in her home at an ungodly hour, but not confident enough to act on the attraction bristling between us.

I stop analyzing when Jacob's deep rumble roars down the hallway. "Ready?"

"Yeah, man, just a minute."

I run into the bathroom, do my business, wash my hands, then jog back out to the small living room, only sneaking the quickest glance at Emily's door on my way by.

When I enter the living room, Lola's massively dilated eyes lock with mine. "Did you find the bathroom okay?"

I nod, put off by the hope in her tone. "Yeah, thanks."

My eyes drift between Jacob and Lola when they gawk at me curiously. I'm confident the sneaky little shits are up to something, but I'm at a loss as to what.

Realizing I'll never get anything out of Jacob when his head is in a lust cloud, I leave the lovebirds to say their goodbyes in private. I make my way outside to have a smoke, hoping a hit of nicotine will stop my thoughts from straying to Lola's sexy-as-sin sister, Emily. I doubt anything will remove her sparkling eyes, beautiful face, and killer long legs from my mind, but I'm willing to give it a shot.

I've got record deals to chase, wannabee groupies to fuck. I don't have time for a relationship—not even a platonic one. Whether filled with sexual tension like my brief encounter with Emily or a friendship with no steam whatsoever, trust me when I say, shacking up with me is asking for trouble. I hated dragging Jacob into my pathetic life, so I'd never let someone as uncorrupted as Emily in without ensuring she knows what she's signing up for.

Considering I never talk about the circumstances that led to me being homeless at the tender age of fourteen, I doubt that conversation will take place anytime in the near future.

I hope one day to move past my grief, but I don't see today being that day.

CHAPTER 2

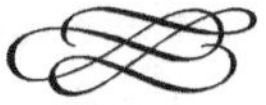

EMILY

"Lola, have you seen my boots?"

I've searched under my bed, in my closet, and next to my desk, but I've yet to locate my favorite boots.

"Here." Lola, my annoyingly frustrating big sis, throws my boots at me from the doorway of my room, narrowly missing my head. From the way she's smirking, I'm reasonably sure she was aiming.

Lola is three years older than me. Although we look similar, we couldn't be more different if we tried. Even when she was my age, she dressed more seductively and was never seen in public without her makeup perfectly in place. I love my sister, but we have very opposite personalities. I'm sure she wants to strangle me as much as I'd like to bury her in the backyard with her beloved cat, Misty, who passed away three years ago.

Most of our love-hate relationship stems from our mom treating us more like twins than sisters. She even dressed us in matching outfits when we were kids, which was utterly ridiculous considering our gap in age.

That was put to rest when Lola and I rebelled like all teenage girls do at one stage during adolescence. Now we're on opposite ends of the spectrum when it comes to fashion... and pretty much anything we can argue about. As I said, I love my sister, but more times than not, I've dreamed about waking up to discover I'm an only child.

I'm the youngest of four, which earns me the dreaded disgrace of being the "baby" of the family. Even being in my final year of high school hasn't stopped my brothers, Aiden and Dominic, from treating me as if I'm ten. When I step back and look at the entire picture, it's comical their protection is finally being offered now. It's two years too late as far as I'm concerned.

Loathing that I'm letting my past spoil my mood, I slip my sock-covered feet into my boots before spinning around to face Lola. My heart beats faster when I catch her disappointing glare. It's so fiery, it burns a hole in my forehead.

"What?"

Her eye roll looks more sophisticated than a twenty-one-year-old should be able to pull off. "Are you seriously wearing that?"

I peer down at my shiny black boots, my super comfortable light blue boyfriend jeans, and my fitted red sweater. Well, it's supposed to be fitted, but since my clothes are handed down from Lola, it's a little loose in *some* regions. Lola and I have similar body shapes, but she's more blessed in the chest department than me.

"What's wrong with what I'm wearing?" I struggle not to return her eye roll. It's a torturous feat. "It's freezing outside, and you're *only* going for a driving lesson, so why do I have to dress up?" My snappy remark has me taking a mental note to check my calendar. I think the Wicked Witch may be visiting soon.

Huffing, Lola saunters to my closet to scan my scarce collection of clothes. While she searches for a *Lola-approved* outfit she'll never find, I drink in her casual, yet sexy ensemble. Her pink fringed denim shorts barely cover her backside, but her black laced shirt and cropped suede jacket add an edge of elegance to her outfit. She's gone all out with her makeup—which isn't unusual. She'd never be caught dead with my regime that consists only of mascara and lip gloss. I won't lie; even though she drives me crazy more times than not, she's a sexpot who knows how to work her assets to her advantage.

When a disgruntled groan sounds from my closet, I flop onto my bed. "Why don't I just stay here? I don't feel like going out anyway."

The fact Lola wants me to hang out with her already has my suspicions piqued. We never do anything together, but for some reason, today she begged me to go out with her. You see, upon hearing my beautiful, talented sister failed her last three driving tests, Jacob, Lola's current squeeze, offered to give her lessons.

Jacob's proposal wasn't made lightheartedly. He had *many* stipulations attached to his offer. The most vital: her lessons take place on the abandoned forestry roads near his house, which is over an hour drive from here.

Lola tosses a pair of skinny jeans I had hidden in the back of my closet next to me. "I need you to back me up, Em. What if Jacob is a weirdo who wants to take advantage of me in the scary dark forest?"

Her eccentric voice makes me smile. She's not the least bit scared. That's not surprising considering she's the toughest girl I know. "As if you wouldn't like that, Lola."

Under my sister's watchful eye, I shimmy out of my favorite boyfriend jeans before squeezing into ones that hug my ass so profoundly, I look like I spray-painted them on.

Spotting my disapproving glare, Lola slants her head to the side, wordlessly daring me to argue with her selection.

"What?" I feign ignorance with a shrug. "I didn't say anything."

She tugs on my low-hanging ponytail before sauntering to my door. "Let's go before I change my mind and keep him for myself."

Even though I'm happy for her to keep Jacob to herself—I don't mind having her hand-me-downs when they're clothes, but that will never extend to men—my interests are too piqued to back out now.

After fixing the mess Lola made to my hair, I snag my purse off my blanket chest then hightail it after her. Her speed is so fast, I have to jog to catch up with her. With years of track under my belt, I could easily catch her, but a portrait hanging halfway down the hall slows my pace.

It's been a little over four weeks since I stumbled upon the hottest man I've ever laid my eyes on. I've never believed in fate, but my almost cringeworthy meeting with Noah makes me less skeptical.

I wasn't supposed to be home that night. My best friends, Jenni and Nicole, begged me to go with them to Tommy's party, but it was the only night left for me to study before spending the next two days busting my butt at Dan's Grocery Store, so a cram session pulled rank on a night out dancing.

I love nothing more than letting go of the strings for a night, but since my parents can't afford to send me to college, I need to maintain good grades so I can score a lucrative scholarship. I had squeezed in a solid four hours of study before I heard Lola arrive home from her first shift at Mavericks. Eager to hear how she did, I abandoned the books for a real-life interaction. I was halfway to my door when I heard Lola giggle. It wasn't her standard girly laugh. It was the one she uses when she has "company."

That took care of any inquisitiveness on my behalf.

With Lola busy, I ditched my textbooks for my pillow. I had worked a five-hour shift after school before exhausting myself even more with a four-hour study session, so my eyelids were feeling heavy. I had considered putting on pants when my bladder niggled, protesting the cans of diet coke I guzzled down to stay awake, but the noises bellowing out of the living room convinced my fried brain that I could make it to the bathroom and back unnoticed.

Bad move.

The last thing I anticipated when opening my bedroom door was the man I assumed was Lola's date. He was laughing at my family portrait—the same hideous portrait I beg my mom to take down daily. He wore a black leather jacket and snug jeans with a chain going from his belt to his back pocket. His legs were long and lean, rising from motorcycle boots, and his dark hair was short at the back and sides.

The longer I watched him, the more my curiosity flourished. He didn't seem like the type Lola usually went for. Her tastes lean more toward school jocks and preppy college boys, but he didn't appear to play a team sport. My stalking meant I couldn't see his face, but his outfit screamed bad-boy, and the only game they play is one that doesn't require a uniform.

When he moved without warning, I jumped in fright. He startled me so much, I bumped my bedroom door, causing it to let out a creak. Not wanting to be busted ogling him like the perverted geek I was, I said the first thing that popped into my head: "Is there something funny about my family?"

I cringed. I was never good at thinking on the spot, and that was a real doozy. Mortified he was caught mocking my hideous family portrait, he stopped chuckling before spinning around to offer me an apology.

I swear to God, I nearly fainted when my eyes landed on his face. He was by far the sexiest man I'd ever seen. His hair was longer on top and styled with messy, *wanna run my fingers through it* spikes. He had chiseled cheekbones, fleshy lips, and gorgeous clear, tanned skin. The gray fitted t-shirt he wore under his jacket revealed an outline of a tattoo, and the parts of his shoulders I could see were bulging with veins.

He was so hot, my skin set on fire. After a disastrous first and *only* date, it's rare for a guy to spark an interest out of me, but he was sparking so much interest, I thought I might soon combust. My dangerously high body temperature only regulated when I mistakenly took him as being my sister's date. Lola may drive me crazy, but I'd never step on her turf like that. I've already handled more than my share of nasty, unfounded rumors, so the last thing I'd ever encourage is a relationship that would turn gossip into reality.

Thank god Noah was quick to set me straight, but not before I had already made a total bitch of myself. I was certain my less-than-stellar introduction would have had him running for the hills, so you can imagine my shock when that same night, hours into me tossing and turning while struggling not to think about his tormented and sad eyes, I received a text message from an unknown number.

The message was as cryptic as its sender's heated gaze.

Never let fear decide your fate. It's inevitable no matter how much it scares you... Noah.

We've exchanged a handful of texts since then. They're only brief, but enough for me to confidently declare Noah isn't a guy I'll ever tame, but I sure could have a lot of fun trying.

I'm still smiling about the flirty message he sent late last night when I enter the living room in just enough time to witness Lola kissing our mom goodbye. She hugs her fiercely before nudging her head to a white car parked in our driveway. "I'll meet you outside."

Nodding, I pace to our mom to replace Lola's arms with my own. I press my glossy lips to her cheek before wrapping her up in a warm hug. With my mom being a few inches shorter than me, her wavy almost-black hair tickles my nose when I draw her into my chest.

I melt when she returns my hug with an equal amount of love. "Be careful, Emily, and try to get Lola back here in one piece."

Pain strikes my chest. She's tired, which is expected since she just finished a double shift, but I'm worried about the hesitance in her voice. I hope she isn't about to have another turn. The last few years have been tough on my mom, but she usually does a better job of hiding it from her children.

"I will, Mom. Love you."

I give her a final squeeze before heading for the door. The quicker Lola and I leave, the faster we'll return, which means our mom will rest. She doesn't sleep until all her children still under her roof are tucked safely in their beds.

My brisk speed down the sidewalk slows when I spot Jacob and Lola making out like teens on their way home from the prom. For two "friends," they seem very familiar with one another.

When they fail to notice I've slipped into the backseat, I slam the door with force, hoping it will announce my arrival. It works. After a final nibble of Lola's kiss-swollen mouth, Jacob cranks his neck to peer at me. My already arched lips curl higher when Lola's expression ruffles from losing his utmost devotion.

"Hey, Em." Jacob greets me with a broad grin, drawing my focus to him. "You ready for this?"

Feeding off the mirth in his tone, I screw up my nose and stick out my tongue. "As ready as I'll ever be."

He throws his head back and laughs. His chuckle is so robust, it could vibrate my heart right out of my chest. Jacob is the size of a giant—the biggest guy I've ever seen—but his laugh gives away his true self. He has a gentle soul.

By the time we make it to the forest, I'm thanking God seat belts were invented. I thought the only time I'd be in fear for my life tonight was when Lola took over the reins. Now I'm petrified. Lola is being taught how to drive by a lunatic. Jacob never goes under sixty, not even in town; he rarely slows down to go around corners, and he finds it entertaining when his car fishtails out of control.

It's not my time yet; it's not my time yet, I chant to myself on repeat, saying anything to calm the nerves dancing in my stomach.

Panic scorches my veins when Lola swaps positions with Jacob. A professional mask slips over her face as she completes the necessary checks of the mirrors before adjusting her seat, but no amount of preparation prevents the bunny hops we do when she floors the gas before releasing the clutch.

"Ease off the clutch more steadily next time, Lola. You're doing great."

Jacob's smile when he praises Lola matches his impressive physique. His bottom teeth are slightly crooked, but with his overbite, you don't notice unless you look at his mouth closely. His blond hair is clipped close at the sides, but the top has more length to it. His intense light blue eyes are the color of the ocean, and his nose is slightly crooked, making me wonder if he's broken it before? He's wearing a blue long-sleeve t-shirt over cream-colored cargo pants.

He's different than Lola's other dates, but I like him, and I hope things work out this time around.

Lola needs a guy like Jacob on her side.

For the next hour, Jacob continues encouraging Lola. He's a great teacher who has nurtured his student so well, we traveled beyond the edge of the forest over twenty minutes ago. Although I'm appreciative of Jacob's dedication, I don't think we should test out Lola's developing skills on the poor, unsuspecting motorists in the town we're approaching.

"Do you think this is a good idea, Lola? This doesn't look like a farming town."

Lola waits for a truck to roar past us before seeking my gaze in the rearview mirror. "It's nearly midnight; what's the worst that could happen?"

Ignoring the hairs on my nape prickling with worry, I sink into my seat, certain something mammoth is about to happen, but having no clue exactly how immense it will be.

CHAPTER 3

NOAH

My teeth grind when Nick, the lead guitarist of my band, asks what time it is for the seventh time the past half-hour.

"Five minutes since you last asked."

I throw my empty cigarette packet at his head, smirking when it hits its mark just above his blond brow. We probably look a little suspicious being parked under the darkness of a railway bridge near midnight, but it's a Tuesday, and we've got nothing better to do, so we may as well help Jacob with his favorite prank.

We've been sitting in Nick's black beast the past forty-five minutes waiting for Jacob to drive past. He's taking Lola for a driving lesson on the abandoned forestry roads. With this being his only way home, we decided to have some fun. It's all about the adrenaline. It gets the girls' hearts pumping while making Jacob look like a knight in shining armor.

We've done this prank a handful of times the past twelve months. Jacob swears it works every single time. He plays it cool, acting like he's so brave, then once he saves the panicked heroine from the baddies in the naughty black truck, his gallantry gets rewarded in some way—more times than not, in a sexual manner.

Jacob swears on his mother's grave that the very minimum he gets from this prank is a blowjob on the drive home. Although pleased Lola is still sparking an interest from Jacob, I'm bored out of my fucking mind. I'm also out of smokes, so if Jacob doesn't arrive within the next five minutes, he'll have to bring out the charm to get into Lola's pants tonight.

When another ten minutes pass with no sign from Jacob, I tell Nick to head off. It may only be a Tuesday night, but there are more entertaining things we could be doing than loitering under an old railroad bridge. My phone feels heavy in my pocket just at the thought of how I could occupy my time.

If you had told me four weeks ago I'd rather spend my night off with my phone instead of my bandmates, I would have said you were crazy. Now I'm always on the lookout for an excuse to get away from the boys and their prying eyes.

I did everything in my power to stay away from Emily, but no amount of alcohol made me forget her number was saved in my phone.

Drunk dialing never ends well. Thank fuck the same can't be said for drunk messaging.

Our messages are as innocent as Emily's face, but they do wonders for a broken soul on lonely and dark nights. I don't intend to take it further than the playfulness we have going on now. I shouldn't even be doing what I'm doing, but there's something about that girl that has me acting differently. Don't ask me if it is a good or bad recklessness because I wouldn't be able to give you an honest answer. I'm still me, just closer to someone I wish I could be.

Just as Nick fires up his truck, Jacob's car pulls around the sharp corner of the railway bridge, arriving for the show with only a second to spare. Flashing a big beaming smile, I bang my hand on the truck's roof, giving Nick the signal to chase Jacob down. We're here, so we may as well accomplish what we set out to achieve.

You'd think with how many times we've performed this stunt, the excitement would wear off. It hasn't. Not in the slightest. I'm buzzing with more energy tonight than I've ever had. It's a weird sensation that's unexplainable but undeniably heart-thumping.

Nick's truck is a big beast, but she's quick off the mark. It doesn't take us long to catch up to Jacob's car, and once we do, Nick's high beams light it up like a motherfucking Christmas tree.

Nick nudges his head to Jacob's car that's sitting a mere inch or two from his chrome grill. "Who's that?"

My heart does an elongated beat when my eyes lock in on a person sitting in the backseat. From her petite frame, I can easily perceive she's female, but with her hand covering her face, I can't see any of her features.

"No clue. Maybe a friend of Lola's?" Usually, there are only two people in the car when we pull this prank. "Jacob will cash in double the benefits tonight."

Grinning at the mirth in my tone, Nick inches his black beast to within sniffing distance of Jacob's bumper. Assuming we want to overtake, the passenger in the back waves her arm through the air, indicating that we're clear of oncoming traffic.

Nick thanks her cordial nature by revving his engine. Its vibrations rumble through my seat as efficiently as my heart thrums against my ribcage when the passenger in the back moves her hand far enough from her face, I can see who she is.

"Oh shit, that's Emily: Lola's little sister."

Nick's eyes snap to mine. "Sisters? Damn! Why does Jacob get to have all the fun?"

Jacob's car veering off the road stuffs my reply down my throat. He kicks up some dust, but not enough for Nick to back off. His truck is so close to Jacob's bumper, one wrong move and his grill will burn through Emily's seat.

"Fuck, Nick, slow the hell down."

"Come on, man, you know Jacob loves this shit. He's swerving the car on purpose to increase the adrenaline rush." Nick floors the gas while idling his clutch. "You do know an adrenaline rush can be as good as an orgasm for some girls."

I grit my teeth, struggling not to wipe the pretentious look off his face with my fists. I would if he didn't divert my attention back to Emily. "She's got spunk."

A smile overtakes the grim expression crossing my face when I spot Emily flipping us the bird. I'm shocked she has the gall. Seeing her brave enough to give us the finger while we're trying to scare the shit out of her makes me wonder if she's as shy as first perceived. Just the thought of exploring her naughty side has my cock turning to stone.

"Jacob will have fun with her."

Nick's comment wipes the smile off my face and softens my cock.

I punch him in the arm—hard! When he rubs the area, feigning injury, I hit him for the second time. The amusement on his face changes to anger, but before he can retort, a much more dangerous situation unfolds.

Jacob's car jerks to the right at full speed, causing his tires to lose traction in the gravel. He maintains control... until he attempts to compensate for his error. His brutal second yank sends his car spinning out of control.

The stench of burning rubber overtakes the dust his car is kicking up when Nick locks up his brakes. "Oh shit."

Our speed is so excessive, we come to a stop a quarter mile from where Jacob's car is spinning like a ballerina. I watch the scene transpire in complete silence. Nothing I can do will stop their twirls; I'm just praying they don't flip. If that happens, Lola's virtue won't be the only thing skating on thin ice tonight.

The more Jacob's car spins, the thicker my blood becomes. I trust that Jacob has this—he drives like a maniac, but he's been behind the wheel since he was ten, so he knows what he's doing—he just needs to keep a cool head.

It feels like the moon circles the sun a hundred times before Jacob's car finally comes to a stop. A dense dust cloud covers it, but miraculously, it's still in one piece.

Thank fuck.

Seeing things the same way as me, Nick returns my jab to the arm. "Jacob is one lucky fucker." He continues with our ruse by flattening his foot to the floor. We take off down the road at a record-setting pace, adding to the dust cloud Jacob's car made.

I'm so stunned by the turn of events, I sit in silence the first few minutes of our trip. I've never seen Jacob take the prank this far before. I get he wants to impress Lola, but I'd prefer he didn't shave years off my life while doing it. I don't know what the fuck he was thinking risking the girls' lives like that, but I do know one thing: I'm not fucking happy.

The rumors about fear thickening your veins with adrenaline are true. My heart is thumping a million miles an hour, and every inch of me is covered with a misting of sweat. I've never felt more alive and more panicked in my life.

When we arrive at a T intersection, Nick indicates to turn left. With my veins still clogged with adrenaline-thick worry, the last place I want to go is anywhere with Nick. That's just asking for trouble. He's not called "One Hit" for no reason.

I sling my eyes to Nick, talking before my adrenaline high wears off. "Can you take me back to Jacob's?"

Nick glares at me like I'm a sex freak who's about to get his rocks off watching his best friend have a threesome... or worse, get his sloppy seconds.

With clenched fists, I return his glare. He shouldn't be giving anyone relationship advice. His ideas about relationships are more fucked up than mine.

Incapable of standing my wrath a second longer, he slams his foot onto the accelerator, fishtailing his car to the right. "Whatever, man, it's your funeral."

CHAPTER 4

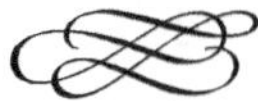

EMILY

While my lungs kick up a stink about the ghastly air they're being forced to suck in, I lower my hands from the roof of Jacob's car to clutch my chest. My heart is raging so fast, I'm shocked it hasn't escaped my chest cavity. We were just run off the road by a lunatic. Well, not technically. Lola's inexperience is partially to blame for our near-death experience, but if we weren't aggressively taunted by two deranged men in a large truck, she wouldn't have pulled into a closed gas station at a speed too fast to be classified as safe.

When my eyes pop open, I gasp in a mangled breath. We're still upright. I have no idea how. From the amount of dust that surrounded us when we spun out of control, I was confident we were cartwheeling. Lola did incredibly well to maintain control. That would have been difficult for an experienced driver, much less someone learning how to drive.

The nerves I'm only just settling flare up again when Jacob roars, "Oh my fucking god!" He pounds the dashboard with his fist, his strength undeniable when he dents the stiff material. "How could they not realize it wasn't me in the driver's seat?!"

I'm impressed by his stamina; he appears more than capable of defending us. Lola is on the other end of the spectrum. She's cowered against the driver's side door, her pupils wide with fear as she stares at Jacob as if he's a monster.

The anxiety hampering her face remains until Jacob throws open his door and darts out of the car. He's not hunting down the culprits responsible for running us off the road—their taillights were the first thing I spotted when the dust settled—he's merely seeking space to throw his fists in the air while biting out a string of obscenities.

While Jacob handles the massive boost of adrenaline lining his veins in a very male fashion, I use a more feminine approach. With a raging heart and sweaty palms, I shift my eyes to Lola. Unease grips my heart when I notice her glossy cheeks. She's crying. I haven't seen her this upset since Misty passed away from old age.

I'm just about to comfort her, but she beats me onto the soapbox. "Are you okay, Em?" Her voice is as rigid as her hands still clutching the steering wheel. "I'm so sorry; I had no idea this would happen."

"I'm fine." I sigh, more concerned about her odd behavior than our near-death experience. She also has no reason to apologize. What happened wasn't her fault, so she shouldn't be taking the blame for it. "It's not like you knew a maniac would be on the loose tonight."

With my nerves still on edge, I lock the car doors. Just because the truck left in a hurry doesn't mean they won't come back to finish the job. I've only just flopped back into my seat when three quick taps hit the driver's side window. Lola and I scream in sync, our frightened squeal loud enough two towns over could hear us.

"Holy shit, Jacob, you scared the crap out of me." Lola cradles her thrusting chest with one hand while the other clears away her tears. She hates crying in general, let alone having the rare occasion witnessed by a man she's interested in.

Jacob does a good job pretending he can't see Lola's tears, but the rattle of his words gives away his true composure. "Sorry. I thought perhaps you'd like to swap places so I can drive?"

"Good idea." Lola bounds out of the driver's seat to plop into the passenger side with a huff. "I need a drink, though. Isn't your home close to here?"

A smile tugs on my mouth when Jacob struggles to repress his. "So it is, Lola; so it is. How about we go back there for a drink?"

Although he's asking a question, he doesn't wait for Lola or me to reply before latching his belt and starting our trip. Our near-fatal accident must have scared him because he drives more responsibly this time around. He keeps well below the speed limit and takes the corners as suggested by the designated signage. He even parks between the lines when he stops at a twenty-four-seven convenience store to grab a few items.

I spend our drive with my forehead braced on the cool window, staring out at the star-filled sky. We've been traveling for over thirty minutes, yet I'm still struggling to get my heart rate back to a safe level.

Any chance of achieving a regular pattern is lost when Jacob glides his car down a wide dirt path. An impressive brick farmhouse with wrap-around porches sits at the end of the long driveway. Its brick and wooden frame is surrounded by manly hedges and rolled turf that stretches as far as my eyes can see.

The traffic that usually keeps me awake at night is nothing but a memory when Jacob shuts down his noisy engine near the front steps. It's eerily quiet but in a serene, calming way. The architectural wonder of his country estate is pushed to the background of my mind when an even more spectacular sight enters my vision. Noah has his shoulder propped up on the front door. He's wearing black satin boxer shorts and a confused expression.

No, I didn't miss anything. That's *all* he's wearing. Boxer. Shorts.

His body is... I'm speechless. There's no possible way to describe what I'm seeing adequately. He's wet, yet angry. Sexy, yet angry. Hot...did I mention angry?

I'm saved from going to hell for my wicked thoughts when Jacob's deep timbre breaks through the lust cloud hazing me. "Can you give me a minute to talk to Noah in private before joining us?"

"Sure." Although Lola is quick to agree to his request, she sounds peeved.

Still speechless by the awe-inspiring visual of a half-naked Noah, I nod.

After silently pleading for me to work on my sister's attitude while he's gone, Jacob throws open his driver's side door, curls out of his car, then hotfoots it to Noah.

With her attention rapt on Jacob, Lola finally notices Noah when Jacob stops to stand in front of him. "Damn..."

I still haven't regained the ability to talk, but even if I had, I'd still be at a loss on how to describe what I'm seeing. Noah's leather jacket and grungy jeans were hiding a masterpiece of a body the night we met. Tonight, his athletic build is on full display. His thick biceps have bulging veins entangled around them, and his left pectoral muscle has a Celtic tattoo covering a majority of it. It appears to have two names woven around it. His six-pack— *or is it an eight-pack, it's hard to see from a distance?* —features a thin trail of hair that's in direct symmetry to his mouthwatering V muscle, and the low hang of his satiny shorts is so scandalous it should be illegal.

An urge to smack Lola into next week hits me when she moans, "Mmm, nice and wet."

Instead, I slap her shoulder. Noah is glistening in the moonlight as if he's just showered, but she needs to keep her eyes on Jacob's assets —not a man I haven't stopped thinking about whether asleep or awake.

Loving that she has me worked up, Lola continues to tease me, "What? He's hot."

"Don't go acting like that tree trunk you're dating is made out of marshmallow." I jerk my head to Jacob, happy to give as much sass as I'm getting.

Lola's manicured brow gets lost in her hair. "One, we're not dating." She gags on her last word. "Two, Jacob has more muscles in his pinky than you have in your entire body."

I slap her again—a little harder this time. I've always been on the slender side, but what I lack in the boob department, I make up for with ass.

The unusual playfulness fueling our exchange is doused when

raised voices sound through the quiet night. "You could have killed them!"

My pulse quickens when my eyes lock in on Noah and Jacob going toe to toe. They've yet to exchange blows, but their thrusting chests connect with every snapped word they shout. I don't see it being long before this escalates from a verbal altercation to physical.

"That's all part of the game, isn't it, Jacob?" Noah's voice is as loud as Jacob's, his anger just as palpable. "Get them so rushed up on excitement, they'll come back here for some more *entertainment?*"

Jacob balks, physically stunned by Noah's reply. He's not the only one shocked. Who the hell are they arguing about? I could be wrong, but my spikes are hackling.

"Get them excited? You scared them to death."

When Jacob's eyes drift to his car, a spasm hits Noah's jaw. Even from a distance, its pulse is undeniable. They continue exchanging words, but since they've noticed mine and Lola's watchful gazes, they lower their volume a few decibels. Noah does most of the talking, but Jacob's anger is evident even without words. His fists are balled at his side, and he looks prepared to attack at any moment. Although he's a good few inches taller than Noah and several inches wider, Noah isn't the least bit intimidated by him. The way he holds himself with confidence would be more impressive in a less hostile environment.

When the aggression in their exchange dulls down, my eyes drift to Lola. "What do you think that was about?"

She's known Noah and Jacob longer than me, so she'd know if this is a regular occurrence for them. I thought they were close friends, but right now, neither appears very impressed with the other.

Lola's lips quirk like she's genuinely unsure. "How about we find out?"

When she curls out of her seat, I mimic her movements. I don't shadow her down the wide sidewalk, though. I prop my backside on the back quarter panel of Jacob's car, happy to watch the scene unfold from afar. It isn't that I'm scared about two large, brooding men going to war; I just don't want to intrude.

Yeah, right.

I'm being the coward who once again lets everyone else take up her fight instead of facing the problem head-on. That's what I did when I found out it isn't just frogs who turn into princes when kissed. Sometimes it's the other way around. Princes turn into frogs more times than not.

Realizing this situation is different than the one I found myself in two years ago, I push off my feet to back Lola up. My determination gets squashed not even two seconds later. Noah is staring at me. It isn't the same intense stare he gave me in the hallway of my home weeks ago. It's brimming more with anger than lust.

Hoping to ease his agitation, I smile at him. He doesn't smile back. Instead, he angrily shakes his head before rushing into the house, slamming the door behind him.

CHAPTER 5

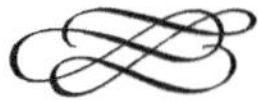

NOAH

I stop tuning my piece of shit guitar when someone knocks on my bedroom door. Raising my eyes, I spot Jacob standing in the doorway. He's casually dressed, but his lips are hard-lined, and his brows are furrowed. He seems hesitant, as if he's unsure if he's welcome in my home. I understand his unease. Things have been tense since our argument a couple of weeks ago. Although it was fueled by a misunderstanding—Jacob assumed Nick and I had left when he failed to arrive at the time we had discussed—it was the most brutal we've had.

I did everything to weaken the adrenaline coursing through my body that night. I paced for over twenty minutes before taking a bitterly cold shower. Nothing worked. So you can imagine my annoy-ance when Jacob arrived home with guns blazing. He was ropeable his prank backfired, but instead of accepting some of the blame, he tried to lump it all on my shoulders. I wasn't having any of it—hence our disagreement.

If that wasn't enough to leave a bad taste in my mouth, after returning home from dropping off the girls, Jacob revealed Lola was driving when his car veered off the road. His confession utterly blind-sided me, and it made me do something I hadn't done in a long time. I ran straight toward the demon who's held my emotions hostage the past six years.

I went home.

The haunting silence of my childhood home is a brutal reminder of why my brother Chris left, but like a ray of sunshine on a stormy day, some good came from my rare visit. I realized I needed to man up and admit my errors like I wish my brother had done instead of taking the easy way out.

With a majority of my agitation centering around Emily's welfare, she was the first person I reached out to. Our phone call was brief, but long enough to soothe the violent storm forming above my head. When she confirmed she wasn't irreparably scarred by her adventurous night, I contemplated telling her the truth—that I was partly responsible for Jacob's car veering off the road—but the idea of disappointing her made me keep my mouth shut. I've disappointed enough people in my life and didn't want to add another name to my very long list. I was acting like a coward, but with my emotions on the edge of a very steep cliff, I palmed off the responsibility for another day.

A smirk tugs on my mouth when I spot Jacob scratching his brow. He only does that when he's nervous. He's a terrible poker player, as his nervous twitch is evident from a mile out.

"Is it safe to come in?"

I wave my arm through the air, indicating that he can enter. He takes two steps before stopping to scan the desolate space for a place to sit. Huffing in disgust, I drag my fingers over my scalp. My home situation is as fucked-up as they come. I have a duffle bag full of clothes lying open, a handful of *Rolling Stone* magazines piled up in the corner, and my stinky old mattress dumped on the floor. Other than that, my room is bare.

My living conditions are nothing new to Jacob. This is the shit hole I've lived in the past six years. It isn't that my mom is poor; the rest of her house is nicely furnished. She just figures if she makes me as uncomfortable as possible, she can finally wash her hands of me.

Her plan was working. For the past few years, I've been at Jacob's house more than my own, but I haven't stepped foot there since our argument. Call me soft, but I've missed Jacob. He's my brother even though we don't share the same blood. I'm just too stubborn for my own good.

Thank fuck Jacob isn't as pigheaded as me.

Happy to accept the olive branch he's holding out, I lean my guitar against the wall, stand from my mattress, then greet him with a fist bump and a pat on his back. My heart beats at an unnatural rhythm when he draws me in for a man hug. "You know you don't have to stay here, man; my home is your home."

Its rapid beat is heard in my words, "Yeah, I know, I just had to sort my shit out." My headspace has been a bit awry the past few weeks. I've always felt a little lost, but it's been more intense this month.

After pulling back, Jacob lowers his eyes to mine. "This is the longest you've been away." He bumps me with his shoulder, almost knocking me over. "Dad keeps asking why the fridge is full."

Loving the roguishness in his tone, I flash him a cheeky grin before throwing a left, right combination into his midsection. Jacob is a huge bastard, but he's a little slow off the mark. If I put enough strength behind my hit, I'm sure I could knock him on his ass. My dad often said, "The bigger they are, the harder they fall," but I've yet to see anyone brave enough to take a shot at Jacob, so his theory could be wrong.

"Maybe if you switched your steroid-loaded shakes for food, your dad would be none the wiser to my absence." When Jacob cocks a brow, denying both my false claims he uses steroids, and the fact a full fridge isn't the only reason his dad has noticed my lack of presence, I murmur, "I'll pop over and see the old man this week."

Although my pledge isn't a lie, it sounds like one. I'm not a guy who likes to sit down and talk shit through— words won't change anything, so why hash out old shit? —but Jacob's dad is a massive fan of expressing emotions. He listens as good as he lectures, but your head needs to be in the right mindset to handle his round of verbal boxing. I'm not there yet.

Jacob smiles a big, beaming grin before returning my jabs. The strength behind his hits has me wondering if he handled our break up as he usually does his love interests. He's got some power behind his punches—more than you'd expect a teddy bear to have.

We go a few rounds of playful boxing before Jacob's thirst gets the better of him. "Wanna grab a beer?"

His smile jumps onto my face. This is one of the reasons we've been friends so long. Our disagreements end as quickly as they begin.

"Sure."

After ruffling his sweat-slicked hair, I snag my guitar and songbook off my mattress before collecting my duffle bag from the floor. I'm not jumping the gun. When Jacob offers you a beer, don't assume he's bartering for an hour or two of your time. Accepting his offer is the equivalent of signing up for a lifetime commitment. Jacob is lucky his personality makes up for his attachment issues, and even more fortunate I lack attachments.

While shadowing Jacob outside, I try not to let it bother me how absurd it is that in a matter of seconds I gathered all my valued possessions. I miserably fail. My life is pathetic.

I stuff my bag into Jacob's trunk before slipping into the passenger seat. While buckling my seatbelt, I glance back at the sizable two-story brick house I used to call home, praying I'll never step foot in there again. No amount of whiskey can drown out the demons in that house. Believe me, I've tried to silence them the past six years. It's impossible.

CHAPTER 6

NOAH

"Thanks for your help today, Noah." Nick slaps me on the shoulder, his good mood reflected in his smile. "This place will get crazy over the next hour. Did you want to stay here or head back to Mavericks?" He nudges his head at the two-way mirror barely concealing the thumping music keeping guests at his brother's nightclub enthralled.

A dance club is not a place where I generally hang out—I'm not a dancing type of guy—but this club has an invigorating vibe. I'm dying to discover why there's so much hype about it. I get you've got the younger patrons who can't go to a standard nightclub, but from what I'm seeing, there are more people here over the age of twenty-one than under.

While giving Nick's offer more thought, I drink in the vibrant surroundings from the manager's office perched at the back of the club. The main walls are black, the perfect contrast to the silver-framed mirrors hung at various heights on each wall. Two silver dance cages shackled to the ceiling by steel chains give the club a risqué touch, but the giant chandelier dangling over the dance floor adds elegance. The burgundy velour curtains draped from the ceiling to the side walls make it feel as if I'm under a giant teepee. Roomy black booths line the outer walls of the club, and a luxurious curved mahogany bar stretches across one wall. In the middle of the bustling space is a large dance floor. Even this early, it's lit up with several dancers.

After taking in the pricy dresses and designer pants on the dozens of people on the dance floor, I glance down at my dirty jeans before doing a quick sniff test under my arm. Trust me when I say it isn't pleasant. I've been working the past six hours, not prepping for a night out. I won't attract anyone in the state I'm in—*not that I'm looking.*

Grimacing, I hint for Nick to look at my filthy, stained clothes. Seeing things as clearly as me, he strolls past his brother's paper-covered desk to reveal a bathroom hidden behind thick wood paneling. "You can grab a shower in Isaac's bathroom?"

Nick's big brother, Isaac, is the owner of this brand-new dance club called the Dungeon. After hearing Isaac had fired his stockman for stealing, Nick offered our help to unload and connect the kegs for tonight. With Saturday night being the busiest day of the week, Isaac was quick to accept his offer. I didn't get a say in the matter, but I would have helped either way. I'm not afraid of getting my hands a little dirty.

"If Isaac is cool with me using his shower, I have some spare clothes in my truck."

Before Nick can reply, Isaac walks into his office. His dark gray business suit makes him appear older than his nearly twenty-six years. I've only met him a handful of times. He's a couple of years older than Nick, so by the time Nick joined my band, he was already in college.

"No worries, Noah, you guys really helped me today, so you're more than welcome to use my shower. I also let Tina know your drinks are on the house," Isaac assures, talking around the cell phone attached to his ear.

After grinning in thanks, I head down to my truck to grab my duffle bag. Getting out of the club is easier than the patrons vying for entrance. A line three people wide stretches halfway down the block and around the corner.

I snag some fresh clothes from my truck before bolting back to Isaac's office. My shower is quick, but it brings me back to an acceptable standard. While dragging my fingers through my wet locks to give them a messy look, I join Nick at the end of the bar. Patrons are swarming the five staff members manning the counter, but Nick is promptly served by a short bartender with a slender frame and an impish glint in her eyes.

"You weren't kidding about this place getting packed." I nudge my head to the dance floor that's growing more crowded with each minute that passes.

Nodding, Nick hands me a bottle of beer before making his way to a booth on our right. From this location, we have a birds-eye view of the entire club. The bar sits on our left; the toilets are down a hall on our right, and the dance floor is front and center. I almost feel like a VIP with such a prime spot.

Over the next thirty minutes, the line outside descends into the club, crowding the dance floor with writhing bodies. People dance provocatively under the strobing lights synced with the music booming out of the speakers above their heads. The seductive scent of sweat on overheated skin lingers heavily in the air. Its intoxicating smell adds to the tantalizing visual. Although I'm still not convinced this is the scene for me, I have more appreciation now than I had earlier.

When a club remix of Nelly Furtado's classic "Man Eater" comes over the speakers, Nick jumps from our booth. "I have to go get myself a man eater!" He waggles his eyebrows. "You coming?"

I shake my head. "No fucking chance."

With a grin that calls me out as a sucker without words, he takes off for the dance floor. He quickly catches the attention of a handful of ladies unaware of his infamous reputation. Nick moved to Ravenshoe after his parents separated. He was sixteen. Rumors are, he initially moved to Florida with his mom, but when she married a wealthy plastic surgeon, her battle to become an elite socialite made her realize she couldn't have both that *and* a teen son, so she shipped Nick off to live with his father.

We often joke that Nick looks like a young Liam Hemsworth—but with his brother's hair when he played Thor. He has the same shaggy blond hair, blue eyes, and chiseled facial features. He isn't the type of guy I'd usually be friends with, but when I heard him playing his guitar one afternoon while walking past the music room of our high school, I knew I had to introduce him to my band members, Slater and Marcus.

His eyes were closed as he played the introduction to Metallica's song "Enter Sandman," but his accuracy was unsurpassed. His fingers strummed the guitar chords with such ease, I was in complete awe.

Slater and Marcus were hesitant to add a new member to the band, but I couldn't continue juggling being both the lead vocalist and guitarist. When Nick handled the inane number of guitar riffs Slater and Marcus requested during his impromptu audition without any hesitation, even they had a hard time denying his talent.

He had so much skill, we were shocked to learn his gift was self-taught. I had begun playing guitar from the moment I was old enough to hold one. My dad was a talented guitarist, and his passion for music was passed down to me. Only a moron would deny Nick's skills, so after a unanimous vote, he was invited to join our band. When he accepted, our group Rise Up was complete. It's been a rocky few years, but I'm confident it will all pay off.

When my gaze returns to the dance floor, it doesn't take long to spot Nick grooving in the middle of it. The club is considerably more crowded than it was when we arrived. A swarm of sweat-drenched bodies move in sync to a thumping beat.

Catching my gaze, Nick waves for me to join him. When I shake my head, denying his request, a flurry of yellow captures my attention. The strobe lights bouncing off the brunette's mini dress make it glow in the dark, while its tight design awards me an uninterrupted view of a perfectly round pair of ass globes.

My cock twitches when she moves toward the dance floor. I'm not the only one eyeing her arrival. Several men—and even a handful of women—avidly watch her and her two friends as they weave their way through the cramped space.

Once she reaches the middle of the packed floor, she swings her hips in rhythm to the music. The seductive sway of her body naturally seduces me, much less the way she dances with both grace and dignity. Although the pulsating disco lights make it hard for me to see her face, her skintight mini dress leaves nothing to the imagination. She's insanely sexy.

I watch her from afar for the next several minutes, my cock too hard to consider joining her. My band is finally getting the recognition it deserves, so I don't want anything tainting that—specifically, me being caught in a packed club with a raging boner.

As the tunes pumping out of the speakers switch from heart-thumping to mellow, a large pair of breasts blocks my vision of the brunette. "Hi, I'm Meg."

A perky blonde wearing a skintight shirt and a microskirt bobs down in front of me, awarding me an uninterrupted view of her more-than-ample cleavage. "Is this seat taken?"

Not giving me a chance to reply, she slides into the booth. She sits so close, our thighs aren't the only parts of our bodies touching. Her erect nipple scratches my bicep as the nauseating smell of bottled perfume smacks into me. If her micro clothing didn't set me straight, I would have assumed she had never heard of the saying "less is more."

Meg twirls her curly blonde hair around her finger as her teeth rake her bottom lip. "I haven't seen you here before."

She clears red lipstick from her teeth as she peruses my body, only stopping her avid scan when her eyes settle on the crotch of my jeans. I wait for her heavy-hooded gaze to return to my face before explaining, "It's my first time here."

When she smiles, wrinkles crinkle the corners of her eyes, revealing she has notched a few more miles in her time than I have. "Hopefully not your last."

My brow arches when she places her hand on my jean-clad thigh to claw my leg. Her eyes are filled with desire, but even if they weren't, I'd still hear her private thoughts. Her needy breaths are louder than the thumping bass keeping the clubgoers raging.

I have to give it to her: she knows what she wants and isn't afraid to go after it—claws and all—but the boner I'm sporting isn't for her. It's for the beauty in the yellow dress still on the dance floor.

With her seductive moves heating my blood, I turn my gaze back to the cramped floor. It doesn't take me long to spot the fluorescent yellow dress I'm seeking in the dense crowd, but instead of dancing as she was previously, the brunette beauty is standing at the edge of the crammed space, staring at my booth.

After squinting to adjust my eyes to the blinding lights thumping in rhythm with my pulse, a grin curls on my lips. A million years could pass before I'd forget the sparkling light brown eyes staring back at me. They belong to Emily.

From the stern look on her face and the thinness of her eyes, it doesn't take a genius to realize she's not as happy to see me as I am her. Actually, come to think of it, she looks pissed.

I shouldn't be pleased by the thought, but for some silly reason, I am.

CHAPTER 7

EMILY

Mortified I've been busted spying on Noah and his busty date, I grab ahold of Nicole's hand then make a beeline for the bar. Jenni, Nicole, and I only arrived at the Dungeon nightclub thirty minutes ago, and although I'm being scorned by an immense amount of jealousy I shouldn't have, I'm not ready to call it quits just yet.

I sat in a salon chair for over two hours having my waist-length locks cut into a fresher, more manageable style before an additional two hours was gobbled up stomping the floors of our local mall to find the perfect dress for a night out on the town. Then I risked death to borrow Lola's ID without permission. That much effort deserves more than a thirty-minute bump and grind on the dance floor. Besides the strength I exuded restraining myself from walking over to Noah's booth to pull the slutty blonde away from him by the strands on her pretty little head, I've barely worked up a sweat, so no matter how many tiny knives are being stabbed into my heart, we're staying.

When Nicole and I reach the bar, we're quickly served by a petite bartender with a fierce pixie haircut. I thought I was daring when I requested for Jenni's aunt to cut nine inches off my hair before adding caramel highlights to my usually bland palate. My boldness doesn't compare to the fieriness this female oozes. She's compact and sexy and one hundred percent aware of her appeal.

After placing an order for two bottles of water, I set my money on the countertop. With the dance floor crammed with patrons eager to spend their Saturday night getting sweaty, my thirst feels unquenchable. Although my throat is burning, its sting is nothing compared to the pain gnawing my chest from seeing Noah getting cozy with his date. It's so scorching hot, my heart will wear its blisters for months to come.

Noah's date appears a few years older than him. Even with my insides twisted with jealousy, I can admit she's attractive. Her tight black skirt and midriff top pairs well with Noah's casual yet sexy look. He's dressed similarly to the night we met. His dark-washed jeans, black motorcycle boots, and white V-neck cotton shirt showcase the impressive ridges of his body in an alluring light.

Upon spotting my inconspicuous gawp through my recently cut side bangs, Nicole nudges her head to Noah's booth. "Who's the hottie?"

I return my gaze to the dance floor, refusing to waste any more time stewing over a guy I have no claim to. We've shared a handful of flirty text messages. That doesn't equal a lifetime commitment. Furthermore, as far as I'm aware, Noah is single, which means he's free to date whomever he pleases. I just wish it could be done without adding cracks to my already fragile heart.

When Nicole arches her brow, wordlessly demanding for me to answer her, I murmur, "He's a friend of Lola's."

Hearing the words I don't speak the loudest, Nicole huffs. "Uh-huh. Whatever you say, Emily."

With a roll of her eyes, she redirects her attention to the dance floor. I can tell the exact moment her eyes lock in on the same suggestive thing I'm seeing as her cheeks bloom with color. A couple is dancing provocatively in a steel cage shackled to the ceiling. The female dancer's blonde hair curtains her face when she bends over to grasp the outer edge of the cage. After adjusting her position so her ass sits higher than her back, a shirtless male dancer grinds against her in beat to the music. The roll of his hips is enticing enough for my olive cheeks to blush.

Nicole, Jenni, and I have sampled a range of dance clubs the past few months, but the vibe tonight is the most electrifying we've experienced. Dampness lingers in the air from the number of sweaty bodies dancing under the warm pulsating lights, making the sexual tension almost palpable. Its moody booths and classical lines of silver add a touch of elegance to an ambiance that screams sex and sensuality.

Noah chose well. The Dungeon is an ideal location for an intimate yet risqué date.

Some of the despair shrouding me leaves when I spot Jenni in the middle of the packed space. She's getting friendly with a handsome blond man whose icy blue eyes can be seen from a distance. I don't know what he's whispering in her ear, but her smile is so broad, it competes with the crystal chandelier hanging above their heads. For the first time the past ten minutes, happiness spreads across my chest, grateful one of us is having some luck in love tonight.

My glee doubles when Nicole grumbles, "The bouncers should hand out sex education pamphlets upon entry. The chemistry in this room is crazy."

When she fans her flushed red cheeks with her clutch, I hand her one of the bottles of water I bought. As she takes delicate sips, she rehydrates, returning her face to its standard Alaska-white coloring. Nicole's wavy red hair falls to her waist like fiery lava spilling from a volcano. Her green eyes seem a little large for her delicate facial features, but they give her an exotic look that attracts a lot of male attention. She's beautiful and utterly unaware of it, which makes her even more appealing.

After lifting my sweat-drenched hair off my neck, I place the bottle of water on the overheated skin on my nape, hoping some condensation will cool the fire roaring through my veins. When droplets of water roll down my back, I close my eyes. The cool water feels blissful on my roasting skin.

My eyes flutter open a short time later when a masculine voice questions, "Can I buy you a drink?"

When my hooded gaze strays to the person propositioning me, my pulse quickens. He has the most unique pair of gray eyes I've ever seen. His mousy brown hair is cut in a trendy style, and his face is lean and long. The dimple in the middle of his chin can't be hidden by the five o'clock shadow on his jaw, and his light gray business shirt looks expensive, but his matching tie is loosened at the knot, giving him a more casual look. His athletic build enhances his dark gray fitted trousers and shiny black business shoes.

His eyes drift from my face to my hand when I lower my water bottle from my neck. Upon noticing my bottle is full, his lips curl into a devilish smirk. "Maybe the next round?"

I offer him a reserved smile before nodding. I'm not shy, but I've been burned in the past, so I've learned the importance of patience. Furthermore, this man is ridiculously attractive, but not all the extra flutters in my pulse belong to him. Some of them are still for Noah —*regrettably.*

Smirking at my skittish response, the man takes a sizable gulp of the amber liquid in his whiskey glass. He swallows the bitter concoction with ease, not the least bit put off by the burn of straight liquor. I never knew watching someone drink could be sexually gratifying, but he makes a quick liar out of me.

I jump out of my skin when Nicole unexpectedly screams, "Oh my god! This is my favorite song!"

She loops her arm around my elbow to drag me toward the speakers blaring Rihanna's latest hit. When I crank my neck back to offer a silent apology to the gentleman I was talking to, out of the corner of my eye, I spot Noah standing at the end of the bar. He's alone, and his dark, tormented eyes are fixed on me.

I flash my eyes to the booth he was seated at earlier, expecting his date to be awaiting his return. Air snags in my throat when I discover she's nowhere in sight.

With quirked lips, I return my eyes to Noah. Turmoil brews in my gut when he shrugs, like it's no big deal he goes through women like toilet paper. Since it's bordering *that* time of the month, my plan to wipe the smug expression off his face forms like a tsunami. It's more dangerous and sinful than any before it.

Spite fuels my motives when I devote my attention back to the man in the gray suit watching me with zeal. I wave for him to join me, fattening up my invitation with a flirtatious rake of my lower lip with my teeth.

When he notices my offer, he guzzles down the remaining liquid in his glass, hands his suit jacket to the bar attendant, then stalks my way. During his short trip, he undoes his gold cufflinks so he can roll up the sleeves of his business shirt. His demeanor is so cutthroat, the crowd parts when they see him coming. He either has the respect of every patron in this club, or their fear.

By the time he joins me on the edge of the dance floor, Nicole has made herself scarce, and my pulse is raging out of control. I was supposed to set a trap, not get snagged by one.

"Hi, I'm Emily."

I offer him my hand to shake, striving to appear more mature than my nearly eighteen years. He accepts my gesture, but instead of shaking my hand, he presses a kiss to the side of my palm.

"Isaac." Not even the thump of bass can take away from his deep timbre.

As Isaac maneuvers us to the middle of the dance floor, I glance over my shoulder, wondering if Noah has spotted our exchange. He has, and he doesn't appear happy about it. His arms are crossed in front of his chest, and his brows are stitched.

Feeling empowered now that I've made him as jealous as I felt earlier, I dance more sexually with Isaac than I usually would. I grind my backside against his groin and swing my hips so scandalously, the only way I'm leaving this club is in handcuffs.

I'm saved from prosecution when Isaac curls his arms around my waist. His new hold keeps me protected from the people crowding us, while also ensuring not an inch of air gets between us. It's a dominating clutch that makes every woman surrounding me green with envy.

Within minutes, Isaac's enticing scent has me forgetting my invitation to dance was merely a ploy to make Noah jealous. I'm so caught up in the moment, I'm giddy when he trails kisses along the sensitive skin on my nape. He licks, sucks, and bites me as if we're not surrounded by hundreds of people watching his every move.

I close my eyes, eager to relish the sensation of being wholly desired. The instant they snap shut, Noah's dark, intense eyes enter my thoughts as they have every night the past two months. With my mind hazy from the electricity firing through the air, I daydream I'm with him instead of Isaac. I pretend he's licking the sweat off my neck before scoring the skin his tongue just traced with his teeth.

My daydream is so vivid, a needy moan rolls up my throat before I can stop it. It's halfway out of my parched lips when a stern cough interrupts my deliriously exotic daydream. When my eyes pop open, I balk, startled to discover Noah standing in front of me. I stare at him, confused about whether my fantasy was real or a figment of my imagination.

It's only when Isaac's tongue soothes the sting of his bite does the truth smack into me. It isn't Noah kissing my neck. It's Isaac—*still.*

With an icy snarl, Noah locks his eyes with Isaac. "Isaac, can I have a word?"

I shouldn't find the bulging veins in his neck attractive, but I do. Very much so.

From the way Isaac continues ravishing my neck, you'd swear he didn't hear Noah's request. "Right now, Noah?"

My eyes bulge when I'm stung by my second realization in under a minute: they called each other by name. Sick gloom spreads through me. Could I be any more stupid? Out of all the men in the club, I pick a friend of Noah's to exact my revenge with. I'm such an idiot.

As guilt rains down on me, I remove Isaac's hand from my waist before stepping out of his embrace. I don't even get two steps away when he seizes my wrist to pull me back his way. "We're not finished yet." His hankering gray eyes bore into mine. "I'll be back in a minute."

Uncertain how to reply while standing across from the man I was fantasizing about, I halfheartedly nod. My stomach launches into my throat when Isaac kisses my hand as he did earlier. I'm not sickened by his gesture; I'm mortified Noah is watching our exchange with murderous eyes.

When Isaac's hand moves to my jaw, Noah's nostrils flare. He looks seconds from detonating, but instead of exploding in front of an audience, he gives me one final glare before storming back to the bar. I feel his jealousy just as intently when the eyes of numerous women follow his every move. They're torn between the two powerhouses presented in front of them. Noah has an edgy rock star look that could grace the pages of every teen magazine in the country for years to come, whereas Isaac has the cutthroat businessman allure that screams of both money and attractiveness. They're both sexy in their own unique way.

I stop watching Noah's rapidly retreating frame when Isaac's thumb traces my top lip. I hardly know him, but I'm certain he's debating whether or not to kiss me. Uneasiness twists my stomach when I assess the potential consequences of his decision. None of them are positive.

Confident I've made enough mistakes tonight, I withdraw from Isaac's embrace, stealing the decision from him. His dark brows tack, but he accepts my unvoiced rejection with the maturity I lack tonight.

After returning my tight smile with one of his own, Isaac pivots on his heels and heads in the direction Noah just went. Once again, the crowd parts when they see him coming. I take in some big breaths before scanning the dance floor, seeking Jenni and Nicole. I need to leave before I make another foolish mistake.

When I balance on the balls of my feet, I spot Jenni dancing with the same blond she was mingling with earlier. Nicole is just to her right, laughing and chatting with another equally attractive specimen. Guilt makes itself known in my stomach. I'm seconds from ruining my friends' night out all because I'm a spiteful bitch.

A nightclub isn't an ideal spot to deliberate, but after a few seconds of silent contemplation, I conclude that I should leave the club alone. With my mood at an all-time low, I won't be the best company anyway, so why not endure it alone.

While Jenni and Nicole slowly approach me, I put on my game

face. Jenni has been my friend since kindergarten, and although my friendship with Nicole is only coming up on two years, she knows me as well as Jenni. If I'm not careful, they'll sniff out my lie before I've delivered it.

Nicole's bottom lip droops when she drinks in the sullen expression on my face. "What's wrong?"

I cough to free the butterflies from my voice. "I'm not feeling very well, so I'm going to take a taxi home and jump into bed."

Jenni joins us halfway through my lie. "We'll come with you."

"No, Jen, I'm not ruining your night just because I have a little headache. Please don't worry about me; I've already called a cab."

Although I hate lying to them, when Jenni peers back at the guy she's been socializing with, my guilt isn't as bad. He has stopped dancing, impatiently waiting for her return, and the excited expression on her face reveals she's more than eager to get back to him.

Jenni's glistening blue eyes return to me when I sling my arms around her neck. "Go on, babe, have fun. I'll call you tomorrow, and you can give me all the details."

"Are you sure?"

Hoping it will ease the worry in her voice, I hug her tighter. "I'm sure. Now go."

I pull back from our embrace, spin her to face her dance partner, then shove her toward him. Her beautiful giggle when she runs back to him is barely heard over the music thumping around us.

Once the sweaty crowd engulfs her, my eyes stray to Nicole. "Please keep an eye on her." I wrap her up in a tight embrace. "And don't forget to have a little fun too." I keep my voice playful, striving to wipe the concerned look off her face.

It works.

She hugs me back minus the shakes Jenni had. "I will. Text me the instant you get home, okay?"

I keep my gaze to the side, ensuring she won't see the dishonesty in my eyes. "Sure, I'll message you after I take something for my headache."

She huffs, aware I'm lying, but also aware of my inability to back down when I have my mind set on something.

After bumping her with my hip, giving her a final assurance without words, I head toward the illuminated exit sign on my left. Just as my black pumps step off the rich mahogany floor, the club goers part, giving me a front row seat to Noah and Isaac going head to head.

Oh no, what did I do?

CHAPTER 8

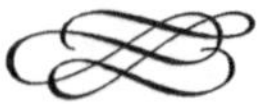

NOAH

Isaac's anger is unmissable. "What the hell, Noah?"

He's pissed at my interruption, but his anger has nothing on the fury pumping through my veins. I'm so fucking jealous, if you were to slice me open right now, my blood would be green.

"Sorry, man, you can't have that one. You can pick any other girl here tonight, but you can't have Emily." My voice is surprisingly firm for how fast blood is coursing through my veins.

Although Isaac and I aren't technically friends, he's a good guy, so I couldn't just storm over and yank Emily out of his embrace, even though I really fucking wanted to. Emily was beautiful the first time I met her, but tonight, she's captivatingly gorgeous. The high rise of her dress paired with her chunky heels make her legs look like they stretch for miles. Her makeup is smoky, giving her light brown eyes a risqué edge, and her long, dark locks have been cut in a shorter, sexy style that has a few highlights added to enhance her already gorgeous olive skin.

Isaac is basically a stranger, but even I know if I let him get too close to Emily, he'll never let her go. And for some fucked-up reason, that notion really bothers me.

"Why the fuck not? She seemed interested in getting to know me."

Isaac arches his brow, his glare picking up. "You should have heard the moans purring from her pretty little mouth when I was kissing her neck."

He rubs his hands together like he's recalling a fond memory. His smug *I'm the fucking king* attitude is too haughty for my liking. It has my anger hitting never-before-reached levels, thickening my blood with furious heat.

It has me unhinged, reckless enough I grab his tie to pull him to within an inch of my face. "Because you can't have her!"

The patrons milling around the bar stop what they're doing to glare at us. They're the least of my problems. Numerous bouncers are charging my way. Realizing I have the club owner by the scruff of his shirt, they push through the throng of people surrounding us without a concern crossing their minds. Their focus is on taking me down.

They don't get within an inch of me when Isaac frees himself from my hold. With the glare of a man on edge, he gestures for the bouncers to stand down. While adjusting his skewed tie, his gray eyes glare into mine. His nostrils flare in sync with mine, and his face is lined with just as much anger.

It takes a few seconds for recognition to dawn on his face. "It's her, isn't it?" He nudges his head in the direction of the dance floor. "She's the one you were telling Nick about today? The one you can't stop thinking about?"

Nodding, I shift my gaze in the direction he nudged. I'm taken aback when I see a pair of panicked light brown eyes. Emily is standing at the edge of the dance floor. Her tiny hands are balled, and she looks seconds from crying.

As much as this pisses me off to admit, I haven't been able to get her out of my head since the day we met. I tried to distract myself, even went as far as not drinking so I wouldn't text her like I did before Jacob, Nick, and I nearly caused her demise. Nothing worked. I've reached for my phone more times than my mic the past month. I barely know her, but she imprinted herself on me so firmly, I feel like I've known her for years.

My eyes drift from Emily to Isaac when he snarls, "Then why isn't she out there dancing with you, Noah?"

Emily only danced with him because she misinterpreted my exchange with Meg. One glance in her eyes told me everything I needed to know. She doesn't hide her jealousy well.

Isaac adds to his cocky statement, "She wanted a taste of sophistication for the night."

Although his tone is mocking, it does little to ease the sting to my ego. I've grown up half my life with people telling me I'm worthless.

"She was using you." Belittling him won't make me feel any better, but it may wipe the arrogant smirk off his face.

Isaac's infuriated gaze snaps to mine as his cheeks redden with anger. "What did you say?"

Foolishly, I repeat, "She was using you," louder this time.

Before I have time to prepare, he lunges at me, shoving me back until I crash into the bar with an almighty thud. I don't register the pain rocketing through my body. I'm too riveted by the rage morphing on Isaac's face to worry about a twinge of discomfort. My words impacted him more than I expected. He's not just pissed. He's ready to go on a rampage.

When the fury in his eyes triples, I brace myself for impact, realizing I've unearthed his weak spot. But I had to do everything in my power to get him away from Emily before she burrowed into his skin so deep, he'd never let her go.

My muscles are tight, primed for the brunt of his onslaught, so you can imagine my surprise when Isaac doesn't let his anger get the better of him. His narrowed gaze shifts to the dance floor for two heart-thrashing seconds before he storms into his office.

My brows furrow as confusion engulfs me. I was anticipating a much fiercer response. After taking a few moments to ease my shock, I glance over to where Isaac was looking. Emily is still standing where she was earlier, except now, her hands are clamped over her mouth, and a handful of the tears once shining in her eyes have trickled down her face.

When I take a step closer to her, she shakes her head, begging me to stop. When I do, she mouths a quick apology before pivoting on her heels and bolting for the club's exit.

"Emily, wait!"

I push off my feet to catch up with her. Due to the large volume of people in one space, five minutes pass before I stumble onto the sidewalk outside the club. With my band's hype picking up, so are our number of fans. Many stopped me on the way, unaware the expression on my face isn't a welcoming one.

I sling my head to the right then left, seeking Emily amongst the crowd. She's nowhere to be found. "Fuck!"

Three girls walking by let out a yelp, frightened by my scream. I wave my hands across my body, showing them I mean no harm. "I'm sorry."

"That's okay." The blonde's frightened expression switches to excited. "Are you leaving?" She twirls a piece of hair around her finger as her eyes rake my body. Her flirting would be better received if she wasn't pouting like a child.

"Yep. I've had more than enough of the club scene for one night."

Ignoring her batting eyes begging me to change my mind, I head to my truck parked at the back of the club. My pride and joy is a rusty 1977 Ford F150. My brother Chris had been helping me rebuild it the past few years. Although she looks like a rust bucket on the outside, her core is strong, and I just refurbished her engine.

After throwing open the driver's side door, I clamber into my seat, then shove my keys into the ignition. A grin curls on my lips when Betty fires up on the first turn of the keys. As she rolls toward the exit, I slip my hand under the bench seat to grab the pack of cigarettes I have hiding there. I gave up smoking five weeks ago, but I kept an emergency stash in case the urge arose. Considering tonight's events, I need a hit of nicotine.

After lighting the cigarette balancing between my quirked lips, I take a long draw of the addictive stick. It tastes like garbage, but the nicotine hits the spot. As my lungs reacquaint with less-than-stellar air, I scan the street for an opening.

I've just found a space I can slip into when I spot Emily. She's standing at the end of a very long line, waiting for a taxi. For the quickest moment, I consider pulling into the slow-moving lane—*it would be better for her if I did*—but when she wraps her arms around her body as she strives to keep warm, I know I'm not going anywhere. I may be an ass who's as confused as fuck, but I'm not entirely heartless.

After pulling my truck to the curb in front of the taxi stand, I roll down the passenger side window. Emily's eyes float up from her shoes when she hears the creak of the rusty mechanism, but she doesn't recognize my truck, so she remains standing in line.

"Do you want a lift?"

"Noah?" When she sheepishly peers into the cab of my truck, excitement beeps in her neck. Although she's excited, she tries to play it cool. "It's okay; I'll wait for a cab."

Over the back and forth game we're playing, I growl, "Get in the truck, Emily."

I don't care if she never wants to see me again, but there's no chance in hell I'm leaving her here, standing in the cold, waiting over an hour for a taxi while she's upset. I'm partially to blame for her watering eyes, so the least I can do is give her a ride home.

When she remains hesitant, I'm on the verge of falling to my knees and groveling. Instead, I try a less weaselly approach. *"Please.* It's just a ride. What's the worst that could happen?"

I can think of many things, but I hope she isn't looking into things as deeply as me. I'm too worked up to think straight, probably because the image of Isaac kissing her neck is rolling through my head on repeat. If he were any other guy, my night would have ended differently. I'd most likely be sitting in a cell instead of my truck. That's how agitated I felt watching another man seduce her.

I'm still pissed, but it eases somewhat when Emily reaches out to open my passenger side door. Her climb into my truck makes her delicious vanilla scent filter into my nostrils. It's a smooth smell that complements the silky skin I see when her mini-dress rides up high on her thigh.

Eager to capture her scent in my truck's cab, and to take my eyes off assets I shouldn't be ogling, I flick my half-smoked cigarette onto the pavement, then roll up my window.

My heart rate kicks into overdrive when her smell intensifies, then it pumps out an entirely new tune when she grumbles, "You should quit that nasty habit. Smoking is disgusting."

CHAPTER 9

EMILY

I clamp my hand over my mouth, mortified. I really need to learn to keep my big mouth shut. Even after my horrendous performance in the club, Noah was kind enough to offer me a lift home, and how do I award his chivalry? I insult him.

With winds whipping in from the coast, I was freezing standing in a very long line, so although I'm stunned he'd desecrate his perfect body with toxins, I'll forever be grateful for his courtesy.

Mercifully, Noah doesn't seem put-off by my scorn. He chuckles at my snarky comment before pulling his truck away from the curb. We're barely half a block down when the winds I was sheltering myself from earlier pump through my open window. Noah's window is up; now I just need to fix mine.

I push down on the rusty window crank near my thigh, but no matter how hard I ram it, my scrawny arms can't get the darn thing to budge. I give it everything I have. It refuses to move.

Deflated by my lack of strength, I slump into the bench seat with a huff, blowing an unruly hair out of my eye in the process. Noah's snickering laughter bounces around the cab as he leans across my body to fix the window into place.

I feel instantly warm. It isn't the window rolling into place responsible for my heated response. It's Noah's forearm skimming the exposed skin on my thighs. He's barely touching me, but even his briefest touch has my heart pumping at double the speed.

Having him so close also fills my senses with his mouthwatering smell, but I don't recognize his scent. If I had to guess, I'd say it is a combination of a spicy aftershave and a smell that solely belongs to him. Eager to quell my curiosity, I suck in a big whiff of air through my nose. Wicked thoughts run wild in my mind because not even the stench of tobacco can dampen his alluring scent. He smells delicious, and my pulse is quickening.

Once he has the window in place, Noah drags his arm back to the steering wheel. Since my chest is expanded from sucking in his tempting smell, he brushes my breasts on the way by. Even if I could palm off my erect nipples as a consequence of the brisk air, nothing could cover up the husky purr toppling from my lips. *Who knew a scent alone could create such a ruckus?*

Wondering if he heard my inappropriate moan, I peer at Noah through a set of thick lashes. His heavy-hooded gaze is fixed on my thrusting chest, and his jaw is tight. He either heard my body's response to his touch or he can sense it.

When his eyes lift from my chest to my face, desire clusters in my womb. His gaze is hungry and wanton—the very look I wanted to see in his eyes earlier. I'm squirming in my seat, completely forgetting how I was an idiot earlier tonight. Nothing is on my mind but ensuring that look stays in his eyes for a lifetime. His mysteriousness is alluring, but it has nothing on his hooded gaze.

Our lust-crazed trance is only lost when a car horn honks. "Shit!"

Noah yanks on the steering wheel, dragging his car back onto the right side of the road. His windows rattle when the opposing car passes us at a furious speed.

He coughs to clear his throat of nerves before stumbling out an apology. "Sorry."

Unable to speak—more because of the heat still teeming between us than our near-death experience—I offer him a tight smile. He accepts by offering up one of his own before shifting his eyes back to the road, where he keeps them for the next several minutes.

Feeling defeated, I sink into my seat before my eyes drift to the scenery zooming past the window. Rejection crashes into me like a tidal wave when I realize he's driving me the most direct route home. The night is still young, yet he's more than ready for it to be over.

That's a slap my ego didn't need.

When my disappointment grows too much for me to bear, my eyes drift to Noah. "Do you have to take me straight home?"

His grip on the steering wheel tightens so much his knuckles go white. After swallowing several times in a row, he stares at me for what feels like a lifetime before his focus returns to the road without a syllable escaping his lips.

Sighing, I lean my flushed cheek on the passenger side window. My overheated skin relishes the coolness of the cold glass, but nothing eases the disappointment burning through me. I never understood how much rejection hurt until now.

The disappointment curtailing my breaths slackens when Noah murmurs, "Where do you want to go?"

I sit up straight as my mind scrambles for the perfect location. Not having the time to evaluate which place is suitable for two strangers with an undeniable connection but a lot of explaining to do, I blurt out the first one that pops into my head, "Bronte's Peak?"

Noah's brows scrunch as his jaw tightens. His response reveals he's heard of Bronte's Peak before. I'm not surprised. It's a beautiful lookout perched above the pristinely beautiful Bronte's Beach. During the day, it's a tourist mecca that sees thousands of people walking its shores every weekend.

Things are vastly different this time of night, though.

Bronte's Peak is the prime hookup location for local teens. The parking lot doesn't have adequate lighting, so its popularity for sneaky rendezvous is undeniable.

If Noah is concerned I suggested Bronte's Peak so we could make out, he has no reason to fret. I don't want a hookup. I just want a chance to explain my actions tonight. I can't stand the thought of him fighting with his friend because I was jealous.

I also want some one-on-one time with him in person. That's not asking too much, is it?

"I thought we could go there to talk?" I mumble with a shrug.

Noah's brows furrow even closer, but his mouth remains tightlipped. When we stop at a T intersection, he takes his time deciding which way to turn. If he turns left, we'll head straight for Bronte's Peak. If he turns right, we'll continue on the most direct route to my home.

With each second that passes, my confidence falters. I begin to worry that the idea of making out with me repulses him so much, he'd rather go home than risk it being a possibility. That hurts—a lot!

After numerous stomach-churning seconds, Noah turns right, and my heart slithers into my stomach. His rejection is a devastating blow that forces tears into my eyes. They're so overloaded, I'm forced to brush one off my cheek when it stupidly slips over the barrier keeping the rest at bay.

Not even two seconds later, my hands shoot out to brace the dash. Noah slammed on his brakes so hard, I either brace for impact or headbutt the windshield. Dust kicks up around us when he yanks his truck to the side of the road. I try not to get my hopes up, but the faintest trickle glitters in my veins.

Noah slants his head my way, his eyes brimming with a vast array of emotions. Optimism. Concern. Anger. They're reflecting so many emotions, I'm shocked I don't hear them when he questions, "What do you want from me, Emily?"

"I don't want anything."

I'm confused as to why he'd think I want something from him. He's been to my house, so he's aware I'm not wealthy, but that doesn't mean I want to use him. I'm *not,* and will never be, a gold digger.

"Then why did you do that tonight?" His clipped tone announces that my actions hurt him.

"I didn't know Isaac was your friend. I would have never done that if I'd known... I'm not like that."

Realizing I'm doing a terrible job of explaining myself, I unbuckle my seatbelt and scoot across the split-bench seat, hoping my eyes will pick up the slack of its weak counterparts. "I was jealous when I saw you were on a date. Instead of figuring out why I was jealous, I lashed out. I'm not proud of what I did, but I looked too deeply into our text messages. I thought they meant something—"

"They did."

He seems as if he wants to say more, but he can't force the words out of his mouth. I don't mind. It gives me a chance to take in all the details of his face I couldn't absorb from a distance. He truly is the most handsome man I've seen.

I stop drinking in the creases I know turn into dimples when he murmurs, "I wasn't on a date."

You'd think my first emotion would be relief. It isn't. Not even close. I'm too angry to be relieved. First, he accused me of being a gold digger—*or even worse, a user*—and now, he's lying to my face. He may not have looked at me while doing it, but he's still lying nonetheless. I didn't hear about his date via the grapevine. I *saw* it with my own two eyes.

With a snarl, I shuffle back to the passenger side to yank on the door handle. I'm at my boiling point, meaning I need some distance before I say something I'll regret. My wish for air is so brutal, the rusted handle snaps off in my hand when I yank it with force.

"You stupid piece of shit!" Frustration bubbles in my chest when it dawns on me that I'm trapped in the truck with Noah and his stupidly handsome face. The door handle is broken, and I'm too weak to roll the freaking window down.

I sling my gaze back to Noah, my anger ramping up when I see his shit-eating grin. "Let. Me. Out."

His gorgeous dimples become exposed when he smirks at the long breaths I take between words. "I'm not joking! Let me out of the fucking car!"

When his eyes spark with humor, I peg the door handle at his head. My teeth crunch when I miss my mark and hit him in the chest instead of his head. My whack is enough to settle the leering expression on his face, but it does little to elevate the smugness beaming out of him in invisible waves.

"Calm down first, then I'll let you out."

Huffing, I fold my arms under my chest. My anger triples when his eyes dart down to my breasts that are pushed up from my strengthened pose.

Nuh-uh. No way, Mister. You lost the privilege to gawk at my breasts when you lied.

I angle my body away from him, denying him the opportunity to look. He tries to hold in his disappointed groan, but I hear it rumbling in his chest, smell it overtaking the scent slicking his skin. He's as frustrated as me at the turn of events.

"I wasn't on a date." He exhales a big breath, hating that he's giving in to the tension firing between us. "Meg invited herself to sit with me."

Hearing nothing but honesty in his tone, I crank my neck back to face him. We've only interacted in person a handful of times, but his eyes are as truthful as his words.

Noah adds wood to the fire I'm extinguishing. "She was pretty friendly, though." I'm two seconds from returning his jealousy with a compliment about Isaac's *friendliness*, but his next set of words steal my retaliation. "But I was too busy watching a sexy brunette in a little yellow dress dancing the night away to pay her any attention."

When his lust-crammed eyes lower to my fluorescent yellow dress. I stare at him in shock. *He wasn't watching me, was he?*

He puts my confusion to rest with a lusty grin. "I'm not surprised you didn't notice my watchful eye. You did have the attention of every man in the room."

My stomach gurgles when I tick off the facts he's giving me. He wasn't on a date at all, but instead of giving him the chance to explain, I turned into a hormonal cow who used Isaac to exact my revenge. *I'm such an idiot.*

I'm confident there's no chance of acting on the inane sexual connection between us, so you can imagine my shock when Noah asks, "So I'll ask you again, Emily, what do you want from me?"

The need in his voice has a light bulb switching on in my head. I wasn't the only one acting jealous tonight—he was as well. That can only mean one thing: he wants this as badly as I do.

With my heart drumming against my ribcage, I crawl across the cracked vinyl seat. "I want you, Noah. I want you."

CHAPTER 10

NOAH

I don't get a chance to register Emily's declaration that she wants me before her tongue lashes my tightly shut lips. She glides it along the seam of my mouth, wordlessly requesting that I accept her kiss.

I've dreamed about tasting her pouty mouth since she busted me laughing at her family portrait, but can I do this? She doesn't know me. No one does—*except Jacob*. I have demons inside of me capable of taking us both down. Do I want to do that to Emily? Do I want to drag her to the depths of hell alongside me? Siding with me never ends well. It doesn't matter who you are, or how strong you appear to be, I'm more toxic than arsenic.

When Emily straddles my lap, I can no longer resist temptation. I'm already going to hell, so I may as well have some fun before I get there.

I bite down on her lip before grabbing a fist full of her silky locks. When my tongue delves into her delicious mouth, her moan has my cock wrangling against the zipper in my jeans, begging to be released.

While I sample every inch of a mouth as sizzling as its owners face, Emily expresses her every want with her tongue, lips, and hands. She tells me how badly she wants this—how badly she wants *me.* It's a crazy, lust-filled embrace that has my cock begging to be freed from my jeans. I can feel her heat against me, its warmth raring up with every second we kiss. It'd be pure torture if it didn't feel so good.

When I adjust myself to ease the ache of my cock, the back of my hand rubs Emily's panties. The tiny pair of panties she's wearing can't conceal her drenched state. She's saturated, meaning it takes everything I have not to fuck this up. Whatever we're stumbling toward isn't anything I planned, but I'm learning that sometimes things are beyond my control. I'm finding myself thinking differently. Nothing drastic, just things aren't as gloomy as they once seemed.

But even if I were wearing rose-colored glasses, I still know I need to slow this down. When, and if, I have sex with Emily, it won't be in my dirty truck on the side of a busy highway.

As I said earlier, I'm not a complete fucking asshole.

Pulling away from Emily's lips is a torturous feat, but I do it —*barely!*

Ignoring the pleas of my raging hard-on, I lift her off my lap and place her on the passenger side. The desire to pull her pouty lips back to mine intensifies when rejection sparks through her glistening eyes.

Although I hate disappointing her, I'm shocked someone so beautiful would ever believe she's being rejected. Her dress is pulled up high, exposing inches of her smooth thighs; she's breathing hard, thrusting her breasts up and down, and her lips are swollen from our kiss. She couldn't be any more beautiful if she tried. Just looking at her has my cock begging to sink into her no doubt tight pussy.

The downward curve of Emily's lips morphs into a smirk when her eyes drop to my crotch. She's pleased with my body's response to our kiss, and she's not ashamed to admit it.

Her smile turns into a giggle when I pull her across the cracked seat to nestle her under my arm. My truck's engine roars to life when I plant my foot on the accelerator. When my tires fail to gain traction on the loose gravel, I panic, but it's soon pushed aside when Emily's lips rise against my chest.

I knew she'd be more than I'd ever be able to handle.

By the time we arrive at Bronte's Peak, the parking lot is deserted. I check my watch, noting it's almost three in the morning, meaning even the locals have called it a night.

When I pull into an empty spot in the moonlit lot, Emily scoots across the seat. She cradles her legs in her arms before her eyes drift to me. The anxiety in them makes me wonder if she's changed her mind about wanting me. She has gone from ravishing my mouth to sitting as far away from me as possible within a matter of seconds... My thoughts trail off when a disturbing notion pops into my head.

"I didn't bring you here to fuck you." I sound like I've swallowed a handful of gravel. My voice is rough and raspy.

I've been to Bronte's Peak numerous times, so I know the reason teens come here after dark, but I'd never do anything she doesn't want me to do. I'm not a fucking monster.

Emily's teeth drag over her lower lip, enhancing the plumpness our kiss initiated. "It's not that." She waves off my concern with a swipe of her hand. "I just realized I never asked if you have a girlfriend."

Although grateful she doesn't think I'm trying to get into her panties, I'm still confused—and perhaps a little snippy. "Do you think I would have kissed you if I did?"

Her assumption gives credit to what I was worried about. She doesn't know me. Even though it's been a *very* long time since I've had a girlfriend, I'm not a guy who cheats.

"No..." She shakes her head, barely concealing her sigh. "I had to ask, though. I'm sorry if it made you uncomfortable. I'd just rather ask than wonder."

The apprehension in her reply awakens my suspicion. Her low tone has me wondering if she's been duped before—quite possibly in the very spot we're sitting. Her spikes didn't hackle until we arrived here. The thought of anyone touching her makes my blood boil, but deep down, I know a girl as beautiful as her would never be untouched. She could have any man she wants. I don't understand why she'd choose someone like me.

In an attempt to lessen the tension between us, Emily lowers her legs before sliding across the bench seat, her vanilla smell getting stronger with every inch. I don't know if it's a perfume or the shampoo she uses, but it's intoxicating. When the moonlight catches her face, it enhances her alluring features: her little turned-up nose, her light brown eyes, the softness of her plump lips. She's so youthful, I grow panicked she isn't as old as I first thought.

"How old are you?"

My cock twitches when a traffic-stopping grin stretches across her face. "How old do you think I am?" She gives me a cheeky wink, her mood drastically improved from seconds ago.

She was at an over-eighteen dance club, so she'd have to be a minimum of eighteen, making her only three years younger than me. "At least eighteen?"

A lump lodges in my throat when she pulls a face. I stare at her, impatiently waiting for her to put me out of my misery. When she delays responding, I bang my head on the steering wheel.

My head smacks the steering wheel harder when she murmurs, "Seventeen."

"Seventeen?!" I peer at her with wide, glossed-over eyes. "Does that mean you're still in high school?!"

My heart slithers into my gut when she nods.

Fuck! The girl who hasn't left my mind the past two months is precisely that—a girl! In high school! She has the body of an adult, but the way she acted tonight might have more to do with immaturity than jealousy.

I stop looking for the police in my rearview mirror when Emily adds, "I turn eighteen in two days. Well, one day now, since it's Sunday morning." Her tone relays the pleasure she gets from teasing me. I'm glad she's having fun, because I'm on the verge of a heart attack. "How old are you?"

I peer at her with mischievous, panicked eyes. "What is this, twenty questions?"

"Uh-huh," is all she replies while folding her legs under her bottom.

Thinking back to my birthday, I answer, "I turned twenty-one a few months back."

I thought your twenty-first was supposed to be a big deal, but other than Jacob and the guys from the band breaking out into a terrible rendition of "Happy Birthday" when I walked into Mavericks for a gig, my day passed without acknowledgment from anyone else.

Realizing it's my turn to ask a question, I lock my eyes with Emily. "My turn to interrogate." She smiles, not missing the playfulness in my tone. "How did you get into the club tonight if you aren't eighteen?"

Isaac would *never* allow someone under eighteen into his club; he'd never risk losing his license—not even for a woman who captivated him as quickly as Emily did. Jesus. Imagine the backlash he could have faced if things went further between them tonight? I shouldn't be smirking at the thought, but I am. Serves him right for touching someone who doesn't belong to him.

The clench of my jaw eases when Emily giggles, swiping the agitation from my veins as quickly as it formed. She might have used Isaac to get us here, but *I'm* keeping her here.

"If you tell her, I'll kill you." She waits, building the suspense. "I borrowed my sister's ID. Tonight was the first time it worked with ease."

My brow becomes lost in my hairline. *Is sneaking into clubs something she does often?*

My chance to ask is lost when she remembers it's her turn to ask a question. "What are you doing right now?"

I give her a frisky wink, revealing the cocky bastard hiding behind my dimpled grin. "Talking to a beautiful lady."

With a roll of her eyes, she slaps my arm. Okay, I'll admit, that was corny as fuck, but if acting like a dickhead makes her smile the way she is now, I'll happily wear the title.

"I meant, do you go to college or work?"

I smirk, aware of what she was asking. "I'm working, if you can call it that."

Her brows stitch, confused by my reply.

I try to alleviate it. "I'm the lead singer of a band my friends Slater, Marcus, and I formed in high school. It kept us out of trouble... for the most part." She smiles along with me. "You can't get into too much mischief when your weekends are tied up rehearsing instead of partying like our peers did."

I watch her closely, gauging her reaction to me not being in school. I'm pleased to say the expression on her face remains neutral. Come to think of it, she also looks a little excited.

"Once we had a few years under our belts, we added a lead guitarist to our lineup, then not long after that, we secured our first paid gigs. A majority of our performances were birthday or engagement parties, but within two years we scored a regular spot at Mavericks."

I chuckle when I think back to how we got our start. "We were mortified when we got stuck with the horrible Tuesday night schedule. Our night was spent singing 80s covers to a bunch of old ladies who finished their day at bingo with a glass of chardonnay at their local watering hole."

A beautiful giggle spills from Emily's kiss-swollen lips at the gag coming with my words.

"Once we showed initiative, we worked our way up to the Friday night spot. We now pick the genre of music we play, and Ollie lets us perform two original songs a night. We don't get paid a lot, but it's enough to get by..." I stop talking, worried I've said too much. I've never spoken so openly before.

Emily doesn't seem to mind. Her smile reveals she appreciates my frankness—and she's eager for me to ask my next question. She's enjoying this communication thing we've got going on way too much for my liking, but there's no chance in hell I'll end it. I have her sole attention. I'm not giving this up for anything.

As I scan the deserted parking lot of Bronte's Peak, the perfect question pops into my head. "Have you been here before?"

The color in Emily's cheeks drains as her eyes rocket to the foggy window next to her head. She silently contemplates, her chest rising and falling as she sucks in sharp breaths.

Just when I think she'll never answer me, she whispers, "Yes."

CHAPTER 11

EMILY

I knew the instant I blurted out Bronte's Peak Noah would ask this question. Bronte's Peak has been the top choice for teens wanting to get hot and heavy after a date for years. This is the exact location I discovered princes can turn into frogs after kissing them.

The excitement I felt two years ago when I was asked out by a senior every girl in our school had a crush on was immense. I thought I hit the jackpot.

I was a naïve idiot.

On paper, Zander was the epitome of the beloved star quarterback. He had long brown hair, washboard abs from the hours he spent surfing, and an ability to lie to my face without a bit of remorse crossing his.

He was damn near perfect... until he got what he wanted.

If I were smart, I would have gone home with Jenni when our double date with Zander and his best friend Christian ended. Unfortunately, I was too caught up in the hoopla of being wanted by the most popular guy in school to see the slimy frog hiding beneath Zander's shiny exterior.

I paid for my mistake dearly.

Not only did I lose my virginity in the back of a dirty old van with surfboards strapped to the roof, I threw myself headfirst into a controversial shitstorm I'm still struggling to find my way out of two years later.

Zander had a girlfriend.

She was a senior at an all-girls school that bordered our hometown. Although she didn't go to our school, it didn't take long for news of my "supposed" slutty ways to circulate between my peers. The Monday morning following the "incident" between Zander and me, I was bombarded without warning. I was slut-shamed, belittled, and attacked viciously by not only Zander's girlfriend, Becky, but by numerous senior girls as well.

I can still recall how badly my scalp stung when Becky wrenched my hair out of my head as she called me a whore in front of the entire school. Do you know what Zander did during her attack? Nothing. Not a single thing. He watched from the sidelines as if I had seduced him, where all I did was believe him when he told me I was the most perfect girl he'd ever seen.

He was my childhood crush, yet all I got for my admiration was hate from those around me. I'm extremely lucky I had the support of Jenni and Nicole. I truly don't know how I would have survived without them. High school is bad enough, let alone when you're labeled the town slut.

Zander was the first and last man I ever dated. Up until now, I've been too scared to trust anyone. Some of my boldness the past few months could be attributed to the fact Becky broke up with Zander because his philandering was too frequent for her to blame the unsuspecting females he liaised with, but most of it can be attributed to Noah.

His texts and phone calls were as cryptic as the man I met in the hall, but they were full of honesty. He never promised a lifetime commitment or made out I was everything he ever wanted. More times than not, his messages conveyed he was as nervous about sending them as I was about responding to them. That made it seem like I was playing on a level field instead of in a stadium filled with vicious, backstabbing people determined to take me down.

I liked the way Noah looked at me in the hallway of my family home—not when I thought he was my sister's date, the seconds leading to me closing the door. I'd give anything to replace the stare he's giving me now with the one he awarded me three months ago, because this one is nowhere near as fire-sparking.

CHAPTER 12

NOAH

After swiping at her cheeks to make sure none of the moisture in her eyes has fallen, Emily alters the course of our conversation. "Can I watch your band play sometime?"

I hardly know her, but I already know she wears her heart on her sleeve. She's doing anything she can to sidestep the can of worms my question opened. Although I'm itching to beat the fuck out of whoever caused her such heartache, I place the urge on the backburner.

We're only just getting to know each other, so I'm not going to force her to tell me what happened. Once I've gained her trust, she'll open up to me. Until then, I'll continue our game of twenty questions while pretending the vein throbbing in my neck is natural.

"I'd love nothing more than for you to watch me perform."

Hearing something I didn't mean to express, she smiles. When I scoot across the bench, her heavy-lidded eyes drop to my lips. The hurt clouding her eyes fades the closer I get. I had planned to tell her it was her turn to ask a question. Now I have other ideas on my mind —these ones aren't as noble.

When I tilt my head to align our lips, Emily licks hers in preparation for our kiss. Her pulse flutters against my fingertips when I grip her nape so I can pull her mouth to mine. Kissing her the second time is even better than the first. I've got all the control this time around, which means my tongue has no trouble sampling every inch of her delicious mouth.

I take my time savoring her delicious mouth, nipping at her lips before stroking my tongue inside her mouth in long, dedicated sweeps. Our kiss barely surpasses a PG rating with our hands at respectable levels at all times, but it doesn't need additional stimulation. It's fire-sparking as it is.

A few minutes later, with reluctance, I withdraw from our embrace. Emily's eyes remain closed, as uneager to return to reality as I am. I watch her brush her fingers over the cupid's bow in her top lip before her eyes slowly flutter open. Upon spotting my envious gawk, she smiles a breathtakingly gorgeous grin potent enough to bring the strongest man to his knees.

Unable to resist the temptation for a second longer, I pull her mouth back to mine. Just as our lips brush, the shrill of a cell phone fills the dead silence surrounding us.

Recognizing the ringtone, Emily yanks back. "Shit! I forgot to message them." As her gaze widens in shock, she snatches her purse off the floor, undoes the zipper, then yanks out a vibrating phone. Fumbling, she raises it to her ear. "Hello?"

Her apologetic eyes dart to mine when a girly squeal roars down the line. "I'm all right... Yes, I know... I'm sorry, I forgot... No, I'm not home yet... I'm a little busy at the moment."

An ear-piercing, "What?!" shrieks through her phone speaker.

It's so loud, Emily yanks her phone away from her ear, tugs on her earlobe, then reattaches her cell. "*Ssh...*" She peers at me remorsefully. "I'll tell you later... I'm fine...Noah will take me home... Yes, that Noah... *Nicole...* Okay, bye... Love you too."

Although I only get one side of her conversation, I can't help the smile stretching across my face. Any heartbreak our kiss didn't take care of, Emily's caller wiped from her face. She smiles a blistering grin while switching off her phone and placing it back in her purse.

After dumping it on the floor of my truck, her amused eyes meet mine. "Sorry about that. That was my friend Nicole. I was at the club with her and Jenni tonight. I told her I'd text the instant I got home. I kind of forgot." The guilt crossing her face enlarges my smile. I can't blame her for being ditzy. My mind went a little hazy after our kiss as well. "Nicole can be a little high strung. I'm shocked the late hour didn't have her sending out a search party."

I balk when she nudges her head to the clock in my dashboard. It's 4 AM. "Then I guess we better get you home before she activates the GPS tracker in your phone."

Although Emily laughs, she still eyes me with suspicion.

———

During our drive home, we continue our game of twenty questions. I discover Emily is the youngest of four siblings. She has two brothers and one sister. Aiden is twenty-three; Dominic is twenty-two, and her sister Lola is twenty-one. Her mom is a nurse at the local hospital and is often fatigued from working double shifts to cover their mortgage. She never mentions her dad, and not wanting to bring up another sore subject, I don't probe her about him.

Her "very best friends in the whole world" are Jenni and Nicole, and she's in her final months of high school, where she's doing everything in her power to get a scholarship to college so she can become a teacher. From the way her face lights up when she talks about her friends, I can easily see how close they are. They have a bond similar to mine with Jacob and my bandmates. They're my brothers, even if it isn't by blood.

Emily asks similar questions: where I went to school, do I have any pets, and how many siblings do I have.

Her question about my family coincides with pulling into the driveway of her home, so I leave my answer short. I tell her I had two brothers named Chris and Michael; my dad isn't around, and my living situation is a little rocky. I could elaborate, but just like Emily, I have secrets I'm not willing to share just yet.

Losing my brothers four years apart turned my life upside down.

Although I live with my loss every day, I've yet to come to terms with it.

Emily takes my hand, her eyes seeking mine. I can see a million questions beaming there, but she keeps things simple. "Are you okay?"

I muster up my best fake smile. "Never better." Hating that I've made things awkward, I give it my best shot to get our night back on track. "Can I take you out tomorrow?"

Nerves bungee jump off my vocal cords, making me sound more skittish than I am. I'm not nervous she'll say no; I've just never asked a girl out before. I've had plenty of hookups and some regular flings, but I haven't had a serious girlfriend since middle school.

"I'd love that." Emily places a peck onto my lips before scooting back to her side of the cab. A grin tugs on my mouth when she yanks on the door handle, forgetting she broke it. Her smile competes with the moon when I run around my truck to help her down.

"Such a gentleman," she teases while jumping down the last step.

She keeps our fingers interlocked for as long as possible before distance forces them apart. Call me a fucking soft cock, but I swear the electricity firing through my body dulls the instant her hand leaves mine.

When she reaches the front door, she pivots to face me. I give myself a mental pat on the back when shock registers on her features. I don't know why she's surprised. I'm not going anywhere—well, not until she's safely entered her home.

Smiling a grin that proves she'll be my biggest challenge, Emily stabs her key into the lock then swings open her front door; her steps are carefree and extra bouncy as she enters.

I wait for her door to close before jumping into my truck and heading home.

The living daylights are scared out of me when I stroll into the living room of Jacob's house. "Where have you been all night?"

With the late hour, I wasn't expecting anyone to be awake. Since the room is shrouded in blackness, I flick on the lamp in the corner of the vast space. My fists clench when the first thing my vision zooms in on is Jacob's bruised and bloody face. His right eye is purple and almost sealed shut. His left brow has a deep gash above it, and he's holding a wad of tissues to a split lip.

"What the fuck, Jake?" I lift his chin so I can inspect his badly bruised face with more diligence. My blood turns black when I take in his extensive injuries. Whoever did this to him will pay. "Who did this?"

He stares up at me with his blue eye that isn't sealed shut. "No one important. It's not as bad as it looks."

He doesn't need to scratch his brow for me to know he's lying. I heard it in his tone. "Not as bad as it looks? Fuck Jacob! You look like you've had the living shit beaten out of you."

Jacob stands from his chair, pissed at my reaction. "You think I look bad. You should see the other guy." His uncomfortable walk reveals the bruises on his face aren't the only ones he was trying to conceal by sitting in a pitch-black room. "I'm going to take a shower."

He makes it two paces into the hallway before he freezes and turns back around. "Please don't tell Lola you saw me like this."

I should say no. I should force him to tell me who did this to him, but he's as stubborn as a mule. No matter how many times I ask, he won't tell me what happened until he's ready.

"Alright, I won't tell Lola."

Relief flashes across his features. It doesn't linger for long.

"On one condition." I hold my index finger into the air. "If this happens again, I'll not only tell Lola, but I'll hunt down the fucker who did this to you and break his fucking neck."

Jacob stares at me for several long minutes, his determination growing with each one that ticks by. I expect him to say something profound, so you can imagine my shock when he simply nods before entering the hallway, not once glancing back at me paralyzed with blackened rage.

CHAPTER 13

EMILY

*J*enni glances at me with amused eyes. "Wear whatever you feel comfortable in."

She snags a chip out of a half-empty bag sitting on my bed while I work through my limited wardrobe acting as if I've been invited to a ritzy gala instead of a rock concert. The skinny jeans and midriff top I'm wearing is the fifth outfit I've tried on since school ended two hours ago.

Noah is on his way to pick me up so I can watch his band perform at Mavericks Bar. If I don't hurry, I'll make a first impression with his bandmates I can't take back. I'm unsure what to wear because the only time I've stepped foot in a bar was to go dancing with Jenni and Nicole. I tried on a range of dresses and skirt and shirt combinations I purchased during my mini makeover, but they were too skimpy, more suitable for dance clubs.

Switching things up, I slid on my trusty boyfriend jeans and a vintage rock t-shirt. It was so underwhelming, when I peered in the mirror, I felt like I hadn't put in *any* effort. I looked how I did every day: plain and boring.

That's when I dug out the outfit I hide in the back of my closet so Lola is none the wiser to its existence. Although it has the vibe I'm going for, I still feel dowdy. I flop onto the bed next to Jenni. "I give up."

She ruffles my hair before darting for my closet with a gusto that matches her tiny frame. She scans a range of shirts huddled in the middle, her head shaking multiple times. Her fashion sense outshines mine tenfold, but even she's struggling to find a suitable outfit for me to wear. It wouldn't be so hard if I knew what genre of music Noah's band plays. For the past month, I've never seen Noah in anything but dark jeans and a black leather jacket. Pairing those with his inky hair and eyes, you automatically assume he helms a hard-core rock group, but something is warning me not to jump to conclusions.

I've seen a different side to Noah the past four weeks. He's dark and mysterious, but also down to earth and loving. His heart isn't as big as the floral arrangement he sent for my birthday, but it's pretty darn close. I'm a little concerned about how quickly I'm developing feelings for him. If he had taken advantage of my eagerness last month when we went on a date to Stony Creek Falls, things would be starkly different.

Our first date was near perfect. I had no idea such breathtaking scenery was a mere hour from my doorstep. Noah took me to Stony Creek Falls for an early morning adventure the day following our back and forth routine at the Dungeon. Stony Creek is a beautiful inland watering hole that has a massive waterfall hidden behind dense rainforest.

After Noah convinced me to jump off a sheer rockface, we spent the remainder of our day making out in his truck. I stupidly thought the only way I'd keep him around was by acting on the inane chemistry brewing between us. That's how things worked with Zander. If I didn't jump to his every whim, he belittled me.

Noah is clearly cut from a different cloth.

The respect he's bestowed upon me the past month has done wonders for my confidence. I feel like the girl I was before I kissed a frog concealed as a prince. Our dates have been squeezed in between Noah's band's hectic schedule and my schooling and shifts at Dan's, but a lack of time hasn't made them any less wondrous. We know our time together is precious, so we make the most of every second we have.

The ginormous grin stretching across my face fades when Jenni throws a sparkly top my way. "Try this with the jeans you have on."

Although I'm not convinced by her selection, I swap shirts before pacing to the mirror in the corner of my room. My pupils dilate when I take in how well the one-shoulder cami matches my jeans. The shimmery black material sits just below my belly button, exposing a sexy yet modest portion of my skin, and the stretchy material hugs my small boobs, making them more voluptuous than they are. It's not a shirt I'd usually pair with jeans, but it brings my outfit together with an oomph of sexiness.

Now I just need to wrap up my ensemble with the perfect pair of shoes. Should I go with my regular boots? Or some leg-lengthening pumps?

Like she can read my thoughts, Jenni hands me my black leather knee-high boots. Once I slip them on, my heart beats double-time. They're the perfect accessory for my risky, rock star approved outfit.

"You're a genius."

I sling my arms around her shoulders and hug her tight. I was hoping she could come with us tonight, but Noah faced an uphill battle getting permission for me to attend since I'm under twenty-one. He's been begging Ollie relentlessly the past month. It was only after he threatened to pull Rise Up from their Friday night slot did Ollie finally relent. Even then, his agreement had conditions attached. The most stringent: I'm not allowed a drop of alcohol. I'm not bothered. I'm a lightweight; it only takes me two glasses of wine to feel tipsy, and I'm not a fan of drinking in public, so I'm happy to follow his rules.

"Now makeup!" Jenni claps her hands together two times, her excitement uncontained.

By the time I'm glammed up but still me, forty-five minutes have ticked by, and a car horn is honking at the front of my house. With my heart beating a million miles an hour, I squeeze Jenni in glee before darting for my front door. Upon exiting my home, I spot Noah climbing out of the back seat of Jacob's car. He's wearing black jeans, a black V-neck shirt, and his infamous leather jacket. He screams bad-boy rocker, and it complements my outfit to perfection.

"Hey, Beautiful." He adds a playful wink to his greeting. "I'm sorry Jacob is an ass." He flips the bird to Jacob, who's gawking at us along with another two men. "I was planning to come to your door, but Jacob has no fucking manners."

Blood pumps through my heart faster when he seals his lips over mine. It's been five long torturous days since we last kissed, so I'm more than ready for our mouths to be reacquainted.

Noah's lips get within an inch of mine when Jacob's thunderous voice booms through my ears. "Come on!" He toots his horn, his laughter picking up. "There's no time for kissing. We're already late."

I immaturely pout when Noah pulls back a mere nanosecond after his lips brush against mine. Smiling at my sullen expression, he guides me to the hanging-open back passenger door. My sagging lips curl upward when he gestures for me to enter before him. For a man whose allure screams bad-boy, he has no trouble bringing out the charm.

A curious pair of green eyes watch me slip into the backseat. Realizing his inconspicuous gawp has been busted, he adds a few words to his silent greeting. "You must be Emily; I'm Marcus."

"Hi. It's nice to meet you."

Marcus's gorgeous African American skin gives his eyes a unique color. His afro is clipped close to his scalp, and when he smiles, dimples indent his cheeks. He's deliriously gorgeous, but lacks the bad-boy edge Noah has.

When Noah slips in next to me, he rests his hand on my thigh. "You've already had the displeasure of meeting Jacob..." Jacob gives him the finger before pulling his vehicle away from the curb. "...and Marcus has already introduced himself." A smile curls on my lips, loving his carefree attitude around his friends. "So that only leaves the douchebag in the front: Nick, our lead guitarist." He points to Nick, who's sitting in the front passenger seat. "Nick, this is Emily."

My pulse flutters from the way he says my name. I'm not a fan of my given name—that's why my friends call me Em—but the way it rolls off Noah's tongue makes it seem like it belongs to a woman instead of the little girl I imagine when hearing it. He gives it a mature edge.

When Nick spins around to greet me with a smirk, I eye him in silence. He's the polar opposite of Marcus. He has pasty white skin, shaggy blond hair, a rugged face, and piercing blue eyes. I'm confident I've seen him before, but I can't pinpoint where.

My eyes flicker as my brain struggles to determine if we've met before or if I'm mistaking him for one of the many blond surfer boys from a beachside community not too far from here. If forced, I could swear on my grandmother's grave that his icy blue eyes belong to the guy I saw dancing with Jenni at the Dungeon last month, but it would be risky. The club was dark, so I could be mistaken.

Anxious about my prolonged gawk, Nick smiles a weary grin before swiveling back around to face the front. I'm still racking my brain for proof of a previous meeting when Noah squeezes my thigh.

"No, he's not a Hemsworth brother—*unfortunately.*"

His chuckle adds to the flighty feeling in my gut. Nick does have similarities to the drool-worthy Hemsworth genes, but I'm more interested in our possible connection. What are the odds of him being who I think he is? Jenni hasn't stopped gushing about the guy she met last month. If he's a friend of Noah's, the possibilities are endless. I now wish more than ever she could have come with us tonight. Nick made quite an impression on her.

Beaming with excitement, I adjust my position to face Noah, eager to update him on the possible connection between our friends. My heart fissures when my wide eyes meet with Noah's narrowed gaze. His jaw is taut, and his hand not resting on my thigh is balled.

"What's wrong?" I keep my question on the down-low, not wanting our conversation overheard. We've communicated more over the phone than in person the past month, but it's never had this level of intensity before.

Noah shoots daggers at the back of Nick's head, his gaze furious. "How do you know Nick?"

"I don't *really* know him per se..." My reply gets stuck in my throat when Noah's narrowed gaze rockets to me. His eyes are the darkest I've seen them, and they set my pulse racing. Don't ask if it's a good or bad rhythm as I wouldn't be able to tell you.

"So you've never..." He licks his lips, hoping it'll ease out his question. "...*slept* with him?"

Bile scorches my throat. Nick is cute, but he isn't my type. Nothing against him, but he reminds me a lot of Zander, meaning if he wasn't Noah's bandmate, I'd steer clear of him. I want to articulate that to Noah, but I can't get any words past my stone-dry lips since I'm so shocked.

Maybe Noah heard the rumors that circulated about me two years ago. For months, I was known as the slut who broke up Becky and Zander's perfect relationship, a relationship I didn't know existed until the morning Becky confronted me. The gossip was that I had helped Zander see what he was missing being stuck in a long-term relationship. After convincing me he was worthy of my virginity, Zander broke up with Becky, citing me in his decision.

Becky was reportedly heartbroken, but instead of handling her heartache as most teen girls do—with the support of her friends and bucket loads of ice cream—she spent the remaining three months of the school year making my life miserable. My locker was vandalized; I was pushed and shoved by her friends when they walked past, and all the senior girls hated me.

The senior guys were on the other end of the spectrum. My newly achieved "slutty" reputation meant I was continuously propositioned. I lost count of the number of times I was asked to be a friend with benefits or invited for a night of entertainment with no strings attached.

No matter how many times I refused their invitations, rumors continued circulating. Supposedly, I had a new guy every weekend. I haven't so much as kissed a man since Zander, but no one was interested in my side of the story.

Although rumors are just that: rumors, the thought of Noah thinking of me in the same manner my peers did fills my eyes with tears. I've matured a lot the past two years, but some burns take more than a lifetime to soothe.

When Noah peers at me through lidded eyes, I shake my head to his highly insensitive question. He sighs—heavily. "Thank fuck."

He kisses my temple before dragging his lips down my cheek and along my jaw. It takes all my restraint not to react to his heart-stuttering embrace, but I give it everything I have. I'm hurt by his accusation, so a little bit of schmoozing won't fix it. After I was burned by Zander, I pledged I'd never let another guy treat me the same way. Although this is different, it does tread close to the line I drew in the sand a very long time ago.

Realizing I'm not returning his embrace, Noah pulls back. Remorse clouds his eyes when he spots the tears in mine. Some of my anger evaporates when his thumbs skate across my cheeks to wipe away tears that have yet to fall.

"I'm sorry; I shouldn't have asked you that—"

"I'm not a slut."

Noah balks, stunned by my snapped comment. "I never said you were."

Honesty is written all over his face, but it does little to weaken the devastation crossing mine.

"No. You just insinuated it."

"No, Emily, I didn't mean it like that." His raging heartbeat almost drowns out what he says next, "I swear, I'd never think of you like that."

CHAPTER 14

NOAH

The instant my question escaped my lips, I knew I had fucked up. I didn't ask Emily if she had slept with Nick because I think she's a slut; it's because I *know* Nick is. He's the very definition of a man-whore, and he doesn't care who he stomps on to maintain his title.

When I introduced them, recognition dawned on Emily's face. She stared at him with her mouth ajar and her eyes wide. I couldn't tell if she was shocked to see him again or happy. She was giving off both vibes. When her eyes twitched, like she was recalling a memory, I began to wonder how well they knew one another.

Out of all of my bandmates, Nick is the biggest player. His ideas about relationships conflict with Jacob's. He's never been in love and isn't planning to fall in love. But that doesn't mean he hasn't had a lot of partners.

He spends his weekends trolling nightclubs and bars for women. A seed of doubt flourished in my head when I recalled Emily saying she had borrowed Lola's ID a handful of times. The idea of Nick touching her infuriates me. Not just because I've developed feelings for Emily I swore I'd never have but because Emily deserves better than a douchebag like Nick. He may be my bandmate, but he is *not* a good person.

I've lost count of the number of women he slept with after Marcus, Slater, and me. I never used to care. If he wanted my sloppy seconds, I was fine with it—as long as it was *after* I had finished with them, but the band nearly broke up after he slept with Slater's fiancée, Nikki.

Nick made out he was showing Slater how slutty Nikki was, but he went about it the wrong way. We all knew Nikki was bad for Slater, but it wasn't our place to say who he should or shouldn't date. Nick is lucky he's fast because if Slater had gotten ahold of him the night he walked in on him and Nikki together, I'm sure Nick would be dead.

Things have been strained with our band since then. That's why Slater now meets us at Mavericks, instead of traveling with us like we used to. I thought the effort Nick put in the past few years had convinced me he was a changed man. Clearly, I was wrong—not just about Nick, but at my beliefs I knew how to swoon. This is *not* how I planned our night to start.

"I'm sorry for what I said, but I swear, I would *never* think of you like that." When Emily's chin balances on her chest, I raise her head back to its rightful place. "Whatever we're forming is new, but I hope you realize I'd never intentionally hurt you."

Before she can reply, Jacob's car pulls into the dusty parking lot at the back of Mavs. When the guys pile out, I ask Marcus to let them know I'll be there in a minute. I take my commitments seriously, but making sure Emily is okay is my only priority right now. What I said is true, our relationship is as fresh as a newborn baby, but the instant connection I felt for her months ago has grown astronomically since she became my girl.

Once the guys have left, I scoot back so I can get a better look at Emily. Her cheeks are dry, but her eyes are brimming with unshed tears. "Are you okay?"

I feel like the biggest asshole in the world. I wanted to spend our night showing her one of my greatest passions, but instead, I've made her feel like shit. This isn't my idea of a fun night and proves I need more than a bit of help in the romance department.

Emily's teeth graze her sexy painted lips before she murmurs, "Can I be brutally honest with you?"

I nod without hesitation. "Of course."

She exhales deeply before telling me about the consequences that arose from her last relationship. Although she tiptoes around the word "virginity," I'm reasonably sure that's what she's referencing. For an ordinary guy, her openness would be troubling, but I'm anything but ordinary. We've talked so much the past month, I'm shocked we have anything left to discuss.

Listening to the first half of her story kills me—I knew someone as beautiful as her wouldn't be untouched, but a small piece of me was hoping I could give her all her firsts—but the last half utterly guts me. How could Zander watch her be attacked in front of half the school and not do anything about it? It reveals how much of a dog he is.

"I swear I didn't know he had a girlfriend, let alone a long-term one." Emily sweeps her hand across her cheeks, ensuring they're still dry. "The rest of the semester, I was bullied by the senior girls all while dodging propositions by guys who believed the rumors."

I struggle to find an appropriate response. Nothing I can say will ease her pain, so instead, I offer her my sympathy with actions instead of words. I press my lips to her temple while running my hand down her smooth, straight locks. I expect her to pull away like she did earlier, so you can imagine my surprise when she accepts my support by nuzzling into my chest so she can drink in my scent.

Although I still want to strangle Zander, a few minutes of silence does wonders for my anger. "I'm sorry you were treated that way." My agitation is subsiding, but my words still arrive with a growl. "High school sucks as it is, without additional drama."

Hearing something I didn't mean to express, Emily's head pops off my chest. She doesn't say anything, but I can see a million questions in her eyes. As I said earlier, we've talked a lot, but I still haven't worked up the courage to tell her about my brothers. I will one day, just not today.

After a few seconds of uncomfortable silence, Emily murmurs, "I'm reasonably sure I saw Nick at the dance club last month." Any awkwardness lingering fades when she smiles. "He was dancing with my friend Jenni."

I inwardly curse when excitement crosses her features. She appears pleased for her friend.

She shouldn't be. If she genuinely cares for Jenni, she should tell her to steer clear of Nick.

I'm about to break a bro-code I've never broken, but if I don't warn Emily about Nick, her friend will get hurt. Usually, that wouldn't bother me, but if Jenni gets burnt by Nick, Emily will get burnt. That's something I won't stand for.

"Your friend should stay away from Nick. He can't be trusted."

Emily's smile falters, but she remains quiet, waiting for me to elaborate.

I follow along nicely. "Nick is a player; your friend will get hurt if she isn't careful."

It feels wrong ratting Nick out like this, but at the end of the day, he deserves it. It might even force him to clean his act up.

"Oh..."

Emily's forlorn face makes me suspicious Nick has already gotten his hooks into Jenni. Before I can ask for more details, Jacob's deep timbre ripples through the air. "Soundcheck in five minutes." His voice projects from the entrance of Mavs. "Ollie said if your ass isn't on stage by then, he's docking your pay."

Like fuck he will. He charges more for a pint of beer Friday nights than any other night of the week because of the hundreds of patrons my band attracts, so he sure as hell won't be slicing the pittance he pays me.

I stop clenching and unclenching my fists when Emily giggles. It's a beautiful thing to hear after such a turbulent start to our evening. "Maybe we should head in?"

"Are you sure you're ready?"

Smiling, she nods. "I'm so excited, I might pee!"

I laugh, loving both her honesty and how at ease she is with me already. It shows that not even a month of turmoil could kill her spirit. I completely misjudged her three months ago. She's not shy. She's a fighter.

After sliding out of the car, I offer my hand to Emily to help her out, her smile turning blinding when she accepts my gesture. We walk into Mavericks hand in hand. I've been here hundreds of times before, but you can tell it's Emily's first. Her eyes bounce around the space, absorbing its eccentric details.

An old wood bar lines a wall housing hundreds of bottles of alcohol on glass shelves. Smoke hovers above our heads from the regulars washing down their beers with a cigarette, and two billiard tables are near the back wall just left of the restrooms. To our left is the stage. Ollie supplies most of the equipment, but we occasionally switch it up by bringing our own. In front of the stage is the dance floor, surrounded by wooden tables with barstools tucked underneath them. At this time of the night, only a handful of regulars mingle around, but within the hour, a younger, more energetic crowd will pack the space.

When I spot Maggie at the end of the bar, I guide Emily toward her. Maggie is the mother hen of the group. She's been working at Mavs for as long as I can remember. She even worked here when my brother Chris and I dragged our dad out of here after he had too many beers.

Maggie's gaze lifts to mine when we stop in front of her. The motherly twinkle in her eyes brightens the longer her eyes bounce between Emily and me.

They blaze when I say, "Maggie, I'd like to introduce you to my girlfriend, Emily."

CHAPTER 15

EMILY

earing Noah call me his girlfriend makes me giddy. You know the feeling you get Christmas morning? Or after a heart-stopping kiss? That's how I feel when he references me as his girlfriend. Although we've been on a number of dates the past month, he never officially asked me out, so I was unsure what our relationship status was, but now I know, and I'm incredibly thrilled to accept the title of his girlfriend.

"Emily, this is a dear friend of mine, Maggie."

Noah waves his hand to a lady standing behind the wooden bar. I'm not overly good at guessing ages, but she appears to be in her mid-fifties. Her wavy gray hair has a few strands of blonde through it, and although a smattering of crow's feet dusts the corners of her stark blue eyes, they still have a youthful sparkle to them. Her Mavericks uniform is the same as Lola's, but she has more material in her red t-shirt and full-length white jeans.

"Girlfriend?" Maggie arches her brow into her hair. "That's a first." She smiles, seemingly pleased for Noah. "Welcome to Mavs, baby girl."

"Thank you." I gently shake the hand she's holding out, afraid I might break it if I grab it too hard.

I have no cause for concern. Maggie's grip is enough for my hand to throb. "How come I feel like I've already met you?"

Hearing the same whip of edginess in her voice, Noah curls his arm around my shoulders. "Emily is Lola's little sister."

Remaining quiet, Maggie drinks in the similarities between Lola and me. The caramel highlights I added to my shorter locks have me at a disadvantage. A few months ago, I would have said our turned-up noses were our only similarities, but now we look more alike than ever.

Once Maggie finishes her avid perusal, she sets back to cleaning the spotless counter she was in the process of wiping before we interrupted her. If her snarled lip is anything to go by, I'm confident she isn't a fan of Lola. For reasons I'll never be able to explain, this makes me like her a little more than I did when I noticed the nurturing glint in her eyes toward Noah.

Noah's body heats my side before his breaths fan my temple. "I've got to prep for the show; will you be okay sitting here with Maggie?"

When I nod, he shifts his focus to Maggie. "Be nice." A ghost of a smile touches his lips, weakening my panic. He's more playful than worried.

Over the next several minutes, Noah and his band complete what I assume is a soundcheck. They fiddle with equipment while Noah occasionally says, "Check one, two, three" into the microphone.

Around five minutes later, a well-built man with long blond dreadlocks enters the main doors. He's wearing sunglasses, a long-sleeve Harley Davidson shirt, black jeans, and motorcycle boots. Pair those traits with the helmet lodged under his arm, and I'm quick to assume he's a biker.

Glancing over at the bar, he dips his chin in greeting to Maggie before stomping to the stage. I swivel my chair in the direction he just gawked. "Who's that?"

Maggie stops wiping the bar to peer up at me. "That's Slater, drummer for Rise Up." She stacks polished glasses under the bar, her smile picking up. "He's a good boy, that one. As are all those young men. Even Nick, who can be a rascal at times, but they all have good hearts."

The pride in her voice makes my chest bloom with warmth. She talks about the boys like a proud mother would.

My happiness cools a little when she locks her anxious eyes with mine. "Be extra cautious with Noah's heart, Emily. That boy has been through enough; he doesn't need more heartache."

Pretending my heart isn't racing a million miles an hour, I nod before slinging my gaze back to the stage. Upon feeling my inquisitive stare, Noah's head lifts from a speaker he's tampering with. He gives me a look that questions, *are you okay?* When I dip my chin, the concern in his dark gaze fades. He takes a few seconds to deliberate before he returns to setting up his equipment.

I watch him in silence, pondering if the heartache Maggie mentioned involves the names tattooed on his chest. Noah explained they were in memory of his brothers, but that's as far as our conversation went. Not everyone is as open and honest as me, so I steered our discussion toward a new subject, hopeful that when he was ready, he'd tell me without me bending his arm.

Doesn't weaken my curiosity though. Not in the slightest.

Over the next hour, the bar goes from a laidback atmosphere to a space thrumming with energy. Excluding one table dead center of the stage, the ones lining the dance floor are full of noisy patrons. Rise Up may not be known nationwide, but they have a massive following in their hometown. I'm impressed, which isn't an easy feat these days. Tell me one teen who isn't cynical?

Mavs' rundown appearance hides the young, energetic crowd it draws this time of night. It's so busy, the four barmaids working alongside Maggie are run off their feet. If I had any idea how to pull a beer, I'd offer to help. Alas, I don't, so I'll continue sitting around, being unhelpful.

I crank my neck when a manly voice greets, "Hey, Em."

After clearing an expansive chest, my eyes land on the smiling face of Jacob. "Hey, Jake." The chirpiness in my voice softens when I notice he has a fading black eye and a scarred lip. "What happened to your face?"

I've only met Jacob a handful of times, but he's a giant teddy bear, so I'm shocked he'd participate in anything violent. Noah, on the other hand...

My inner monologue tapers when Jacob mumbles, "I ran into a door."

When Maggie *tsks* him, Jacob's eyes narrow. "Is Lola working tonight?"

Maggie rolls her eyes with the attitude of a teen. "No. *Thank goodness.*"

Just like Noah, Jacob finds her dislike amusing. His throaty chuckle chops up his words when he rumbles, "Be nice, or you might offend Lola's little sister, Emily."

He bands his arm around my shoulders to squeeze me tight. Even with me sitting high on a barstool, I'm swallowed by him.

He's barely hugged me for a second when his arm is yanked away. "Keep your hands to yourself."

After snarling at Jacob, which increases his laughter, Noah stops to stand in front of me. "Do you want to stay here or up front at the band's table?" He nudges his head to the empty table I mentioned earlier.

Considering tonight is the first time I'll hear him play, I want to be as close to the action as possible. "The band's table."

I leap off my barstool, my eagerness on full display. I'm excited to see Rise Up perform, but the fact Noah will be front and center the entire time has my pussy throbbing with anticipation.

CHAPTER 16

NOAH

"*N*oah..." Emily turns to face me. Tears are welling in her eyes, but I'm not worried, because she also has the biggest smile stretched across her face. "I love it." She leaps into my arms to curl her legs around my waist. "I love you."

My heart strums against my ribs. Not once the past three months has she directly said she loves me. She toyed around with it, expressing it in a non-direct manner when her head gets hazy with lust, but she's never directly said it like she did now. Although I'm ecstatic, I'm too stunned to say it back. I love her too, but for some fucked-up reason, I can't get the words out of my mouth.

Instead, I kiss her.

It starts an avalanche of hands, lips, and teeth. We've made out like this many times the past twelve weeks, but there's a new friskiness in the air tonight. We're alone at the fancy hotel I saved up for so I could show Emily how *real* men treat a lady.

I crave Emily like solar panels crave the sun, but no matter how intense my cravings grew as we tiptoed from a forming relationship to one with enough intensity to electrify Ravenshoe, we've never slid past third base. She's constantly worried I'm rejecting her. I'm not—*I never would.* I just wanted our first time to be special. She lost her virginity in the back of a van with a douchebag who had no clue of her worth. I refuse to disrespect her like her scumbag ex did.

Although it was torture stopping our make-out sessions when they stepped over the line I deemed acceptable, it was best for all involved. It supplemented the feelings we've developed for each other with a massive boost of respect, convincing me nothing will ever come between us.

Renting a hotel room doesn't sound romantic, but with Emily still living with her parents and me boarding at Jacob's house, there isn't any other place for us to go. Furthermore, you couldn't see Emily's face when I opened our hotel room door. I spent the afternoon lighting candles on every surface; her favorite flowers are on the bedside tables, and her crush, Adam Levine, is crooning in the background. I've got all my bases covered... and then some.

After kicking the hotel room door closed with my boot, I walk Emily to the king-size bed to place her down, our tongues dueling the entire time. Her chest rises and falls in a steady movement when I undo the latch on her boots before sliding down the hidden zipper. Although she's clearly nervous, we've both wanted this for so long, excitement is far exceeding nerves.

I dump her boots on the ground before nudging my head to the pillow above her head. "Lie back."

While she scoots up the mattress, I toe off my shoes then drag my shirt over my head. Emily has seen me naked a good dozen times the past three months, but she still drinks me in as if it is the first time.

Her appreciative gawk has my cock roaring to life. Things have always been crazy intense between us, sometimes a little too fast to be seen as more than lust, but what newly forming relationship isn't? If you're not attracted to the person you're with, why are you with them? And if you didn't have an *instant* fascination with them, how did your relationship get off the blocks?

Don't get me wrong. I'm still skeptical about insta-love, but my stance lessens with every day I have with Emily. Even before we become an official couple, she was on my mind, so imagine how bad it became once she was my girl.

Eager to relieve the pain of my zipper biting my cock, I unbutton my jeans and slide down the zipper. The hissing of metal adds to the tension brimming between us, which lengthens my tease. Emily is glaring at my crotch, impatiently waiting for me to free my cock, but I can't help teasing her. She hates waiting nearly as much as she hates being tickled.

"Noah…" She appears seconds from crawling across the mattress to help herself to me. "If you don't hurry up—"

Her words falter when I tug down my jeans enough the cropped hairs across my pelvis peek out from my low-riding boxers. "Better?"

While Emily nods, her pupils dilating, my boxer shorts have a meeting with my jeans, which are huddled around my feet. My cock is as hard as the pining expression she's giving me. I take it in my hand, giving it a long, determined stroke before jerking my chin up to the baggy jeans she's wearing.

"Your turn."

Precum wets the crest of my cock when her top is the first thing to go. Her vintage rock shirt is closely followed by the removal of her jeans. I tighten my grip on my shaft when it twitches. She dressed for the occasion, and I'm fucking ecstatic. Her bra and panties are like the pair she wore when we jumped off the cliff at Stony Creek Falls on our first date but fancier, with lace making up a majority of the design.

"Do you want to play around first?" I need her wet enough to take all of me, but I'm as impatient as fuck. The dampness of her panties won't curb my eagerness. She's drenched.

Emily shakes her head. "No. We've waited long enough. Please don't make me wait any longer." As predicted, she crawls across the mattress to add to her request without words, pulling me down until I'm lying on top of her. My cock creates delicious friction with her damp panties. "I want you, Noah. I want you so much."

Her eyes squeeze shut when I grind against her. I go extra slow, ensuring she knows we're not fucking. We're making love.

I suck her lips into my mouth before slipping my tongue between them. I kiss her like I wish I could her pussy. I want her juices on my chin, but not as badly as I'm dying to make her mine.

After a final drag of my tongue along the ridges of her mouth, I pull back and glance down at her. "Are you sure?"

"Yes," she answers without hesitation, her confirmation coming with a nod. "I've never wanted anything more."

Smiling, I nip at her lips, her budded nipple through her bra, and her stomach as I make my way to her panties. They're lacy and completely soaked through. Although she said no to foreplay, I can't hurt her. I need to make sure she's fully prepared, so with that in mind, I slip her panties away before spearing my tongue through her seductive heat.

Fuck me.

Heaven. I must have died and gone to heaven.

It doesn't take many lashes of my tongue to get her ready for me. She's so wet, not only does my chin bear unmissable evidence, but Emily's thighs are trembling.

Before crawling back up to her flushed face, I snag a condom from the many I hid in the drawer when preparing our room. Emily watches me roll it down my cock in revered silence as she licks her lips. She's thirsty for my cock, but unlike the times I drive her home after our dates, she doesn't want it between her pillowy lips.

Once everything is in place, I position myself between her splayed thighs. Fuck me, there aren't any words to describe what I'm seeing. I've never seen her as beautiful as she is now, and I've often been caught staring in admiration.

I nestle my cock at the entrance of her pussy before returning my eyes to Emily's flushed face. "Are you sure you're sure?"

She hates that I'm double-checking, but I want to be sure she's not being coerced by smoke and mirrors. I want her to do this because she wants to, not because she feels forced.

When she nods for the second time, I spend the next several hours enjoying every delectable inch of her. It's pure fucking heaven. Pert tits, a pussy that's sweeter than honey, and eyes that see through to my soul. I couldn't get better than this, and for the first time in my life, I feel lucky—almost at peace.

A couple of hours later, Emily rests her head on my chest so she can trace her finger on the outline of my tattoo. "Will you tell me about them?"

She knows I lost my brothers in unrelated incidents, but I've never talked about the event that led to their deaths.

Sensing my hesitation, she whispers, "Please," before placing a kiss on Chris and Michael's names integrated in my tattoo.

I roll onto my hip, hoping her blissed-filled eyes will lessen the pain I experience any time I share the story of how I lost two of the most incredible people I had ever met within years of each other.

"On the surface, my family looked like an ordinary family. In reality, we were far from it. My mom got pregnant with Chris when she was seventeen. Because she refused to have an abortion, and my grandparents wouldn't allow her 'bastard' child in their house, she became homeless. My dad's band was well known in its early days. He often shared stories about how they were offered a record deal worth thousands of dollars, but with my mom pregnant and homeless, he left his band to work at the local sawmill." My thoughts drift to the sawdust-covered overalls still in my dad's closet. It forces a smile onto my lips.

"For years, my parents appeared to have a perfect marriage. I joined the trio a couple of years later, making Chris a big brother and completing our family. Things were ideal, but when my dad's band went on to have some minor success, his regret for leaving soon burned a hole into his soul."

My smile slackens. "By the time I was in middle school, he had begun drinking heavily to drown his sorrows. He'd often come home late, collapse onto the sofa for a cat nap before going to work the next day. It didn't take his bosses long to realize he was working drunk. They had no choice; they had to let him go. My parents had only been together for two months when she got pregnant, and although my dad would never admit it, everyone could tell he blamed my mom for forcing his decision to leave his band."

When I stop to take a breath, Emily offers me an encouraging smile.

"Not long after my dad got fired, my mom got a job as a receptionist at the local doctor's office. Her long hours meant we rarely saw her, so Chris and I were mainly raised by our dad. I don't know whether Michael was conceived as an attempt to save their marriage, but he did make our family closer. Because of the age difference, Chris and I doted on him. He had the most inquisitive brown eyes that absorbed everything around him. My dad said that meant he was an old soul who had been here before."

I lick my dry lips, praying a bit of moisture will help ease out my next set of words. "Although dad's drinking improved after Michael was born, it was still rare to see him without a beer in his hand. Because I had grown up around it, I didn't know any different. I loved my dad, even though he was a drunk. He often came to Marcus's house to help my band practice, and he even worked on a few tracks for some lyrics I had written down."

The fractures in my heart are heard in my words. "One afternoon, a few months after my fifteenth birthday, a huge storm rolled in. Usually, I'd walk home after rehearsals, but because it was pouring rain, and I had borrowed my dad's pride and joy, his vintage Gibson guitar, I called the house hoping Chris could pick me up. Chris had already left for work, so my dad offered to get me. I had grown up most of my life with an alcoholic father, so I didn't think about him driving drunk."

I peer up at the ceiling, blinking rapidly in hopes it will stop tears from forming in my eyes. "I was waiting for him at the front of Marcus's house when a massive bang boomed into my ears. I dropped my dad's guitar case and ran into the street. I had only sprinted a few yards down when I saw a mangled mess of metal and broken glass. It was my parents' van. As I sprinted toward the wreckage, I witnessed my dad climbing out of the driver's side window. He was dazed and confused, but relatively unharmed."

My words choke when I force them out of my mouth. "My heart stopped beating when he yelled out Michael's name while yanking on the crumpled rear driver's side door. I ran to his side, fruitlessly trying to help him free Michael from the wreckage, but that side of his car had so much damage, the door wouldn't budge. I screamed Michael's name over and over again, hoping he'd say something back. If he had made some kind of noise, I would have known he was okay." I shake my head. "He never made a sound."

Emily burrows her face into my chest, her lips quivering.

"A few minutes later, the fire department freed Michael from the wreckage with the jaws of life. When they pulled him out of the car to perform CPR on him, he was limp and lifeless. I knew he was gone the instant they shined the light into his eyes. All the spark they'd held had vanished. The police report said my dad lost control of his vehicle in the heavy rain. He veered into oncoming traffic before colliding with a van on the opposite side of the road. Michael was killed on impact. He was only four years old."

I try to regather my composure by taking several long, ragged breaths. The memories of that day are still so raw for me. Even though it happened six years ago, and my nightmares have lessened, that day will forever haunt me.

I continue before I lose my nerve. "Michael usually had preschool on Thursdays. My mom picked him up on her way home from work. I had left for school that day not knowing he'd been up most of the night with a fever, so he stayed home with dad. If I had known he was going to be in the car, I would have never accepted my dad's offer to pick me up. I would have walked in the rain or waited for the storm to pass, but I didn't know... honestly, I didn't know he was in the car."

My hand flies across my cheek, wiping away a rogue tear before Emily notices it.

"My mom was brought to the hospital by a local police officer. When she saw me lingering at the side of the emergency department, she stormed over and slapped me hard across my face. I knew then and there that she'd never forgive me for asking my dad for a ride that day. If I had just walked home, both Michael and Chris would still be here—"

"No, Noah, no. You are *not* to blame for his death." Emily cups my cheek with her hand, the truth in her eyes easing the pain shredding through my heart. "You did nothing wrong. *Nothing* at all."

I want to believe her, but I can't. I am partially to blame for what happened that day. My dad was charged with operating a motor vehicle while intoxicated. His blood alcohol level was five times over the legal limit. He pleaded guilty to all charges and was given a ten-year sentence at the Parkwood State Prison.

My sentence was much more severe. Even now, with my girl in my arms and my heart the fullest it's ever been, I can't help but wonder how much longer it will be before I lose everything again. I can only hope paranoia is fueling my worry, because I barely survived losing Chris and Michael. I won't survive that type of loss a third time around.

CHAPTER 17

EMILY

"*W*here do you want this box?"

Jacob walks into my dorm room, juggling a box marked with "lingerie and sex toys." Noah thought he was hilarious when he labeled my box of books with that. He knew Jacob was helping me move this weekend, so he picked the heaviest box, hoping he'd fool Jacob into believing he has a massive selection of sex toys at his disposal.

Our relationship has undoubtedly increased its heat level the past three months, but the only toys at Noah's disposal are the ones attached to his body. If I had to explain our relationship with two words, I would say: mesmerizingly perfect. Take our immediate connection the night we met, multiply it by a hundred, then you'll be within ten percent of how sparking things have become between us. Noah is affectionate, sweet, protective, and has me one hundred percent convinced the only slimy thing about him is his sweaty hair when he finishes wooing his fans on stage.

A smile creeps across my face when Jacob asks, "What the hell have you got in here, Em? It weighs a ton."

Noah slaps down the flap of the box a mere second before Jacob peeks inside. "That's for me to know and you to never find out."

He yanks the box out of Jacob's grip, causing him to chuckle. "Come on, man, don't be a tease."

Stealing Noah's chance to reply, Jacob heads back to his car to collect the remaining two boxes. My pulse quickens when his departure coincides with Noah strolling toward me. He drops the box onto my desk before curling his hands around my jaw. My thighs press together as his lips arrow toward mine. He kisses the living shit out of me, leaving no doubt that I've been on his mind all day. I pout when he withdraws from our embrace way before I've had my fill. We've been apart for over eight hours today, which is the longest since summer break started.

As Noah peers at me with confident, cocky eyes, I drink in all his gorgeous features. His dark, stormy eyes, the beautiful dimples he flashes as he smiles his panty-dropping grin, and the plumpness of his kiss-swollen lips. My god, he's handsome—and entirely mine.

"I missed you so much, Beautiful." His frisky wink makes my panties wet. "Are you moving in okay?"

He takes in the minuscule dorm room Jacob and I have been moving me into the past four hours. Although nervous, I'm excited to begin my studies at Parkwood State College. I initially planned to attend Columbus University, but being eight hours away from Noah was more than I could bear, so I chose Parkwood instead. Our commute is still an hour, but I'll see Noah every weekend instead of the six-week blocks we were looking at.

I follow Noah's gaze around my damp-smelling room. "We're getting there... *slowly.*"

My room is extremely bland. Two full-size beds take up one wall, separated by a bench desk that looks suitable for dual occupants. The light gray walls haven't seen a coat of paint in years, and there's a funky smell in the air, but mercifully, I have a private bathroom, meaning I won't need to use the communal showers down the hall.

Although I would have loved a private room off-campus, my budget doesn't allow it. I'll only sleep and study here, so this is more than adequate—even more so since we're alone.

Noah grins when I tug him onto the bed we're standing next to. "How was your meeting?"

For the past six months, we've spent every Sunday together, but we had to skip today because he had a meeting with some music executives interesting in signing Rise Up. Although I'm dying to hear how his meeting went, I have lost time to make up for.

"Hmmm. It was good."

Noah's moans vibrate my core when I suck, nibble, and kiss his neck. I feel their thrum when I straddle his lap. His cock is straining against the zipper in his jeans. He's primed and ready to go.

We kiss for a few more moments before the number of clothes between us becomes annoying. After a final lick of his lower lip, I fist his shirt to raise it over his head. With some assistance, I have him shirtless not even two seconds later.

The heat bristling between us turns scorching when I place feather-like kisses along his jaw, down his neck, and over his chest. I stop briefly to press my lips to Michael and Chris's names inked on his chest before continuing my mission.

My lips rise against his skin when Noah's six-pack contracts with every kiss I place. I lavish each perfect bump before sliding my tongue down the thin seam of hairs running from his belly button to the crotch of his jeans.

With his eyes arrested on me, Noah props his arms behind his head, giving himself a prime spot to watch the show about to occur. He drinks in my dedication to his body with a patience he doesn't often have in the bedroom, and his watchful eye adds to the sticky situation between my legs.

While one hand fiddles with the button on his jeans, the other slides down his zipper. I'm about to free his cock from its tight restraints when a cough echoes into my room. "That was supposed to be my bed?"

When my head flings in the direction the amused voice came from, I spot a beautiful blonde standing in the doorway. Her hands are splayed across her hips, and she's grinning broadly.

I gulp. I've been dying to meet my new roommate, but when the clock struck three, I assumed she wouldn't turn up until Monday morning with the remaining freshmen.

Noah groans when I dive off my bed. I don't know if he's devastated because our make-out session was interrupted, or because my knee got a little friendly with his groin during my dismount. I'd say it's a bit of both.

Ignoring the wobble of my thighs, I head toward the blonde to offer an introduction. Although my strides are confident, I'm dying on the inside. Things could be worse. Imagine if she had arrived a few minutes later? "Sorry about... *that.*"

I can't believe I'm meeting my roommate this way. Adjusting back to sharing a room will already be difficult, so I don't need additional problems. Once the dust settles, we'll have to work out how we'll handle situations like this in the future. Surely I won't be the only one wanting privacy? She's incredibly beautiful, just in a wholesome, down to earth way that's hard to explain.

"I'm Emily, your roommate."

After returning my hands-off greeting with a smile, she glances over my shoulder to Noah, who's propped on his elbows, watching our exchange with curious eyes. When her gaze drifts back to me, she gives me a brazen wink. "I can't blame you." She giggles, her cheeks inflaming.

I can't blame her either. Much to Noah's disgrace, Jacob has dragged him to some work out sessions at his local gym, meaning his muscles are more defined. Although I'd prefer she keep her eyes off Noah's assets, surprisingly, I don't feel threatened by her. She reminds me a lot of Jenni, whom I'll miss dearly since she's studying in New York.

There are no decent fashion courses at Parkwood State College, so Jenni and I said a tearful goodbye last Friday when I drove her to the airport. My heart pangs just thinking about her living in a different state, but we promised to visit as often as possible, and Wednesday nights between five and ten are blocked solely for each other. No interruptions. Just us.

My eyes drop when the blonde thrusts out her hand in offering.

"I'm Crystal. I dropped off some things yesterday and had planned on that being my bed, but I guess you can have it."

I smile, loving her carefree attitude. She seems genuinely fun, but with an edge of mysteriousness—just like Noah.

When I wave for Noah to join us, he hops up from the bed, yanking on his shirt in the process. When he stops at our side, I gather his hand in mine, preparing to introduce him, but Crystal steals my opportunity.

"Please don't do that for me. You're more than welcome to walk around shirtless any time you like." Her teeth rake her lower lip as her flirtatious gaze drinks in an up-close Noah. "It isn't like I haven't seen it all before."

My heart falls from my ribcage. If I find out she's slept with my boyfriend, I'm going to need a new roommate. Noah has been upfront about the hookups he had before we got together, but there's no chance in hell I'll share a dorm room with someone he's slept with. That's *way* above my level of understanding. Just the thought has me wanting to slap someone.

My eyes drift to Noah when his thumb glides over the hand crushing his so powerfully, I'll be surprised if he can play guitar this month. When he gets my focus, he shakes his head, wordlessly assuring me my sudden shift in demeanor isn't required.

Relief swamps me. Noah doesn't lie—*not even when he should*—so I have no reason to distrust his silent assurance that he doesn't know who Crystal is.

As Noah settles my paranoia as only he can, Crystal rummages through a box sitting on our desk. I don't know what she's looking for, but her face lights up when she finds it. With glee lining her face, she rushes back to Noah's side. The reason for her giddy response comes to light when she hands Noah the demo album Rise Up created three months ago.

"Can you please sign this? I'm a huge fan; I haven't missed a show all summer."

Noah smiles a beaming white grin. "Sure."

My heart rate soars, loving that I get to witness him signing his very first album cover. Crystal's request also reveals how she's seen Noah shirtless before. I've watched Rise Up perform every Friday since the month we began dating. Noah's sex appeal on stage is blistering—that may have something to do with him performing shirtless for a majority of the show.

When I questioned why, he said the lights on stage are so hot, it's more comfortable performing without a shirt. It was only after his band members snickered behind him did he confess it also helps bring in the female fans.

Noah's bandmates are an odd match, but they have a massive following of female fans. That's not surprising considering each member is gorgeous in his own way. Although their handsome faces and panty-wetting bodies get their fans in the doors, their talent keeps them coming back for more.

I'm not biased when I say Rise Up is extremely talented. I swear to god, it took everything I had to keep my hands off Noah after watching him perform for the first time. The entire experience was exhilarating.

Once Noah finishes signing Crystal's CD, he hands it back to her. She jumps into the air, squealing like a jubilant teen. "Thank you so much." She shifts on her feet to face me. "Could you ask the rest of the band to sign it for me? I'd die a thousand deaths."

Her excitement jumps to my face. "Sure..." I pause, building the suspense. "Or I could introduce you to them after one of their gigs, and you could ask them to sign it for you."

Her mouth gapes open, shocked by my offer. She shouldn't be stunned; the guys would be thrilled to meet her. They always have time for their dedicated fans.

"Thank you so much!" She squeezes my arm, her joy uncontained. "I need to tell my friend Trish."

After squeezing me to within an inch of death, Crystal spins on her heels and rushes out of our room. I'm not a part of Noah's group, but excitement still thickens my blood. I'm so incredibly proud they're starting to get the recognition they deserve. They've worked relentlessly the past six months writing enough songs to fill two albums.

They don't have a label yet, but they scraped together enough coin to organize a demo album.

Ricco, the sound engineer they hired, printed off an additional hundred CDs to sell to their fans on the condition that they'd remember him when they're famous. If today is anything to go by, I don't see that being too far off.

Feeding off the hype, Noah bands his arms around my waist to spin me around the room. "Can you believe it? I just signed my first album cover—in front of my girl. Life can't get better than this."

He continues spinning me until dizziness overtakes the euphoria pumping through my veins. "Please stop."

If he doesn't adhere to my demand, my room will be decorated with vomit instead of the hundreds of collages Jenni and I put together during Noah's many rehearsals this summer. A mere second before barf lands on his shoes, Noah stops spinning me mid-twirl. He holds me flush against him for several minutes, as if panicked I'll disappear.

"Are you okay?"

I want to say sudden changes in his mood are uncommon, but unfortunately, that isn't the case. His emotions at times can seem like a rollercoaster: soaring to great heights before crashing to devastating lows. His past has a lot to do with that. Although he has no reason to, he feels guilty any time he's enjoying life. After placing me down, Noah saunters to the rumpled bed we were making out on.

"I'm alright." He pats the comforter, offering up the spot next to him. When I plop down, I drape my arm over his shoulders, tightening my grip when he confesses, "I was just thinking about how much Chris would have loved witnessing me sign my first cover."

My heart breaks for him as it does every time he talks about his brothers. He told me about the accident responsible for his little brother's death the night we made love for the first time. I was devastated for him—so much so, uncontrollable sobs shuddered through my body. I should have been comforting him, but it was Noah who rubbed my back for hours, consoling me.

Although that night was both the best night of my life and the lowest, some good came from his confession. It made me realize the months of torment I endured from my peers was barely a blip on the radar compared to the heartbreak he had suffered. I was convinced nothing could be worse than being hated by my classmates, but now I feel foolish I let them get the best of me. Don't get me wrong, at the time, their cruel words stung like a thousand bees, but it also made me a better person by ensuring I'll never treat anyone how I was treated.

That's why, when I woke hours later still cuddled into Noah's chest, recalling that he never said what happened to his eldest brother, I refused to break his heart for the second time that night. Instead, I worshipped his body, matching his earlier intensity, showing him how courageous and loved he was using nothing but my body. It turned our night around in an instant, and made me fall in love with him even more than I thought possible.

Knowing how brutally broken he was, but still having the courage to be gentle and kind to those around him shows how much of a badass he is. His heart was broken, but big enough to still work despite its cracks.

A few weeks after we made love for the first time, I found out from Jacob that Noah's eldest brother committed suicide on the fourth anniversary of Michael's death. They don't know if it was the combination of the drugs in Chris's system, or because he couldn't take the pain any longer that lead to his decision.

Chris was only twenty-one years old, the same age Noah is now. He was so young. I couldn't imagine losing Noah at the same age. Just the thought has tears pricking my eyes.

The heat of my breaths fans Noah's neck when I murmur, "I love you."

He sucks in a ragged breath like my words are too much for him to bear, but not even a hurricane could stop him from replying. "I love you too."

When my eyes rise to his, my heart swells. They're nowhere near as troubled as they were moments ago. Surrounding him with the people he loves will show him that he's not alone, but just in case it doesn't, I sweeten the deal by sealing my mouth over his.

Our tongues have barely tangled when Jacob enters my dorm, his swagger more felt than witnessed. "Get a room."

My lips curve against Noah's mouth before my eyes pop open. A giggle rumbles in my chest when I spot Noah giving Jacob the finger. For two friends who are as thick as thieves, they get an immense amount of pleasure teasing one another.

"These are the last two boxes, Em." Jacob dumps them on my bed, either oblivious to Noah's taunt or not caring.

When Noah stands, taking me with him, my dorm shrinks in size. With the three of us standing shoulder to shoulder, it's even smaller than initially perceived. It's a rabbit warren.

I can't believe this is it. My entire life packed up into a handful of moving boxes. Excluding books and clothes, I don't have many personal belongings. A majority of my savings went toward my 2001 VW Beetle. It's light pink and my *second* most valued possession. Can you guess who has the number one spot? It's the same man who refuses to drive my car because it's the most un-masculine vehicle he's ever seen.

Even getting Noah into the passenger seat is an effort. I don't know whether he's afraid it will ruin his bad-boy reputation, or if his six-foot-two frame makes it hard for him to fit. With Noah and Jacob finishing the rebuild of Noah's truck two months ago, Noah insists we take it whenever we go on a date. I never argue with him. I'm not insane. The large bed in the back means we have plenty of room for our heavy make-out sessions.

"How was your meeting, Noah?"

Jacob's question reminds me that I never got an answer from Noah earlier. Well, I did. It was just more a moan than an actual response.

A huge smile carves on Noah's mouth. "Good, *real* good."

He bounces on his feet, his excitement brewing. Rise Up had a meeting this afternoon with Isaac's music executive friend, Cormack McGregor. After watching Rise Up perform a few weeks ago at Mavs, Cormack spoke to Noah after the show. He told Noah he works for Destiny Records and was scouting for new talent. He enjoyed the two original songs they played that night and was interested in discovering how many more songs they had developed. Noah gave him one of their CDs free of charge. Two weeks later, Cormack arranged for Rise Up to meet with other executives of the label. That meeting was today.

"They enjoyed the sound we created and want to experience it live. They're coming to watch our gig this Friday."

I throw my arms around his neck and hug him tight. "They'll love you guys!"

I can't contain my excitement. This is precisely what the guys have been aiming for. Once the executives see them perform live, they'll sign them to their label. They're morons if they don't.

"That's great news, Noah." Jacob slaps him on the shoulder. His smile is as large as mine, his joy just as notable. "This is what you've been working toward your whole life."

He takes his praise one step further by wrapping Noah up in a man hug. A grin curls my lips when Noah returns his embrace with a pat on his shoulder before stepping back. Noah isn't a hugging type of guy, and Jacob is aware of that. That's why he stays holding on tight, refusing to acknowledge the annoyance flaming Noah's cheeks.

Regrettably, Noah is just as aware of Jacob's dislikes. "Alright there, big guy, don't start crying."

Jacob pushes Noah away from him with a grunt. "Whatever."

Before I realize he's dropping one of Noah's neuroses for another, he bands his arms around my torso. I've noticed the last few months that Jacob loves using me to rile Noah up. Every time he says a lewd comment or hugs me inappropriately, Noah takes his bait, hook, line, and sinker.

When Jacob spins me around, the dizziness I felt earlier returns full pelt. "Emily loves my big hugs. Don't you, Em?"

My pupils turn massive when he glides me down his body after four full twirls. His size has people fooled into believing he's cushiony under his long shirt and trousers. He isn't. Layers of clothes hide his impressive muscles.

"Get off her, Jacob!"

Noah drags me away from Jacob, giving him the exact reaction he was aiming for. His laughter bounces off the paint-peeling walls, his swagger cocky. I hate that he uses me as bait, but I love that even after months of dating, Noah still gets jealous.

"Bye, Emily." As he walks to my door, Jacob daintily waves.

Noah saunters to the same door, his rock star swagger in full effect. "Fuck off!"

When he slams the door in Jacob's face, strangers may mistake his actions for anger, but the shit-eating grin stretched across his face reveals otherwise. He's loving their tit for tat routine as much as Jacob.

My smile fizzles to a sultry smirk when Noah pivots to face me. Is it wrong of me to say I love when he's riled up with jealousy? Any time his feathers get ruffled, his efforts to ensure I'm thoroughly satisfied ramp up to never-before-reached levels.

Remind me to thank Jacob the next time I see him, because if the hankering look in Noah's eyes is anything to go by, I'm about to have an extremely adventurous afternoon.

CHAPTER 18

EMILY

My first week of college was a complete mess. I spent the majority of my week aimlessly lost. I barely made it to class on time and haven't eaten a decent meal in days. If Crystal didn't have the same English Lit class as me, I wouldn't have made one class on time. Let's hope things don't continue on this path. If they do, I'd rather spend my next four years with my head in the sand.

I've only been in college for a week, and I'm already seriously considering calling it quits. My gloomy mood probably has more to do with my crappy phone reception than being a freshman. Its signal is barely existent, meaning I've missed numerous text and calls from Noah the past week.

Noah calls me every night, so when Monday came and went without contact, I was devastated. It was only while walking to class Tuesday morning did I discover my phone has no reception in my room. I had twelve unread text messages and even more voicemails.

Although grateful he hadn't cut contact, I had no clue how much our lives had become enmeshed the past six months. I took advantage of him always being there when I needed him. I was so desperate to hear his voice Wednesday night, I lay in bed, listening to Rise Up's CD on repeat. Crystal thought it was romantic. I was on the other side of the fence. I felt pathetic.

I'm extremely homesick, and it will only get worse when Crystal gets her new roommate. Crystal is from Oklahoma, and she and her best friend Trish picked Parkwood State so they could be roomed together. Unfortunately, a mix up with their applications had them bunked in different dorms. They submitted requests for a room change but have not yet heard if it's been approved.

I offered to swap rooms with Trish, but since she's in an apartment dormitory, I had to withdraw my offer. Offsite apartments don't come with a dining plan. Since I can't afford my own meals, I have to stay put. With Trish's roommate, Rochelle, refusing to downgrade to the dormitory-style room, Crystal and Trish are stuck living in separate locations. I'm sure it won't be long until their request is granted, just like I'm sure it won't take too long for me to settle in.

Although my week hasn't gone as planned, I woke up this morning incredibly ecstatic. Today is Friday, which means I get to spend the next two days with Noah—and my classes are dragging even more than usual. I'm enjoying the lessons I signed up for, but the number of times I've checked my watch makes it seem as if time is standing still.

When the clock finally strikes three, I gather my textbooks and bolt out of my ancient history class. I sprint down the stairs of my building, eager to get my weekend started. I don't expect Noah for another two hours, so you can imagine my surprise when my gallop down the stairs has me stumbling upon him. He's leaning against his truck, his smile picking up when he notices my frozen gawk.

When he pushes off his feet to head my way, I drop my textbooks with a squeal before dashing for him. He grins when I leap into his arms. "I've missed you so much!" I cover his face with feather-like kisses before leaning in to suck in his delicious scent. "You smell just like I remember."

He laughs, loving my eagerness. I wasn't joking. I've missed his scent so much, I'm going to steal a handful of his shirts, then I can wear them when I'm lonely. Just being surrounded by his scrumptious scent will soothe my agitation.

Still smiling, Noah jibes, "You do realize it's only been a few days, don't you?"

Although he's teasing me, his kiss reveals our week apart has been as torturous for him as it's been for me. He kisses me in front of my peers until the sadness haunting me the past week fades. He doesn't care that I'm being dramatic. He's too happy seeing me again to let a little bit of teen drama dampen his mood.

After a final nip of his lip, my eyes roam over the face I've missed so much. His cut jaw is clean-shaven, and his dark locks are styled like the night we met, but they have a rock star edge to them. He won't just woo the music executives tonight with his musical talents. He's putting all his best attributes on the table—gorgeous face included.

Once he's placed me back on my feet, he collects the books I dumped on the sidewalk. For a guy who swears he's not romantic, he has a funny way of showing it. With my books huddled under one arm, he wraps the other around my shoulders before walking toward my dorm so I can collect my overnight bag.

Several hours later, Noah pulls his truck into Mavericks' parking lot. Because of the rush hour traffic, the drive took two hours longer than usual. It's been a long and exhausting trip, but it gave us plenty of time to talk about all the things we missed due to crappy phone service.

Noah disclosed the band has been practicing sun up to sundown in preparation for tonight's gig. They persuaded Ollie into letting them perform four original songs, so they've got the perfect opportunity to showcase their talents to the execs coming to watch them play. Noah just needs to get his head into game mode. His nerves are getting the better of him. His shoulders droop when we walk into the bar hand in hand.

The importance of tonight smacks into me when I notice Slater and Marcus setting up their own instruments, convinced they perform better when they use their own equipment. They're also nervous. Slater's near fumble over his drumkit is proof of this.

I remember the first time I walked into Mavs. It felt so foreign. It wasn't an establishment I'd generally hang out at. Now it feels like home. Mavs doesn't have so many regulars because its old, rundown vibe. It's the people inside who bring patrons back, people like Maggie, who is standing behind the bar, washing down the already clean countertop with her infamous red dishcloth. She only stops scrubbing when she notices Noah and me approaching her.

"Hi, baby girl."

I wave a greeting before leaning over the bar to hug her. Although things are fine between us now, it took her a little while to warm up to me. Only once she realized looks were the only similarity Lola and I have did she give me a chance to prove my worth.

I don't know what happened between Lola and Maggie. Maggie never brings it up, and any time I ask Noah, he just shrugs and smiles. If I had to guess, I'd say it has something to do with Maggie being a motherly figure to Jacob and the guys in the band. She loves them fiercely as if they're her children. Once she was convinced I wouldn't hurt Noah, she welcomed me into her family with open arms. Perhaps Lola hasn't earned her trust yet?

My deliberations stop when Noah asks, "Will you be alright if I help the guys set up?"

I realize how bad his nerves are getting to him when our eyes connect. They've lost their spark, and his smile is basically non-existent. Usually, excitement is pumping out of him in invisible waves. Fridays are his favorite nights of the week.

Hating the change in his personality, I fist his shirt then pull him toward me. "You've got this, baby." I lock my eyes with his so he can see the truth in them. "It's in the bag." I spin him to face the stage, and with a huge slap on his glorious ass, I shove him toward it. "Now go show them how much of a rock star you truly are."

CHAPTER 19

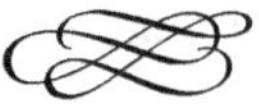

NOAH

The stupid ass nerves fluttering in my stomach vanish when Emily thrusts me toward the stage. I've never experienced this level of anxiety before. I guess things are different tonight. It's not every day bigwigs from a record label travel to an unknown bar to hear a band play. I thought I was doing a good job hiding my worries, but Emily's pep talk proves I should never give up singing for acting.

After winking my thanks to Emily, I climb onto the stage to help Slater and Marcus. They're pulling down the old stage equipment so we can set up our own. It's easy to use the instruments supplied, but since we have special guests coming tonight, we're polishing the silverware and dusting off the porcelain. It's time to put our best foot forward.

We have the stage dismantled by the time Nick rocks up. "About time, fuckface."

Nick retaliates to Slater's taunt by giving him the finger before crouching down to hook his guitar into his amp. "Sorry I'm late; I had some shit to sort out."

When it takes him several attempts to connect his wireless guitar cable into the input hole, I peer at him in shock. His face is gaunt and white, like he's seen a ghost. Nick is the baby of our group; he only turned twenty-one last month. Usually, he cruises through life, happy to see where things take him, but I'm beginning to suspect I'm not the only one being hammered with nerves tonight.

I try to ease his panic by slapping his shoulder, praying he'll snap out of his odd mood before the executives arrive. When it doesn't work, my eyes stray to Emily. With the band's table reserved for the music execs, she's sitting at the bar, talking with Maggie. I hate that she's not front and center as she has been the past six months, but she was the one who suggested seating the music execs in her spot. She's adamant it's the best seat in the house, so it's the prime spot for us to woo them with our talents.

After advising Slater I'll be back in a minute, I head to the bathroom to take a leak. On my way, I notice only one table remains empty. It's the one Ollie put a special reserved sign on for the record label hotshots. It's noticeably empty since every inch of Mavs is filled with dedicated Rise Up fans. Even a handful of newbies have arrived to watch us perform.

While doing my business, I tell myself time and time again that the execs are stuck in traffic, and that they'll be in their chairs waiting for me once I'm done.

My optimism gets squashed when I catch sight of myself while washing my hands in the sink. Black circles are plaguing my eyes, and my pupils are massive. The drive back from Emily's school was long, but that's not the reason for my tired appearance. I haven't been sleeping the past week. With the anniversary of my brothers' deaths getting close, nightmares I'm ashamed to admit I have are haunting my dreams.

After splashing cold water on my face, I rake my fingers through the haircut Jacob made me get this morning. He said I had to look "fresh" for the music executives. "If you look like you have money, they'll give you money."

Like that makes any sense. If I had money, I wouldn't be panicked about getting a record deal. I'd produce our own album. I just wish my panic about failing would fuck off. That's what is frustrating me the most. Failing the boys, failing myself, but most of all, failing Emily. If Rise Up gets the big break we've been striving for, I'll be able to give her the world. She says she only wants me, but I want her to have more than that.

If she hadn't been offered a scholarship for college, she wouldn't have attended, just like me. I hate that. Two people who work so hard shouldn't have to struggle like we do. That's why no matter how bad I need to vomit, I have to give tonight everything I've got.

With a newfound spring in my step, I exit the bathroom. It's time for our set to begin. As I walk through the mass of bodies mingling around the dance floor, I keep my eyes off the empty table. If we don't get a record deal tonight, we'll try again and again and again until we do get one.

When I step behind the mic, I crank my neck back to make sure the guys are ready to go. They're all in their correct positions: Slater is behind me on his drums, Nick is on my right with his electric guitar, and Marcus is on my left with his bass guitar.

Realizing our set it about to start, the crowd surges toward the stage. It's heavier tonight than usual. The first two rows are filled with scantily clad women who push and shove each other our whole set as they vie for the band's attention. The dedicated Rise Up fans are packed like sardines on the dance floor, and Mavericks regulars and a handful of newcomers congregate at the back near the bar.

I like to stir the crowd up before each performance, and tonight is no different. "Are you guys ready to raise the roof?!"

The crowd lets out a roaring chant, but it's only half the cheer I'm aiming for. I sling my eyes to Nick, my disappointed sigh enough to silence the crowd. "Do they sound ready to you?"

Nick pulls a face while strutting over to snatch the microphone out of my hand. "Hell no! Those fuckers don't sound ready!"

The crowd erupts into boisterous laughter. I laugh along with them, glad Nick has reverted to his usual self.

"How about we try that again? Are you guys ready to raise the roof?!"

A deaf man could hear the crowd's cheer, and it sets my heart racing. I do the same thing every Friday night, but they eat it up every single time. "Now you sound ready!"

I tap my boot on the wooden floor, counting out the beat for my bandmates. We begin our set with Hinder's "Lips of an Angel." It's a classic from a few years back, but I couldn't stop thinking about Emily's lips when I heard it. After performing an acoustic version of it for Emily one afternoon—and greatly benefiting from my performance—it was added to our playlist. It's been a glorious few months.

Once that song is finished, we transition to "Under Your Scars" by Godsmack. As dampness increases in the air, the crowd sways in sync to the beat of the music. They're loving tonight's performance just like they do every week. There's no better way to start your weekend than blowing off the cobwebs of a workweek with music.

Sweat rolls down my back when, in the corner of my eye, I see Jacob heading toward the front doors of Mavs. Cormack and two elegantly dressed people are standing just inside the bar. The only lady in the group appears to be in her mid-forties. She's wearing a black pants suit with a white silk top. Her blonde hair is pulled back into a tight bun, and her face is densely covered in makeup. The man on Cormack's left is significantly older than him. His hair is silver, his face lined with wrinkles.

After introducing himself, Jacob guides them to their reserved table. Even though Mavericks is not a table service bar, Maggie sends a bartender over to take their drink orders. I wait for them to be served their beverages before signaling to the guys that at the end of this song we'll perform the four songs Ollie agreed to let us play.

The first original song we perform is "Surrender Me." It was penned the night I made love to Emily. It's about surrendering yourself to the possibility of being loved. Because of what had happened with my brothers, I refused to let anyone in. Whenever anyone got close, they left—so why put myself through that?

No matter how hard I fought, I couldn't get Emily out of my head. Within weeks of us becoming a couple, she shattered the walls I built to protect my heart, leaving me no choice but to love her back. "Surrender Me" reveals the struggles I went through the weeks I tried to pretend she didn't exist.

The next song we perform is one I wrote after my brother killed himself. I know Chris was hurting, but the pain I faced being left to battle my demons alone was truly devastating. This song reflects the pain I felt.

When I open my eyes at the end of "Hollow," I see Emily brush away the tears it always incites. Although I hate seeing her cry, if "Hollow" doesn't move you to tears, I should hang up my mic.

Trying to lighten the mood, we move on to a fan favorite: "Player." It's a light-hearted song that was supposed to call out all the players in the world, but it didn't take our fans long to realize who it was penned for. Nick fucking loves it. He struts around the stage, more than happy to announce it was written for him.

As I break into the chorus about broken hearts and missing panties, my eyes stray past the people bobbing along to the funky tune. My heart kicks out an even more jazzy beat when I witness Emily fumble off her seat. She sways uncontrollably, clutching the bar with two hands to ensure she stays upright.

While she runs her hand down her face, I seek Jacob's gaze, hoping he'll check on her. This isn't like Em. She rarely drinks in public, and even then, she'd never consume enough to make her so woozy.

Because Jacob is schmoozing a cute blonde at the far end of the dance floor, I fail to get his attention. As I continue belting out the tune, I return my eyes to Emily. She's no longer at the bar. She's pacing toward the restrooms, her steps slow and sluggish.

My grip on my mic tightens when she stumbles into a man around the age of my dad who is standing amongst the pool tables. He doesn't appear to be paired with any of the college students playing, and he isn't holding a cue stick. Our band attracts a wide range of fans, but his handknitted sweater makes him stick out like a sore thumb. With Slater's drums taking up every bit of my hearing, I can't hear a word Emily speaks to him, but the quick movement of her lips convinces me she's apologizing for bumping into him. That's just like her, even when she isn't at fault, she'll still take the blame.

I continue singing without missing a beat... until the middle-aged man Emily skirted by pulls her close to his body. He's not righting her unsteady strides. His grip is too firm to be helpful. He's holding her body like I do—like he's hoping for the same level of closeness.

Lyrics I know as intimately as Emily's body slip from my mind when she is dragged toward the back exit. She fights to free herself from the man clutching her, but the more she resists, the tighter he grips her.

With my pulse pounding into my temples, I throw my microphone stand out of the way then dive off the stage. My mad dash across the beaten wooden floors alerts Jacob to my worry. He also barges through the mosh pit of sweaty bodies, but his strides have nothing on mine. A freight train of devastation is crashing into me, my mind void of any thoughts beyond getting Emily away from her attacker before smashing his fucking teeth in.

I seize Emily's wrist to yank her away from the man who has dragged her halfway out the back entrance. Once she's out of harm's way, I punch her attacker in the face. I hear his nose crack, but nothing slows my onslaught. I pound my fists into his unprotected face on repeat, my anger unlike anything I've ever experienced. Nick yells for me to stop, but I can't. Now that all the anger and rage I've built up the past six years is being unleashed, I don't have a chance in hell of reeling it back in.

After another three jabs to the man's face, Nick grabs me by my shoulders to yank me back, panicked I'm seconds from killing him. I probably am, but I can't stop. He was hurting Emily right under my fucking nose, so who's to say what he would have done once he got her alone. The thought makes me furious, flooding my blood with a second bout of anger.

When my knuckles collide with the man's left rib, blood splatters my cheek. His lungs wheeze as they fight for air, but my beatdown doesn't stop. He was taking Emily away from me, just like everyone I've ever loved was cruelly taken from me.

That's unforgivable.

He must pay for his stupidity.

I continue beating him without remorse, only stopping when Nick screams that Emily needs me. I stop swinging my fists, my eyes darting up to where I left Emily standing, except she's no longer upright. She's lying on the floor with her lolled head in Jacob's lap.

No!

I crawl across the wooden floor on my hands and knees. My heart thrashes as I carefully remove her from Jacob's lap to cradle her in mine. "Em, baby, open your eyes." I remove the strands of her hair stuck to her temples before tracking my finger down her stark white cheek. Whatever made her woozy also drained all the color from her face. "Come on, Beautiful."

Her chest rises and falls as she takes shallow breaths, but her eyes remain shut. I take comfort in the fact she's breathing, but I'm beyond panicked she won't wake up.

I raise my eyes to Jacob, who's standing above me with his cell attached to his ear. "What's wrong with her?"

He cups his phone with his hand. "I think he slipped a roofie in her drink."

My eyes snap to the man holding together his broken nose and sunken cheeks with his trembling hands. He should count his lucky stars I have Emily cradled in my arms, or I'd finish what I started. What sick fuck roofies girls half their age? And what was he planning to do with Emily when he got her in the alleyway...

Oh my god... if he touched her like that... if he'd... *I'd fucking kill him.*

The chances of me going on a rampage are squashed when Emily whispers my name. Her eyes are still closed but are rapidly moving under her eyelids as if she's dreaming.

"It's okay, baby, I'm right here. I'm not going anywhere," I assure her as sirens filter into the bar.

CHAPTER 20

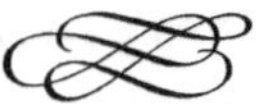

NOAH

"Her admission is a precaution; with her high heart rate and shallow breaths, she should be monitored by professionals."

I understand what the paramedic is saying; I also agree with it, but it doesn't make it any easier handing Emily over to him. Deep down inside, I know he can look after her better than me, but it takes everything I have not to argue with him.

The blond medic I'd guess to be mid-twenties nudges his head to his ambulance just outside Mavericks' doors. "You can ride with us. She won't be out of your sight for even a second."

That seals the deal for me. I learned a hard lesson tonight about leaving Emily alone. I won't do it again.

When I nod, the EMTs carefully remove Emily from my lap to place her onto their gurney. It's lucky they arrested the man who drugged her because having her torn away from me for the second time tonight instills me with a mammoth amount of rage. This is why I fought so hard to stay away from her when we first met. Being involved with me in any way always ends disastrously. But I can't give her up now. I love her too much.

As I follow Emily to the ambulance parked outside, my eyes stray to the police officers working the scene. From what I've gathered, Emily was given a near-lethal dose of GHB. It's a liquid form of ecstasy. Because she's so tiny, it didn't take much for her to overdose. The EMTs stabilized her stats rather quickly, but they want to admit her to the hospital to ensure her heart rate and breathing stay within safe levels.

I've barely climbed into the back of the ambulance when a male officer in his late thirties tells me I can't leave. "You need to be questioned about the incident. You can't assault a man and not expect any repercussions."

He wiggles two fingers in the air, demanding I exit the van. I shake my head. There are over three hundred witnesses who can testify I had a good reason for beating him. Furthermore, he drugged my girlfriend with the intention of raping her. He should be grateful he's still breathing.

When I refuse to leave Emily's side, the officer sends in two plain-clothed patrolmen to forcibly remove me. My blood boils with anger, but mercifully, before I can act on any of the thoughts in my head, Ryan's deep timbre rumbles through my chest. "Let him be. He has nothing to answer for, and even if he did, we will question him at a *more* convenient time."

A female officer with wiry black hair and wrinkles of a woman a good twenty to thirty years older than Ryan requests to have a word with the officer snarling at me. When he agrees, but not without a frustrated squint, Ryan closes the doors of the ambulance then taps on the roof, signaling for the EMTs to go.

Ryan is a good man. He's the rookie officer who brought my mom to the hospital after Michael died. I hate that he witnessed my mother slapping me, but ever since that day, he's kept an eye on me. I think his close watch is more because he was a friend of Chris's before he died, but I can't testify to that.

Not long after Emily is admitted to the hospital, Jacob arrives on scene. When he called Lola to tell her what happened, Lola reached out to Emily's mom. Since Patrice was working a late shift, she came straight to the floor where Emily is and was here for two hours.

I only persuaded her to go home ten minutes ago. She was exhausted from working a double shift, and there wasn't anything she could do for Emily that I wasn't already doing. I won't lie; I felt smug as fuck when she trusted me to look after Emily. I'm sure it wasn't an easy thing to do, but I appreciate it more than she'll ever realize.

I stop watching Emily's eyes rapidly move under her eyelids when her hospital room door swings open. Ryan is standing just inside the sanitary-smelling space. He has a recording device in his hand that is a little outdated for the swanky suit he's wearing.

"Can I have a word?" He nudges his head to the corner of Emily's room, advising I won't have to leave her side during our conversation. For that alone, I agree with his request.

The first half of our conversation is the standard one you'd expect a detective and a man brandishing bloody knuckles to have. He asks me to run him through the events that occurred while he jots down an occasional note in his notepad. I guess a voice recorder can't pick up the nervous fidgeting liars do.

Once I've finished my statement, Ryan switches off his recording device before running his hand over his freshly trimmed hair. He seems uneasy. I understand why when he murmurs, "The DA wanted to charge you with assault."

My heart sinks into my stomach. I knew I wouldn't get off scot-free, but I hadn't considered the possibility I'd be formally charged for defending my girlfriend from a rapist.

Ryan looks as pissed as me when he discloses, "We've been hunting the man who did this for a while. The canister of GHB we found in his possession had enough liquid to drug another ten girls. If he wasn't under arrest, who's to say another person wouldn't have been assaulted tonight."

My teeth grind together. I'm shocked he needs to drug girls to get them to sleep with him. It isn't like he's hideous-looking—well, he wasn't until I got ahold of him. He seemed like a regular guy in his forties. He could even have children around Emily's age.

I take a step back when Ryan says, "It took a lot of convincing, but the DA will consider dropping all charges against you if this was self-defense."

My eyes bulge, shell-shocked by his statement. I must have misheard him—surely.

"Jacob's on-scene statement indicated that the man you assaulted swung at you first."

My confusion triples. That doesn't make any sense. The guy didn't lay a hand on me.

It takes a few moments for the truth to smack into me. Jacob lied in his testimony so I wouldn't face charges.

Ryan steps closer to me. He's about my height, but with my shock at an all-time high, he seems much wider. "It's true he attacked you first, isn't it, Noah?"

He stares straight at me while nodding. Although I hardly know him, he doesn't need to be my best friend for me to see the plea in his eyes for me to follow his suggestion, so, with my heart in my throat, I copy his movement.

Ryan smiles. "Great! Then lets re-record your statement from the beginning where *he* swung at *you* first."

My shock about the lengths Ryan and Jacob will go to save my ass is heard in my voice when Ryan retakes my statement. They saved my tail tonight with their quick thinking. I'd never survive staring at four walls all day. I don't even visit my dad because I can't stand the idea of being trapped in one place for a prolonged period.

Happy he has a plausible recollection of events, Ryan stores his recorder in his jacket before holding out his hand in offering. After everything he just did for me, it doesn't feel right only shaking his hand. Instead, I curl my arms around his shoulders and give him a quick hug. At first, he stiffens, but it doesn't take him long to return my embrace.

"I'm glad you showed restraint tonight. If you had killed him, we would have never gotten you off charges." He hugs me tighter, reminding me just how close he was with Chris before he died. "Please don't let what happened tonight ruin all the good you've done the past three years. You've worked so hard for this. Don't let one minor thing fuck it up."

He steals my chance to reply by pulling back from our embrace, pivoting on his heels, and exiting Emily's room. I stare at the swinging door he raced through at the speed of a bullet, shocked into silence. He came into my life under the shittiest of circumstances, but I'll be forever grateful he's a part of it.

Jacob and the guys from the band filter in and out of Emily's room most of the night. The first time they entered, their mood was subdued. They stood at the back of her room, quiet and respectful. This time around though... they're upbeat and excited. Between performing for the music execs and Emily being roofied, it's been a rollercoaster night, so their odd moods can be excused. I just wish they'd do it a little more quietly. The nursing staff said Emily can only have one visitor, and it's supposed to be her next of kin, so I don't want to give them a reason to kick me out.

"Shut the fuck up," I growl when they get a little rowdy. They're so hyped up, I'm sure three wards over can hear their chatter.

"Sorry, Noah." Marcus slaps my shoulder, his wordless apology more sincere than his articulated one.

Nick slips into the chair next to me. "We learned some exciting news that's hard to contain."

I assume he's referring to me escaping charges, but I'm proven wrong when Slater roars, "They fucking loved us!"

I stand from my seat, warning him if he doesn't shut the fuck up, I'll shut his mouth with my fists.

He backs away with his hands held in the air. The boys aren't used to seeing me so worked up, but they never had the opportunity.

Before Emily, I only ever cared about myself, and I didn't do the best job at that either.

Marcus waits for me to sit back down before bumping me with his knee. "Cormack wasn't happy when you jumped off the stage, but he said they heard enough to warrant offering us a record deal."

My pulse beeps in my neck, but I can't bring myself to be happy about it. At least not while Emily is lying in a hospital bed unconscious. She would have never been in a place like Mavs if she weren't with me, and if I hadn't agreed to give her spot to the music execs, I might have noticed the guy spiking her drink. Then we could have avoided hours of heartache.

"Did you hear him, Noah? They want to sign us to their label." Nick's slap of his knee is half the volume of his voice. "We did it. We got a fucking record deal!"

"I don't care." My squinted gaze bounces between my bandmates, who are staring at me with concern slashed across their faces. Anger is pumping through my veins, overheating my body with more heat than I know what to do with. "I just... I need..."

I curse under my breath, hating that I'm blubbering like an idiot. I've never handled these types of emotions before—not by myself, anyway. Emily has a way of calming me down when shit gets the better of me, so I'm not only struggling without her, I have no fucking clue what I'm doing.

The mad beat of my heart somewhat settles when I catch the faintest whiff of the vanilla oil Emily dabs on her skin every morning. It's nothing compared to the comfort she generally offers, but it's enough for me to realize I'm taking my anger out on the wrong people.

After licking my lips, I murmur, "I'm sorry. It's great news. I'm glad I didn't scare them off."

I swallow several times in a row before my eyes float up from the floor. Nick, Slater, and Marcus are all staring at me, their faces covered with shock. Anyone would swear I just told them I love them. I do, but I'll never openly admit it. I merely overreacted to their excitement, so they deserve an apology.

When Emily wakes up, she'll be ecstatic to hear we've secured a record deal. Then, once the dust settles, I'll use my first endorsement check to buy her a big, beautiful engagement ring, because she deserves so much more than the dainty one I've been carrying in my pocket all day.

CHAPTER 21

EMILY

"It could be another hour; it could be five. She'll wake when she's ready."

As my mouth works through its dryness, I struggle to open my eyes. I'm experiencing the same sensation I felt when my parents drove through the darkness of night to beat traffic on the family adventures we took every year when I was a child. I don't know where I am, and I'm not sure how I got here, but there's an unusual sensation thickening the air.

I feel as safe and as protected as I did back then. That probably has something to do with the hand curled around mine. If the alluring scent I'm sucking in is anything to go by, I'm confident it's Noah comforting me. If only my eyes would cooperate, then I could satisfy my curiosity. Alas, no matter how hard I fight, my eyes refuse to open.

It's probably for the best. My head is pounding so badly, it feels like someone is jackhammering my brain. It's worse than the hangover I had when Jenni and I got tipsy at Phillip's eighteenth birthday party three years ago, but I didn't drink anything last night, did I?

My memories are a little vague. I remember Noah picking me up from school, but I have no recollection of what happened after that.

Perhaps I've fallen asleep on the drive back to Ravenshoe, and I'm dreaming?

Wake up, Emily! You don't want to miss Noah's performance.

A blinding light streams through my eyes when they finally follow the prompts of my brain. It's the low-hanging sun bouncing off the stark white walls surrounding me. I'm lying in a rock-hard bed, and an annoying beep is making the pulse in my head more noticeable.

Although I've never been a patient at a hospital, I'm fairly sure that's where I am. My mom has worked in the health department for years, so I'm well aware of how they look.

A grin overtakes my grimace when my eyes stumble onto Noah. He's sitting in a hard blue plastic chair. The top half of his body is slumped over the bed. He's sleeping—but not peacefully. Lines are etched into his forehead, and the veins in his arms throb with every twitch of his muscles. I hope he's not having a nightmare. With the anniversaries of his brothers' deaths approaching, his nights are growing more restless.

Although I hate seeing him so edgy, his twitching exposes a water jug on a table at the side of my bed. My throat is on fire, so I'd sell a kidney for a glass of water. Not wanting to wake up Noah, I stretch out my arm, praying I can reach the jug without freeing my hand from his grasp. I get within an inch, but it does little to relieve my thirst.

Like magic, the jug lifts. I lick my parched lips before raising my eyes to my savior. Jacob greets me with a smile, not missing my slack-jawed response. "Jesus, Em, you scared us half to death."

I shush him. Not because we're in a hospital, but because Noah is sleeping. With a grimace, Jacob pops a straw into a cup before raising it to my lips. The cold water trickling down my throat gives me instant relief.

I suck greedily, guzzling down the entire cup before Jacob can pull it away. "Thanks, Jake." My voice is husky, but my gratitude can't be misplaced. "I'm sorry I was short with you. I just don't want to wake up Noah. He hasn't been sleeping much the past month."

Jacob gives an understanding nod at the exact moment Noah lets out a groan, leaving no doubt to my theory his sleep is being interrupted with horrid real-life nightmares.

Once the crinkle in Noah's brows smooths, I return my focus to Jacob. "What happened? I don't recall anything after Noah picked me up from school."

Other than my throbbing head, I'm relatively uninjured, so I couldn't have been in an accident, but what other reason would have put me in the hospital?

I suck in a sharp breath when Jacob discloses, "You were roofied at Mavs. The doctor said the excessive dose he spiked your drink with is the reason you've been out so long. Usually, you're unconscious for an hour or two. You've been out for over eight hours."

My heart rate climbs to a dangerous level as my woozy head struggles to decipher what he is saying. Isn't a roofie a date rape drug? If so, why was it given to me...

My inner monologue trails off as panic makes itself known with my gut. Was I raped? Is that why I'm in the hospital?

Although I'm panicked I've been horrendously violated as no woman ever should be, not all my worry stems from that. Nothing but consoling Noah is on my mind. He's already endured his share of trauma in his short twenty-one years. He doesn't need more atrocious things added to his overflowing plate.

Jacob touches my arm, easing the heaves of my failing lungs. "He didn't touch you, Em. Noah got to him before he could."

Gratitude hits me first, but it's closely followed by panic. With my heart clutched in fear, my watering eyes drift to Noah. I scan every inch of him, fretful I missed something during my earlier perusal.

I didn't—*thank god.*

Other than busted knuckles, he's unharmed—physically. I'll have to wait for him to wake to check his mental state.

Tonight was Rise Up's big chance to impress the music execs, so I can only pray their performance ended before I was drugged.

Realizing I have the answer standing directly in front of me, I relock my eyes with Jacob. "What happened with the music executives? Did Rise Up finish their set?"

Jacob shakes his head. "They were halfway through 'Player' when Noah leaped off the stage." His words grind out of his mouth as he works his jaw side to side. "I was talking to Melissa when Noah missed a line in the chorus. If that wasn't enough indication that something was amiss, the fury on his face was a surefire sign. When I followed his gaze, I noticed a man was dragging you toward the back exit. I rushed for you, but Noah beat me. He fucked the guy up pretty bad."

He scratches his brow as he shuffles foot to foot. "You collapsed within seconds of Noah pulling you away from him."

The guilt in his voice shocks me. What does he have to feel guilty about? *I* stupidly left my drink unattended, meaning *I* most likely ruined Rise Up's chance of securing a record deal. Jacob has nothing to feel guilty about. I'm the only idiot in this room.

Jenni, Nicole and I were forever cautious about date rape drugs when we went dancing. We never drank from a drink left unattended, and we refused any offers to buy us drinks, but the one night Noah needed to concentrate solely on his band, I slacked off on my observations. I'll never forgive myself if my stupidity ruins everything he's worked so hard for.

When tears blur my vision, my hands dart up to catch them before they can fall. Like I need any more proof of my idiocy, my abrupt movements wake Noah. He lifts his head, his tired eyes as reluctant as mine were to open. For two seconds, he appears confused. It's only when he spots the cannula in my hand suspended halfway in the air does lucidity form.

"Thank fuck."

The sheer relief in his voice adds more moisture to my already brimming eyes. When he leaps up from his chair, I scoot across the bed, wanting him to sit next to me so I can rest my head on his chest. Just hearing his heart will calm down my swirling stomach.

He accepts my offer before drawing me in close to his chest. "You scared the shit out of me." I can barely hear a word he speaks since his heart is raging so fast.

"I'm sorry. I don't know what I was thinking."

Out of excuses, I burrow my head into his pecs, praying his scent will stop my tears from falling. I feel terrible about what has happened, but I don't want him to see my tears. He hates when I cry.

My breath snags halfway to my lungs when my eyes zoom in on specks of blood dotting Noah's shirt. My stomach launches into my throat when my head darts off his chest. "Are you hurt?"

I fist his shirt, seeking any bruises or cuts that may be responsible for the blood. My woozy head doesn't appreciate my brash movements, but I don't care. I need to make sure he's okay.

Noah drags his shirt over his head before bunching it up and hooking it across the room. My eyes float over his torso, seeking injuries. The panic burning me alive soothes when I fail to notice any marks. He appears unharmed.

Noah backs up my confirmation with words. "It's not my blood."

I want to say his comment fills me with relief, but it doesn't. Now, instead of worrying he's injured, I'm petrified he's minutes from being arrested.

While taking a moment to calm down, I return my eyes to Noah's. I want to ask what happened to the guy who drugged me, but I also don't want to know. The longer Noah stays in my protective bubble, the longer he's safe from threats. It's bad enough I ruined his chance of getting a record deal, much less destroying his life. What if he ends up in jail like his dad? He'd never survive that. Noah is the strongest man I've met, but he'd go crazy in a four by four cell for years on end.

I stare at Noah, wondering if he can hear my thoughts when he murmurs, "The police aren't pressing charges."

I have a million questions in my head, but I can't articulate one of them. I'm too shocked. How can you beat a guy half to death and not face charges? Don't get me wrong, I'm grateful, but I'm also stunned.

"Can I go home?" There's too much turmoil in Noah's beautifully tormented gaze for me to relax in a hospital bed.

Noah takes a few seconds drinking in the plea in my eyes before shifting his focus to someone behind my shoulder. "Can you grab the nurse, Jake?"

I was so caught up, I completely forgot Jacob was in the room with us. After a quick nod, Jacob heads for the door, closing it behind him. He's barely stepped foot into the corridor when Noah pulls me back down until I'm nuzzled in his chest. "Are you sure you want to go home?"

I nod without pause. Other than my throbbing head, I'm perfectly fine.

"Because the doctor advised staying until the drugs wear off."

I understand the doctor's concerns, but I don't want to spend the only full day I have with Noah this week in a hospital room. That would be more detrimental to my sanity than being drugged.

Upon spotting my shaking head, Noah presses his lips to my temple. "Alright. We'll see what the doctor says. If he's happy for you to go, we'll get you signed out as soon as possible."

The nurse arrives not long after Jacob comes back. After the nurse completes a set of observations on me, the doctor strongly advises that I stay under observation for a few more hours. With Noah refusing to take my side over the doctor's, I accept the pain medication the nurse gives me before snuggling back into Noah's chest.

CHAPTER 22

EMILY

I didn't anticipate falling asleep, so you can imagine my shock when I wake up to discover it's a little after 11 AM, and I'm back to my usual self.

"Good morning, Beautiful."

Noah's voice is raspy from waking up. Apparently, he snuck in a couple hours of sleep as well. I have no clue how. He's sitting upright in a rock-hard bed with me drooling all over his chest. I'd be mortified if I didn't love waking up in his arms.

"Morning." I keep my lips close to his chest, not wanting to kill him with my horrific morning breath. My throat is raw, so I'm relatively sure it smells like I ate roadkill for breakfast.

When Noah's finger slips under my chin to lift my head, wanting to give me his daily kiss, I yank back. "No! I haven't brushed my teeth."

As quickly as a flash of lightning brightening a dark sky, Noah flips us over until he's positioned on top of me. The girly giggle erupting from my mouth switches to a moan when the thickness his jeans fail to conceal rubs my aching core. My thin hospital gown ensures I feel every delicious inch of him. Every. Rock-hard. Inch.

Worry about rotten breath becomes a thing of the past when I soak him in. He hasn't replaced the shirt he removed earlier this morning, meaning he's wearing nothing but ripped jeans and a sultry smirk. His thick biceps, tattooed pecs, and stacked abs already have my head in a tizzy, much less his handsome face.

When he tilts his head to align our lips, I no longer care how bad my breath may smell. I pull him toward me to ravish his delicious mouth without a single thought crossing my mind.

I've barely sampled half his scrumptiousness when a voice remarkably similar to my mom's filters into my room. "I guess you're ready to go home?"

When I glance over Noah's shoulder, I spot my mom standing in the entrance to the room. She's wearing her regular concerned motherly face; it's just more taut today. My admission scared her.

Hoping to put her worry to rest, I answer, "*Very* ready. I feel great!"

My tingling lips drop into a pout when Noah rolls off me so he can stand next to my bed. He has the same worried expression my mom is wearing, but his is due to my mom seeing us getting frisky in public.

He has no cause for concern; my mom loves him as if he's her son. The moment I introduced them, she considered him family. That has ensured he's never worn his shoes inside our house like he did the night we met. My mom is pedantic about cleanliness, but she also has a nurturing side that is proven without a doubt when she greets Noah with a kiss on the cheek.

My brow arches when her hug coincides with her whispering something into his ear. I strain to hear what she says, but she's too quiet. I can't make out a word she is speaking. It must be important, because shock crosses Noah's features before he nods.

Pretending she hasn't noticed my inquisitive glare, my mom squeezes my hand. "How about we get you signed out of here so you can enjoy the rest of your weekend?"

I nod eagerly.

———

An hour later, I was discharged from the hospital under the watchful eye of both my mom and Noah. Noah wanted to take me straight home so I could rest, but I felt fine and didn't want to waste a beautiful day, so I convinced him otherwise.

We spent the majority of our day at Bronte's Peak. It was packed with people just as eager to enjoy the splendid blue sky day. We explored hidden caves and made out on the white sandy beach. I love spending the day by the water with Noah. It's rare to see him out of his beloved grungy jeans. The first time I saw him in board shorts, I laughed. I didn't mean to be cruel; it was just so foreign. He looks out of place on the beach, but that doesn't stop women of all ages ogling him when he walks by.

Bronte's Peak has become our favorite hangout spot the past six months. We spent a majority of our summer there before school started, but no matter how late in the afternoon we arrived, Noah ensured we left before the sun set. I've told him on numerous occasions that Zander is in the past, and I no longer care about what happened there, but Noah is adamant Bronte's Peak will never be our hookup spot.

With the rest of our time spent at Jacob's house, Noah is only dropping me back to college now, early Monday morning. We're nearly pulling into the street my dorm is located on when the nervous bob of Noah's knee gets the better of him. "We got a record deal."

I freeze, sure I heard him wrong. "What?"

He smiles in a way that restarts my heart. "Cormack was pissed I dove off the stage, but he liked what he heard so much, he offered us a record deal."

"How long have you known?" A gleam in his eyes answers my questions on his behalf. "You've known all weekend and didn't tell me." I slap his arm, more in play than anger. "Noah Gibson Taylor!"

He laughs, loving that I used his full name.

Unable to contain the buzz thickening my veins, I throw off my seatbelt before diving over the seat to give him a congratulatory kiss. He swerves toward incoming traffic, startled by my sudden arrival.

"Jesus Christ, Emily! Put your seatbelt back on."

With a grimace, I slide back to my side of the seat before clipping my belt into place. I was so excited, I didn't register how stupid it was to scare him like that. Any time we travel, he always makes sure my belt is fastened, yet I go and undo it while he's driving down a busy road.

Poor guy. I nearly gave him a heart attack.

Once he's happy my seatbelt is back where it should be, Noah shares the information he got in dribs and drabs from his bandmates Friday night. "There are only four songs on our demo CD the label wants to work with, so they're arranging for us to meet with a song-writer who will help me develop enough songs to fill an album. We'll work from their studios in Hopeton..."

I'm stoked for them, but also a little panicked. Does his new schedule mean we won't see each other as regularly as we have the past six months?

Noah settles my panic. "For the first few months, our schedule will follow the routine the band has had since it was founded. We'll just work from a studio in Hopeton instead of the one in Marcus's grand-ma's garage."

I laugh when he discloses the song he wrote about Nick was cut from their album. Nick was reportedly devastated. It serves him right. Anyone who happily admits they're a player doesn't deserve someone as talented and beautiful as Jenni. I'm just grateful she heeded my warning about Nick. If she hadn't, who knows how far the carnage would have spread.

When Noah pulls into the parking lot of my dorm, the gloomy cloud just clearing from my head returns full force. Even being drugged, I enjoyed my weekend—so much so, the last thing I want to do is return here.

Upon hearing the heavy sigh I couldn't stifle, Noah shuts down his engine before jerking his chin up. "Come here."

When I scoot across the cracked leather bench, he adjusts me until my back is leaning against his chest and his arms are curled around my front. He wraps me up so firmly, I feel every inhalation he takes.

"Remember your dreams, Beautiful. That's why you're here."

My heart clutches as tears wet my eyes. I've wanted to be a school teacher since the first grade. My teacher, Ms. McMahon, was the loveliest and kindest person I had ever met. She taught me how to read and put a Band-Aid on my skinned knee after I fell off my bike while riding to school. I admired her for years, and I was adamant I'd have the same connection with my own students one day.

When she died of breast cancer when I was in eighth grade, I was gutted. Not just for myself, but the hundreds of students who'd miss out on being taught by a person born to teach. With my early goals still in mind, I studied hard throughout high school. My parents couldn't afford to send me to college, so I did everything in my power to get a scholarship.

I was ecstatic when my goals panned out, yet here I am moping like a spoiled little brat because my cell service in my room is crap. Noah is right; I need to pull up my big girl panties and stop acting like a baby.

I suck in a big breath, confident I've got this. Hearing my silent pledge as loudly as me, Noah gives my shoulders a gentle squeeze. With them lighter than they were only seconds ago, I tilt back to kiss him goodbye before sliding across the seat and hopping down from his truck.

I'm about to twirl back around to add to my goodbye with words, but the creak of a car door opening stops me. Noah is no longer behind his steering wheel. He's jogging around the bed of his truck, his smile as blinding as the sunrays bouncing off the silver box he's holding.

"I've gotta walk my girl to her door."

With a playful wink, he clasps my hand in his before guiding me toward my building. I don't know why I'm shocked. He may be an up-and-coming rock star, but he's been a gentleman a lot longer than that.

When we stop in front of my paint-peeled door, I shove my key into the lock and swing it open. "Home sweet home."

I pace into my room with Noah following closely behind. While I place my bag on my desk, he peruses the many photos I have of him and me together on my bookshelf.

"I like this one." He twists around a photo Jenni took of us at

Bronte's Peak. It was the first time we got our friends together for a BBQ. We're standing waterside, peering lovingly into each other's eyes. We were so enamored with one another, we didn't notice Jenni was taking our picture.

After setting down the frame, Noah sits on my bed. The silver box he's clasping contrasts with my dark bedding, making it even more noticeable.

"What's in the box?" I've always been impatient, so the suspense is killing me.

Noah arches a brow into his hairline. "Come here, and I'll show you."

As I stroll toward him, I try to act as seductive and sexy as him. I feel ridiculous, but Noah's smile reveals he appreciates my effort. With my dorm room being teeny tiny, it doesn't take many strides to reach him, meaning my hips didn't achieve half the swing I was aiming for.

When I sit down next to him, Noah places the box on my lap. "Is it for me?" I sound shocked. Rightfully so. It isn't my birthday, so I wasn't anticipating a gift.

When Noah nods, curiosity gets the better of me. Carefully, I undo the ribbon before cracking open the lid. My heart sings when I notice a tiny silver object inside. It's shiny, sparkly, and brand-spanking new.

"Noah..." I add to my excitement by hugging him tightly. "Thank you so much!"

He snatches the box off my lap. "Here, let me get it out for you."

My eyes bounce between him and the box, my happiness uncontained. "I can't believe you bought me a phone!"

I still have the dated phone Lola handed down to me years ago. This one is shiny and new, and way more technical than I'm used to.

Noah sounds like he's talking from experience when he says, "You need to get a cover for it, because if you drop it, the screen will shatter. Jacob swears this brand has better reception than your old phone, so it should work in your dorm."

I'm so excited I can barely contain myself. I should be angry he spent his hard-earned money on me, but I'm so relieved we can resume our nightly chats, I'll accept his gift without too much guilt.

Noah grins before spinning around the screen to face me. "There you go, two bars."

With the scream of a teenage girl much younger than me, I snatch my phone out of his hand and dial a number known by heart. I nearly cry when my call connects without the message I've heard on repeat the past week.

Noah chuckles while digging his ringing cell out of his pocket. He may be sitting right next to me, but he'll always be the first person I'll call on both good and bad days.

CHAPTER 23

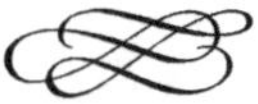

NOAH

When Nick and I break through the double glass doors of Destiny Records, a brisk wind blasts into us. "Damn, it's freezing!"

A chill runs down my spine when the wind blowing off the ocean cuts through me like a knife. I zip up my leather jacket. Nick wasn't joking; it's fucking freezing. We don't usually get snow around these parts, but with how frosty it is, I'm beginning to wonder if Ravenshoe is about to experience its first white Christmas.

Crisp air puffs from my lips when I bid farewell to Nick. "See you tomorrow."

I pat him on the shoulder before heading to my truck parked at the back of the studios. When we signed our contract, I thought it would only be a matter of months before our songs were on the radio. Let me tell you, it's been a longer, more drawn-out process than I was anticipating. We haven't even stepped foot inside a recording studio yet.

Thank fuck that is about to change. Although our last four months have been tied up with logistical red tape, we did compile enough songs to fill an album. After a two-week break over the upcoming Christmas-New Year period, we'll start laying down tracks. It's been a torturous few months, but I'm still excited about what's to come. I've always loved the music industry, and my admiration grew when I learned how much effort goes into every song produced.

After cranking the heater in my truck to full pelt, I head home. Commuter traffic is at its worst, meaning I don't pull into the driveway of Jacob's house until 6:30 PM. I usually call Emily at seven, so I'll wash off the funk I'm feeling before calling her. I can't call her while agitated. She can tell when something is bothering me, and I don't want to place this burden on her shoulders.

Today has been an uphill battle. Mickie, the songwriter the execs hired to help find lyrics from our album, wanted to change "Surrender Me," the song I wrote for Emily. He wants it to be a song about heartbreak instead of repair.

No matter how fucking angry Mickie got, I flatly refused. He's a colossal bastard, nearly the height of Jacob, but he's Sudanese, so compared to Jacob's pasty skin, his is as dark as night. We get along most of the time, but today I wanted to strangle the huge son of a bitch. Although today I had a win, it wasn't done without carnage.

While rubbing a kink out of my neck, I cross my bedroom floor, heading for my attached bathroom on the far right. My breath hitches when I raise my eyes in just enough time to spot Emily. She's sleeping in my bed, wearing nothing but panties and one of my shirts. Today is only Tuesday, so I'm not only shocked by her unexpected arrival, I'm panicked.

Walking over, I kneel next to the bed so my eyes can rake her enticing body. Even snoring, she's undeniably beautiful. Her face is fresh and radiant, revealing she hasn't been crying—her eyes go puffy when she's upset—and her forehead is free from lines. Neither her face or her body reveal the reason for her impromptu sleepover.

I lose the chance to deliberate further when her eyes flutter open. She startles for the quickest second, shocked to see me crouched in front of her, but she pushes away her surprise, replacing it with a blinding smile.

"You okay?" I keep my tone neutral, even though I'm beyond panicked.

Her smile enlarges.. "I'm fine."

Any concerns I'm having vanish when she leaps out of my bed to seal her mouth over mine. She kisses me senseless, a kiss so mind-hazing, I forget my name, what day it is, and what planet I live on.

My head is still woozy when she pulls back and raises her eyes to mine. "Happy birthday, Noah."

A smirk furls my lips. I should have known she'd realize today is my twenty-second birthday. Not only is she a snoop, but she also makes big deals out of the little things others forget. I haven't celebrated my birthday in the last seven years. Even before Michael died, my parents weren't big on celebrations. I usually got new school clothes or shoes, and on special birthdays we had a cake after dinner.

Upon spotting the shocked expression on my face, tears prick Emily's eyes. "Did you really think I'd forget your birthday?"

It isn't that. I just had no clue she knew today was my birthday. I should have known better. She would have made it her mission to find out my date of birth the instant we started dating.

Moisture fills Emily's eyes, fretful I'm mad about her unexpected visit. I'm not. I'm stoked she's here—so much so, I don't hesitate to show her how appreciative I am. Her pulse quickens when I shrug off my jacket and slip into the bed next to her so I can spend the rest of my birthday enjoying every inch of my most valued possession.

"I'm so fucking happy you're here."

Goosebumps pepper her skin when I guide her shirt over her head, exposing a lusty set of tits too perfect for a mere mortal. Dropping my head, my tongue darts across her budded nipple. It hardens more when I blow air on it, encouraging its stiffened response.

"Now I get to end my birthday with my ultimate gift."

I lavish her left breast with the same attention I bestowed on her right before dragging my stubble-covered chin down her quivering stomach. My zipper digs into my cock when her vanilla scent adds to the smooth palette of her skin. She tastes as good as she smells.

When my tongue lashes the skin high on her thigh, her knees curve inward. "Noah..."

My lips lift against her skin before I suckle it into my mouth, encouraging her to open up for me. When she does, I kiss her from her thigh to her ankle. I return back to her midsection by caressing her opposite leg from her ankle to her thigh.

By the time my head is within an inch of her panties, they're soaked through. She's not the only one making a mess. Precum is seeping into my boxer shorts as my cock begs to be released from the tight constraints of my jeans.

His pleas will have to wait. I've got more urgent matters to attend to.

With my hooded gaze locked on Emily's face, I press my lips to her panties, which are erotically exposing her arousal. A moan topples from her mouth as her hips thrust upward. I smirk, loving the effect I have on her. I honestly feel like a god when she's panting beneath me.

Impatient to taste her again, I hook my thumb into her panties and slip them away, revealing her pretty pink pussy to my keen eyes. My veins thicken when her beautiful scent infuses the air. I could get drunk off her smell.

Her breathing labors as her light brown eyes stare down at me, wordlessly begging for me to consume her. I move close enough to her my heated breaths add to the sticky situation between her legs, but I ignore her silent demands. I'm dying to taste her again, but can't help but tease her a little.

A grin curls on my lips when her eyes taper into tiny slits. If you want to piss Emily off, tease her. She hates it.

Her anger becomes a forgotten memory when her scent gets the better of me. As my tongue darts out to lash a pussy that tastes sweeter than honey, her back arches off my bed. A rough, indescribable moan tears from my throat when her seductive taste fills my taste buds. Her pussy is the sweetest thing I've ever eaten.

She grips my hair to hold me hostage to her pussy when I suck her clit into my mouth. Her worry is unwarranted. I have no intention of leaving until she's screaming my name—not once, but twice.

I bring her one step closer to the brink when I slip two fingers inside of her. Even though we fool around like this a minimum three times a week, the tightness of her pussy is undeniable. As she rides my fingers with steady grinds, her pussy sucks at me. Her rolling hips match the flicks my tongue is doing to her clit. It's a slow, teasing pace that adds to the fire forever sparking between us.

"Noah..." This cry is similar to the one she released earlier, but needier and more urgent.

I eat her with slow, lazy licks, knowing whether we're fucking like wild animals or being gentle and sweet, the outcome never alters. She's my girl, and I'm her man. Nothing will ever change that.

Emily's body tightens all over as the heat I'm eating like a starved man grows musky. She stills for barely a second before the most beautiful noise shreds from her throat. Her body spasms as her orgasm rips through her with unforgiving shakes. I guide her through the darkness by slowing the grinds of my fingers and easing off on her clit.

By the time she comes down from her high, my chin is dripping with her juices, and her face is glowing. While crawling up her sweat-dotted skin, I wipe away evidence of her arousal before freeing my cock from my jeans. They're barely huddled around my knees when my tongue spears between her parted lips at the same time my cock nudges the folds of her pussy.

We breathe as one when I rock my hips forward, sinking into her with one fluid movement. We still, the sensation unexplainable. No matter how many times we make love, the emotions attached to it never wane. It's a blistering, heart-strangling time that makes me wonder what the fuck I ever did to deserve her.

Feeling the sentiment in the air the same as me, Emily drags her tongue along the roof of my mouth before pulling back. She peers up at me with wide, lusty eyes, but not even the width of her pupils can take away from the message hidden beneath them. She loves me, wholly and without restraint. And I love her too.

"Happy birthday, Noah."

Happy birthday indeed. There's no greater gift I could be given than this.

A few hours later, Emily stops tracing the outline of my tattoo. Her leap out of my bed causes a near catastrophe. One inch to the right and she would have taken off my cock. "I forgot about your present."

She tosses her clothes back on before fumbling to the door. I'm pissed the body I spent hours admiring has been stolen from my view, but I'm also excited. Excluding Jacob, no one has given me a birthday present in years.

My excitement ramps up when Emily's voice projects from behind my half-closed door. "Close your eyes."

Although amused, I do as instructed. A few seconds later, I hear her tiny feet padding across the floor. "Are they closed?"

If I know Emily as well as I think I do, she's waving her arms in the air, assuring I'm not being a spoilsport. She hates when people ruin the fun. The thought alone makes me smile.

The already brisk speed of my heart shifts into a gallop when I catch the quickest whiff of her vanilla scent. She must be close.

My instincts are proven right when coolness brushes my legs. She has rested something on my thighs. It's not overly heavy, but it definitely weighs more than a standard gift.

"Okay, you can open them now."

After swallowing to relieve my parched throat, I open my eyes. The first thing I see is Emily's beautiful face. She's beaming with so much excitement, a vein in her neck looks seconds from bursting. The second thing my eyes lock in on traps the air in my throat.

"Emily..." My near-choked response is compliments of the original sunburst vintage J-45 guitar resting in my lap. It's a replica of the guitar my dad had—the guitar stolen from me when I ran to Michael's wreckage.

I run my hand down its perfectly crafted body, mesmerized by its craftsmanship. I've been eyeing one at my local music store the past few years, but it was too expensive for me to buy. This would have cost Emily a fortune.

I give it one final glance before locking my eyes with Emily. I hate what I'm about to do, but it must be done. "It's beautiful, but I can't accept it."

Emily's smile transforms into a frown. "Why?"

"It's too much. I appreciate the thought, but I can't accept something so expensive." She can barely afford to live, let alone give me a guitar worth thousands of dollars.

When tears trickle from her eyes, I set down my guitar before pulling her into my lap. I feel terrible that I've upset her, but she can't afford to spend this much money on me.

"I saved for weeks so I could get you a gift I knew you'd love."

The rattle of my hands is audible in my words. "You saved that money for you, Beautiful, so you wouldn't need to work while attending college. I appreciate your generosity, but it's too much. I'll get a guitar like this one day, just not until *we* can afford it."

I lift her head, my thumbs at the ready to clear her tears. Their efforts double when I murmur, "I love you, Beautiful. Just you being here is the best gift I could have received."

I give her a gentle kiss, praying she doesn't pull away from me. She doesn't, but her hurt radiates in our kiss. It's as fire-sparking as ever, just dampened by her wet cheeks. It kills me that I've made her cry. There's nothing I hate more in the world than seeing her upset, but she can't afford the gift she purchased, so it would be selfish of me to accept it.

After withdrawing from our embrace, I clear away a handful of rogue tears our kiss missed. "We'll take it back in the morning. Because it's in the same condition you purchased it, they'll have no reason to refuse a refund. Okay?"

She takes so long contemplating a reply, just when I think she'll never answer me, she nods. "Okay."

***

When I walk out of the steam-filled bathroom the following morning, wrapped in a towel, Emily greets me at the door with her usual big, beautiful smile on her face. "It's time for me to go. I love you."

When she plants a chaste peck to my mouth, I tug her in close for a steamier embrace. The heaviness my shoulders have been carrying the past six hours lightens when she returns my kiss with as much love and tenderness as she bestowed upon me last night.

I'm glad she isn't leaving angry. Just getting her to hand over the receipt for my guitar took a lot of persuading. She only caved a mere second before I hopped into the shower. We're leaving at the same time this morning, just in different directions. She's going back to college, and I'm heading to the studio.

I nip at her lips until I get enough of her taste to last me until Friday before walking her to her car. "I love you too, Beautiful. Drive carefully."

Nodding, she slips into her hideous pink car before guiding it out of Jacob's driveway. I wait for her taillights to blur before heading back to my room to get dressed. It's so fresh outside, it feels like my toes are about to drop off. Serves me right for standing outside in only a towel.

After throwing on my standard outfit, jeans, fitted shirt, and my leather jacket, I collect my keys from the bedside table, then grab the guitar so I can return it on my way to the studio. Unable to ignore its beauty, I run my hand down its smooth woodgrain surface for the last time. It's nearly as beautiful as Emily when her face is flushed with ecstasy. I wish I could keep it, but that would be wrong of me to do.

I give it one last glance before packing it away in its case. Halfway there, I spot a hand-written inscription on the very bottom left-hand side.

It's rude not to accept a gift.
I love you
Emily xx

My heart beats double-time when I scrub at the black ink, praying it will come off. It doesn't budge an inch no matter how hard I scrub. My teeth crunch when my step back has me bumping into my bedside table. The permanent marker teetering back and forth exposes Emily's ruse. She tainted my guitar, so I couldn't refund it.

That witch! I'd kill her if I didn't love her so much.

As a smile crosses my face, the truth smacks into me. I'm now the proud owner of a vintage 1957 Gibson J-45. Although some people might say it's less valuable since it's been inscribed, to me, it's even more precious.

It's my second-most valued possession. Do you know who has the top spot?

CHAPTER 24

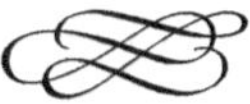

EMILY

Noah will kill me when he discovers I marked a rare guitar with a permanent marker, but I really wanted him to keep it, so something had to give. It's partly his fault. He let it slip that the store wouldn't let him return it if it wasn't in its original condition. I probably made an expensive guitar worthless, but it'll be worth it. Just the look on his face when he spotted it justifies every penny I spent.

I've seen Noah eyeing a similar guitar for months. It was more expensive than the one I purchased, but the three thousand dollar price tag on his guitar already stretched my budget thin. My brother Dominic negotiated an awesome deal from a family friend. He expressed concern about me spending so much money on a gift, but when I explained to him the reason why I needed that specific guitar, he soon understood.

The day Michael died, Noah dropped his dad's 1957 Gibson J-45 guitar to run into the street. By the time he remembered he had left it in the front yard of Marcus's grandma's house, it had been stolen. That was the guitar Noah's dad taught him to play on, and it was the same guitar Noah had been teaching Michael to play. Just seeing Noah's face when he ran his hands over the smooth wood surface made it worth working full-time at Dan's Grocery Store during my summer break to afford it.

My eyes divert from the road when my phone beeps, announcing I've received a text message from Noah.

Noah: *You're naughty...But I still love you xx*

I squeal in jubilation, stoked he's keeping the present I brought him. If it weren't for being a snoop, I wouldn't have known yesterday was his birthday. He never mentioned the actual date he was born, and when I would ask, he'd say things like, it's in a few months, or it's a few weeks away; he never gave me an exact date. I knew his birthday was toward the end of the year because when we began dating, he told me his twenty-first birthday had been a few months earlier.

A couple of months ago, when my snooping nature got the best of me, I snuck a peek in his wallet. His license told me everything I need to know. He was born on the eighteenth of December, and his middle name is Gibson—now do you understand why I went to such lengths to force him to keep his gift?

While sneakily placing Noah's license back into his wallet, I stumbled upon a ring in a compartment at the back. There were two white gold infinity symbols on each side of its thin band, and a modest diamond in the middle. It looked very much like an engagement ring, and it set my heart racing.

You have no idea how hard it's been pretending I'm none the wiser to its existence. I've known since the week we started dating I want to spend the rest of my life with Noah, so discovering he felt the same way was euphoric.

After hugging the ring as if it were worth a million dollars, I slipped it back into his wallet, hoping to see it again soon. I spent the rest of my night snuggled into his side, dreaming about becoming Mrs. Emily Taylor.

It has been a few months since I discovered the ring. As far as I'm aware, it's still sitting in Noah's wallet, gathering dust. Although I hope it gets to sparkle one day soon, I don't want Noah to propose before he's ready. We're young; we've got plenty of time for weddings and babies.

I just need my sentimental, snooping ass to get the memo. This isn't a Hallmark movie. It's real life, and damn near perfect as it is, so why rush something we have years to cherish?

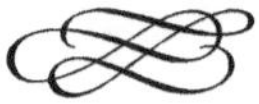

CHAPTER 25

EMILY

$\mathcal{N}$oah laughs while shadowing me into my childhood bedroom. "Your family is great, Emily."

When he slips out of his jeans and slides into my bed, I grimace. It kills me knowing he'll be half-naked and I won't be able to touch him. It isn't that I don't want to feel his heated skin under my hands. I just respect my mom enough not to have sex in her house. That's the sole reason Noah and I spent the first few days of Christmas break at Jacob's house. I can't be near him and not touch him—sue me.

"Slightly crazy, but great." His laughter grows louder.

We've just spent Christmas Day with my family. After I let slip that Noah's family never celebrated Christmas, Mom went all out. We had a massive feast for lunch before gathering around the tree to exchange gifts. I couldn't stop giggling when Noah opened Lola's gift. She bought him the tightest pair of black leather pants imaginable, explaining that modern rock stars wear leather pants— not jeans.

My laughter trapped in my throat when Noah bragged that his cock would be on display for his fans. That wiped the smile right off my face and had me determined that Noah would *never* wear leather pants.

Well, not in public anyway.

With the gift-giving taking longer than predicted, the sun fell from the sky before any of us were ready, so instead of preparing a second feast, we ate leftovers and played board games. It was all fun and games until our night ended with charades. For some reason, I suck at that game. Keeping my big mouth shut is already asking too much—I like to talk—but when Lola can't work out what my flapping arms mean, it agitates me to no end.

My family should be banned from playing charades. Every game ends in an argument. If Noah didn't get between them, Dominic and Aiden would have damaged more than the Christmas tree.

After wrangling off my sweatpants, I slip into my bed next to Noah and snuggle into his chest. "They're a little bit crazy, but what family isn't it?"

While watching me spin the charm bracelet he bought me for Christmas around my wrist, he sees something on my face I didn't mean to express. "Do you not like it?"

"I love it."

I'm not lying. I love the bracelet—truly, I do. The clasp has my birthstone in it, and it's crafted with the same yellow and white gold combination my other jewelry has. I'm just being silly—like every girl is when presented a jewelry box. I gave his gift too much thought while opening it. It was small and lightweight, the perfect size for an engagement ring. Although my present wasn't quite what I was hoping, it's still a thoughtful gift.

Leaning up, I press my lips to Noah. "I love it, thank you."

"But...?"

"No buts, I love it."

"Em..."

He stares at me, aware I'm lying, but having no clue I can't tell him the truth without sounding like a selfish brat. Furthermore, I don't want him to propose because our first Christmas together would enhance the love story I plan to bore our grandchildren with one day. I want him to ask me to be his wife because he wants to, not because he was forced.

When his glare becomes too much for me to bear, I shimmy down the mattress until my eyes are level with his tattoo. Seeing firsthand how much he's already lost in his short life has the words I don't want to speak stumbling out. "When I saw the box, I thought maybe there was something different inside."

I wait for him to respond.

It's a long-ass thirty seconds.

Sheepishly, I lift my head off his chest. The narrowed eyes and flaring nostrils I expect to see aren't there. He's smiling—broadly.

"How long?" He cocks his brow, his heart rate picking up. "How long have you known about the ring in my wallet?"

I bite my lower lip, acting coy. He doesn't buy my act. He knows I'm the world's biggest snoop. Even as a kid, I snuck peeks at the presents my mom *thought* she hid around the house.

"A few months." I hide my flushed cheeks in his chest, mortified.

"You little snoop."

I stiffen when he tickles my ribs. There's nothing I hate more than being tickled. If you're the youngest in your family, you'll understand. Dominic and Aiden always ganged up on me. One would hold me down, while the other tickled me until I wet my pants. I still hate them for it, and Noah knows that.

"Noah, don't!" With a squeal, I maneuver away from his torturous hands. It does little to stop his onslaught.

"Stop!" I scream louder this time, my legs kicking out to emphasize my statement.

"Fuck!" Noah grabs ahold of his crotch before curling into a ball. His face fills with pain as his eyes clamp shut. I've hurt him—bad.

"I'm so sorry."

He might believe my apology if I weren't giggling. I should feel bad I've kneed him in the balls, but part of me thinks he got what he deserved. He tickled me even knowing I hate it. Karma works in mysterious ways.

When he stays down for longer than predicted, I grow worried I've really hurt him. "Are you okay? I didn't mean to whack you in the nuts; I just got a little flustered." I rub his back in a circular motion, soothing him like he usually does me when I'm upset.

After several long heartbeats, the redness on his face recedes, and his eyes open. "Jesus, Em, you weren't joking when you said you hate being tickled." His words are rickety, still laced with pain.

"I'm sorry—truly." I add to my apology by pressing my lips to his. He wants a more sincere request for forgiveness. With his hand woven through my hair, he takes control of our embrace. He whips his tongue along my lips, wetting the dryness my panicked breaths caused, before delving inside my mouth. He kisses me until I'm breathless.

Pulling back from our embrace, I stare into his dark eyes. Warmth spreads across my chest when I notice how peaceful he seems. I've never seen him so down to earth and happy. I'm glad he's finally found some peace in the world. He was dealt a rough hand, and I'm doing everything in my power to fix. No one should go through the pain he has — not even a monster.

I gaze into his eyes, my love unmissable. "I love you."

Projecting how deeply I care for him with three little words doesn't feel adequate, but they're all I have, so they're what I use.

Noah smiles, flashing his gorgeous dimples. "I love you too, Beautiful."

His lips brace my temple before climbing out of bed. A groan rumbles in my chest when he bobs down to snag his wallet out of his jeans. His backside... hot enough to cook an egg on.

My heart stops beating when the quickest shimmer of gold catches my eye. He's removed the ring from his wallet to clutch it tightly in his hand. "No, Noah."

I shake my head as my eyes seek his. I don't want him to ask me to marry him now. I want him to do it when he feels the time is right, not because I expected a different gift Christmas morning.

Pretending he can't see my rapidly shaking head, Noah slides back into the bed, then rolls onto his hip. He lies so close to me, our chests compete with every breath we take. Although the sentiment in the air is heavy, I'll never forgive myself if he proposes because he feels forced.

"Don't propose until you're ready—"

"I've known since our very first date that you'd be the girl I'd marry one day. I purchased this ring before I booked our hotel room."

His confession utterly blindsides me. In a good way, but I'm still shocked all the same.

"I had planned to ask you after the band performed for the music execs, because I knew even if I had failed that night, I'd still have the brightest future with you. It doesn't matter if I sell a million records or work in a suit nine to five, all that matters is that you're at my side while doing it. I love you, Emily; I always have, and I always will, so will you do me the honor of becoming my wife?"

My heart beats wildly as I struggle to compile a response. It isn't that I don't want to say yes. I've practiced screaming that exact word for months. I just want to make sure he's proposing because he wants to, not because I snooped.

When my delay fills Noah's eyes with panic, I realize he only asked because he wanted to, freeing me to say, "Yes, Noah, I would be honored to be your wife."

With a dimpled grin, he slips the ring he's clutching for dear life onto my finger. "This ring is temporary. I've been waiting to propose until I could get you a nicer one, but it'll do for now."

I shoo away his suggestion, my eyes watering as I take in the sparkling diamond on my hand. "I love it. It's perfect just as it is."

It's a beautiful ring. The infinity symbols on each side represent how long our love will last, and the diamond reveals that no matter how insignificant something seems, in the right eyes, it's priceless.

I stop gawking at my ring when Noah says, "I love you, soon-to-be Mrs. Emily Taylor," before sealing his mouth over mine.

Unlike me, he has no qualms expressing himself. He pours his heart and soul into our kiss, articulating his love without the three little words I always use. It's a knee-buckling kiss that sees us breaking more than my no-sex rule in my mother's house... We also break my bed.

CHAPTER 26

NOAH

*A*fter six tireless months, we've finally achieved the seemingly unachievable. Our album is done! It took longer to wrap up than anticipated, but budget restraints meant we didn't have as much time in the studio as we needed. Delays were inevitable. The reward far outweighs the agony, though. I'm not being showy when I say our debut album is a fucking masterpiece. I cannot wait to share it with our fans.

Next week will be huge for Rise Up. Just reaching this stage has our excitement hitting peaks never reached before. We can barely contain ourselves as we wait to be called into the boardroom at Destiny Records' head office. The meeting we have scheduled today will be life-altering. I can't explain it any more simply than that.

Electricity infuses the air when Cormack pops his head out of the boardroom. "Come on in."

His smile says it all. He's just as excited as us. After clearing the sweat from my palms with my jeans, I nudge my head to my band members, gesturing for them to enter before me.

"Boys, this is Delilah Winterbottom." Cormack introduces us to a lady with jet black hair cut in a fierce bob. "Delilah, this is Marcus, Slater, and Nick."

The boys shake Delilah's hand in greeting before taking a seat around the boardroom table, leaving me with the final introduction.

"And this is Noah Taylor, lead singer of Rise Up."

My chest swells with smugness at the pride in Cormack's voice, but not for long. Delilah's narrowed eyes are already off-putting, much less the snarl she gives before accepting my hand. If first impressions are anything to go by, she'll be a real ball breaker.

Remembering Marcus's pledge to play nice, I mumble, "Nice to meet you," before sliding into the empty chair next to Slater, who's gorging down sandwiches like he's never been fed.

Cormack has gone all out for our meeting. There's an impressive spread of sandwiches and cakes in the middle of the table, and the half dozen cans of soda the boys haven't demolished already are to their right.

Just like every other meeting we've had the past eleven months, Cormack and Delilah sit opposite of the band. I don't know if they're doing it on purpose, but I take offense to this arrangement. It's like they're pompously stating they're in charge of the game, and we're little pawns they use to play.

With introductions out of the way, Cormack gets straight down to business. I appreciate that about him. I hate weaving through the trivial shit. "Delilah will be responsible for all of Rise Up's public relation matters—"

"What do you mean 'public relations'?" Slater asks with a mouth full of food.

I shake my head when he takes another bite of his sandwich, not the least bit concerned that he's talking with a mouthful of food. I swear the fucker doesn't have any manners.

Slater's throat struggles to swallow his sandwich when Delilah glares at him. "It means I handle all media on behalf of the band. I'll be in charge of organizing radio and television interviews, and my articles will be printed in publications around the world." She straightens her spine as her jaw grows taut. "I'll also be responsible for the band's image."

"Image?" Marcus scoots to the edge of his chair, his brows furled.

"As in, how we're perceived by the public? Or what we wear?"

Cormack swivels his chair to face Marcus. "Both. Her role will encompass what clothes you wear at events to how the public perceives you."

My head slants to the side as confusion stirs in my gut. The image presented before me now—the guys chowing down on sandwiches and slurping on soda—proves a little help in public etiquette would be helpful, but I don't want to change who we are because we got a record deal. The fans love us because of our music, not how we look.

Moving matters along, Delilah discloses, "We'll be marketing your album to audiences in the thirteen to thirty-five demographic."

When her squinted eyes swing my way, I sink into my chair, wondering what the fuck I did wrong. The demographic she's aiming for sounds spot on. Our fan's average age is mid-twenties. We didn't get a chance to tap into the younger market as anyone under twenty-one wasn't allowed in Mavs. Potential older fans were too busy being parents or working, so nights out were a rarity, but that doesn't mean they won't buy our CD. I'm glad we're striving to reach new fans. The more people who hear our music, the better.

My eyes float up from the ground when Delilah pushes our meeting into a direction I wasn't expecting. "Noah, I understand you became engaged over the holidays?"

I smile. The day Emily agreed to be my wife was the happiest day of my life. I cannot wait for us to wed on our second anniversary. As far as I'm concerned, it can't come quick enough.

Taking my smile as confirmation, Delilah snarls, bearing teeth. "The band needs to be attainable to its fans, which means we cannot publicly announce that you're engaged, let alone broadcast that you're in a relationship."

"What?" My mind is blank for a better reply. I'm truly shocked. How can being engaged affect the band's album launch?

When I ask Delilah precisely that, her glare ramps up. She scowls so hard, wrinkles line her forehead. It's the exact look my mother gives me any time I'm in her presence. Not once since Michael's death has she looked at me without disgust on her face.

Anger sluices through my veins, overheating my already sticky skin. This woman doesn't know me, yet she already hates me. That's fucked.

My annoyance reaches fever pitch when Delilah flattens her palms on the table and sneers, "It's the *fans* who download songs, listen to them, and share them with their friends—not fiancées. Furthermore, when women hear a love ballad, they imagine they're the woman in the song. If they learn you're engaged, that won't happen, which in turn means they won't download your song, fall in love with it, and dream of the day they'll marry the man promising them a lifetime of happiness with lyrics designed to do exactly that." She angles her head to the side, hoping it will hide her vindictive smirk. It doesn't. Not at all. "That's why whatever silly little thing you *think* you're planning next year will not only remain a secret, it will *not* occur. Not on my watch."

Spit flies out of her mouth like venom when she speaks, only magnifying my anger. "I'm not hiding Emily away!"

I'll rip up our agreement before I'll ever do that. We've already begun planning our wedding. It's set in stone.

I glance around the table, seeking support. Slater and Marcus have stopped eating and are leaning low in their chairs. Their wide eyes drift between Delilah and me, but they don't appear eager to jump in to back me up. Nick is sitting on the edge of his chair. His brows are furrowed, and the tight hold of his jaw can't conceal its tick, but he's also mute, leaving the fight solely on my shoulders.

After huffing my annoyance at their lack of assistance, I turn my focus back to Delilah. Before I can tell her to row up a creek without a paddle, Cormack rejoins the conversation. "We're not saying you have to break up with Emily. We just can't have the public knowing you're in a relationship."

He peers at me with nurturing eyes, begging me to calm down. He did the same thing numerous times during the production of our album, but those arguments were different. They were creative disagreements; they weren't personal.

I'm interrupted from expressing my thoughts for the second time when one of my bandmates finally backs up my campaign. It's the last person I expected, but I'm grateful all the same.

"This is bullshit. We don't make music so immature idiots can daydream about marrying us. We do it because we're fucking good at it." Nick stands from his chair to flatten his palms on the table. "You don't pick who you love, so leave them alone!"

His outburst stuns me. He's adamant he'll never fall in love, yet he's the only one defending my right to publicly declare who I love. I never thought I'd see the day. Nick, the world's biggest player, is defending love. My eyes would get misty if I weren't so pissed.

My chance to slap him on the back in congratulations is lost when Delilah roars, "This is *not* negotiable! You either agree to our terms or the record deal is off the table!"

Cormack drags his hand down his face when she storms out of the boardroom. He looks tired, but not enough to leash Delilah's campaign for another day. "She could have put it across a little smoother, but her terms are nothing new in this industry. It's a publicist's job to let the public know what *they* want them to know. It doesn't mean you love Emily any less. It's just business, and our job..." He gestures his hand to the door Delilah just rocketed through. "...is to sell as many of *your* albums as we can."

I understand what he's saying, but it doesn't make it any easier to swallow. Emily is someone I never knew I wanted but now crave more than anything. Although she'll most likely support Delilah and Cormack's decision to keep our relationship out of the public eye, I don't want to ask her to do that. Her confidence has flourished so much the past twelve months, I don't want anything affecting that.

Certain he's getting through to me, Cormack smiles uneasily before advising he'll give us the rest of the afternoon to think things over. He's barely out of the room when Nick's angry roar bellows through my ears. "Fuck this shit! This is bullshit, Noah. You can't let them do this!"

It's only when I spot the regret in his baby blues does reality dawn. He's not defending my right to declare who I love. He's in love!

Holy fucking shit, how did I miss this?

Spotting my wide eyes and gaped mouth, Nick snarks, "Shut up, Noah." He storms out of the room, kicking a chair on his way out. "Just shut the fuck up."

I stare at the door he walked through for several heart-thrashing seconds, struggling to work out if I'm the only one in the dark about his personal life. When I crank my neck back to Slater and Marcus, I realize how well Nick has kept his relationship hidden. They're as stunned as me.

"Holy shit, Nick's in love?!" Slater slaps his knee, his voice cracking from how hard he's laughing. "The world's biggest fucking player finally got played."

Marcus's nudge to Slater's shoulder nearly sends him toppling to the floor. "Don't be an ass."

When Marcus scoots his chair closer to me, my teeth grit. I'm not up for one of his pep talks right now. He's always been a *let's sit down and talk shit over* guy, but I'm too angry to listen to anyone.

"You can do what you want with my advice once I've given it, but you're going to listen," he warns when I attempt to bookmark his lecture for another day. "I get you're pissed; I understand why you want to throw this deal in the trash, but you need to think about this with a clear head. Hate it or not, what they're saying is true. It might not be right, but it is true. You've been in this industry for years, Noah; you know how it works."

"I'm not a fucking puppet who performs on demand, Marcus. Why can't the fans just listen to our music without fantasizing that they'll marry the man singing the lyrics?"

He shrugs. "I don't know. It's fucked." His rare use of a curse word shocks me. I've never heard him swear before. Clearly, this is frustrating him more than he's letting on. "Why don't you talk to Emily and see what she thinks? If she's fine with it, maybe you will be too."

He doesn't wait for me to respond. He just slaps my shoulder in support before exiting the boardroom, passing Slater who's still pissing himself laughing about his "player got played" comment.

CHAPTER 27

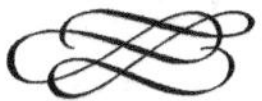

NOAH

Although I hate even considering the idea of siding with Delilah, my two-hour trip to pick Emily up from school has me examining both sides of the coin. I can't hide my relationship with Emily; we've already booked the church, but the album the boys and I created is a masterpiece. It deserves to be heard. Years of blood, sweat, and tears went into its creation. I can't let that much creativity be wasted.

This pains me to admit, but my deliberations prove what I've always known: no matter which path I take, I'll come out of this deal a loser.

With Emily's last class today being English Lit, I pull my truck into an empty spot at the front of the building her class is held in. When I jump down from my truck and round the hood, you have no idea how badly I'm itching for a hit of nicotine. Twelve months ago, smokes were my go-to when I was stressed. Now, I work through my agitations with a beautiful brunette whose skin smells as sweet as it tastes. Just the thought of Emily's lazy smile when I drag my stubble over the skin high on her thighs has my first smile of the day raising my cheeks.

It doubles in size when Emily pushes through the double doors of the building I'm loitering in front of. Her long, dark locks swish across her back when she notices me leaning on the quarter-panel of my truck. She races my way, as eager to see me waiting for her now as she was the first time I picked her up. I love that even though we've been together a little over a year, excitement still takes hold of my senses every time I see her.

Her vanilla scent engulfs me when she leaps into my arms to mash our faces together. After smothering my cheeks, lips, and jaw with kisses, she sucks in a massive breath before breathing out with a sigh. "I've missed you so much."

"I've missed you too, Beautiful."

I show her precisely how much by sealing my mouth over hers. Our kiss is anything but innocent. If the wolf whistles surrounding us aren't already a sign, the numerous requests for us to "get a room" are a surefire indication.

Emily's lips rise against mine before she pulls back. She doesn't care about the attention we've gained. She just wants to take our gathering somewhere more private.

She's not the only one.

Although her dorm room is close, I assist her into my truck. Jacob's house may not be the house I was raised in, but it's my home.

I've barely pulled my truck away from the curb when Emily's inquisitiveness gets the best of her. "Did you bring it?"

She's so excited, she can hardly sit still. She, along with the thousands of fans we've amassed on our Facebook page thus far, have been impatiently waiting the reveal of our album cover. Although social media won't get it for a few more days, I promised Emily her own special reveal the instant it came off the press. It's so fresh, the ink was still wet when I plucked it from our producer's hand.

"Yep!" I give the P an extra pop, my excitement as palpable as Emily's.

She has seen concept covers, but I'm dying to show her the final product. The creative director of our shoot wanted us to be as appealing as possible, which means we're all shirtless, wearing only jeans with the top buttons undone. We're formed into a diamond pattern, and the guitar Emily gave me for my birthday is draped in front of me.

Emily's eyes dart around the cab of my truck. "Where is it?"

I love that she's so excited, but I can't help but tease her a little. It keeps things exciting.

It takes all of two seconds for Emily's impatience to be announced. "Noah Gibson Taylor."

I grin. She only uses my full name when I'm in trouble, which I'm pleased to say isn't very often. We don't fight. We've had a few misunderstandings fueled by jealousy, and the occasional disagreement about what movie to watch, but other than that, we have nothing to argue about.

That may change when she folds her arms under her chest with a huff, forcing me to bow out of my tease like a weasel. "It's in the glove compartment, *Emily Faye McIntosh.*" I use her full name on purpose, knowing it will rile her up. Serves her right for being so impatient.

Emily doesn't dislike many things, but the top two items on her hit list are indisputable. She hates being tickled and utterly despises her middle name. Faye is her grandmother's given name. Emily swears she's the meanest old cow you'll ever meet, so she's flabbergasted as to why her parents lumped her with such a hideous name. I think it's cute, but I'll never tell Emily that. I barely survived the last time she kneed me in the nuts. I'm not eager for round two.

A grimace screws up my features when Emily yanks open my glove compartment with so much force, I'm afraid she's broken old Betty's hinges. A little vein in her neck pulsates as she drinks in the recently printed cover.

"Yay! I can't believe it's finally here! You look so hot!" I scold myself for getting jealous over a CD cover when she hugs it close to her chest. "How much longer until we hear your songs on the radio?"

Her question reminds me why my pits are sweaty even though it's winter. "There's a bit of a problem."

Dust kicks up around us when I maneuver my truck into the emergency shoulder at the side of the road. Emily is great at hiding her true feelings, but only when I'm not looking at her. I can't maintain eye contact and her safety at the same time, hence me pulling over.

After turning off the ignition, I twist my torso to face Emily. Even though she is frowning, she's still the most beautiful girl I've ever seen. "We met with a lady today... *if you can call her that.*" The snark in my tone can't be missed. Delilah rubs me the wrong way. It's still early, but I doubt we'll ever have an amicable working relationship. "Cormack brought her onboard to look after Rise Up's public relation matters." I swish my tongue around my mouth, loosening it up for my next set of words. "She was *extremely* adamant that the band needs to remain attainable to its fans."

Emily's eyes bounce between mine, confusion filling them.

Recognizing I'm doing a poor job of explaining myself, I try a new tactic. I rip the Band-Aid off with one quick tear. "She wants the public to believe I'm single."

Emily remains quiet, contemplating what I've told her. It doesn't take her long to hear Delilah's request in the same manner I did. "Are you breaking up with me?"

"No, Emily, God no." Just the thought has me twisted up in knots. I couldn't live a day without her in my life. "I'm not breaking up with you; that will *never* happen."

I know without a doubt she'll be my wife and the mother of my children one day.

When I seize her wrist to pull her to my side of the bench, she grips me tightly, as if she's afraid I'll vanish. "I don't understand what you're saying, Noah. I don't understand what you mean."

Explaining it for the second time doesn't make it any easier to swallow. "They want to keep our relationship a secret, so the public doesn't know we're together."

My body slicks with sweat as anger from my meeting resurfaces. I can't believe I'm even considering this. It's not even confirmed yet, but I can already feel cracks forming between us. If that isn't proof enough of what I need to do, I don't know what is.

"I'm not doing it. I'll tell them no."

My hand slips from Emily's back when she draws back to peer at me. "What happens if you refuse?"

I shrug. "I don't know."

I hate lying, but I'm not even sure I am. The Ice Queen said her terms weren't negotiable, but was that just a threat, or something she plans to follow through with if I don't conform?

"Will you lose your record deal?"

Once again, I shrug.

Emily calls out my deceit without a word seeping from her lips. Her head slants to the side as her brow cocks. She's angry I'm coasting over important facts, but panicked about why I'm doing it. Usually, I'm brutally honest.

With a sigh, I murmur, "We may."

When fresh tears loom in her eyes, she draws herself into my chest to hide them from me. I don't need to see them to know of their arrival, though. The quiver of her lips on my torso tells me everything I need to know.

I hold her close for several long minutes, lost on what to do. Just as everything pans out as I've been planning the past six years, it's close to being snatched away. And no, I'm not solely referring to my record deal.

After a few more minutes, Emily's head pops off my chest. The weight on my chest eases when I spot her dry cheeks. Her eyes are close to bursting, but she's given it her all to hold back her tears. "We can do this." She nods like the ideas I see rolling through her head make sense. "We just can't get married right now. But we will. *Eventually*. Won't we?"

Her confidence plummets with each word, assuring me I'm doing the right thing. Fuck them and their record deal. I won't let them break Emily's heart.

"I'll tell them no. We'll get married like we're supposed to. I'm not changing who I am so fans can live in a fantasy world."

I expect Emily to be relieved, so you can imagine my surprise when her reply is on the other end of the spectrum. "No, Noah. I refuse to become your mother." Her tone is firm and to the point.

"When your dad gave up his dreams, it ate his soul. I won't let that happen to you. You've worked too hard for too long to give up now."

I agree with what she's saying—my dad's decision to leave his band was the beginning of his dreaded life—but our circumstances are vastly different. I won't blame her like my dad blamed my mom. This isn't her choice. It's mine, and I'm choosing her over the band.

"I can't live without you, Emily; it will tear my life apart. It's not your choice; it's mine, and I'm telling them no."

"I'm *not* your mother, and you will *not* force me to be her!"

Anger so black it almost chokes me curls around my throat when she pushes away from me. I'm trying to save us, yet she pulls away from me. *What the fuck?*

"I love you, Noah, but you're not giving up your dreams for me—"

"Then what do you want me to do, Emily?!" I shouldn't be lashing out at her, but I'm so fucking angry, I'm holding on by a thread. "I can't give you up, but you won't let me fight for you either!"

I smash my knuckles against the steering wheel, my anger too intense to be dispelled with just words. After hitting it enough times my knuckles bust open, I throw my head back to suck in some ragged breaths. I feel like I'm being torn in two. Our record deal is everything I've been working toward for years, but now it sits dangling on a piece of thread because they want me to give up the one thing I crave more than anything: to be loved.

The throb in my knuckles transfers to my heart when Emily crawls onto my lap. She cradles my sweat-drenched head into her hands before weaving her fingers through the hair stuck to my temples. She soothes me as only she can, her silent affirmation assuring me I can have both her and my musical dreams.

She backs up her unspoken words with spoken ones. "You don't have to give anything up." She raises my head until our eyes meet. "We just can't let anyone know about us."

"I can't keep quiet about you like you're a dirty little secret."

Her smile has my heart skipping a beat. "Why not? It will be fun. We've just got to be more inventive than we've been. We're still getting married. It's just on hold for a couple of months. Gives me more time to plan."

"Em…" I try to say more, but I can't. I still only have a very minute hold on the thread I've been clutching since Chris killed himself.

This kills me to admit, even more so since I hate talking about my feelings, but I've struggled hard with depression since Chris died. There were days when I didn't get out of bed and times where I believed it would be best if I never did. If it weren't for Jacob, I doubt I would have survived, so can you imagine the burden of a life without Emily in it? I've already lost so much, I'd never survive a third bout.

I run my thumb across Emily's beautiful face before tracking it over her lips. They're extra puffy from the number of times she has dragged her teeth over them. "Are you sure this is what you want?"

She nods without hesitation, proving what I've always known. Only the strong can drag the weak out of the darkness. She did it twelve months ago, and she continues to do it every day she's mine.

CHAPTER 28

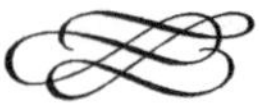

EMILY

My heart stops beating as my pupils widen. I stare at the radio in Jenni's pride and joy, certain I'm not hearing what I *think* I'm hearing. That can't be Rise Up's song "Hollow" blaring out of the speakers—surely.

When the tears the heartbreaking lyrics always produce well in my eyes, they snap to Jenni. She's as stunned as me, her mouth gaped and her eyes wide. With a squeal, she yanks her car off the road before cranking the volume to the highest setting.

Only four weeks ago, I didn't think this was possible. Noah was on the verge of letting Rise Up's album sit on the shelf gathering dust. I'm so glad I talked him out of it.

I'll admit, when Noah said the record label wanted him to appear single, I assumed he was breaking up with me. We have a great relationship, but he's been working his butt off for a record deal for years, so it was understandable that my first thought was panic that his career was more important than me.

I had no reason to fret. Noah was ready to give up *everything* for me. His dreams, his career—even his band. Although relieved he proved without doubt I'm his number one priority, I couldn't watch him throw away years of hard work. I love him too much to see years of his life wasted like his father. Trevor gave up his dreams for his girlfriend, and now he sits in jail, praying to be released so he can see the only son he has left.

I retaliated when Noah told me he'd tell them no, but that was only because I know how much he despises his mother. I'd never want him to look at me in the same light he does her. If he'd given up his dream, it would have killed his soul, and the depression he's kept buried the past seven years might have resurfaced. Not even I could see him through that.

Rise Up is incredibly talented, so it will only take a few songs before their fans grow more interested in their music than their personal lives. If we have to wait a few months for that to happen, that's what we'll do. I'll wait a lifetime for Noah.

My thoughts revert to the present when Jenni grips my hand so hard, her French nails pierce my skin. She's back home for the long weekend so she can join the festivities Noah and the band organized this weekend. Noah rented a cabin on the cliffs of Bronte's Peak. He wants to get everyone together for one last hurrah before things get crazy. We were halfway to the cabin when Noah's soulful voice filtered through the speakers.

Once lyrics about being left behind to face your demons alone fade into another song, I lock my moisture-filled eyes with Jenni's. "They did it."

She bites on the inside of her cheek, praying the sting of her teeth will stop her tears from falling. "They did it."

With a waggle of my brows, I yank my bag from the floor to fetch my phone. I have to call Noah to tell him we just heard his song on the radio. I've been waiting for this day for over a year. My fingers fumble over the screen, punching in a number I know by heart, before I raise it to my ear.

Noah's seductive voice rumbles down the line not even a second later, "Hello, Beautiful."

"Hi—"

"Are you crying?"

While sweeping my hand across my cheeks to make sure they're free of moisture, I smile. I love that he can read my emotions only hearing one teeny tiny word.

"I am, but I'm okay. They're happy tears."

He releases a deep breath in relief. I'm not surprised. He hates seeing me cry, which sucks since I'm a bit of a sookie la-la. "Jesus, baby, you scared me."

My gratitude for his concern is audible in my voice when I shout, "I just heard you on the radio! They played 'Hollow'—just now. Like two seconds ago. Can you believe it?!"

When Noah's chuckle barrels down the line, my heart squeezes. He has an important meeting this afternoon, so he couldn't pick me up from school like he usually does. I missed the chats we have every Friday afternoon during our drive.

My spine straightens when Noah discloses, "We heard 'Surrender Me' on Monday when we were driving to the head office."

"Why didn't you tell me?!" I try to act mad. It's all a ploy. I'm too happy to let anything dampen my mood.

"I wanted you to hear it yourself." A rustle sounds down the line like he's shifting foot to foot. "It's more exciting hearing it by coincidence than sitting around, waiting for it to come on."

This pains me to admit, but he's right. Because I wasn't expecting to hear his voice, the excitement was ten times more intense.

My ears prick when I hear an unfamiliar voice in the background, closely followed by Noah's deep timbre. "I'm sorry, Beautiful, I have to go. I'll call you once I'm done."

"Okay, I love you."

"I love you too."

I wait for him to disconnect our call before lowering my phone from my ear. I angle my torso to face Jenni. She's also on a call. To whom, I don't know, but she's quick to shut down their conversation when she realizes I'm no longer distracted.

She dumps her state-of-the-art cell into the console before clearing away the tears slipping down her cheeks. I'm hoping they're happy tears, but just in case they aren't, I ask, "Who were you talking to?"

Confusion overtakes some of my happiness when she glances at me beneath lowered lashes. She seems torn, like she's struggling to tell the truth. That's a very odd response for her. She's usually so forthright, sometimes it comes off as blunt.

I'm pummeled with my third emotion of the day when she pleads, "You can't tell anyone, okay? Promise me."

The fear clutching my throat makes it hard for me to breathe, but I manage a squeaked, "I promise."

Panic hits me like a hard blow to the chest. We never keep secrets from each other, so I'm beyond worried something is horribly wrong.

Jenni's chest rises and falls three times before she pushes out, "I was leaving a message for Nick."

Nick? Nick who?

My eyes dart between hers as my brain runs through all the names she's introduced me to her first six months at college. Nick is a common name, but I'm reasonably sure she hasn't mentioned one.

When guilt mars her beautiful face, the truth smacks into me. She's not talking about a new Nick; she's referring to Noah's Nick. I thought they hadn't been in contact since the night they danced up a storm at the Dungeon.

"Nick, as in Nick from Rise Up Nick?" I sound stupid, but there are plenty of Nicks in the world, so maybe I'm mistaken.

When she fidgets with her skirt, I realize I've hit the nail on the head.

"How long?"

I grimace when my question comes out more sternly than I expected. It can't be helped. We pinkie promised back in kindergarten that we'd never keep secrets from each other, so I'm somewhat upset about her deceit.

The pain intensifies when she murmurs, "A while."

"Why didn't you tell me? Everything I've been dealing with the past four weeks, you've been going through as well, except you're not just deceiving the public, you're lying to me, your *supposed* best friend."

My words hurt her, but they don't stop her from saying, "I wanted to tell you, Em, I just couldn't."

Guilt sits heavily on my chest when tears splash down her cheeks. This is also not like her. She's always been the strong one of our duo, so to say I'm fearful of her tears isn't an overreaction.

"I'm sorry. I shouldn't have snapped." I want to engulf her in a big hug, but her car is too compact for that. Instead, I rub my thumb over her hand clutching mine. "I just wish you felt comfortable talking to me. We were so close before college. I don't want distance to change that."

"We *are* close. This is just... hard." Pain scours her beautiful face as she struggles to lessen her sobs. "I love him, Em, but I can't be with him, and it's killing me inside."

My heart bleeds for her. "Why can't you be with him? If he is who you want, why can't you love him?"

Hiccups separate her words. "It's...complicated."

When she rests her head on my shoulder, I comfort her the best I can in the tight confines of her car. "It's okay. I promise you everything happens for a reason. It'll work out."

When I add to my assurance without words, my mind wanders to Noah. He is around Nick a lot more than me, so he may have more of an idea of what's going on.

Just as quickly as Jenni's tears arrived, they leave. She pops her head off my shoulder before clearing away the mascara stains marking her cheeks, then her eyes float up to mine. "I can't talk about what's happening right now, but when I can, I'll tell you everything. Okay?"

I want to help her, but she's as stubborn as a mule. Instead, I nod. I'm worried, but the best thing I can do is be there when she needs me. I learned the hard way what happens when you force someone to open up. I won't make the same mistake twice.

"When you need me, call me. I don't care if it's the middle of the night or during class. If you need me, I'll be there for you no matter what."

A heartbreaking sob ripples from Jenni's lips, its robust vibrations almost drowning out two words I never expected her to speak: "I'm pregnant."

My pupils enlarge to the size of dinner plates, but before half my shock can be absorbed, Jenni adds more sauce to the plate. "Nick can't find out, so you can't tell Noah. Promise me, Em, promise me you won't tell Noah."

I stare at her, shocked. She doesn't understand the pledge she's asking me to make. I've never lied to Noah, so I don't know if I can keep this from him.

"Please, Emily. I know it's asking a lot, but once you know all the details, you'll understand why Nick can't know about our baby." She stares me straight in the eyes, killing my hesitation with a pair of glistening baby blues I've known for almost fifteen years. "Please, Em."

I hate what I'm about to do, but I have to trust she knows what she's doing. She wouldn't ask me to keep quiet unless it was extremely important.

"I promise I won't tell Noah."

CHAPTER 29

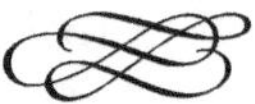

NOAH

Cormack rests his elbows on the table, his excitement uncontained. "As you guys are already aware, "Hollow" and "Surrender Me" have secured radio airtime the past two weeks. If that isn't already exciting, "Surrender Me" is currently sitting at number sixty-eight on the Billboard charts, and "Hollow" is closely riding its coattails."

A grin curls on my lips. I've been monitoring the Billboard charts daily with the hope of seeing our songs in thick black ink. I can still recall the excitement I felt when "Surrender Me" made it to the ninety-nine spot two weeks ago. "Hollow" is following quickly behind, but only just entered the charts at number ninety-eight earlier today.

"Getting two songs onto the charts so quickly is impressive, but we need to expand on it. After schmoozing some contacts in the industry, Delilah arranged a handful of radio interviews along the West Coast over the next six weeks. Things will be hectic, but we need to ride this wave all the way to the shore."

I swivel my chair to face the guys. Excitement is beaming out of them. Marcus slaps my shoulder as Slater and Nick high-five each other. If that isn't proof of the electricity firing in the air, you'll never be convinced. That's the first time I've seen them interact positively in over three years. Good things are coming. I can feel it.

Some of the happiness is stripped from my face when Cormack says, "Delilah will travel with the band. Her role will be to ensure you represent not only the record company to the best of your ability, but yourselves as well."

He hands us our schedule for the next two months. He's right; it does seem brutal, but I agree we've got to milk this cow for all it's worth. Although a majority of our schedule is blacked out, I'm stoked to see most Sundays are clear, meaning I'll still have my weekends with Emily.

Emily called just before I entered our meeting. I could tell she was crying. It wasn't because of her voice; it's the short intakes of breath between sobs that give it away. I was glad to find out they were happy tears from hearing us on the radio. Delilah screwed up her nose when I asked Emily if she was okay, but mercifully, she held in her snarky comment. It's been a day of miracles on all accounts.

Although I'm going along with the record company's ruse that I'm single, I made sure they know without doubt that I'll *never* break up with Emily, and that this situation is only temporary. Cormack seems to have gotten the message, but Delilah is a little slow on the uptake.

"If you have any questions, please come see me. If not, I'll see you boys bright and early Monday morning." Delilah mimics Cormack's movements when he rises from his seat. "Enjoy your weekend, boys, as things are about to get a little bit crazy."

Marcus waits for them to exit the room before he throws his fist in the air. "Here it is! Everything we've been waiting for is just outside those doors!"

Slater slaps his shoulder before backing up his excitement. "Now let's go blow out the cobwebs before we're stuck smelling each other's stinky socks for the next two months."

The ruckus we make as we exit Destiny Records makes it seem as if our song hit number one overnight. We're loud and vocal, and not the least bit sorry about it.

Who has time to feel regret? We have the perfect weekend

planned. The boys and I rented a beachside cabin for three nights. We've got booze, friends, and enough food to feed an army. I can't fucking wait.

Usually, Emily and I spend her college breaks together, but with the studio needing me to lay down new tracks, our time was cut short, so I'm more than itching to get her alone for a night or three.

An hour or two later, Nick and I pull into the cabin we rented. His place isn't too far from here, but for some reason, he asked to drive here with me. He's been a little weird since his outburst a few weeks ago. I've tried several times to get him to talk to me, but he keeps telling me to shut the fuck up, that it was nothing, and that he's fine.

I even went as far as offering for him to bring his girlfriend here with us. He was quick to shoot that down as well. I'm not sure what is going on with him, but I hope he gets over it soon. He's miserable to be around lately, and that's saying something. Slater's normally the only grumpy grouch in our quartet.

As I slide out of my truck, I scan the cabin. It's an exact match to the pictures online. A massive wrap-around porch surrounds all four sides, and there's a loveseat hanging on the front veranda. A set of wooden stairs on our right lead to the white sandy beach below. Even though I have fond memories of Bronte's Peak from my early days with Emily, we'll spend a majority of our weekend in the infinity pool. It's heated, and when swimming in it, it'll seem as if we have the entire ocean at our feet.

My eyes stray from the fire pit to Nick when he asks, "What time did Emily say she and Jenni were arriving?"

"Should be any minute..." My words trail off when tires crunching over gravel sound through my ears. A smirk curves my lips when Jenni's BMW turns into the pebbled driveway. "Here they are."

Who knew three little words could cause such panic? For how fast Nick's face pales, anyone would swear I told him the dads of all the girls he's screwed are hunting him down. He's got no reason to be nervous. He and Jenni met at the Dungeon nightclub over a year ago. Emily told me they hit it off, so I'm at a loss as to why he's so rattled. Perhaps he heard about how I ratted him out all those months ago?

"You alright?"

Nick jerks up his chin. "Yeah, I'm good." He throws a case of beer onto his shoulder "Better get these inside before they get hot."

He darts for the cabin so quickly, his feet kick up more dust than Jenni's car coming to a stop. Noticing the girls are in deep conversation, I hang to the side, not wanting to interrupt them.

It's a good ten or so minutes before Emily cranks open her door. She greets me in her usual way—by throwing her arms around my neck and hugging me tight—but something seems off with her. She's more skittish than usual.

"What's going on?"

When she burrows her head into my chest, I take a step back. My breath hitches when my eyes zoom in on the red, puffy rings circling her eyes. She's been crying. She was teary when she heard our song on the radio, but that was nearly an hour ago.

"Em...?" My silence asks more questions than my words ever could.

Her lips quiver as she begins to speak, "I'm fine; I've just missed you, that's all."

When she returns to nuzzling my chest, I swing my eyes to Jenni. She's emerged from her car, but is standing frozen just inside her hanging-open door.

"What's going on?" I mouth to her.

She shrugs before skirting past us to enter the cabin with the speed Nick used only minutes ago. I've only interacted with her when Emily is around, but I still know her well enough to know when she is lying.

Anger envelops me as horrible notion after horrible notion fills my head. "Did someone hurt you? Are you hurt?!"

I don't mean to yell at her, but I need to know why she's upset, and I need to know now!

"No. I'm fine." She'd have more chance of me believing her if she weren't shaking so much. Recognizing I'm seconds from going on a rampage, she tries to settle my agitation. "I'm upset, but not because anything happened to me." Worry bristles in her eyes as her teeth rake her lower lip. "I promised not to say anything. Please don't make me break my promise."

Although I hate that she's upset, I can't demand she break someone else's secret when I'm keeping ones of my own. "It's alright; you don't need to tell me. As long as you're not hurt, I'm fine with you keeping your promise."

She stiffens as her breathing levels, shocked I've given in so easily. She's also suspicious. "I want to tell you; I just can't."

"I know." It's the same for me. I've been struggling for months not to share Jacob's secret with her. It's not like we're intentionally lying to each other. We're just being good friends to the people trapped outside of the bubble we've lived in the past thirteen months. "But I can't handle any more tears, Em. You've got to put them away for the rest of the weekend."

Giggling, she nods before sweeping her hands across her cheeks. Once they're moisture-free, she lifts her glistening eyes to mine. "Better?"

"Much."

I tighten my grip on her petite body before nibbling on her lips. This weekend is about letting go of the bigger picture and appreciating what's in front of you. My entire world is standing before me, but we're letting others come between us. Not anymore. For the rest of the weekend, it's just us.

Emily's brow quirks when I step back, curl my hand around hers, then guide her toward the entrance of the cabin. "Where are we going?"

"I thought we should get a head start on christening each room before the rest of the gang gets here."

She slaps my chest, but her pace doesn't slow.

Thank fuck.

After testing out every solid surface of the master suite and attached bathroom, Emily and I spend our afternoon and night with our friends. We fired up the grill to cook hot dogs before enjoying the star-filled sky. It's been a perfect start to our weekend—even better than I was hoping.

As I glance around the table we're sitting at, my heart beats out a tune I've never heard before. It belongs to a content man.

Directly on my right is Slater and his current squeeze, Kylie. Kylie's mousy-brown hair sits just below her shoulders. Tiny freckles adorn her nose, and her red cotton dress and brown boots are an odd combination to see sitting across from Slater. A hardcore biker paired with a humble cowgirl should seem odd, but they get along really well.

Marcus is on my left. He arrived alone like usual, although he's had no issues chatting up Nicole most of the night. Nick vanished not too long ago. I think he went to check on Jenni. She left the table citing an upset tummy as an excuse for an early night. I hope she's not coming down with something. Neither the band nor Emily has time for her germs.

Sitting next to Marcus is Emily. I've been stalking her all night like a creep. I still can't believe someone as perfect as her will be my wife. I must have been a good man in another life because nothing I've done this lifetime renders me worthy of her.

My stalking ramps up when Emily's giggle jingles into my ears. She has a beautiful smile, but she's self-conscious of it. When she thinks she's smiling too big, she covers her mouth with her hand. The only good thing that comes from her insecurity is the hues of light her diamond ring bounces across the table.

Last weekend, I took Emily to the jewelry store to pick out a new engagement ring. Our royalty checks are slowly rolling in, meaning I could keep the promise I made to her when I proposed.

Not only did she blatantly refuse every ring I suggested, but she also cried when I steered her toward a pink three-carat princess cut masterpiece—and not in a good way. She said the only ring she wanted was the one she had, and that the size of the diamond didn't represent how much I loved her.

I'm ecstatic she loves the ring. I picked it because the infinity symbols on the sides reveal how long our love will last. Two souls joined together for eternity. I have a lifetime to spoil her, so I can live with her keeping her small, dainty ring if that's what makes her happy.

My attention shifts from all the non-monetary ways I can spoil her when a screen door slamming shut booms through my ears. Looking over at the cabin, I spot Nick storming out. His face is taut; he seems both angry and in pain.

Emily shoots up from her seat, mouths, *"I love you,"* then dashes into the cabin.

She's barely out of view when shattering glass fills the silence of the night. I crank my neck to the noise, my mouth gaping when I realize what is going on. Nick is swinging a baseball bat at Jenni's BMW as if he's receiving pitches at home plate.

What the fuck?!

I dive out of my seat and sprint to his side. His face is lined with anger I didn't know someone as easygoing as him had, and his veins are bulging with furious adrenaline. With a grunt, he swings his bat into Jenni's headlight. It crumples like tissue paper being dunked into a glass of water.

"What the fuck are you doing?! Stop!"

Ignoring me, he lines up his bat with the driver's side window. He isn't as big as the rest of us, but he spears his bat through the window without breaking into a sweat.

As he moves to the rear driver's side of the car, the muscles in his arms flex as violently as his jaw clenches. "They can't do this! I won't let them!"

When the window shatters beyond repair, my eyes drift to Slater, wordlessly requesting he give me a hand. He shakes his head, cautious of Nick's unprecedented violence, but not enough to put an end to it.

Air snags halfway down my throat when I shift my eyes back to Nick. Tears are streaming down his face. I've never seen him cry. Not once. Not even when Slater knocked him out with one hit.

"They can't force her to do it!" His words are more brittle than the glass covering his shoes. "They have no say in what she does! It's her fucking body!"

When he lifts the bat, preparing to take another swing, I charge for him. A grunt ripples through my lips when I hit his torso with the same force he used on Jenni's car the past five minutes. We land on the ground with a thud, my hit enough to dislodge the bat from his grip.

It also steals the air from my lungs. I roll off him, wheezing. "What the fuck, Nick?"

I probably shouldn't have charged at him so hard, but I needed to take him down mid-swing so he didn't knock my head off. I've never seen him lose control like this. He's the easy-going one, the goofball who cruises through life, but now something — *or someone* — has screwed with his head.

My brows lower as the facts stack up. Jenni was the only person in the cabin with Nick. Is she responsible for his outburst?

My eyes stray to Nick, who is lying next to me. "Jenni?"

He throws his hands over his face, his words coming out in a sob. "I love her so much it hurts."

I'm glad he's finally admitting he's in love, but this isn't how it's supposed to be. You can have moments of jealousy; sometimes you may even have little tiffs, but if he's in love with Jenni, why the fuck did he take a baseball bat to her car?

Everything makes sense when he murmurs, "She's going to kill my baby."

"She's pregnant?"

When my eyes scan Nick's face, nothing but turmoil reflects back at me. We've never been overly close; he's the equivalent of an annoying younger brother I'm forced to put up with, but even I can comprehend how fucked up this is. He's finally fallen in love, but the person he's in love with wants to terminate his baby. That's fucked. He might be a player, but not even he deserves to be treated like this.

After scrubbing his cheeks, Nick locks his pleading eyes with mine. "Can you ask Emily to talk to her? She's the only person Jenni will listen to. I don't want her to kill our baby, but without your help, I won't be able to stop it. Please, Noah. I'll do anything you ask if you do this one thing for me."

My eyes turn to the cabin. Emily is standing at the second-story window, peering down at Nick and me. Her face is marred with pain, and she's weeping. I stare at her, struggling to comprehend how I can force her to convince her friend to keep a baby she doesn't want.

Once again, I've drawn the short straw. I won't leave this dilemma with fewer scars than my previous scuffle.

CHAPTER 30

EMILY

A Few Months Later...

The first few weeks of Noah's West Coast radio tour were rough. He arrived home grouchy and frustrated, and our calls went from being over two hours of nonstop chatter, to strings of worthless sentences. His dour mood was understandable considering his time away was spent with Nick.

Misery loves company.

Weeks passed before we had a conversation that didn't involve Jenni and what she was planning to do with the baby she conceived with Nick. Noah thought I had the answers he was seeking. I didn't. I was as much in the dark as he was.

He'd never admit it, but I know my lack of knowledge annoyed him. It created tension between us and had me dreading our daily calls instead of looking forward to them. He was mad I stuck by Jenni's side as I had pledged months earlier.

I've known Jenni over half my life, and even though I was shocked she'd consider having an abortion, I still love and respect her. She was being judged enough; she didn't need me adding more angst to her life.

It was my support that led to me attending an appointment with her a couple of weeks after Nick demolished her car. Jenni wasn't as pedantic about tracking her cycle as I was, so she had no clue how far along she was.

It's funny how life is one giant circle. While waiting for Jenni to be called in, the lady behind the reception desk caught my eye. She seemed familiar, even though I hadn't been to that practice before. It was only when she smiled did I realize who she was.

Noah got his dimples and dark eyes from his mother.

It was hard watching his mom be courteous to strangers when she was so callous to her own son. Noah isn't a man of many words, but the stories he had shared left no doubt on how cold and heartless his mom was to him when he was growing up.

You wouldn't know that from watching her at her workplace, though. It seemed as if she was an entirely different person. When she noticed me staring at her, she offered me the same polite smile she had been giving patients all day. No matter how hard I fought, I couldn't return her gesture. She caused Noah years of misery, so she didn't deserve to pretend as if she had a perfect, happy life.

Thank god the doctor called Jenni in when he did. If I had to watch her fake act for a second longer, I wouldn't have left the waiting room without ensuring everyone there knew what a terrible, two-faced bitch she is.

When Jenni's doctor, Dr. Morgan, offered to do an ultrasound to see how far along Jenni was, everything changed in an instant. Her baby was only the size of a jellybean, but its heartbeat was robust. It only took Jenni hearing it for two seconds to know she could *never* destroy the precious gift growing in her tummy.

With news that she was a little over twelve weeks along, and pictures of their blob, Jenni flew to Nick to tell him her decision in person. I thought with their struggles over, things would improve between Noah and me.

Unfortunately, that hasn't been the case.

Our relationship continued to slip as the band's schedule significantly increased.

For the first few weeks, Noah came home every weekend as he originally planned, but as their album climbed the charts, his visits began to wane. At first, he came home every second weekend, then his visits decreased to once or twice a month.

You don't want to know how long it's been now. My heart shatters like glass just thinking about it. I understand he's busy. Just last week, "Surrender Me" snuck into the top twenty on the charts, and "Hollow" is following closely behind at number twenty-seven. I'm super proud of everything Rise Up has achieved, but I can't help but feel isolated and alone.

Crystal's transfer request was approved the month before Noah and I went to the cabin with our friends, so I've had my dorm room to myself the past five months. I had no idea such a homey-sized space could feel so lonely.

Thank god Crystal took me under her wing when she did. She introduced me to people with the same major as me and invited me to tag along with her and her friends when they went to parties. For the most part, it was a godsend, but it all came toppling down when Noah and I had a brutal fight in the middle of a frat party.

Crystal's friends are lovely, but some of them get a little overzealous when they've had too much to drink. I had just started talking to Noah on FaceTime when Matt, a football player for Parkwood State, wrapped me up in a bear hug. He twirled me around while loudly declaring he had missed "his baby" at the top of his lungs.

That was nothing out of the ordinary for Matt. It was how he greeted every female friend he had. It was innocent... Regrettably, Noah didn't take it that way. By the time I wrangled out of Matt's grip, Noah had disconnected our call. I dialed his number on repeat. He didn't answer one of my thirty-eight calls or return any of my many text messages.

I understood he was frustrated, but he wasn't the only one annoyed. The fact he expected me to wait around for him to show up pissed me off. I needed to interact with others, or I'd go stir-crazy.

When Noah finally returned my call later that night, it was apparent he had been drinking. He was slurring so severely, I barely understood a word he said. Our confrontation became heated pretty quickly. We both said a lot of things we didn't mean, and our call ended without the terms of endearments we usually exchanged.

Thinking arguments like that are normal for couples our age, I tried my best not to let it affect our future conversations, but that was a woeful waste of time. Every call we've had since then has been cold and distant. I can only hope his visit home this weekend reignites the flame we've lost, as I don't think I can take much more. It honestly hurts just thinking about how distant we've become.

While wiping my cheeks to ensure they're dry, I drop my eyes to my watch. I've spent a majority of my economics class staring at it, impatiently willing the big hand to strike three. Only eight minutes to go, but they're the longest, most torturous eight minutes of my life.

The big hand barely reaches the twelve when I leap up from my seat to shove my textbooks into my satchel.

"Eager to be somewhere, Ms. McIntosh?"

After bobbing my head at Dr. Kurt's question, I gallop down the stairs of my economic class. I'm halfway out the door when he dismisses the rest of the class for the weekend.

When I push open the double doors of my building, all the worries I've been having the past few months vanish in an instant. Noah's truck is parked at the end of the concrete path. He's waiting for me like he did when I began my studies last year.

My heart riots against my ribs as I break into a brisk jog. My dash is anything but glamorous, but I'm dying to see him again, so I'll happily look unattractive while doing it. As I get closer to his truck, my confusion grows. Noah isn't leaning against the front like he usually does. Maybe he's worried about being recognized? He has caught the attention of the paparazzi lately. It's how I've kept updated on all things band related—I cut out clippings from the magazines they're in.

Pushing aside my disappointment for a more appropriate time, I leap in front of Noah's partially cracked open window and scream, "I've missed you so much, baby!"

Pain stabs my heart when the dark eyes I'm anticipating aren't there. These eyes are blue and full of remorse. "I'm sorry, Em, Noah couldn't make it."

Jacob peers at me from the driver's seat of Noah's truck, praying my tears stay at bay. He hates when I cry just as much as Noah—*if Noah even cares anymore.*

As I beg for my tears to remain in my eyes, I walk around to the passenger side door to climb inside. My steps are more sluggish than moments ago. Noah usually calls first thing in the morning when he's canceling, so when 7 AM came and went without a phone call, I was certain my disappointments of the past few months were finally coming to an end.

How stupid was I?

Just as I finish buckling my seat belt, my phone rings with the "Surrender Me" ringtone I have set for Noah. I consider answering his call, but with disappointment still raring through my veins, I hit the decline button instead. After shutting down my phone, I throw it into my satchel on the floor of the truck then shift my focus to the scenery whizzing past the window. Jacob watches me cautiously but remains silent. What could he possibly say? He doesn't deserve to be in this predicament any more than me.

The tunes pumping out of the radio keep my mind off my swirling stomach for the first twenty minutes of our trip. Jacob has always had a lead foot, so we're nearly halfway home in the time it generally takes for Noah to exit the parking lot.

My throat works hard to swallow when the introduction of Rise Up's song "Surrender Me" comes over the radio. As memories of how that song used to make me feel filter through my head, a massive sob tears from my throat. I'm beyond devastated, meaning I'm no longer capable of concealing my heartache.

Although I try my hardest to keep my sobs to a bare minimum, Jacob must hear them. He switches off the radio before turning his remorseful eyes to me. "Noah would be here if he could—"

I cut him off by swiping my hand through the air. As much as it would be nice to believe what he's preaching, weeks of disappointment don't award me the privilege. It's been so long since I've seen Noah, I'm beginning to forget what he smells like.

Gut-wrenching heartache rings true in my tone when I finally submit to the feelings tearing me in two. "I can't do this anymore, Jake. I love Noah, but I can't hold on to someone who's no longer there for me to grasp."

I've wondered for weeks if this is the outcome Noah was hoping to achieve from his absence. He's always said he'd never break up with me, so maybe this is his way of forcing me to break up with him? I love him, but perhaps I need to let him go so he can live the life he wants without continually worrying about me.

"Em...don't...you need to think about this."

Jacob's plea is interrupted by his ringing cellphone. When he peeks at the screen, I know who is calling. It's Noah.

"I have to answer him. He's probably freaking the fuck out." After giving me a sympathetic look, he hits the connect button then raises his phone to his ear. "Hey... calm down... She's sitting next to me. She's safe."

They talk for a few more seconds before Jacob shifts his big cornflower blue eyes to me. "He wants to talk to you."

I nearly reach out for his phone before my backbone rejuvenates. I deserve better than how I'm being treated.

Tears fling off my cheeks when I shake my head, denying his request. Jacob wordlessly begs for me to take his phone, but I refuse. This hurts, but it's not any more painful than what I've experienced the past few months.

After a tense staredown, Jacob reverts his focus to his cell. "She doesn't want to talk to you."

CHAPTER 31

NOAH

 stare at a speck of dust floating in the air, sure I heard Jacob wrong. What does he mean Emily doesn't want to talk to me? We've coasted over a couple of rocky bumps the past few months, but even during our hardest battles, Emily has always answered my calls—even the ones she knows will leave her disappointed.

"Put her on the phone, Jake!" My racing heart is heard in my low tone. I do not mean to sound angry with him; I'm just panicked, which generally means I'm irrational.

I hear Jacob's muffled voice before the static on the phone clears. "I'm sorry, Noah. She's adamant she doesn't want to talk to you."

"Put her on the fucking phone!" I kick a steel chair in front of me, sending it flying across the room. It stops just to the side of Marcus, who is watching me with concern. "I need to talk to her—*please.*"

I hate that Jacob is in the middle of this, but he's the only one close enough to Emily to force her to listen.

My tone is less harsh this time around, but it does little to hide the knot in my stomach. "Please, Jacob. Even on speakerphone. She doesn't have to talk to me; she can just listen."

A stretch of silence crosses between us before Emily's faint sobs come down the line, adding to the heaviness on my chest. "Em, baby, are you there?"

When her sniffles increase from hearing my voice, I flop onto the sofa in the green room to cradle my head in my empty hand. "I'm so sorry, Beautiful; I would have been there if I could..."

My words trail off when I realize what I'm doing. It's the same pathetic excuse I've given her the past couple of months. She deserves better than bullshit excuses. I need to stop lying. I fucked up. I got so tied up in the band's success, I thought canceling on her would be okay because she'd be there waiting for me once the hype died down. I miss her every fucking day, but I wanted to ensure our album was a surefire hit. I told myself it would be okay to disappoint her now as long as I made up for it once I was filthy rich.

Now I may not get the chance.

"Em... please talk to me."

My heart cracks more with every sob that bellows down the line. It also reveals what I've always known: I'm a fucking idiot. She's supposed to be my number one priority, yet I fucked it all up for someone who has only ever cared about himself.

I stop staring at my clenched fists when Emily whispers, "I can't do this anymore."

I'm grateful she's finally spoken to me, but it doesn't linger long. I don't know what to be more panicked about: what she said, or the fact she disconnects our call immediately after saying it.

While gripping my phone in a white-knuckled hold, I redial Jacob's number. My teeth grit when my call goes to voicemail.

I redial again.

And again.

And again.

Jacob answers on my fifth try. "You need to give her some time."

What he is saying makes sense, but isn't a majority of our problem because I haven't given her enough of *my* time? So how will giving her more space help?

While running a shaky hand over my hair, I deliberate. It doesn't take me long to separate the pros and cons of Jacob's suggestion. As much as it hurts to admit, he's right. I need to give Emily time.

With that in mind, I push my phone close to my ear. "Tell her I love her, Jake, and that I'm sorry. I never meant to hurt her."

Hating that the cracks in my heart are heard in my voice, I disconnect our call by throwing my phone onto the tiled floor. It shatters on impact, proving not only were Jacob's assumptions right over a year ago, they're just as factual today.

"What the fuck?" Missing the first half of my conversation, Slater bends down to pick up my broken phone. I'd laugh at him trying to piece it together if I weren't on the verge of having a meltdown. "We're due on stage in thirty minutes, don't go fuckin' it up by acting like a diva. We're rising stars, not Hollywood Walk of Fame famous."

Even though he's joking, all I hear is angst. I can't be playful with the dark shit creeping into my veins. I've once again let Emily down, and for what? A chance to get "Surrender Me" into the Top Ten of the billboard charts.

That's what today is about. Delilah pulled some strings allowing us to snatch up a lucrative spot when another band canceled last minute. We're hoping our live performance on MTV will help "Surrender Me" sprint toward the number one spot we've been aiming for the past few months.

"Is everything okay?"

My eyes float up from the ground to Marcus, who is crouched next to Slater. "I don't know. Em said she couldn't do this anymore; what does that mean?"

Marcus is good with his emotions, so if anyone knows what Emily meant, it will be him. When remorse settles in his misty green eyes, it dawns on me that he took Emily's statement the same way I did.

The love of my life just broke up with me.

My heart slithers into my gut as the pain in my chest turns crippling. Desperate to drown away the despair clutching my soul, I grab the closest bottle of brown liquid I can find. It burns my chest when I unscrew the cap and swallow down several big mouthfuls, but I don't hold back. The burn of whiskey is nothing compared to the pain stabbing my heart..

When I balance the bottle against my lips for a second gulp, Nick snatches it out of my hand. "You're not your dad, Noah."

He screws the cap back on, then places it on the bar, not the least bit concerned about how much his comment guts me. It still kills me knowing my brothers and I weren't enough for my dad to pull himself out of the depression that ate him whole, but who am I to talk? I let fame and a man not worthy of my time take me away from the one person who means the world to me.

"Emily fucking left me," I growl through gritted teeth.

Nick can't understand what I'm going through. His fiancée is having their baby in a few weeks. They live together in a house purchased with profits from our album, and he gets to travel home to see her while I'm stuck here picking up the slack only a lead singer can.

His life is perfect, where mine is going down the fucking toilet.

When I skirt past him, he steps back into my path. It pisses me off, but the determination in his eyes is enough to keep me out of the dark pit I'm galloping toward. "One step at a time. Perform the shit out of this song first, then tomorrow morning, we'll go sort this shit out —*together.*"

He'd never admit it, but I know he feels guilty about how his relationship with Jenni affected mine with Emily. We spent weeks worrying more about them than ourselves, and although his pledge of assistance won't repair the fuckups I've made, it's a step in the right direction.

While jerking my chin up in agreement with his suggestion, I scrub my tired eyes. I had no clue how tiring it is to be a musician until I was pulled from one side of the country to the next—every single fucking day. Weekends are ideal times for radio interviews, but they're the only days Emily has off school.

When my mental and physical exhaustion got the better of me, I took the easy way out. I started canceling on Emily. The first few times, she sounded upset, but she said she understood my obligations went further than my bandmates. Then, as I canceled over and over again, her disappointment switched to frustration. That's when I should have stepped back and looked at the entire picture.

I would have if it were only dollar signs flashing in front of my eyes.

No matter how we got here, one fact never alters: I have to win her back. This isn't an option; it's a requirement. She owns my heart, and I have no intention to ask for it back. Instead, I'll do everything I can to prove why she's its rightful owner.

Suddenly, it dawns on me what I need to do.

CHAPTER 32

EMILY

Jacob comforts me the best he can the remainder of our trip, but not even his corny jokes can stop the sobs ripping through my body. Thirty minutes ago, I did something I never thought I would do. I broke up with Noah.

It feels like someone has lassoed a rope around my heart to strangle it along with my lungs. I've barely caught a breath the last half of our trip, and I've shed more tears than I care to admit. But even with the pain, I'm confident I've done the right thing. Unclipping Noah's wings is probably the kindest thing anyone has ever done for him. At least I can say I gave him that.

When Jacob's turn signal flashes at the T that leads to Ravenshoe, my eyes stray to his. "Can you please take me to Jenni's?"

Even his multiple assurances that Noah and I will work through our hiccup without too much heartache, the last place I want to go is to his house. Jacob is my friend, but his home is Noah's home, so I can't go there right now—*if ever.*

Jacob gives my hand a gentle squeeze. "Are you sure this is what you want, Em?"

The concern in his ocean blue eyes blurs my vision with fresh tears, but I don't need 20/20 vision to express my wishes. When I nod, he squeezes my hand for the second time before turning left.

Five minutes later, he pulls into the driveway of Jenni's house. Not even two seconds after that, Jenni waddles down the front steps of her porch. Even with my eyes brimming with moisture, I can't miss how radiant she looks... until she spots my tear-stained face. Concern washes over her as her wave "hello" suspends mid-air.

I mouth to her that I'm fine before pressing my lips to Jacob's cheeks. "Thanks, Jake."

Jacob's lips tug into an uneasy grin as he watches me climb down from Noah's truck for the last time. Who knew something so trivial only a few months ago could seem so big now?

Jacob waits for me to trudge to Jenni's side before he reverses out of the driveway. His taillights have barely disappeared when Jenni curls her arms around my shoulders to hug me tight. Her hot breath on my neck when she asks if I'm okay adds more wetness to my cheeks.

I pretend my world isn't falling apart as we climb the stairs of her front porch and enter her house, but once we're inside, the avalanche starts.

By the time I update her on everything that has happened, an hour has passed. Even with her knowing a majority of the story since I've called her crying many times the past two months, I leave nothing on the table. I tell her everything.

It feels good getting it off my chest, but it adds to my heartache. Although Jenni has faced the same isolation issues with Nick being on tour, she can't deny she's still seen Nick every two weeks at a minimum the past two months. I haven't seen Noah once. If I needed more proof that I did the right thing pulling back on the reins, I just got it.

"That proves it was Noah's choice to stay away." I blow on the cup of the tea Jenni just placed in front of me, praying it will hide the quiver of my lips.

It's pointless when she replies, "He's the lead singer, Em. He has more on his plate than the other boys do."

I almost snap back until our eyes collide. Even though it sounds as if she's defending Noah, her eyes reveal otherwise. She's also angry at him.

"Did he tell you why he canceled today?"

I shake my head. "No. I haven't talked to him."

I knew hearing his voice would have me backing down on my decision to leave him. It was a close call when Jacob put him on speakerphone.

"Oh..." Jenni's brows pull together even tighter, revealing she knows why he canceled. When I give her a look, one demanding she spill the beans, she murmurs, "They're performing on MTV. It's set to air tonight."

My chest swells with pride. Rise Up has been working toward this for a long time, but whether it's a big deal like MTV or a small radio gig, Noah would have still canceled on me.

"That's great; I'm pleased for them." My voice is as uneasy as my facial expression.

Jenni paces around her kitchen table to wrap me up in a hug like she did earlier. Although my heart is splintering, my first smile in days curls on my lips when her belly wiggles against my back. Her firm hold has the baby protesting about a lack of space. "You'll work this out, Em. You can't love someone as much as you love Noah and walk away from it."

After pressing her lips to my temple, she trudges out of the kitchen, her steps as clunky as the irregular arrhythmic beat of my heart. I love Noah. I always have, and I always will, but sometimes love just isn't enough. He needs more than I can give him, so the best I can do is give him the freedom to discover what that is.

Blinded by a migraine and heartbroken beyond repair, I decide to have an early night. When I update Jenni on my plans, she begs me to watch Rise Up's performance on MTV. I refuse. It would kill me watching Noah sing "Surrender Me" to screaming fans. I've grown stronger the past two years, but I'm not *that* strong.

After hiking the stairs to the second level, I careen toward one of two guest bedrooms in Jenni's house. I'm so exhausted, even tugging down the duvet takes effort. I kick off my shoes and yank down my jeans before slipping between the warm sheets. I'm expecting it to take me hours to fall asleep, so you can imagine my surprise when I crash the instant my head hits the pillow.

By the time I wake the following morning, it's a little after nine. I slept over twelve hours straight. Jenni must be awake because fresh towels are at the end of my bed. With the shower beckoning me to it, I head to the guest bathroom. The scorching hot water comforts my weary muscles while soap washes away the sorrow slicking my skin.

When the water turns frigid, I switch off the faucet and clamber out, my teeth chattering. While wrapping a fluffy pink towel around my body, I stroll to the vanity to brush my teeth. When the steam from the mirror clears, I grimace. Even twelve hours of sleep hasn't made me look presentable. The girl reflecting back at me is still the same Emily McIntosh I'm used to seeing, except this Emily is broken on the inside.

I brush my drenched hair but leave it to dry naturally before slipping into a pair of denim jeans and a black Led Zeppelin shirt. Winter is approaching, but Jenni has adequate heating, so I don't put on a jacket.

I gallop down the stairs, taking them two at a time before turning left at the hall. No matter the circumstances, today will be a good day because it's Jenni's baby shower. I refuse to let whatever is happening between Noah and me ruin my best friend's special day.

When I round the corner of the kitchen, I spot Jenni standing near the sink. She's a good foot back since her tummy is so large. While approaching her, I muster a huge fake smile on my face. "Happy baby shower d..."

My words fail when I detect I'm being watched. With my heart in my throat and my tears burning from a sudden rush of moisture, I jackknife to my right. As my body predicted, Noah is sitting at the breakfast bar, staring at me. The dark rims around his eyes make him appear as exhausted as I felt yesterday, but he's still the most handsome man I've ever seen. Although this is everything I've ever wanted, it comes too late.

My eyes drift back to Jenni, hating what I'm about to do, but I have no choice. "I'm sorry, I have to go."

She loses the chance to protest when I dart out of her kitchen as quickly as my quivering legs will take me. I hear Noah call my name, but I don't stop. My focus is on one thing and one thing only: going anywhere I can cry without witnesses.

A frustrated squeal bubbles in my chest when my stomps across Jenni's driveway fail to lead me to my car. With my mind fritzed, I forgot Jacob dropped me off. After cursing the cool morning air, I rack my brain for another solution. My first thoughts are to ask Jenni to drive me back to school, but she has friends arriving in a few hours for her baby shower, so that option isn't viable. But I have to leave because seeing Noah again hurts too much. It feels like my heart is being torn in two.

My deliberations are cut short when Noah shouts, "Em, wait!"

With my heartache overtaking my smarts, I race down Jenni's driveway. It's mid-morning on a Saturday, so I'm confident I'll bump into someone I know eventually.

I'm not even halfway out of the driveway when Noah catches up with me. I scream my anger into the street when he bands his arm around my waist and pulls me back. Since he's several inches taller than me, my feet lift from the ground from his hold, freeing them to lash out in violence. I kick and roar with all my might, unleashing all the anger I've built up the past few months.

"Let me go!" I'm fighting so hard my words are barely coherent. "Let me fuckin' go!"

I scream so loud, anyone having a lazy Saturday morning sleep-in no longer is. I claw him with my nails while jabbing my boots into his shins. I do anything and everything to free me from his hold, but no matter how hard I fight, he continues to hold me close to his body.

"I'm sorry, Emily; I'm so fucking sorry." He draws me in tighter, but it does little to stop my onslaught.

He gave up on us. I can't forgive him for that. "It's too late; we're done. I can't do this anymore."

"It's not too late; I'll make it up to you. I promise. I just need you to give me the chance—*please*."

I try to stay angry, to not melt into his embrace, but the longer he begs for forgiveness, the faster my anger fades. He sounds as heartbroken as I feel.

As heartbreak overtakes my anger, tears splash down my face. I stop fighting to be freed. I can barely breathe through the wetness flooding my cheeks, let alone resist a man I'll never stop loving no matter how badly he hurts me.

Recognizing I'm no longer fighting, Noah lowers us to the ground before drawing me in tight enough we almost become one. "I'm so sorry, Em," he repeats over and over again. "I never meant to hurt you. Hurting you was *never* my intention. I just..." He sighs. "I fucked up."

I don't know how much time passes with us sitting outside on the frosty, frigid ground. I'm not cold. Noah's body assures mine remains nice and toasty. I just wish I could stop crying. Every time I catch a whiff of his delicious scent, I tear up all over again. He's always smelled like home to me.

It takes several long, tedious minutes to get my crying under control. Once I do, I use my sleeve to wipe my nose before popping my head off Noah's chest. Fresh tears burn my eyes when I see the devastation in his beautifully tormented gaze. He's miserable.

He cups my cheeks before lowering his forehead to mine. No words escape his mouth, but he doesn't need to speak for me to hear them. His remorseful eyes relay his sympathies.

"I'll make this right, Em; I promise." His eyes bounce between mine as the plea darkening them picks up. "I just need you to give me a chance."

I stare at him, expressing my worries with as many words as he used to show his remorse. I've craved precisely this for months, but will it be enough to get me through our next span of time apart?

Fear grips my heart when a new emotion overtakes the remorse in Noah's eyes. He's hurting—badly. I've never seen him so insecure in his own skin. He truly believes losing me is the worst thing he'll ever face. After everything he's been through, that's truly shocking.

Ignoring the shake of my hands, I cup his jaw before sealing my mouth over his. His lips stiffen in surprise for the quickest second before they part at the invitation of my lashing tongue. Our kiss expresses the words we can't speak. It represents our love, understanding, and my added request for forgiveness.

The past two months have been the lowest of the low for me, but can I truly hold a couple of bad months against him when he has given me so many wonderful ones before?

It's pure torture pulling back, but I'd endure a thousand scars if they produced the same results. Noah's eyes are nowhere near as troubled as earlier. My kiss settled the violent storm in them.

"I'm truly sorry, Emily. I thought what I was doing would help us. I would have never done it if it meant I wouldn't have a future with you."

CHAPTER 33

NOAH

Emily bites on the inside of her cheek as she struggles to control her tears. She has no clue everything I've been doing the past few months is for her. I want her to have the fancy things neither of us can afford. I'm just thankful she's giving me a second chance to prove that.

When she ran away from me, I wasn't sure she would come back. Usually, she runs into my arms.

My seven-hour flight home after pre-recording my performance on MTV became the longest seven hours of my life. I knew I was in for a battle when I touched down on home turf, but I had no clue Jenni would be my first obstacle.

She was pissed, hormonal, and didn't give a fuck that I was the lead singer of her fiancé's band. I only got through her barricade when I swore not only to fix all the errors I'd made, but also not to wake Emily. She wanted her to sleep off the tears she had shed the night before.

I know she was looking out for her friend, but her comment tore my heart to shreds. Knowing Emily was crying while I wasn't there to comfort her was bad enough, but knowing I was responsible for her tears utterly gutted me.

Although it was a hard feat, I kept my promise to Jenni when I entered the guest room of her home. Emily was sleeping on her side, her hair a mess, and her cheeks showing signs of crying herself to sleep. The remorse strangling my heart doubled when she whimpered my name. It wasn't the husky purr she usually makes. It was full of pain and anguish.

Right then and there, I pledged to make things right between us. I don't care what it takes, or how much I have to give up; I'll give everything away before I'll ever let her go.

When I tell Emily that, she balks like I did when she cursed earlier. I've only heard her swear once in the near two years we've been together, so I was not only shocked, I was devastated. Her rare use of a curse word proved how badly I hurt her.

I'll fix my mistakes though. Starting now.

Emily's sunlit brown eyes bounce between mine when I curve my hand around her jaw. A spark of relief darts through them when I angle my head to align our lips. I get them within touching distance when a tormented scream shreds through my ears. "Noah, hurry!"

Cranking my neck back, I see Nick walking down the front stairs of his home, cradling Jenni under the crook of his arm. Jenni's face is constricted as though she's in an immense amount of pain.

Reading things more clearly than me, Emily jumps to her feet. "The baby!"

When she races across the dew-covered grass, I shadow closely behind. She fusses over her friend, soothing Jenni and comforting as only a woman would know how.

"It's too early, Em..." Jenni's declaration shifts to a scream as her hands dart down to her stomach. I don't know much about labor, but I'm reasonably sure her cry means she's being hit with an intense contraction. "He... can't... come... yet."

Emily waits for Jenni to stop grinding her teeth before helping her into the passenger seat of Nick's big black beast—the same black beast that nearly claimed her life two years ago. "It's okay, Jen; babies come early all the time. He'll be fine. You just need to breathe." She makes *hee, hee, hoo, hee, hee, hoo* noises like a Lamaze instructor would.

Jenni copies her until another revelation pops up. "My bag! I haven't packed my hospital bag!"

She barely gets her sentence out before another contraction rips through her. I'm not an expert, but if her contractions are this close, Nick needs to get her to the hospital right now, or she'll deliver in their driveway.

Eager to get them out of here, I tug Emily back from the door, slam it shut, then tap on the roof three times, giving Nick the signal to leave. "Emily will pack your bag; then we'll bring it to the hospital for you."

I'll hand Nick the rights to "Player" if he'll get her the fuck out of here. I love him like a brother, but I do not want to watch his fiancée giving birth.

"Thanks." Nick throws a set of keys at me that I catch mid-air before he dives into the driver's seat, backs out of the driveway, then takes off down the road like a maniac.

Emily and I peer in the direction they fled for several long minutes with our mouths hanging open. That's not exactly how I predicted my morning to go.

When I shift on my feet to face Emily, a grin tugs my cheeks high. She's smiling brightly, her excitement unmissable. "I'm about to become an aunty!"

Caught up in the hype, she leaps into my arms and kisses me hard on the mouth. She tastes so fucking good, it takes everything I have not to ravish her against the front door of Jenni and Nick's house. I wouldn't hold back if she didn't need to be there for her friend, and I didn't need to stop being so selfish.

"We better get Jenni's bag ready," I mumble over Emily's plump lips. "If her screams were anything to go by, she may need it sooner rather than later."

Emily yanks back, her eyes bulging. She was so enamored by our kiss, she forgot her best friend just left here in labor. I shouldn't love that I can make her so daft, but I do.

Over the next ten minutes, I shadow Emily around Nick and Jenni's house as she packs a bag. After gathering the necessities every overnight bag needs: toothbrush, comb, soap etc., she shifts on her feet to face me. Her nose is screwed up in the most adorable way, and wrinkles are indenting her forehead. "What do you wear after you've had a baby?"

I shrug; I have no fucking idea. "Pajamas?" Even a stranger would hear the hesitation in my voice. After my mom had Michael, she spent most of her day in her pajamas, but she also had postnatal depression, so I'm not sure if that is the norm.

I think I'm on track when Emily smiles. "Good idea. PJ's will work."

She grabs several nighties out of drawers on our right before shoving them into the overloaded suitcase on the bed. It's so fucking heavy, it takes both Emily and me to carry it down the stairs, then more than double the muscle to ram it into Jenni's car's trunk. She no longer drives her navy-blue BMW. It's been replaced with a much more compact car.

After wrangling the bag into the tight confines, I naturally veer toward the driver's side door. Even with Emily having her license, I've always done a majority of the driving in our relationship.

I slip into the leather-lined seat before yanking it back as far as it can go. Even with the seat being at the last notch, my knees sit around my ears.

Recognizing we aren't going anywhere soon, Emily offers to drive. It takes more effort for me to peel out of Jenni's car as it did to enter it. I even honk the horn with my crotch a handful of times, which Emily finds amusing. I don't mind hearing her laughter. It's a beautiful way to repair the damage her heartbreaking sobs did to my ears.

As we make the twenty-minute trip to the hospital in silence, I watch Emily's profile. Any time she notices my stalker watch, her teeth rake her bottom lip to hide her smile, but she keeps her focus on the road. I don't know how. The sexual chemistry that forever bounces between us is still in abundance. It may even be more intense because of our weeks of absence.

Emily's eyes turn from the road for the first time the past twenty minutes when I murmur, "I missed you so much, Beautiful."

She smiles in a way that sets my heart racing before she whispers, "I missed you too."

CHAPTER 34

EMILY

On December third at 9:53 AM, Jasper Nicholas Holt entered the world five weeks early, weighing a tiny five pounds, one ounce. His face is an adorable mix of both Nick and Jenni, but he has Jenni's strawberry blonde hair and Nick's elf-like ears.

Although shocked by his sudden arrival, Jenni and Nick's expressions speak volumes when we're ushered into their room to meet their brand-new son. "Do you want to hold him?"

Not waiting for me to answer, Jenni gestures for Nick to hand me baby Jasper. I stand frozen, equally awed and in shock at the little person staring up at me. A mere hour ago, he was nestled in his mother's womb. Now he's peering up at me with big blue eyes and the heart of a stallion.

The miracle of life truly astonishes me—so much so, I grin like a kid at a candy store. Thankfully, I'm not the only one smiling. Noah is watching me as intently as he did during our drive to the hospital. He's got the same sentimentality on his face, but it has a touch of pride to it now. Even though he's scared shitless about having children, he'll be a fantastic father one day. His parents showed him the wrong way to raise children, but with the right guidance and trust in his self-worth, his offspring will grow up in a nurturing, loving environment.

I just hope I'm the one who makes him a daddy.

Images of a young Noah stop running through my head when Jenni fails to stifle a yawn. My mom has often said that my quick delivery wasn't any less exhausting than Lola's sixteen-hour labor, so I'm not surprised Jenni is zapped of energy. Her body just ran a marathon in under forty-five minutes. I'm tired just thinking about it.

After pressing a kiss to Jasper's gooey head, I carefully hand him back to his mother. I fumble to keep his neck protected, but Jenni takes it all in stride. She's a natural already.

"You did so well." I beam proudly at my best friend. "He's perfect."

Noah moves to stand next to me. "He sure is, guys, congrats."

He thrusts his hand not clutching mine toward Nick. I smile when Nick slaps it away before counterbidding his offer by holding his arms out wide for a hug. Proof beyond reasonable doubt that Noah is trying to fix the wrongs he made is shown when he accepts Nick's offer. Only six months ago, he would have decked Nick just for trying to hug him.

As Noah and I make our way out of Jenni's hospital room, my steps reluctant, I sling my eyes back to Jenni. "I'll come visit you this afternoon, okay?"

When she smiles and nods, my eyes drift to Nick. "You also did well."

For the smile on his face, anyone would swear I told him he's a better kisser than Noah. Although I never want to be the judge of that, I don't need to be to know the results. Nick would never win—not in a thousand years.

Noah and I walk through the multistory hospital parking garage hand in hand. My heart is beating triple time, excited my nephew is here and safe, but a small part of me is a tad bit jealous that Jenni became a mom before me. I've always loved kids, but just like I didn't want Noah to propose before he was ready, I don't want to force him into the dreaded parenthood talk either.

Just as we reach Jenni's car, my cell vibrates in my pocket. Pulling it out, I peer down at the screen. I don't recognize the number, but that means nothing these days.

Shrugging, I swipe my finger across the screen before pressing my phone to my ear. "Hello—"

A cranky voice interrupts my greeting, "Is Noah with you?"

"Yes, he is—"

"Can I speak with him?" She's demanding, not asking.

Noah's dark eyes bounce between mine when I hand him my phone. The confusion on his face changes to annoyance when he scans the number on the screen. I don't recognize the voice, but he clearly recognizes the number.

"Do you mind?"

I shake my head. "Not at all."

I untwine our fingers, preparing to wait for him in the car. He tightens his grip on my hand before I even get two steps away from him. He doesn't say anything, but his eyes plead for me to stay.

With my feet planted next to his and a fake smile on his face, he presses my phone to his ear. "Hello, Delilah."

Now his hesitation makes sense. Noah gets along with everyone... except the Ice Queen in charge of the band's public relations. She reminds him too much of his mother for their relationship to ever be amicable, much less the pressure she places on him every week.

I try to keep my nose out of Noah's business but miserably fail. I've always been a snoop. "Yes... No. That was not my intention... I understand... I said I fucking understood." When he loses his temper, his eyes dart down to me to give me a silent apology. "Uh-huh... yep!"

He hangs up without saying goodbye. I doubt his quick disconnection saved Delilah from hearing the string of curse words he bites out while his thumb repeatedly jabs the end call button. He's frustrated but trying his best to project his anger at the person responsible for it.

After sliding my cell into his jeans pocket, he bands his arms around my shoulders and pulls me in close. The mad beat of his heart subsides when he burrows his nose into my hair and inhales deeply. "You smell so fucking good."

My cheeks rise against his chest, loving that he enjoys smelling me as much as I love smelling him. "As do you." I'm not lying. He smells like a freshly laundered shirt left on a sandy beach to dry. It's a manly yet unique scent.

I could stay in his protective bubble for years, but lose the chance when he bursts it by disclosing, "Delilah is pissed about the stunt I pulled on MTV. She pulled a lot of strings to get us that spot, and I 'supposedly' fucked it all up. She threatened to toss my ass to the curb if I do it again."

I pull back far enough to glance into his eyes. I need to see them while pondering if I want to ask about the stunt he pulled. His reference to Delilah threatening to fire him is nothing out of the ordinary; she did that a minimum once a week their first few weeks on the road, but the MTV part of his confession, I'm more than interested in unearthing what that is about. The half-smile he's wearing assures me he didn't throw his career down the toilet, but there is a gleam in his eyes I can't ignore.

"What happened on MTV?"

His half-smile turns blinding. "It's a secret."

With a flirty wink and a tap to my backside, he slides into the passenger seat of Jenni's car, leaving me gobsmacked on the sidewalk. I'd be all up in his business in an instant if I truly believed it was a secret; unfortunately for him, nothing the band has done the past three months has occurred quietly. I'm so confident his "stunt" is plastered all over the internet, checking my Google alerts for Rise Up will be the first thing I do when we return to Jenni's house.

That, and steal a handful of Noah's shirts from his luggage. I don't even care if they're dirty. It will better if they are.

Eager to both snoop and replenish my wardrobe, I slide into the driver's seat of Jenni's car and crank the ignition. Noah has barely latched my seatbelt into place when I tear out of the parking lot like a maniac. My speed is so excessive, we get airborne when I hit a speed bump too fast to be safe.

"Jesus, Emily."

I laugh at the fake panic in Noah's tone. He's a revhead, so it takes more than a few miles over the speed limit to get his heart truly pumping. I'd give him more of a thrill if I was confident in my driving skills. Regrettably, I'm not. I'd never forgive myself if I lost control. The last thing Noah needs is another wreck to contend with. He's handled his fair share of carnage, so I refuse to add more to his plate.

With my heart beating slower than it was, I lighten my pressure on the gas pedal. It fully ascends when we reach the T intersection separating our hometowns. When I indicate a left turn, Noah asks, "Can you take me to Jake's so I can pick up my truck?"

I assume his awkward phrasing is compliments of the tight confines of Jenni's car. It's so compact even I struggle to fit comfortably, so I can imagine how uncomfortable it is for him. But his next set of words corrects my misconception. "And maybe once we're there, we can talk?"

Noah hates talking about *anything*, much less his feelings, but if we want any chance of getting our relationship back on track, we need to do this.

When I nod, the concern hampering Noah's face fades. If only it could work its magic on the worry flaring through his eyes.

***

A few minutes later, I guide Jenni's car down a gravel driveway. A gentle breeze blowing from the west adds to the dust cloud the tires make, but not even a murky haze can't reduce the blueness of the sky. A new day has dawned, and I plan to make the most of it.

After parking next to Noah's truck, I swivel my torso to face him. "Where do you want to talk?"

When his lips curl into a panty-dropping grin, my eyes narrow. He won't tell me where we're going because he'd rather tease me. He gets an immense amount of pleasure from forcing me to be patient. Usually, it's only in the bedroom. *Thank god.*

"Come on."

With the core of a gentleman but the face of a sex god, he assists me out of Jenni's car before aiding me into the passenger seat of his truck. Heat spreads across my chest when he fastens my seatbelt before jogging to his side of the truck and hopping into the driver's seat. He's wearing a smile I've only seen a handful of times before. He's nervous, yet relaxed—if that makes any sense?

When Noah takes a left at the end of Jacob's street, my eyes stray to his. "Alright. Fess up. Where are we going? There's nothing but cow dung and pastures this way."

He smiles but not a word seeps from his lips. It's only when he turns down familiar-looking streets do I realize where we're going. He's taking the back roads to Bronte's Peak. Only locals know this way.

We haven't been to Bronte's Peak since last summer. Things with the band got so hectic, we didn't have time to visit our favorite spot. Although it's usually overrun with tourists every weekend, since it's winter, the crowds shouldn't be as bad.

With us entering the parking lot from the opposite end, Noah finds an empty spot rather quickly. After turning off his ignition, he grabs a blanket from under the seat—the same blanket he wrapped me in on our first date—then comes around to help me down from his truck.

"Are you sure this is okay?" I whisper, worried people may recognize him. It may not be as packed as it usually is, but there are still a few hundred people taking in the spectacular manmade creation.

"I have my disguise." Grinning, Noah flicks open a baseball cap he had stuffed in his back pocket before lowering it onto his head. It's the Parkwood State cap I gifted him months ago when he visited my campus. I hate that it hides his eyes from my view, but by looking like a regular college student, he has a better chance of remaining incognito.

He just needs to simmer down his rock star swagger.

As we walk hand in hand to the wooden staircase that leads to the beach below, a few people look our way. I don't know whether they recognize Noah, or if they just appreciate how incredibly handsome he is. I'd say it's a combination of them both.

After trekking across the white sandy beach, we merge into a cave at the very end. We discovered this hidden beauty nearly a year ago. If you brave the darkness, your courage is rewarded with the most spectacular view. There's an opening at the end of the cliff edge. It hangs just above the crystal-blue water of Bronte's Peak. It's a view money can't buy.

Noah lays down the blanket on the slippery rock surface, sits down, then gestures for me to join him. I take up the spot between his legs before resting my back on his chest. When he cocoons me with his arms, his heart pounds out a hearty tune against my back. I assume the awe-inspiring visual in front of us is the reason for his heart's strenuous beats, but I'm proven wrong for the second time today when he murmurs, "I'm sorry about everything I did, Em. I never meant to hurt you."

"I know."

Noah is a talented man, but spiteful will never be on his list of attributes.

"I just thought if I put in the hours now, I wouldn't have to work so hard in the future." He swallows away the roughness in his voice before continuing, "It just never occurred to me that you wouldn't be there waiting for me once I was done."

"I would have waited for you. I just didn't think you wanted me anymore." Tears well in my eyes as I confess words I never thought I'd speak. "My heart could only take so much rejection before my head took control of my feelings. That's what happened yesterday. My head did what it thought was right for both of us."

"Em..." His grip on my waist tightens. "You're all I've ever wanted. I'll never want anything or anyone more than I want you—"

"Not even your career?"

"Not even my career," he answers without delay. "I made a mistake, but it wasn't until I lost you did I realize how stupid I've been." The panic his eyes held earlier reignites as his throat works hard to swallow. "But that will be done with now. It's time for you to learn the truth."

CHAPTER 35

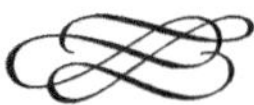

NOAH

Emily lifts her head off my chest, her eyes widening. She heard the panic in my tone, felt it slicking my skin. She knows what I'm about to tell her will hurt, but is also aware this needs to happen so we can step out of the fog clouding our relationship. I hate what I'm about to do, but I need to stop lying to her like I've been for the past nearly two years.

"Jacob made me promise not to say anything to you, but you deserve to know the truth."

The instant Jacob's name seeps from my lips, the concern on Emily's face alters. She doesn't like that I'm keeping things from her, but her mind went in a different direction than the revelation I'm planning to confess. I guess that's my fault. I've kept her in the dark so long, trust is bound to be an issue. I'm just hoping once everything is out in the open, we can start afresh. A clean slate, as they say.

"Once we have everything on the table, I promise there'll be no secrets between us ever again."

When Emily nods, I exhale a big breath before the confession purge begins. "Jacob has been fighting in an illegal underground fight circuit the past two years. He was fighting in a professional circuit, but was banned from competing when he was charged with assault and battery."

Emily's pupils widen. She's as stunned about Jacob's fighting career as I was when I found out. He's always been more of a lover than a fighter. "Why was he charged with battery? Cage fighting might be scary, but it's legal."

I swish some spit around my mouth, hoping it will ease out words I swore never to speak. "Because he beat up Lola's ex-boyfriend, Callum."

Her eyes flicker as she struggles to work out why Jacob would hurt any of Lola's previous squeezes. When she fails to find a reason, she locks her moisture-filled eyes with mine. "Why would he do that?"

I reposition her so she's straddling my lap, needing to peer in her eyes while telling her news I know will devastate her. "Because Callum assaulted Lola—more than once."

Anger sluices my veins as memories of what happened to Lola roll through my head. There's nothing I hate more than pathetic scum who put their hands on women. They're the worst of the fucking worst.

"What?"

I wipe away the tears sitting high on Emily's cheeks. "Jacob noticed Lola flinched a lot when they first met, but you know how stubborn Lola is? Anytime he tried to bring it up, she shut both him and his questions down." Emily nods, more than aware how opinionated and strong her big sister is. "A couple of weeks after we started dating, Callum turned up at Mavericks looking for Lola. He rough-handled her in front of Maggie. After Jacob took Lola home, I drove him to Callum's house."

"Because you wanted Jacob to hurt Callum, like you wish you could have done to Zander?"

I nod. "But this was different. Callum *physically* hurt Lola, but since she refused to press charges, Jacob had no choice but to take matters into his own hands. I would have tried to talk him out of it if I had known he was fighting professionally, but he kept it a secret from everybody, including me."

Emily rubs at the groove between my brows, comforting me as I should be her. "What happened to Callum?"

"He got his ass whooped." I laugh a tormented chuckle. "Then he had Jacob charged with first-degree battery. Jacob plead guilty. Because it was his first conviction, he got two years' probation. His conviction is the reason he lied when I beat up the guy who drugged you. His lawyer tried to say Callum hit him first. Jacob wouldn't have any of it. He wouldn't give Callum the satisfaction of thinking he laid a hand on him."

Emily remains quiet as she absorbs the information I've just divulged. After a beat, she lays her head on my chest. "Although I hate what happened to Jacob, I'm glad he stood up for Lola."

Emily and Lola weren't overly close growing up, but they've been working hard on building a better relationship since Emily left for college. Emily will most likely be upset she's finding this out from me instead of Lola, but Lola refuses to talk to anyone about what happened. I'm not even sure if she knows I know what happened to her. That's how quiet she keeps her private business.

"There's still more to confess, Em."

Emily peers up at me with wide tearful eyes. "More." She only says one word, but the ones she doesn't speak are the loudest. She's unsure if she can handle much more.

With that in mind, I confess to something more lighthearted than the original admission I was planning. "Do you remember Jacob teaching Lola how to drive in the state forest near his house?"

Emily's brows stitch before she faintly nods. She has no clue where I'm going with this.

"Well, I was in the black truck that—"

"Oh my god!" She slaps me on the arm two times. "You asshole. Why would you do that?" The giggle that comes with her question weakens the intensity of it. "Whose truck were you driving, anyway?"

"I wasn't driving; Nick was. It was his truck." I grimace. "The same truck he drove Jenni to the hospital in this morning."

She shakes her head in disbelief. "So the entire event was staged?"

"Yeah, but Jacob was supposed to be driving, and I didn't know you were in the car until it was too late. That's what Jacob and I fought about that night."

"I still don't understand why you would want to do that? What benefit would you get from scaring the living daylights out of us?"

I'm unsure whether to protect my crotch or my face while admitting, "It's about the adrenaline rush. Jacob swears his bravery gets rewarded in the bedroom when he saves his date from the naughty black truck."

Emily gags, sickened at the lengths some guys go to to get a girl to sleep with them. "That's disgusting!" She whacks my chest two times, but they're not the cause for the panic bubbling in my blood. It's what she says next: "I'm also telling Lola."

I stiffen. Jacob will kill me when he finds out about all the secrets I've confessed, but I promised to no longer lie to Emily, and I plan on keeping my promise.

With that in mind, I get back to the real reason we're here, and the person at the forefront of our break up. Before a syllable can escape my lips, a much more urgent sound rumbles from Emily's midsection. It's the loud grumble of her hungry tummy.

"Sorry. I'm starving. I haven't eaten since lunchtime yesterday." She stands before pivoting to face me. "Can we take a raincheck until we've had something to eat?"

Although there's no doubt she's starving; her stomach's growls are unmissable, a glint in her eyes exposes she isn't up for any more confessions today. She's not only reached her limit, but she needs time to process the ones I've hit her with so far.

"Burgers and milkshakes?"

When excitement flares through her eyes, I jump up and grab the blanket. By the time we've climbed the wooden stairwell of Bronte's Peak, my hunger is as paramount as Emily's. I'm seconds from chewing off my own arm.

As we walk to a café at the side of the parking lot, I notice a handful of people peering at me in recognition. They snap my picture with their phone and giggle with glee, but they don't approach me.

Thank fuck.

I'll forever love and appreciate my fans, but I've just won Emily back, so I'm not ready to throw her into the craziness of my life just yet.

We're seated in a booth in the middle of the diner by a cheerful waitress with crazy blonde locks and a huge smile. Since we've eaten here multiple times before, we give her our food order at the same time she jots down what drinks we would like. As she walks away to prepare our milkshakes, Emily gestures for me to remove my cap. I hesitate. Without my disguise, I'll most likely be recognized.

When the love in Emily's eyes revs up to a level I haven't seen before, I can't deny her request. Within half a second of removing my cap, whispers circulate from the tables surrounding us. A few patrons shyly wave, and a handful look close to peeing their pants, but unlike the paparazzi who follow me around LA, they respect my right to privacy.

Over the next fifty minutes, Emily and I talk like we've never been apart. She updates me on everything happening with her at school, and how she's been taking extra classes so she can graduate early. I rib her about how "dorky" she is, but in reality, my chest puffs with pride, smug as fuck that I got a beautiful and smart girl who isn't afraid to get her hands dirty.

Emily would never expect anything to be handed to her on a silver platter. She works hard for everything she has. That's why as much as I'd love for her to come on the road with me, I'll never ask her to do that. She craves independence, and whether she is in a relationship or not, she has the right to achieve that. I just need to be more flexible so we can work around her school schedule. When she graduates, the world will be our oyster.

Once we finish eating, the waitress delivers our bill to the table. I place my credit card in the leather wallet before handing it back to her. She cracks it open as she strolls away from our table. Not even a second later, her squeal gives me permanent hearing loss. "I knew it was you!"

When she twirls around to make her way back to our table, I dip my chin in greeting, but try to simmer down her eagerness. If she doesn't settle down, I'm seconds from being lynched by a mob.

"Hi, nice to meet you, but can you keep it down? I don't want anyone to know I'm here."

Emily smiles throughout our exchange. She thinks it's cute for me to be recognized, but she doesn't realize how quickly the tides change. Once one fan gets a little eager, they *all* get a little eager.

"Sure, no worries." The waitress runs her hand down her apron as she takes in some big breaths. "But can you *please* sign an autograph for me? My best friend Michelle will never believe I served you if I don't give her proof. She's weird like that."

"Sure." I laugh, amused at her reference to her friend. Marcus is like that as well. "Do you have anything in particular you'd like me to sign?"

After nodding, she skips away from our table to ring up our bill and gather something for me to sign. Once she's out of eyesight, I return my focus to Emily. The jealousy I'm expecting to see in her eyes isn't there. Nothing but happiness is radiating from her gorgeous light brown eyes. "How often does that happen?"

I take a moment to bask in the pride beaming out of her before answering, "Too often."

Her eyeroll isn't even halfway around when the waitress appears like magic. I jump out of my skin, startled by her nimbleness. "Here's your receipt, and if you could you sign this, I'll love you forever?"

After taking in the name on the tag of her mock-seventies diner uniform, I scribble an inscription onto her Rise Up CD.

To Molly
Thanks for your fantastic service today!
Noah Taylor

CHAPTER 36

EMILY

My excitement doubles when I watch Noah sign Rise Up's debut album cover for Molly. Although he expressed dislike for how often this happens, he'll never tire of his fans—especially the ones who have followed his journey from Mavericks to MTV.

When Noah hands Molly her CD, she smiles before hugging it close to her chest. I'm sure he wrote something more than just his name. Noah has a knack for making people feel special, which is endearing considering how poorly he was treated as a child. I guess that explains why he got caught up in the hype of the entertainment industry. For years, his mother told him he was worthless, so the endless praise he's received from reporters and fans the past five months is unfamiliar but reassuring. After years of being pulled down, who wouldn't want to ride the high they worked so hard for?

I've always been a hard worker. It's a trait I learned from my mom. She works tirelessly to provide for her family, and I want to do the same for mine, but only now am I realizing my stubbornness is hurting my relationship with Noah.

I hate the idea of being "kept," but Noah and I can't continue on the path we're on now, or there'll be no "us." Noah's weekends are booked with obligations required for the band to achieve the success they deserve, and my school has the standard Monday to Friday schedule. I don't know an immediate solution for our predicament, but once things settle down, Noah and I will buckle down and work something out, because our relationship deserves more thought than we've been giving it the past few months.

I'm dragged from my thoughts when Noah stops to stand beside me. "You alright? You appear deep in thought."

"Yeah, I'm good. Just thinking."

"About...?"

I smile, loving the touch of panic in his voice. "Us, and where we go from here."

He smirks in a way that makes my knees weak. "Did you come up with anything good?"

"I have a few ideas up my sleeve." I give him a flirty wink before standing. "But we should probably take this elsewhere... I'd hate for you to get arrested for public indecency."

Molly offers Noah a friendly wave when we pass her on the way out, but he doesn't pay her any attention. He's too busy hiding the bulge in his jeans to act cordial. It's not his fault he's hard. The sexual tension between us has been so intense, it overcooked the eggs on our burgers. Then add the suggestiveness in my tone, and someone was bound to get horny. Mercifully, I can hide the excitement thrumming through my veins. Noah can't.

Some of my sass is squashed when we break through the double doors of the café. I can barely see two feet in front of me because of the bright lights being shoved into my face. They're so blinding, I doubt I'll see anything but white circles for the next week.

As my arm darts up to protect my eyes, questions are screamed at Noah.

"Noah, who's your date?"

"Noah, how long are you back in town for?"

"Is this the person you declared to love on MTV last night?"

"Noah, this way, Noah?"

I startle when I'm clutched from the side by a sturdy pair of hands.

My panic recedes when I recognize the scent of the person holding me. It's Noah. "Keep your head down and don't say anything."

He uses his leather jacket as a curtain to shelter us from the paparazzi lights while weaving us through the swarm of men double my size and age. I can't see anything but the gravel at my feet, but I don't need to see to know the paparazzi are following our every move. Their repeated questions are evidence enough, much less the way they push and shove me as they try to get to Noah.

Relief fills me when the sidesteps of Noah's truck enter my vision a few minutes later. After opening the passenger door, not without the shove of several paparazzi, Noah helps me inside. The smell of his heated skin smacks me in the face when he clips my seatbelt into place.

Once he has me buckled in, he drapes his jacket over my head, jumps down from the cab, then slams my door shut. Cameras click like crazy, the paparazzi grateful his face has finally been exposed. They hone in on him, their eagerness to get the perfect shot stepping over an acceptable level.

I can't see a damn thing under his leather jacket, but I'm confident Noah has wrangled his way through when his driver's side door flings open a few seconds later. I'd never mistake the grumbling under his breath when he's frustrated. I don't know if he realizes he does it, but it's super cute.

Not long after the motor kicks over, I hear the gearshift crunch into reverse before Noah's fingertips tickle my nape. "Move, you fucking idiot!"

He honks three times before gravel crunching under tires sounds through my ears. The speed I reached in Jenni's car this morning is nothing on Noah's pace when he flattens his foot to the floor. We race out of the parking lot at the speed of a rocket. It's both exciting and scary.

We travel for a few minutes in silence before Noah eases up on the gas pedal. "You can come out now."

When he tugs his jacket off my head, I remove the strands of hair stuck to my temples before turning my eyes to him. It doesn't take a genius to realize he is angry. His jaw is ticking, and I hear his teeth grind over the healthy purr of his motor.

I'm dying to ease his agitation, but since I don't want to scare him like I did months ago, I use words instead of actions. "Are you okay?"

He scrubs the stubble on his chin. "Yeah, I'm just trying to figure out how they knew I was home?" He tightens his grip on the steering wheel as his face reddens with frustration. "They never leave me alone, but I hoped they'd dial back the obsessiveness when I'm not attending public events." He huffs, his eyes rolling. "Clearly, I'm a fucking idiot."

"It's frustrating, but try and think of it from their side. They're just doing the job they're paid to do?"

Noah throws back his head and laughs. Considering the circumstances, it's either the most beautiful noise I've ever heard or the craziest. "Only you would defend the paparazzi, Em."

"I'm not defending them; I just don't know how else to explain their crazy tactics."

"Crazy would work. Crazy is good."

I whack him in the arm, unappreciative of the mirth in his tone.

After rubbing his arm, feigning injury, he winks. "I love you, Beautiful."

Such simple words, but their importance is unsurpassed. He has called me beautiful since the day we started dating. Even though it's conceited for me to say, I love my nickname.

"I love you too."

You have no idea how hard it is not to slide across the bench and plant my lips on his when dimples pop into his cheeks. He's smiling his panty-wetting grin, yet I can't do a damn thing about it. Thank god Jacob's house is only around the corner because I'm not strong enough for this. The chemistry between us has been insane today, but since we were in public, we've kept our usually high level of PDA on the down-low. It's killing me, and that's putting it nicely.

My eyes stray to Noah when he pulls his truck down Jacob's driveway. It's not because I'm hopeful I'm seconds away from having my every wish granted; it's because Noah is yawning. As he parks next to

Jenni's car, I take in the dark circles plaguing his eyes and the low hang of his eyelids. He looks exhausted.

"Did you sleep last night?"

Guilt clutches my heart when he shakes his head. It's nearly two in the afternoon.

"Not at all?"

"No, Em, not at all. I needed to fix the mistakes I'd made before I worried about sleeping."

When he lets out another yawn, I climb down from his truck. "Time for bed, Mister."

His chuckle bounces around the interior of his truck before he joins me outside. Not even his laugh is the same since he's so tired.

In silence, he walks us through Jacob's vacant house, his steps urgent. When we enter his room, he spins around to fix the lock into place. The click is still ringing in my ears when he creeps up behind me to plaster his front against my back. I fail to stifle a moan when I feel how thick he is. His cock is bulging against the zipper in his jeans.

Desire surges through me when he slips my hair to one side so he can kiss and suck my neck, but knowing he hasn't slept for over thirty hours dampens my excitement.

He needs sleep.

My body screams at me in disgust when I pull away from him. I hate myself too, but this is the right thing to do. After spinning around on a wobbly pair of knees, I fold my arms in front of my chest and jerk my chin to his bed, giving Noah his marching orders.

His shocked expression nearly has my ruse coming undone. If his slanted head and wide eyes are anything to go by, this is the first time he's felt the sting of rejection.

"You need sleep."

He arches a brow into his luxurious hair. "Do you truly think I'll sleep a wink without making you come first?"

Slickness coats my panties. Noah is always a gentleman...until he enters the bedroom. There, he isn't just a gifted musician, he has many other *talents* as well. One happens to be sex.

"Come here."

When he summons me with the crook of his finger, I try to maintain my ground, to uphold my integrity. It does me no good. The fire in his eyes is too much. I'm not strong enough for this.

I stroll toward him with my hips swinging and my lips parted. There's barely three feet of air between us, but I make it seem so much more. I seduce him without words before adding touch into the mix. He eyes me curiously when I raise his summoning hand to my mouth, pop his index finger between my lips, then suck down hard.

His growl has my knees clanging together. "Now that's what I'm talking about."

He cups my thighs to guide my legs around his waist. I grind down on the hardness his jeans are failing to conceal as his tongue sweeps across my lips, demanding they open. When they do, he samples every inch of my mouth with slow, tantalizing licks. I return his kiss with just as much intensity, biting at his lips before suckling his tongue into my mouth.

After adjusting the tilt of my hips, I grind down again, desperate for more direct contact. Intuiting my needs, Noah places me on my feet before fiddling with the button on my jeans. I become lost in his dark gaze when he guides the stiff material down my thighs with his eyes never leaving mine.

When he has them far enough down my cotton panties are exposed, he places a teasing kiss on the damp material. I feel his lips rise against my pussy when my hips jerk. He loves how receptive my body is to him.

After wrangling off my jeans, he stands from his crouched position to remove my shirt. Air whistles between his teeth when he drinks in the tiny pair of panties and a mismatched lace bra I'm wearing. When my day started, I never expected it to end like this, so I didn't prepare. I never thought I'd experience such raw emotions again.

Noah must be feeling the sentiment in the air as strongly as I do. His eyes scorch my skin as he stares at me as if it's the first time he's ever seen me. I love that. I love that even with our second anniversary approaching, nothing has changed. His hunger for me is just as voracious as it was years ago. As is mine. I'll never get enough of him.

My eyes go crazy when he removes his jeans and shirt. I take in his stacked abs, smooth pecs, and the thin trail of hair flowing down the bulge protruding from his satin boxer shorts. While fanning my flushed cheeks, I return my eyes to Noah.

"Beautiful. So fucking beautiful," he murmurs, expressing my feelings to a T.

The heat raging through my body doubles when he unclasps my bra and dumps it onto our rumpled clothing on the floor. It turns catastrophic when he hooks his thumbs into my panties to glide them down my quaking thighs. They join the rest of our clothing, but not until he's given them a quick squeeze to assess their dampness. I should be ashamed of how wet I am, but I'm not. Noah has taught me there's nothing wrong with being adventurous if you're with the right person.

My hair fans out on the pillow when Noah lays me down on his bed so his lips can travel the path his eyes just took. He showers my skin with feather-like kisses and gentle bites, like I'm his most treasured possession. I watch him in bewilderment, excited to be at his complete mercy.

By the time he reaches the area aching for his attention, I'm on the edge of hysteria, seconds from toppling into the abyss. Thankfully, his hunger is as potent as mine. He doesn't tease me or make me beg, he just spears his tongue through the folds of my drenched pussy before worshipping it as only he can.

He gives it his all, holding nothing back until I crumble into a mind-hazing climax. His name tears from my throat, and my body shakes as euphoria pumps through my veins hard and fast. It takes several long, pussy-clenching minutes for me to return from hysteria, and even then, I'm still woozy.

After a final lash to my clit, Noah climbs up my body so he can pay the same attention to my breasts. The calluses on his fingertips from playing guitar for years add to the teasing tweaks he does to my nipples. He plays my body like it's an instrument, not stopping until I'm singing in ecstasy for the second time tonight.

My head is just returning from the clouds when a condom

wrapper being torn open resonates through my ears. Like I could get any more horny, a second wave hits me from watching Noah roll a condom down his densely veined cock. There's nothing sexier than seeing him as he is now. Relaxed, mouthwateringly hot, and hard enough to make me panic that no amount of wetness will prepare my body for his invasion.

My nerves are set aside for euphoria when he nestles his big cock at the entrance of my core. He sheaths me slowly, notching in each inch during a slow, painless thrust. Once I'm fully hilted, a vibrating moan ripples through my lips. I love how full I feel. It's painful, yet delicious at the same time.

After adjusting my thighs, Noah withdraws to the very tip before sinking back into me. He does the same thing over and over again until the rim around his cock has the nub inside me tingling beyond doubt. He brings me so close to the brink before dropping his eyes to mine to whisper the words he knows will push me over the edge for the third time.

"I love you, Beautiful."

CHAPTER 37

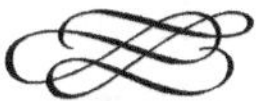

EMILY

*N*oah didn't lack an ounce of stamina our first two hours home, but once he ensured I was thoroughly satisfied, he collapsed from exhaustion. Although I'm tired from our bedroom antics, I can't sleep. I got twelve hours straight last night. If you add that to the excitement still thrumming through my veins, you've got a person who is very alert and very much awake.

Since Noah needs sleep, I do what every teen does when they've got hours to kill: I scroll my Facebook wall. That's where I stumble upon an article my friend Crystal shared. It's about Rise Up's performance on MTV last night.

Curious, I click on the link. It takes me to a well-known and respected gossip site. The headline screams, "Noah Taylor's Acoustic Performance Sets Tongues Wagging."

I scroll down to read the article underneath.

Noah Taylor, lead singer of Rise Up, has set tongues wagging after announcing he is in love during his heartfelt performance on MTV last night. We've been informed by an anonymous source that Noah has been in a relationship the past few months, but he has kept it on the down-low out of respect for his new love. Sources believe Noah is dating small screen actress

Hope Bennett, who recently broke her engagement to movie producer Tom Dempsey. Although Hope's publicist has yet to issue a comment, we wish both her and Noah the best with their budding relationship.

Jealousy has me punishing the screen on my phone a little more than intended. It isn't that I don't trust Noah, I've just never heard of Hope Bennett before, so I'm googling her to ease my curiosity.

Yeah, right.

Wikipedia informs me that Hope Bennett is a twenty-two-year-old starlet of a daytime soap opera on CBS. She was recently announced as the lead actress in a romantic comedy being filmed in the summer. She's beautiful, but I don't see how anyone could connect her with Noah. There are no photos of them together, and she's based in New York, whereas Noah's band obligations keep him on the West Coast.

After scrolling back to the original article, I click on the video link of Noah's performance. Any jealousy still wreaking havoc with my stomach clears away when the video zooms in on Noah. He's sitting on a metal chair, and the guitar I bought him for his birthday is on his lap. He's staring down the camera with remorseful eyes.

Tears burn my eyes when the hostess announces his performance, "Ladies and gentlemen, tonight we have something a little different for you. I'm sure you've heard the sensational hit songs 'Surrender Me' and 'Hollow' by Rise Up that have been climbing the charts the past few months. Well, tonight, I introduce Noah Taylor, lead singer of Rise Up, performing their hit song 'Surrender Me' acoustically."

With his eyes shut and his foot tapping, Noah pours his heart and soul into the song he wrote after we made love. It's the most endearing and riveting performance I've ever seen. Not just from Noah, but from music icons across the globe. It's so beautiful, I can't stop the tears from springing into my eyes. This song has always meant the world to me, but I'm seeing it in an entirely new light now. It's not a pop song. It's a love ballad.

At the end of the performance, Noah opens his eyes and peers straight down into the camera. "I love you, Beautiful."

Not only does his performance prove I've always been his number one priority, it unlocks the answer I've been seeking the past few hours. I now know what I must do. I'm scared, but Noah has always been worth the risk.

CHAPTER 38

NOAH

The light taps of a keyboard draw me from my slumbering state. I'm not sure how long I've been asleep. The drool on my pillow hints at a couple of hours, but the thump of my temples says otherwise. As I take a lazy stretch, I drink Emily in. She's sitting at my desk, tapping frantically on the laptop she splurged on last year. It's secondhand, but she loves it as much as she does her hideous car.

I watch her with interest when she stops what she's doing to jot down something in a notebook at her side before she starts tapping again. She has the sexy naughty librarian look going on. Her hair is contained in a messy bun, and a pencil is stabbed through the middle of it. Although she's not wearing glasses like all the teacher/student fantasies I've had, her sexy-as-fuck lips are gnawing on another pencil.

There is only one way this visual could get more appealing: by acting on my fantasies.

"Hey, Beautiful."

My voice is hoarse from waking up, but it's enough to gain Emily's attention. Smiling, she walks over to slip into my bed. "Hi, baby."

My cock twitches when her teeth graze my earlobe before she sucks it into her mouth. I've spent more time devouring her today than I have sleeping, yet she still hasn't had her fill. I love how insatiable she is.

After pressing a handful of pecks to the stubble on my chin, she slips back out of my bed, leaving me hanging. Upon spotting my dropped lip, she smiles. "You've only been asleep for two hours. You need a lot more than that."

I hit her with the same look I gave her earlier. Since she came more times than I can count, she doesn't fall for it this time around.

Fuck it!

She kisses my forehead. "While you catch up on missed sleep, I'm going to visit Jenni and Jasper at the hospital." The sparkle in her eyes exposes how smitten she is with Jasper. I can't blame her. He's pretty cute—even if he looks like his father. "I'll be back in a couple of hours."

Refusing to let her leave without a proper sendoff, I tug on her wrist until she lands on top of me, then snuff her squeals with my tongue.

By the time I pull back, baby cuddles are the last thing on her mind. "You're a tease, Noah Taylor."

It's the fight of my life not to bring out my best tricks when she stands, wobbling, from my bed. I'm as smug as fuck about how woozy I can still make her.

The egotistical grin stretched across my face is wiped off when she whips back around to face me. "Before I forget, I'll leave my phone on your bedside table. I switched it off because the Ice Queen has been calling it nonstop the past hour."

Delilah is most likely having a coronary that I've been off the grid for so long, but she'll have to wait a few more hours. I'm too fucking tired to deal with her shit right now. I can barely keep my eyes open, let alone face World War III.

After gathering her purse and my truck key from my desk, Emily returns to my side to kiss me goodbye.

"I love you, Beautiful." Since I'm covering a yawn, it sounds more like, "I bub you, bubaful."

She giggles. "I love you too. Now go to sleep! I'll grab dinner on my way home."

I'm back asleep before she breaks through the door of my room.

With a mouth as dry as the Sahara Desert, I swing my legs over my bed and grab my phone off the bedside table to check the time. My brows stitch, confused as to why I'm clutching Emily's phone. It takes several hazy minutes to recall that I smashed my phone the night before.

When I switch on Emily's cell, I see that it's 8:23 PM. As much as I want to sleep until noon tomorrow, if I go back to bed now, I'll be wide awake at 1 AM—guaranteed!

As I throw on a pair of boxer shorts, Emily's phone buzzes like it's possessed. She has thirteen voicemail messages and twenty-three unanswered texts. Although they could be from anyone, even my sleep-deprived head is screaming at me not to be an idiot. Delilah doesn't know the words "back down."

I could return her calls, but she's waited this long, so another thirty minutes won't hurt, right? Even on my best days, I need a coffee IV before I get to work on battling the dragon who despises everything I do.

As I walk through the living room, I rub a kink out of my neck. My muscles are aching, but none of their wails are from a lack of sleep. Emily often says that jealousy sex is the best sex there is, but I'm no longer quick to agree. Being scared shitless of losing someone will have you bringing out your best moves. You'll fuck like a monster with the hope they'll panic, worried they'll never be satisfied in such a way again, so they'll put up with your shit.

My eyes float up from the ground when Jacob's voice drills through my ears. "Hey, Noah." He's sitting at the dining nook at the side of the kitchen, fiddling with his laptop.

"Hey." I scrub my hand over my eyes, urging myself to wake up while spanning the distance between us. "How're things?"

"Good." He smiles a slick grin while jerking his chin up. "Saw Emily leaving earlier. I'm glad you guys worked things out. She was a fucking wreck."

I hate that he was in the middle of our fight, but I'm also grateful. I don't want to think about the circumstances if I hadn't sent him to pick her up Friday afternoon. I'd most likely be waking up hungover and depressed instead of sexually exhausted.

My brow cocks when Jacob scratches his brow. He only ever does that when he's nervous. "What?"

"Who's Hope Bennett?"

Yep, he spits it out just like that. No pause. No delay. A straight jump out of the gate without hesitation.

I shrug. "No fucking clue."

"Alright, but I wouldn't recommend reading the latest gossip sites then."

Unease curdles in my guts when he spins his laptop around to face me. It's open on an article declaring that I'm in love, which is true. An anonymous source quotes that I've been in love for months, which is also true, but it's been more than a few months. And my rumored love is Hope Bennett, a silver screen actress who recently broke off her engagement to a hotshot movie producer.

"What the fuck? How do they even come up with this shit?" When Jacob shrugs, my eyes stray to his. "You believe me, don't you?"

I shouldn't care what he thinks, but for some fucking reason, I do.

Mercifully, he doesn't leave me hanging for long. "Yeah, I do. You might be as annoying as fuck, but you know to keep your cock in your pants...or Emily's...whichever suits more."

"I just hope Emily doesn't read this before I tell her about my performance—"

"Em showed me this article on her way out." He doesn't seem the slightest bit concerned by what he has just said. I'm the only one shitting bricks.

"And...?" I encourage, wanting him to elaborate on his response.

He twists his lips. "She didn't seem worried."

I take a step back, shocked. That's not the reply I expected. Emily trusts me—I've never done anything to break her trust—but I still thought she'd be upset reading gossip about me schmoozing another girl. Rumors are just that, rumors, but they plant seeds of doubt not even the most self-assured person can ignore.

I learned that the hard way three months ago.

I cough up half a lung when Jacob throws his fist into my stomach. "And will you *please* call Delilah Winterbottom? She's been calling the house nonstop the past four hours. She's driving me fucking nuts!"

Growling, I pivot on my heels and head back to my room. I may as well get the inevitable over with. Upon entering, I discover Emily's cell vibrating on my desk. Surprise, surprise, it's *another* call from Delilah.

After hitting the connect button, I press Emily's phone to my ear. "Hell—"

"It's about time! I've been trying to reach you all day!"

I pull the phone away from my ear to wiggle out her shriek before reattaching it. I swear to god, this lady is worse than a dragon on heat. She's always riled up. "Sorry, I've been a little busy on my *days off*. You do know what days off are, don't you, Delilah?"

"I'm well aware of what they are. They're things people have when they're *not* striving to get their debut album to the number one spot in the country!"

Touché—I guess. I hate what she is saying, but we knew getting our album off the ground wouldn't be a walk in the park, but there won't be a follow up if I'm exhausted of material. Emily is my muse. Excluding "Hollow," every song on our album is about her in some way.

I jackknife back, certain I heard Delilah wrong when she snarls, "I need you back in LA as soon as possible. We have several gigs lined up over the next four weeks. I've scheduled you a redeye for tonight. I've spoken with Nick and understand he had a baby this morning, so he won't honor his commitments for another week, but I'm sure you can hold down the fort while he plays house husband." She gags during the last part of her rant, like she's sickened as to why anyone would have a baby.

"I can't catch a flight tonight—"

"You'll either find yourself on that flight, or find your contract with Destiny Records null and void!"

My back molars smash together as I struggle to keep a rational head. It's impossible with this woman. She sure knows how to push my buttons—and not the good ones!

"I'll get on a plane tomorrow, but I'm *not* getting on one tonight. I have priorities that are more important than the band."

"Huh?! Like what?"

She knows what, so I'm not spelling it out for her. "It's called a compromise, Delilah. Come on, I'm sure you've heard of those before." I keep my tone flirty, hoping a little bit of niceness will have her verdict swinging in my favor for once. "Please."

After a long pause, she huffs. "Fine! I'll reschedule your flight for tomorrow afternoon, but if you miss that flight..." The warning in her tone finalizes her threat.

"I won't miss it. I promise."

I'm not sure if she catches my pledge since she slams her phone down into its receiver.

"One battle down, many more to come," I mumble to myself.

I'm walking into the living room when Emily's phone vibrates in my hand, showing a text from Jenni. Any annoyance bristling my skin from my confrontation with Delilah floats away when I read the text message.

Do you want Chinese or pizza? Emily xx

I reply back:
Chinese with dessert? Noah xx

Okay, what do you want for dessert?

You! ;)

I think I can arrange that :) I'll see you soon xx.

Although panicked about what her reaction will be when I tell her I have to get back on the road, I refuse to let it dampen our night. Until I work out a way I can have both Emily and my career, our schedules will be tight, but I'll make it work. She means too much to me to give her up. I'd even leave the band before I'd give her up.

I trip over the rug in the living room when Jacob's angry roar booms into my ears, "You lying bitch!"

He's no longer sitting in the dining room. His backside is planted on his dad's beloved recliner right in front of the flat-screen TV broadcasting from a house that looks remarkably similar to my childhood home.

Bile creeps up my esophagus when the cameraman zooms out, revealing not only my worst nightmare, but the person responsible for it. My mother is standing on the front steps of the home she inherited when my grandfather passed away conducting an interview with an entertainment reporter who's been hounding me the past three weeks.

I step closer to Jacob just as the reporter throws back her segment to the main hosts. "As you just heard from the mom of Rise Up's lead singer Noah Taylor, Noah has not been in contact with his family since his rise to fame began. Noah is the only surviving son Maree has left. Her youngest son Michael was killed in a traffic accident nearly eight years ago, and her eldest son Chris committed suicide four years after that. We can only hope for all involved that Noah will hear the pleas of his heartbroken mother."

"Rewind it."

Jacob pulls the remote out of my reach when I attempt to snatch it out of his hand. "Don't get tied up in her bullshit, Noah. Just let it go."

"Re...wind...it!" My demand is separated with big, growling breaths. When that fails to get him jumping to my command, I add a glare to my threat. I'm two seconds from lodging my boot up his ass before rewinding the footage myself.

Jacob's huff reveals he'd like to see me try, but he rewinds the footage all the same. The interview takes place on the front porch of the house that caused me years of pain. My mom wears a black and white floral-printed dress with a matching cardigan, and she's clutching a school photo of me taken the year Michael died in one hand and a handkerchief in the other. She appears as if she's been crying, which I know is full of shit. She didn't even cry at the funerals of the sons she liked.

My jaw gains a tick when she begins her interview by telling the reporter she only agreed to it because she's so desperate to reach out to me. "I'm speaking to the media in the hope of establishing contact with my son, Noah Taylor, the lead singer of Rise Up. I haven't seen Noah since the band shot to fame a few months ago. I've tried many times to contact him, but he's yet to return my calls. Noah is the only son I have left; his brothers were tragically killed..." The cameraman zooms in real close to her face when a sob steals her words. "...I'm begging you, Noah, please don't shut me out. You're the only family I have left. I love you, Son."

Peeved as fuck about the lady who abused me for years acting like a saint on TV, I rip the television's cord out of the wall before attempting to throw it across the room. Although hate is turning my blood black, something holds me back. It could be the sympathetic look Jacob is giving me or the smell of Emily's skin on mine, but whatever it is, for the first time in years, I don't respond to violence with violence.

CHAPTER 39

EMILY

Chinese takeout swings in my hand when I enter Jacob's house. With Noah and Jacob having huge appetites, I purchased nearly every item on the menu. I'm more broke than I've ever been, but I owed Jacob for easing my mind earlier today.

Out of curiosity, I asked him if he knew Hope Bennett. He was as clueless as me. When I showed him the article, I read it along with him. During my second read-through, I noticed the report said Hope's publicist had yet to confirm their report. Nothing was mentioned about waiting on a statement from Noah's publicist, Delilah Winterbottom.

Like lightning brightening a black sky, clarity formed. Delilah is so evil, she'd have no qualms fabricating a story to ward off questions about Noah's declaration of love. She's been meddling with our relationship from the get-go. She has me at the end of a tether, but since I refuse to stoop to her level, I'm brushing off the article as nothing but idle gossip. Noah loves me. He declared his love in front of millions of viewers. I don't need more proof of his loyalty than that.

After balancing the Chinese on my hip, I increase my speed. My mood has dramatically improved the past twenty-four hours. First, reconnecting with Noah after months of absence, then my visit with

Jenni. Not only did I get lots of squishy baby cuddles, but we worked out a way I can support Noah's career *and* finish my studies. It's not the degree I was hoping for, but my career choice won't work if I'm married to a rock star.

While Noah was sleeping, I matched the courses I'm studying with flexible career options. By staying on a similar schedule, I won't need to restart my scholarship. I just need to make a handful of adjustments. Although I haven't narrowed down a field I'm interested in, I did schedule a meeting with the Dean of my college for Monday morning. Once I'm closer to graduating, I'm sure the perfect career will fall into my lap. If not, the extra classes I took to ward off loneliness will come in handy.

When I walk into the living room, I spot Noah talking on my cell. His shoulders are squared, and grooves are scouring his forehead. He seems a little tense—but he still tracks me as I cross the room. Even from a distance, his hunger can't be missed.

I wave at him like a naïve idiot before continuing to the leather sofa Jacob is sitting on. "Hey, Jake."

"Hey... Ohhh, what have you got there?"

Jacob rubs his hands together while eyeing the Chinese. Even with the hunger in his eyes coming from food, he can't help but tease Noah by planting a sloppy kiss on my cheek. Just as he does every time Jacob riles him up, Noah takes his bait hook, line, and sinker. He arches his brow before glaring at Jacob, giving him clear signs to fuck off.

Jacob's chuckle rumbles through my chest, pleased he got a rise out of Noah, before he assists me by loading the containers of Chinese onto the coffee table. Once everything is staged for a night in front of the idiot box, Jacob flops into his seat and starts devouring a box of fried rice with chopsticks. He's as playful as he always is, but there's a heaviness in the air I can't ignore.

"Is everything okay?"

Jacob stops eating mid-chew to scratch his brow. "Yeah, I think so."

While Noah continues his call, Jacob tells me about how his mother held a press conference hoping to guilt Noah into contacting her. I want to pretend I'm surprised by her ruse, but I'm not. I've been waiting for this to happen; she just did it sooner than I anticipated. It's the same for anyone when they become famous. Family you didn't know exist come out of the woodwork, let alone ones you previously cut ties with.

In all honesty, I'm unsure how Noah will handle his mother's attempt to steal his limelight. I'm reasonably confident he won't have any contact with her, but there are ways this can be handled without establishing a line of communication.

Not long after Jacob consumes a box of fried rice, Noah joins us in the living room. He presses a kiss to my temple before helping himself to the Chinese. Unlike Jacob and I, he uses a fork. He's never mastered the art of eating with chopsticks.

In even less time than it took to cook our dinner, Noah and Jacob polish it off. Not a single morsel of rice remains.

"Thanks for dinner, Em; I was starving."

When Jacob stands to clear away the empty containers, I jump to my feet to help him. He shoos me away. "You cooked; I'll clean."

He disappears faster than a man his size should be able to move. Although I'm grateful to have Noah all to myself, what Jacob disclosed earlier isn't sitting right with me. I could pretend I don't know what Noah's mom did, but only today we pledged not to have any more secrets between us, so I'm going to uphold my side of the deal.

"Jacob told me about your mom. I'm sorry she's doing this to you now."

"By talking about it, we're giving her exactly what she wants. Don't waste your breath on a woman not worthy of it, Em."

To a stranger, Noah's reply may seem callous, but to me, it's spot on. Noah loves his mother—she's the only one he has—but that doesn't mean he can't also hate her. She caused him years of pain. That's not easily forgivable.

My eyes dance between Noah's dark gaze when he stands from the sofa to hold out his hand in offering. With a smile, I accept his courteous gesture. The worry lingering in the back of my mind fades when he plucks me from my seat with a yank on my wrist, then it completely disappears when he nibbles and sucks on my lips.

I'm lust-drunk by the time he pulls back, but no amount of haze can take away what he says next, "Marry me, Emily?"

I wiggle my ring finger in the air, the diamond in my engagement ring bouncing rainbow hues across his face. "I already agreed to marry you." I playfully bite on his lower lip before dragging my tongue across it. "A very long time ago."

"I mean marry me now, like right now. We could fly to Vegas or go to the courthouse, but I want you to be my wife tonight."

I get giddy at his eagerness... until I realize he's being serious.

"We can't ..." My words trail off when his shoulders deflate in defeat. "...Yet." His eyes snap back to mine. "Don't get your hopes up. We need to apply for a marriage license first. That can take a few days, but once it's processed, I'll meet you in Vegas at a time and date of your choosing."

"You'll do it? You'll elope with me?"

A dull ache hits my chest. I hate seeing him like this, so vulnerable and lost. His mother's ploy to steal his limelight must be affecting him more than he's letting on. I wish he'd open up to me. I'm on his side no matter what, and if marrying him proves that, I'm all for it. We were initially planning to wed soon anyway, so what's a few weeks between friends?

"I can't wait to be Mrs. Noah Taylor," I talk over his lips before kissing him hard on the mouth.

My boldness starts an avalanche of hands, lips, and teeth. We stumble into his room, our clothing discarded during our short trip. The lock on his door has barely clicked into place when Noah hoists me against it, slips my panties to the side, then impales me with one ardent thrust. I call out, the sensation unlike anything I've experienced.

Unlike earlier today, when he cherished me by making slow tantalizing love to me, he fucks me hard and fast. He screws me senseless until his name is torn from my throat in a ragged scream, and I'm determined nothing will ever come between us again.

Later, while in my favorite position, in the crook of Noah's arm with my head resting on his chest, he updates me on the phone calls he took while I was visiting Jenni.

"Delilah was adamant my ass was to be on a red-eye tonight." He gags, expressing his annoyance without words. "I managed to get a stay of execution, but not for long. I'm sorry, Em, but I have to fly back tomorrow afternoon. I've missed so much the past two days, Delilah is going batshit crazy."

He sounds concerned, panicked I'll take the news of him leaving harshly. Although I hate that we're parting again so soon, he's not the only one who has important matters to attend to.

"It's okay; I have to get back to school anyway. I have a few things to sort out."

The concern in his eyes fades, pushed aside for a more excited gleam. I find out why when he discloses, "After talking to Delilah, Cormack called to advise the lead guitarist from Redemption was in a motorbike accident—he broke his leg in three places. With Rise Up's recent success, Redemption's record label asked for us to fill the remainder of their concert tours. They've been the opening act for the O'Reilly Brothers and have another six weeks of concerts scheduled."

Excitement whooshes through my blood. I'm equally shocked and thrilled. "That's fantastic!" I hug him tight. "I can't believe you're going to be the opening act for the O'Reilly Brothers!"

The O'Reilly brothers are multi-platinum, award-winning artists who won three Grammys last year alone. They're my favorite band next to Rise Up.

"I'm so proud of you."

My excitement dampens when I notice the panicked expression on Noah's face. He's worried about us being apart for the six weeks of the tour. He doesn't need to be. I'm working on a solution to fix that. I just can't tell him my plans yet because I don't want his hopes dashed if things don't work out.

"We'll be okay. I promise you. This time, we'll make this work."

He runs his index finger down my cheek before tracking it across my lips. "I haven't agreed to anything yet. I told Cormack I wanted to talk to you first. I understand if you don't want me to do this."

"I want you to do it. It's a fantastic opportunity for the band. You can't give this up..." My words trail off as true panic pumps into me. "What about Nick?" Jenni just gave birth, so there's no way Nick can leave tomorrow afternoon.

"Nick will stay here while we finalize the stage production. He'll join us on the road just before our first gig in San Francisco."

I sigh, grateful. Although it isn't ideal, I'm glad adjustments were made for the first-time father. "Everything is falling into place as it should, proving it's meant to be."

"Meant to be?" I giggle when Noah flips me over before pinning me to his bed with his hips. "The only thing meant to be is me and you."

I'm about to tease him about how romantic he is—he hates when I jeer him about his bad-boy persona only being a disguise for the big softy hiding beneath—but the movements of his lips stop me. He isn't talking. He's devouring—*me*.

We didn't get dressed after a joint shower to clean away the mess our fuck on his bedroom door caused, so there's nothing between us but the bit of air he lodges between us as he moves his lips down my body. He kisses every inch of me, only stopping when he reaches regions deserving of more than a peck.

Then, after a mind-hazing orgasm, I return the favor. I drag my lips down his smooth pecs, over the rigid bumps in his abdomen before following the thin trail of hair down his midsection.

Noah props himself on his elbows, ready for the show when I wrap my hand around his shaft. After licking my lips, parched from the screams I released during climax, I hover over his crest. I'm dying to lap up the bead glistening at the end, but I'm trying to maintain his steady pace, so I relish the heaviness of him in my hand and his delicious scent instead.

Only once he's on the verge of begging does my tongue slither across the crest of his cock.

"Fuck, Em—" He hisses out a groan when I slide my lips over his head to swallow him down gently. His cock pulsates when I accept him inside me as far as I can without gagging. I can't take all of him, but he doesn't seem to mind.

"That feels so good, Beautiful. Your lips were designed for this."

Within minutes, I have him at my mercy. His shoulders slacken when he leans back, his eyes rolling. The salty goodness dripping from his crown increases with every suck as I take him deeper, faster, almost greedily. My hunger for him is so intense, I've forgotten about his earlier worshipping pace. I want him moaning my name as his cock pulsates with need. To taste him in my mouth before feeling the heat of his seed inside me.

Just as my prayers are about to be answered, Noah's cock pops from my lips. He flips me over again, then lies on top of me. As his weight pins me to the bed, he lavishes my mouth with long, precise licks while guiding my legs around his waist.

"We're not fucking, Beautiful. We're adoring. Worshipping." His eyes stray to mine, bristling with lust and admiration. "Loving."

Excitement zaps down my spine when he lines up his cock with the entrance of my pussy, giving my clit two welcomed swipes during the process.

The friction is so torturous, I beg, "Please, Noah. I need you."

With his fingers woven through my hair and an adorable grin on his face, he sinks into me slowly. It's a slower pace than my buzzing clit was hoping for, but nothing can take away from its brilliance. I'm full all over. My heart, my body, and my soul.

After wrapping my arms around his neck, I match the rolls of Noah's hips. We move as one, the sheer pleasure unexplainable. This isn't about him or me. It's about us. Together. As a couple.

My breathing shallows when he lowers his hand to scrub his thumb over my clit. He places the perfect amount of pressure, circling it in a way that has every muscle in my body heightening for release. I moan, unable to keep my eyes open for a second longer. The sensation overtaking my body is out of control. I'm heating up everywhere.

"That's it, Beautiful, just like that."

Even while making love, Noah's voice is pure heaven. It serenades me into a trance-like state, one where I'm certain my body can't endure another orgasm in such a short period. We've had weekends where we did nothing but fool around, but not even those had me hitting the record-breaking number of orgasms I've experienced the past ten hours.

When a quiver shudders through me, an egotistical grin morphs onto Noah's face. It's more wondrous than arrogant. He feels my race to the line approaching, and he won't let anything stand in its path.

"Leg up, Em, take all of me."

He positions my right leg higher on his sweaty hip before increasing his thrusts. It adds to the tingling sensation racing through my veins while also allowing the last inch of his cock to sink into me. His moan when he's fully seated is the hottest thing I've ever heard. It spirals me into a madness that makes stars dance in front of my eyes.

"Ah! Oh... oh!" I sound like a feral animal!

Noah pumps into me another three times before he growls my name in a husky grunt while shuddering all over.

Several hours later, Noah pulls his truck into the multi-story parking garage at Ravenshoe Private Hospital. After hearing Nick's complaint about the hospital's food being as bland as cardboard, Noah thought it would be nice to bring the new parents some of their favorite take-out for lunch. I jumped at the chance. I'd never turn down an opportunity for more baby cuddles.

News of Jasper's birth must be circulating the gossip sites, as there are over a dozen paparazzi waiting outside the main entrance. The crowd looks similar in size to what we handled yesterday at Bronte's Peak, if not a little heavier.

After pulling his truck into the first vacant spot, Noah shuts down his engine, then swings his eyes to me. "You go in first, then I'll follow in a few. I don't want them barging over you to get to me."

"Okay. I love you."

I press my lips to his cheek, hoping it will ease the agitation in his tone, before slipping out of his truck. Butterflies take flight in my stomach as I make my way to the double doors, my hands slicking with sweat, my heart racing. I'm beyond nervous the paparazzi will recognize me from my date with Noah yesterday.

I had no reason to fret. Other than an appreciative gawk from men older than my dad, they don't pay any attention to me. I enter relatively unscathed.

I don't see Noah being quite so lucky.

CHAPTER 40

NOAH

A grin tugs at my lips when Emily walks past the paparazzi unnoticed. I kept an eye on social media the past twelve hours, worried our run-in yesterday would have her name circulated by the media, but it was unwarranted. Excluding the shots they got when we exited Bronte's Peak Café, Emily's face was sheltered by my leather jacket.

If they took the time to sit down and study the blurry, wide-eyed image, they'd eventually put two and two together, but with the paparazzi being more annoying than smart, I don't see that happening within the next week or two, and by then, it will be too late. My relationship with Emily will be public knowledge.

At the start of our agreement, I explicitly stated the record company's ruse of making the public believe I'm single would only be temporary. I did what they asked; now it's time for them to uphold their end of the deal. I'm going public with my engagement mere weeks before marrying the love of my life.

With a smile on my face, I narrow a black cap down until it covers my eyes. The paparazzi's lights aren't just annoying; they're blinding.

I've barely stepped down from my truck when they spot me.

Camera flashes hinder my vision a mere second before I'm hit with a range of questions.

"Are you the reason Hope broke her engagement to Tom Dempsey?"

"How long have you and Hope been in love?"

"Are you rushing down the aisle because Hope is pregnant?"

I remain silent, not answering any of their questions, but my curiosity is piqued as to why I've been linked to Hope Bennett. I don't even know who the fuck she is.

I give two security officers a grateful dip of my chin when they stop the paparazzi from following me into the hospital lobby. They usher them outside as I head to the elevator banks on my right to head to the maternity ward on the third floor.

With the hospital on near lockdown status, the elevator doors ding open not even a few seconds later. As I enter the sanitary-smelling space, I spot Emily leaning against the wall, seemingly waiting for me. That's a shock. I didn't think even I could trump her wish to squeeze Jasper to within an inch of his life.

When I notice the concerned wrinkle popping between her brows, I increase my pace. "Everything okay?"

Emily shakes her head. "No. Yes." She huffs. "I don't know. Jenni is upset. Nick just told her about the tour. She's not taking it well."

I understand how she feels. I'm struggling with the idea of leaving again, so I can imagine how torn Nick and Jenni feel. She only gave birth to their son yesterday.

"If worse comes to worst, we can look into alternative arrangements until Nick can join us on the road. It may not be this tour, but I'm sure we'll add more soon."

As Emily nods, I guide her to the hard plastic chairs lining the corridor. In silence, we wait for Nick to give us the all-clear to enter. I'm not overly patient, and I hate that I'm wasting precious time with Emily before my flight this afternoon, but this isn't a decision Nick and Jenni should make in haste. They deserve some time to deliberate.

Approximately twenty minutes later, Nick exits Jenni's room. His brows are hanging as low as his shoulders, and his eyes are crammed with moisture. He appears as devastated as he was the night I drove him to the hotel after Jenni told him she was getting an abortion.

"I'll meet you in there." I kiss Emily's lips that are still swollen from our night of lovemaking before nudging my head to Jenni's room.

She reads me as only she can before nodding. When she enters Jenni's room, I gesture for Nick to join me on the chairs as hard-lined as Delilah's lips when I piss her off. He slumps into the chair with a groan, his hand shooting up to scrub his watering eyes.

"I can't leave now. She needs me." He keeps his emotions at bay, but his crackling voice gives away his true response. He's stuck between a rock and a hard place. "Just the thought of leaving Jenni already sucks, let alone wondering how much Jasper will grow while I'm gone. I don't want to leave them."

"Then bring them on the road with you."

Nick scoffs, either shocked by my suggestion or annoyed he didn't come up with it himself. I realize it's the former when he groans, "I can't take a baby on tour."

"Why? I don't know much about babies, but I'm reasonably sure they just eat, sleep, and poop. Can't they do that anywhere?"

Nick's teeth graze his bottom lip as he considers my response. After a few seconds of pondering, he sits up straight in his chair as his eyes stray to mine. They don't look as pained as they were moments ago. "Do you think it could work?"

I shrug, truly unsure. "It can't hurt to try though, can it?"

"It could work." He sounds as if he's trying to convince himself more than me, and just like every decision he makes, he escalates it rather quickly. "It could work. Noah, you're a genius!"

Grabbing my face with both of his hands, he plants a kiss on my lips. I yank back, disgusted beyond words. "Get the fuck off me!"

I wipe my lips with my shirt as he bolts into Jenni's room. The grimace crossing my face morphs to a grin when he declares my genius state to Emily and Jenni so loudly, two towns over hear him.

Emily and I stay at the hospital for nearly two hours before time gets the better of us. I'm due at the airport in an hour, and I haven't started packing. I hate that I'm leaving again, but this time, I won't let others influence my decision. I'm a grown man, so it's time for me to start acting like one.

Emily and I have a little ways to go before we're back to how we were months ago, but with the blame for our stumble falling solely on my shoulders, I'm the one who is responsible for getting us back there. Then, once things are back on track, I'll explain the real reason for my absence. It will seem ridiculous when I admit my stupidity out loud, but at the time, I felt like my world was crumbling.

When the elevator dings, announcing we've arrived at the foyer, my eyes drift to Emily. "Wait for me out front, and I'll pick you up on my way out."

Grateful to skip a second gauntlet run with the paparazzi, Emily nods before stepping out of the elevator car. Our fingers remain entwined until the very last second, only unlocking when flashing bulbs brighten an eerie afternoon sky.

"Be careful," Emily whispers before breaking away from my side.

I sign in relief when she makes it through the media contingent without incident. I'm nowhere near as lucky. I once again get hammered. The questions flung at me are identical to the ones I got on the way in. They all focus on Hope Bennett. I'm eager to find out about our supposed connection, but not enough to let it gobble up my remaining hours with Emily.

After picking her up from the front of the hospital, I make my way back to Jacob's to pack. It's done between feather-like kisses and playful touches. Neither of us want to separate again, but there's a new understanding bristling between us. We're both determined to make this right again. We stumbled, but it's how we rise from our fall that proves how strong we really are.

Once I'm ready to go, Jacob travels with us to the airport. He'll take Emily back to school once I've boarded my flight. When we reach my boarding gate, I shake Jacob's hand and pull him in for a man hug before shifting my focus to Emily. While kissing her goodbye, I try to convey how much I love her and that I'll miss her more than she'll ever realize.

I've always expressed myself without words, but I'm finding it difficult today. I have so many things I want to say, but not enough time to say them. That's the most frustrating part of my life lately. Not having enough hours to achieve all the things expected of me.

When I pull back, Emily has tears in her eyes, but her next set of words proves she understood the meaning of our kiss. "I love you too, Noah."

I swipe at the blobs of moisture close to falling down her cheeks. "No tears, please. It'll kill me to walk away from you while you're crying."

"Sorry."

After scrubbing her eyes, she forces a fake smile onto her face. It's not her breathtakingly beautiful smile, but it lessens the pain tearing me in two when I spin on my heels and walk away from her, only glancing back six hundred trillion times at the woman I'm going to marry one day. *One day soon.*

———

The flight back to LA is long and uneventful. With Jacob always one step ahead of the game, he set up a new cell phone for me earlier today, but with the wi-fi in flight on the fritz, I've got nothing to do but twiddle my thumbs.

While scrolling through my new phone, I chuckle out loud. Jacob not only arranged for me to have the same number, but he added all my contacts as well. He's great like this. I just wish he'd give my offer to become my assistant more thought. I may be riling him, but in reality, if he said yes, I'd jump at the chance.

As I walk down the gangway, I call Emily to let her know I've arrived safely. She's been back at school for a few hours and is already in bed. Clearly, my efforts to exhaust her were spot on.

We talk until my phone beeps with another incoming call. "Sorry, Em, I've got another call coming in. Can I call you tomorrow?"

"Of course. I love you."

After returning her declaration of love, I lower my phone from my ear to connect my second call. My brow cocks when I notice it's Cormack calling. With the late hour, I expected it to be the fire-breathing witch I've been ghosting the past twelve hours.

I hit connect before pushing my phone to my ear. "Hey—"

"You're a fucking genius!"

My ego gets stroked from Cormack's shouted words. This is the second time today I've been told how terrific I am. They better be careful, or I might start believing them.

My already high chest sits a few inches higher when Cormack advises the reason for his call. "Your acoustic performance of 'Surrender Me' is receiving rave reviews. It just hit the number one spot on the Billboard charts."

I stop walking just as I hit the sidewalk of the airport. The tingling of goosebumps flutter over my arms. "What?" I mumble, not believing what I've heard.

I must have clogged ears from the flight. Surely, I heard him wrong. "Surrender Me" only just hit the top ten this week, and we've been plugging it relentlessly the past four months. There's no way it's jumped nine spots in twenty-four hours.

I'm proven cynical when Cormack shouts, "You did it! You got the number one spot! You have the number one single in the country, and your album is the highest-selling album this week!"

My heart beats super-fast as my feet leave the ground. "Holy shit!" I'm so excited, I'm not bothered by the dozen or more paparazzi snapping my picture. "Do the rest of the guys know?"

"No, I thought I'd leave the honor to you."

"Awesome. Thanks."

I stumble out a goodbye to Cormack while peering past the swarm of paparazzi to spot my driver. I find him a few seconds later standing in front of a black Escalade, holding out a board with my name on it.

During our drive to the hotel, I call the boys one at a time to tell them our news. Since Marcus has been with me from the start, I call him first. I get to kill two birds with one stone when I discover Slater is with him at the bar, sampling a range of LA throat-burning concoctions.

Marcus is quietly reserved—that's not unusual; he's always been the humble one of our group—but Slater goes crazy. He tells everyone around him that he's a chart-topping artist before declaring the next round is on him.

After reminding Slater we've got a few months before the royalty checks roll in, I call Nick. For a man known for his eccentrics, his reply is odd. He gasps briefly in surprise before ruffling sounds down the line. It's only upon hearing the murmur of a baby annoyed at being moved do I realize why he's being so quiet. He must have Jasper cradled on his chest.

Once Jasper is handed to Jenni, the response I expected barrels down the line. Nick hollers loudly, his shouts coming with several *woo hoos*!

I laugh at his response before promising to call him at a better hour tomorrow. When he hangs up, I call Emily. I wanted to tell her first, but she hates taking the fanfare away from the boys. She's yet to realize she's just as integral to the band as the rest of us. Without the support of our loved ones, we'd still be playing at Mavs every Tuesday night to a bunch of old ladies with lipstick smeared on their teeth.

It takes Emily a few seconds to answer, and when she does, she sounds tired. "Hey, baby."

"Did I wake you?"

I hear her lips rise over the phone. "Maybe... but it's okay; I love hearing your voice." Her husky voice pops images of the fun we had last night into my head. It stiffens my cock, but not as much as what she says next: "Come on, out with it. The last time I heard you this excited was when you told me you booked us a hotel for my nineteenth birthday."

I try to remain humble. I miserably fail. "We did it! We finally fucking did it. 'Surrender Me' is number one on the Billboard charts, and our album is the number one selling album in the country!"

"Noah..." Emily takes in a sharp breath like she always does when she's about to cry. "I'm so proud of you. I knew you'd do it."

"I couldn't have done it without you, Em."

A gush of wind sounds down the line, like she's shooing away my 100% accurate statement. "Forever prepared for insults, but compliments leave you baffled."

Her level of smarts is too much for me to handle this late at night.

When I tell her that, she laughs. "It means you earned this, so you deserve to enjoy it. Stop worrying about everyone else and lap up the glory."

"I'd rather lap you up."

She laughs again.

We talk for a few more minutes before my Escalade pulling into my hotel cuts our conversation short. I bid Emily goodnight with the promise of celebrating my success with those equally as deserving. I have no clue what my promise entailed until Slater and Marcus lock onto me like a missile aiming for its target when I try to slip past the hotel bar unnoticed. Slater is well past intoxicated, and Marcus is looking a little worse for wear.

With my recent promise still ringing in my ears, I accept their invitation for a celebratory drink. Before we know it, one drink turns into four, and dusk transforms to dawn.

I roll over with a grunt, my hand stretching out to slap the annoying drone bouncing across my bedside table. No matter how many times I smack my phone, its annoying buzz won't shut up. I wouldn't be so aggravated if I weren't paying for the celebratory drinks I had with the guys last night. My head is thumping like someone is jackhammering in there, and my mouth feels like it's been wiped clean with cotton balls.

"Alright. Fuck me! I'm up."

I throw off my duvet with a growl before picking up my once again ringing phone. The worst hangover in history can't compete with the bile scorching my throat when I peer down at the screen. Delilah is calling me—again.

She's the last person I want to speak to while hungover, but if I keep skirting her like I did yesterday, it will be more than my job on the line.

After neighing my lips like a horse, I press my phone to my ear. "Hello."

"Sorry, Princess, did I wake you?"

I yank my phone away from my ear, her screeching voice too much to bear this early in the morning. "Uh-huh," is all I can mumble.

I badly need some Advil and should probably wash it down with a few gallons of water. If my scaly skin is anything to go by, I'm severely dehydrated, which is surprising considering the copious amounts of liquor I drank last night.

I need more than pain medication when Delilah barks down the line, "I need to brief you before our press conference this afternoon. I'll be in your room in fifteen minutes."

She steals my chance to advise I'm not presentable for company by slamming down the receiver. As I dump my cell on the bedside table, I notice it's a little before eleven. Although I'm dying to call Emily, she'd be in her sociology class by now. Instead, I send her a text before dragging my sorry ass out of bed for a steaming hot shower.

I've barely soaked my head in one-tenth of the liquid I guzzled down last night when I hear Delilah banging on my hotel room door. If I weren't anticipating her arrival, I'd be worried I'm seconds from being raided by the police. That's how hard she's knocking.

I throw on a pair of boxer shorts before racing to the door to let her in. Things got a little rowdy with Slater, Marcus and me last night, so the last thing I want is another disturbance notice.

"It smells like a brewery in here."

Delilah screws up her nose before entering my room. After taking in the empty bottles spread across the coffee table, she moves to the two-seater table in front of a floor-to-ceiling window to take a seat. I usually eat my breakfast there while enjoying the scenery.

Delilah might not have any appetizers in front of her, but that doesn't mean she isn't taking advantage of usually unseen scenery. Her eyes rake my body for several nauseating seconds before they return to my face. The lust in them almost makes me barf. I've never felt more ill in my life.

Hell no, dragon lady, you're not allowed to sample my goods.

When I snag a shirt off my bed and throw it over my head, her eyes return to their normal, narrowed squint. She tries to play it cool, like she wasn't just ogling me like I was cake and she's been on a diet for three years. Now I know why she helps the talent. She's a shit actor.

After doubling my protection with a pair of jeans, I take a seat across from Delilah before accepting the piece of paper she is holding out for me. "You have a press conference at three where you'll read this statement before opening up questions to the reporters in attendance."

I scan the document, my blood pressure notching up the longer I read it.

Good afternoon, I'm Noah Taylor, lead singer of Rise Up. First, I'd like to thank you for attending our press conference today. I understand how hectic things can be. Our lead guitarist, Nick, welcomed a baby boy into his family Saturday morning—his fiancée, Jenni, is recovering well—and our song Surrender Me *climbed to the number one song on the Billboard charts late last night.*

If that isn't already exciting, on Saturday afternoon, Rise Up was signed on as the opening act for the O'Reilly Brothers for the next two months of their West Coast tour. Tickets are available for all shows; the details can be found on our record label's website. Rise Up is excited to work alongside such talented artists, and we thank them for the opportunity they have given us.

I'll now open the floor to any questions, but I will not be answering any questions in regards to my relationship with Hope Bennett.

My eyes snap up from the paper I'm clutching. "What the hell? The last part insinuates I'm in a relationship with Hope. I don't even know who the fuck she is, so why would I be associated with her?"

"After the stunt you pulled on MTV, I've been fielding endless calls from reporters wanting to know whom you're in love with."

"Then tell them the truth!" I throw my arms in the air. "I'm in love with Emily, my *fiancée*, not some starlet I've never heard of!"

"My job is to ensure the public perceives you in a manner that helps your career. Admitting you're engaged to a suburban hick would be ludicrous."

Fury blackens my veins. I've never wanted to slap a woman, but Delilah is my first exception to that rule.

"*This* makes sense." She nudges her head to the press release she wants me to read. "Two up and coming stars find both love and stardom together. The gossip sites will have a field day with it. A rock star and an actress. It's every publicist's dream."

"I don't give a fuck if it's a pot of gold under a rainbow, it's not happening. I'm not going through with this anymore." I look her dead set in the eyes. "I love Emily. She is going to be my wife. *This...*" I toss her document to her side of the table. "... is done. We're done."

CHAPTER 41

EMILY

I skip out of the Dean's office. Our meeting went better than expected. He couldn't answer all my questions but promised to have them tied up by the end of the week. That's also when he'll make his final decision about my proposal. It will be a nerve-wracking week, but with a heavy course-load to keep me occupied, I'm hoping it will go quick. If not, I'm sure the upcoming Christmas/ New Year festivities will pick up the slack.

As hoping, my week flew by. Unfortunately, I haven't heard back from the Dean in regards to my application. I'm a little disheartened, but understand the upcoming holiday season may delay the process. I'd be more upset if Noah hadn't kept his promise about maintaining regular contact like we did when I first started college. We've FaceTimed every night the past five days, and our texts could fill the pages of a romance novel. He's extremely busy prepping for his tour, but he's always in a positive mind frame when we talk.

With Noah needed on the West Coast, I visited Jenni, Nick, and Jasper for the weekend. With Jasper being premature, they weren't discharged from hospital until Friday night. Jenni is a nurturer, so parenting has come easy to her. Just looking at her, you wouldn't know she only had a baby a week ago. She's positively glowing.

My trip had many great benefits. I got squishy cuddles and had plenty of time to daydream about the traits I hope my children will inherit from Noah. I really hope they get his dimples and dark, stormy eyes. Then, while Jasper was sleeping, Jenni and I worked on the surprise I'm planning for Noah's birthday.

It's so top secret, everyone involved has been sworn to secrecy. Although I hate keeping things from Noah after recently promising to have no secrets between us, this is different.

It's not a secret when it will give him everything he's ever wanted.

***

My gallops down the stairs of my economics class slow when my cell phone plays its 'Surrender Me' ringtone. Grinning like a giddy idiot, I slide my phone out of my pocket, hit the connect button, then press it to my ear. "Noah..." I breathe excitedly into the phone.

"Hey, Beautiful, how are you?"

I walk down the concrete sidewalk and head for my dorm. "I'm good, thanks. Just finished my last class of the day." I only have classes until midday on Mondays. The other half of my day is allocated to study or make-up courses.

"How was your economics class?"

My heart beats double time. He paid careful attention to my class schedule last year, but I thought that would be over now that he's so busy. I love how considerate he is. Having him follow my routine makes it seem as if he's studying right alongside me.

"It was good." I smile while rolling my eyes. I'm not a fan of economics. I just love the many doors it could open for me in the future. "How's your day been?"

My steps taper when he murmurs, "Long... but it'll be worth it."

He sounds tired. That's not a surprise. He's been working nonstop the past week preparing for their debut concert Saturday night. It will be a massive week of firsts for him, and I'm not solely referring to his career either.

"How's the weather?"

I stop walking to look up and admire the brilliant blue sky. "Umm... good. It was a little windy this morning, but it has settled down this afternoon." It's weird he wants to talk about the weather, but I'd talk to him about the odd color of Jasper's poop if it means I get to hear his voice.

"Compared to LA, the wind here is like ice. You really should be wearing a jacket."

My heart skips a beat when the entirety of his reply hits me. He's talking as if he's here, with me. With my hand on my chest to keep my heart in its right spot, I spin in a circle, seeking Noah amongst the crowd. For a Monday, the quad is more packed than it usually is, but I don't spot Noah.

I lick my dry lips before forcing out my words through the excitement clutching my throat. "How do you know I'm not wearing my jacket?"

Noah warned me to be cautious about being followed after the paparazzi captured half my face at the café last week, but the closest I've come to a camera the past eight days was when Jeremy Mitchell snapped my picture unaware last week. He was quick to delete it when I said I'd report his "Hottie or Not" website to the Dean. My ego was stoked at the 99.9% rating I achieved when he added me to his site last month, but I'm not a fan of women being judged online like we're pieces of meat.

I stop thinking up ways to have Jeremy's website pulled down when Noah growls, "I know your Van Halen shirt is one of your favorites, but sometimes even the greats have to take a step back when it comes to your health."

My heart squeezes in my chest when I peer down; I'm wearing my favorite Van Halen shirt. My tearful eyes drift over the students socializing in the quad. There are hundreds of them, but I scan every single face. *He is here; he has to be. I can feel him.*

Thirty seconds later, my breath hitches. A gorgeous pair of intense dark eyes are peering at me from beneath a Parkwood State cap—the same Parkwood State cap they hid under only days ago.

"Noah."

If I needed any more proof, the pop of his dimples when he smiles leaves no doubt who is standing before me. "Hi, Beautiful."

He's standing next to the economics building stairs I just galloped down. I feel like an idiot that I walked straight past him, but my stupidity can be easily excused. He's wearing a Parkwood State sports jacket, matching slacks, and a low-hanging cap, making him blend in with the rest of the male population.

Blood surges through my body when I push off my feet to race his way. When I reach him, I throw myself into his arms, equally shocked and ecstatic that he's here. His visit will throw a wrench into the surprise I'm planning for him, but I'll work through the ripple effect after I've worked through my shock.

For now, nothing but reacquainting our lips is on my mind.

CHAPTER 42

NOAH

hen Emily leaps into my arms, I'm engulfed by her delicious vanilla scent, closely followed by the plumpest pair of lips I've ever sampled. She kisses me without the snicker I expected when her ex-roomie, Crystal, helped me plan a disguise so I could greet Emily outside of her class like I did before our album broke record sales. I feel like an idiot wearing an outfit jocks happily wear even on the weekends, but I'd do it all again if it achieves the same outcome. The surprise on her face when she spotted me was priceless. Only a few weeks ago, I saw nothing but stress on her face when we video chatted.

After kissing me senseless, she pulls back. "How are you here?"

"It's my last day off before our tour begins, so I had to visit my favorite girl."

Her eyes glisten with happiness, but it only lingers for a few seconds before changing to panic. "Does Jacob know you're here?"

I shrug, but the chance of giving a verbal response is lost when I notice how quickly we're gaining attention. Emily attracts the eye of many admirers as it is, but with her knocking my cap off, we've got more than admiration directed our way. We've got overzealous fans.

"Can I please take a photo with you?" one girl practically begs.

"How about an autograph?" asks another before she's barged aside by someone doing a live broadcast on Facebook.

I'll always love and appreciate our fans—they made our album number one—but I only have hours before I'm due back in LA. I can't have that time wasted on fans when I'm already giving them so much of me.

I'm about to decline their request when Emily nudges me closer to them. "It's okay."

"Em—"

"It's fine. They can only have you now. I get to have you for a lifetime."

What the fuck did I ever do to deserve her?

After pressing my lips to her temple, a clear sign to the girls giving me heart eyes that I'm taken, I pose for selfies and sign a few shirts and the odd piece of paper. When one shy girl asks Emily if she could take a photo of us together, Emily agrees without any hesitation. She even gets in on the act when we take a handful of Snapchat pics with funny filters. It's nice seeing my fans respect and admire her as much as I do.

After signing until my hands cramp, I thank them for their support, tug Emily under my arm, then dash to her dormitory. Mercifully, the college girls at Parkwood State are more subdued than their LA counterparts. Only a handful follow us, and they're soon lost when we dash by other dorms and sororities before reaching Emily's dorm.

By the time we reach Emily's actual room, I'm sweating like a pig, and she's giggling like she's at the comedy club. I smile along with her... until I spot the packing boxes scattered around her room.

I shift on my feet to face her. "Did you get a new roommate?" I sound disappointed. Rightfully so. It will be hard seeking privacy if she's been assigned a new roomie.

Emily smiles before shaking her head, but her mouth remains tightlipped. That's very unlike her.

"Are you moving?"

Her smile increases before she nods.

"Where to?"

She sighs. In my worked-up state, I can't tell if it's a good or bad sigh.

I'm really fucking hoping it's a good one when she murmurs, "I was hoping I could move in with you. If you'll have me."

I wiggle my ear, confident my hearing is still damaged from the screams we endured while racing through her college grounds like Peter Rabbit running away from the farmer hoping to dock his tail.

Concern crosses her features the longer I delay in replying. I'm shocked, as confused as fuck about what's going on. Emily wants a career. She can't have that *and* come on tour with me. It's not possible, is it?

"What about your studies?"

She smiles an uneasy grin, grateful I've finally replied, but put off that it isn't the response she was hoping for. "I requested to study via correspondence. I applied last week. The Dean called today saying it's been approved."

"Are you serious!? We can have the best of both worlds?"

When she nods, I band my arms around her petite waist to spin her around the room. "Fuck yes, Emily, you can move in with me! This is everything I've ever wanted."

She squeals with laughter mere seconds before her giggles switch to pleas. "Oh god, please stop. I'm going to be sick."

Usually, she pretends to be green at the gills. Today, she looks green at the gills. If I don't stop twirling her, she'll smear my preppy boy shoes with vomit.

"Sorry." I tug her into my chest before dropping my eyes. She still looks a little unwell, but not enough to make me pull back. "Are you sure this is what you want? It's a little crazy on the road—"

She ends my interrogation by giving me a scorching hot kiss.

Once she has me as dizzy as she feels, she pulls back. "It's everything I've ever wanted." She sucks my lower lip into her mouth before releasing it with a pop. "*You're* everything I've ever wanted."

She drags me onto her bed to show me exactly how much.

<hr />

Later that night, we sit on the floor in Emily's room, eating the pizza her ex-roomie bought for us. Crystal heard from numerous reliable sources that Noah Taylor was camped in one of the dorms, so she knew we'd face issues if we left to get something to eat. Although no one will ever replace Jenni and Nicole in Emily's life, I'm glad she's found a good friend in Crystal.

While taking a bite of the greasy pizza, I peer over at Emily. She's wearing the shirt I removed earlier. Her hair is a tangled mess, and her cheeks are still flushed from our activities before Crystal arrived. She's so incredibly beautiful, it takes everything I have to let her eat. She needs her energy—even more so after the news she gave me earlier today.

I still can't believe she's coming on the road with me. I'm as happy as fuck.

I stop grinning like a lunatic when Emily's singsong voice trickles into my ears. "Do you want kids, Noah?" She folds her legs under her bottom before screwing up her little nose. "We've never talked about it before, so I'm a little unsure of your thoughts."

Her nose crinkles more when I run my index finger down it. "Yes. I can't wait for us to have kids... The instant you give me the nod of approval, I'll be more than happy to have you barefoot and pregnant."

She laughs. "Such a caveman."

I gnaw at my pizza as if I'm exactly that.

After swallowing down the big chunk, I ask, "What about you? Are you ready for dirty diapers and a screaming boobie monster?"

She smiles in a way that takes my breath away before nodding. She looks so happy I can't help but ravish her delicious mouth. She melts into my embrace, as gooey as the cheese I taste on her lips.

When I pull back, I peer into her dazzling eyes. "I love you."

I've spoken those exact three words over a million times already, but I'll say them a trillion times if it gets across how much she truly means to me.

"I love you too," she replies in a husky whisper before standing to her feet.

When she yanks me from the floor with a tug on my arm, I realize she's going to use more than words to express how much I mean to her.

How lucky am I?

The next morning, with Emily sleeping peacefully, I call a taxi to take me to the airport. She offered to drive me, but I don't want to wake her. Instead, I leave her a note before tiptoeing out of her room.

The regret I usually feel when I leave her isn't as strong today, because in a matter of days, she'll be joining me on the road. She has everything worked out, meaning she'll be standing in the wings of the stage during my very first concert.

I'm fucking ecstatic.

As I exit LAX, my phone buzzes with a text message. In all honesty, I don't remember much of my flight. I've trekked across the country more times than I can count the past twelve months, so one trip must be hazing into another.

Spotting that I have a voicemail, I hit play before pushing my phone to my ear. A grin tugs at my lips when Emily's voice comes down the line. "I'm so sorry I didn't take you to the airport. Someone wore me out..." She giggles before continuing. "I love you, baby; I'll see you real soon."

It's just past midday, so I dial Emily's number. She should be at lunch, but it rings out on repeat. After my fourth redial, I leave a message. "Hey, Beautiful, I just got your message. I landed safely." While raking my fingers through my damp hair, I chuckle. "I'm heading to the studio to lay down some tracks, so I'll call you tonight. I love you."

After sliding my phone into my jeans pocket, I dart through the double glass doors, prepared to outrun the paparazzi who follow my every move. My brisk pace slows when I realize they're not waiting for me like they usually are. I guess they were as surprised about my impromptu trip as Emily was yesterday.

When I jump into the back of a taxi, I give the driver the address for the studio Rise Up has been working out of the past few months. His green eyes reflecting at me in the rearview mirror are familiar, but I can't pinpoint where I've seen them before.

I'm still working through my confusion when he drops me off at the studio. I'm not the only one having a slow start today. The usually bustling space is quieter than a ghost town. I don't mind. It gives me a chance to get down the lyrics that have been playing on repeat in my head since last night. It's a ballad I want to perform for Emily after we wed. "Surrender Me" is our song, but it's been shared with millions of people. This new masterpiece will be solely for Emily. It will never be released to the public.

I've been working in the studio for a few hours when a commotion outside its soundproof doors gains my attention. Someone is shouting, but I can't understand anything they're saying. After setting down the guitar Emily bought me for my birthday, I head for the door. All musicians have creative arguments, but this seems like more than that.

My already high heart rate kicks up another notch when I spot Ryan on the other side of the door. He's a detective in Ravenshoe, so what the fuck is he doing in LA?

When he cranks his neck my way, I wave for him to join me in the studio. He does, albeit hesitantly.

"What are you doing here?"

I slap his shoulder two times before pulling him in for a man hug. I feel like I haven't seen him in ages. The last time would have been around the time he helped me escape conviction when I beat the man who drugged Emily.

Ryan returns my hug but seems stiff and robotic.

After wiping the suspicious gleam from my eyes, I take a step back. "What's up?"

Fear clutches my throat when our eyes lock and hold. His eyes are brimming with tears, and his face is gaunt and horrified. I haven't seen him cry in the eight years I've known him. He didn't even cry when he informed me Chris had committed suicide.

The veins in my neck thrum, panicked at what has him nearly sobbing. "Did something happen to Lola?"

My first thoughts go to Jacob. If Callum has hurt Lola again, I doubt I'll be able to stop Jacob from killing him this time.

As I bend down to grab my phone off the floor, I notice Ryan is shaking his head. "I'm sorry, Noah."

Unease settles in my gut as my lungs burn for air. I feel like I'm drowning, that I'm seconds from death. When Ryan steps closer to me with nurturing, sorrowed eyes, dread overwhelms me.

Oh god no. Please don't do this to me again. I can't go through this again.

"It's Emily..."

Rage floods my veins, blocking out what Ryan says next.

"No!" As pain shreds through my chest, I grab the chair next to me and throw it across the room. It shatters through the glass door, forcing Jacob and my bandmates to duck out of the way of flying shards of glass. "This can't be happening again; it can't be true. Not Emily—please."

I look Ryan straight in the eyes. If he wants to break my soul and shatter my heart, he can maintain eye contact while doing it. "Please, I'm begging you, please tell me Emily is okay."

The remorse in his eyes says more than his words ever will. "I'm sorry. She's gone."

"No! Not my beautiful Emily. I can't live without her! I won't live without her."

I pound my fists on Ryan's chest as I scream "no" on repeat. When he fails to flinch, I grab anything I can find and swing it against the tiled floor. I trash the studio, the pain tearing through me too much to bear. It hurts so much I feel like I'm being torn in half.

Emily can't be gone; I was watching her sleep only hours ago. She'll be with me in a few days. She's coming on the road with me. I'll finally have everything I've ever wanted. She can't be gone. I refuse to believe it.

As the room spins around me, all I can see is her beautiful face. She's calling out for me, begging for me to save her, yet here I stand, useless and fucking helpless.

When the dizziness becomes too much, I hit the wall with a thud before sliding down. I slap myself over the head on repeat, urging myself to step out of the haze and grasp reality. I need to wake up, to pull myself out of this nightmare.

I don't wake up. I remain on the ground, bleeding from the wounds my fists caused my head.

As I peer at my blood-stained hands, Ryan crouches down in front of me. His lips are moving, but I can't hear a word he's speaking. It's a blurry haze—nothing makes any sense. All I can hear is Emily's voice, and all I can see is her beautiful face.

That's what I want. Her in front of me. Safe. Protected. *Alive.*

Except she's not.

She's gone. Forever.

I don't know how long I stay huddled on the ground. It could be an hour, it might even be three, but once I lift my eyes, I'd give anything to take back what I'm seeing. There are shards of wood scattered across the floor matching the grain and varnish of the material used to make my guitar—the guitar Emily gifted me for my birthday...

No!

As I crawl to the splintered remains of my guitar, my heart breaks like glass. I broke the gift she worked so hard to buy me—*me.* I destroyed it.

With tears sliding down my cheeks, I vainly try to piece it back together. There are hundreds of tiny pieces, but my hazy mind refuses to give in. This is all I have left of her, so I can't give up. I have to fix the mistakes I made. I have to bring her back.

When my brain finally realizes that my guitar is broken beyond repair, I'm no longer capable of holding in my utter devastation. After gathering the splintered remains close to my decimated heart, I sob uncontrollably about the girl I surrendered my heart to only to have it destroyed as violently as I destroyed the gift she gave me.

CHAPTER 43

NOAH

I'm bitch-slapped from my sleeping state when freezing cold water drenches me head to toe. I attempt to barge past Jacob, but he stays standing solid like a brick wall, blocking my exit from the shower stall. I don't know why he's being such a prick, but I do know one thing: I'm not fucking happy about it. I'd throw a punch at him, but I'm so weak, I can barely lift my arm.

"You need to sober up."

When I glance into Jacob's eyes, the remorse settled behind them has memories crashing back into me hard and fast.

My beautiful Emily is gone.

As despair overwhelms me, I fall to my knees with a howl. All I can see is her beautiful face. That's why I've been drinking so excessively. I want to forget. The pain is too much. I'm not strong enough to survive this.

I hide my tear-stained face under the now warm water since Jacob turned the faucet to hot. The effort to hide my devastation triples when memories I keep buried with alcohol resurface. The last words we spoke. Our final kiss. They all filter through my mind until they're torn from my grasp by the realization that I'll never experience any of those things with her ever again.

She's gone. Never to be returned. And I'm once again alone.

The sobs hammering me lessen when Jacob sits on the ground outside the shower stall. He braces his back against the soap scum-coated wall before his eyes stray to me. He watches me intently, reminding me that I'm not alone, even though I've never felt more isolated.

"Do you want some water?" he asks a short time later.

Unable to speak, I shake my head. My head is pounding, but it has nothing on the pain in the area where my heart once pumped.

"Why Emily, Jake?" My voice wavers when it cracks. "Why did they take her? Why couldn't they have taken me instead?"

"I don't know." Jacob stands to his feet to fill a glass of water. After removing a bottle of Advil from the cabinet, he spins around to face me. "This will help your head."

He hands me the glass of water and three white tablets. I don't want to take anything, but the pleading look he's giving me has me swallowing them without protest.

When I stand from my crouched position, I sway like a leaf on a windy day. I'm not surprised. I shouldn't be able to stand after how much I drank last night.

As I yank my soaked jeans down my thighs, Jacob exits the bathroom. He's not giving me privacy. He just wants it to appear that way. He's been my shadow since Ryan told me what happened to Emily. He knows I can't be trusted, and in some ways, he's right.

After dumping my jeans outside the shower stall, I dry myself with a towel before stumbling to the bathroom cabinet. My brows stitch when I soak in the hollow man reflecting back at me. I barely recognize myself. Dark rings are circling my eyes, and thick stubble covers my chin. My face is gaunter than usual, and my pasty skin seems dull compared to my black, soulless eyes.

"Do you remember where we're going today?"

My eyes drift in the direction the voice came from. Jacob has his shoulder propped on the bathroom doorjamb, his eyes revealing his wariness. He's worried about how I'll react to his question. It's been four days since Emily left, and although I haven't stopped drinking, I know today is the day she's laid to rest.

Incapable of speaking, I nod before returning my eyes to the vanity mirror. Anger brews in my gut when I scrub my hand over the wiry hair on my jaw. I look repulsive. Thank god Emily never saw me like this, or she would have realized years sooner that she deserved someone better than me, and our time together would have been even shorter.

Wanting to clean myself up for her, I remove a razor from the bathroom cabinet. I glance down at the blade when it sparkles in the bathroom light. It has the same gleam Emily's eyes held every time she smiled. I'm so captivated by it, I accidentally nick my thumb when I run it over its sharp edge.

When droplets of blood smear on the white porcelain sink, Jacob steps into the bathroom. "Noah..."

He knows me so well. At times, it's as if he can read my thoughts. I'd be lying if I said I hadn't considered suicide. That was my immediate thought when Ryan told me what had happened to my beautiful Emily...

With my heart as shattered as Emily's gift, Jacob took me back to my hotel. The instant we walk into the dated room, he pours me a generous helping of scotch in a plastic cup. I swallow the double shot in one hit, praying it will ease the pain tearing me in two.

It does nothing. Emily's beautiful face is still everywhere I look.

I go to the liquor cabinet for another shot.

It's closely followed by another.

And then another.

Once I've finished a fifth of scotch, I stagger into the bathroom to take a leak. In my drunken state, I can barely stand, let alone aim, so I not only piss all over the floor, I make a mess of myself as well.

While toeing off my boots so I can remove my soiled jeans, a flashback of Emily holds me hostage. It was of our final night together. We had just finished eating the pizza Crystal bought for us when Emily ushered us into the attached bathroom of her dorm room. She made out her ruse was inno-

cent by washing her hands in the vanity sink, but the look she was giving me was anything but innocent.

With a wink as playful as the gleam in her eyes, she switched off the faucet then spun around to face me, raking her eyes down my half-dressed frame as her teeth got friendly with her lower lip. Even with her long locks tousled from our earlier antics, she was incredibly seductive, and for once, she knew it. Her confidence was the highest I'd ever seen.

Incapable of holding back for a second longer, I entered the bathroom. Her room was incredibly small, but I made my steps half their natural stride to add to the tension brimming in the air. Once I stopped to stand in front of her, I curled my hand around her nape and pulled her delicate lips to mine. The throaty moan she released when our tongues danced in perfect rhythm had my cock bulging through the slit in my boxers.

When Emily stood back, her eyes dropped to the only article of clothing I was wearing. She licked her lips as she unclipped the button stopping my erection from bouncing out of my boxer shorts. Once my cock was freed, she returned her eyes to mine, where they stayed as she placed butterfly kisses down my chest and over my abdomen before lowering herself to her knees so her tongue could trace the V muscle peeking out of my shorts.

I shuddered when her tongue skimmed across my engorged knob. She lapped up the beaded drop at the end before lowering her lips down my shaft. Unlike the slow, steady pace we used the week before, she sucked me hard and fast, bringing me to ecstasy in a shameful amount of time.

Thankfully, with youth on my side, that wasn't the end of our exchange.

After hoisting Emily from the ground, I spun her around. She clutched the vanity in a white-knuckled hold when I notched in my still rock-hard cock at a speed faster than we usually go. I fucked her from behind, loving that I could watch every expression crossing her face in the vanity mirror. There was nothing more beautiful in the world than Emily's face in the midst of an orgasm.

When my memory fades, I glance into the mirror in the hotel bathroom. I don't recognize the man staring back at me. All I see is a worthless shell of a man who is selfish and always puts himself first. Resentment overwhelms me when I realize how I wasted my last months with Emily. If I weren't so self-centered, all of this could have been avoided.

I swing hard at the pathetic man standing in front of me, my fists making quick work of the vanity mirror. It shatters into a million pieces, spraying the sink and my feet with dangerous shards of glass.

While gripping the vanity to stay upright, I gulp in some ragged breaths. Unease spreads through me when my eyes lock in on a fragment of glass resting to the right of my hand. I want the pain to stop. I want to be free of the burden, so with my head in lockdown, I gather the glass into my hand and hold it tightly.

It digs into my palm, sending droplets of blood rolling down the cracked sink. I hear Jacob banging on the door. He's hitting it so fiercely, he's seconds from breaking it down, so I dig the glass into my wrist. I want to be with Emily. My life isn't worth living if I have to live without her.

Just as the glass pierces my skin, Jacob barges into the bathroom, splintering the doorframe. He tackles me as he did years ago on the football field, dislodging the glass from my hand in the process. We hit the floor with a sickening thud, the air in my lungs forced out with a brutal grunt.

"Let me fuckin' go!"

I fight to get away from him, but Jacob is a huge fucker, so no matter how hard I fight, his hold never weakens.

"No, Noah!"

Acting as if I am as light as a feather, he drags me out of the bathroom to throw me onto the hotel bed, which he frantically paces in front of with his fists clenched as tightly as his jaw.

Even with his anger at a level I've never seen, I can't stop. I don't want to live my miserable life anymore. "Why won't you just let me go? I can't do this anymore—"

"Because you're my brother, Noah!" Jacob roars as his sorrow-filled eyes dart to mine. "You can't leave me because I won't fucking let you."

"I have nothing left to live for. They're all gone."

The pit in my chest enlarges with each word I speak. The pain of losing everyone I've ever loved is crippling me.

"What about me?!" Jacob pounds his thrusting chest. "What about fucking me?! You're my brother, Noah. You hate that Chris left you, yet now you want to do the same thing to me. I won't fucking let you leave me like he left you; I won't fucking let you!"

Chris's death is the reason I wrote 'Hollow.' When people commit suicide, they don't consider the loved ones they leave behind, what they trudge through: the hurt, the anger, and the years spent wondering if there was something they could have done so they would have stayed—so they would have lived.

"You have to fight, Noah; you have to fight to live. Emily would want you to live." He kneels on the ground next to me to clutch my hand in his. "Promise me you'll fight. Promise me, and I'll promise that you won't go through this alone. I'll be there for you every day. I'll fight alongside you. You will survive this, Noah. It'll never stop hurting, but you will survive this."

Jacob has always been there for me, just as I have for him, but what he is asking is too much. I want to deny his request. I want to finish what I started. Instead, I stare into the eyes of a friend who's always been more like a brother to me while murmuring, "I'll try."

Now, four days later, he still watches over me as haunted memories race suicidal thoughts to the forefront of my mind.

CHAPTER 44

NOAH

"You're not going through this alone, Noah." Jacob removes the razor from my hand before placing it on the edge of the blood-smeared sink.

"I know."

Jacob and the boys from the band will always support me, but nothing can soothe my devastation. For the past four days, I've reverted back to the coping mechanism I used when my brothers died. I appear to be functioning, but I don't live—because I'm dead on the inside. My emotions are so out of whack, my moods can swing from depressing lows to scorching anger within minutes. Emily could subdue the demons raging inside me, but now that she's gone, I'm left to battle them on my own once more.

After a cautious glance warning he is always watching, Jacob exits the bathroom. "We leave for the church in thirty minutes."

He leaves my bedroom door hanging wide open because my saying I would try isn't the same thing as promising. I never make a promise I can't keep. That's why I never promised to fight.

Today isn't about me, though. It's about Emily. I don't know any of the details of her funeral. I was kept out of the planning. I'm okay with that as long as they have white lilies on her coffin as requested.

They are her favorite flowers. She told me how much she loved them after they were included in the floral arrangement I ordered for her eighteenth birthday. They were also the flowers scenting the air in the hotel room the first time we made love.

She told me she loved me that night. I didn't think anything could top her beautiful smile when she noticed the candles I had lit for her, but those three little words made a quick liar out of me.

Desperate to hear them again, I snag my cell phone off my bedside table and log into my voicemail. My hands shake when her singsong voice comes down the line, "Hey, baby, I'm so sorry I didn't get to take you to the airport this morning. Someone must have worn me out last night. I love you, Noah. I'll see you real soon."

I listen to her message three more times before shutting down my phone. I miss her voice and her laugh every second of every day. I swear when I sit really still, I can sense her near me. Her vanilla scent, the smell of her recently shampooed hair. Everything around me has absorbed her scent, making it seem as if she is here with me, even though she isn't.

My eyes lift from my hands when someone darts past my bedroom door. Jacob must be checking on me since I've been unattended for five minutes. He doesn't leave my side for long.

As my eyes stray back to my phone, I spot a suit bag hanging on the front of my closet. It's black and looks flashy. After staggering to the bag, I lower the zipper, my breath hitching when my eyes roam over a black suit with dark gray pinstripes. There's a matching dark gray dress shirt underneath and a swanky tie.

I don't recall much of the past four days, and have no clue how I arrived back in Ravenshoe, so I assume the suit is from Jacob for me to wear today. I may be a selfish, heartless man, but even I know you don't wear jeans and a leather jacket to the funeral of your fiancée.

Once I put on the suit, I shift on my feet to face the only mirror in my room. The heaviness on my chest grows when I stare at my reflection. This isn't an outfit anyone should wear to a funeral. It's more suitable for a man standing at the end of an aisle, waiting for the love of his life to walk toward him.

I can imagine how beautiful Emily would have looked. She would have hated the fanfare, but I would have forced her to relish it. She loved things understated because she was anything but. I was all about the hoopla, and look where it got me.

Pretending anger isn't overtaking my heartache, I slip my feet into the black dress shoes I found next to my bedroom door. Now I'm ready to go, except instead of attending the wedding I've dreamt about since the week I started dating a shy, wholesome girl with the face of an angel, I'm going to my beautiful fiancée's funeral.

When I round the corner separating the living areas from the bedrooms, I spot Marcus and Slater at the dining room table. Marcus notices me first and fumbles out of his chair before bridging the gap between us.

"Noah," is all he whispers. When he pulls back from our embrace, his green eyes reveal the words he can't speak. He's sorry for my loss and will be here for me no matter what.

Slater replaces Marcus's arms with his own. "I'm so sorry." His rumbling baritone breaks through the haze surrounding me. "But you'll pull through this."

He tugs me tighter before giving my head a noogie. These men are my brothers before anything else. They've been there for me through thick and think. Marcus dragged me away from Michael's wreckage when the ambulance arrived, and his grandmother drove me to the hospital so I wouldn't have to travel in the ambulance with Michael's body. They've been at my side for every unfortunate event that's happened in my life, but even they won't be able to pull me out of this. I'll never recover from losing Emily.

My eyes float up from my shoes when Jacob enters the dining room from the kitchen. He stops dead in his tracks when he sees what I'm wearing. I understand his shock. I was just as stunned when I noticed Slater is also wearing a suit. I shouldn't be surprised. No one could meet Emily without falling in love with her. Even someone as rough and rugged as Slater was no match for her affections.

After gathering his keys and wallet, Jacob spins around to face me. "Ready?"

I nod, even though no one will ever be prepared to say goodbye to someone they love.

We drive to the funeral service in Marcus's car. I keep my eyes planted on the scenery outside, watching puffy white clouds form in the blue sky. They have me wondering what heaven is like. It would have to be beautiful since Emily is there.

Once we arrive at the church, my second coping mechanism kicks in. I block everything out: the attendees patting my shoulder as I weave through them, the flowers lining the aisle, and the hum of churchgoers offering their condolences. None of it matters. My focus is on one thing and one thing only: the white casket at the end of the aisle.

Emily's coffin has the lilies I requested surrounding a photo of her in a large white frame. I recognize the picture; it's one Jenni took of us at Bronte's Peak. We're gazing into each other's eyes and smiling. She looks so happy. She was back then because it was before I let my dreams take me away from her—before I fucked up in a way I can never fix.

I find it hard to tear my gaze away from her picture. That beautiful, smiling, happy Emily can't be the same person lying in that coffin. How can a bright, hopeful future get squashed without any warning? Why take someone like Emily when there are millions of monsters in the world every day? Murderers, rapists, and pedophiles breathe every fucking day, but Emily's life gets ended way too early. How is that fair?

Tears burn my eyes when I recognize the song playing faintly in the background. It's about being in the arms of an angel. I wish I could wrap my arms around Emily, who is now an angel in heaven.

I don't know how much time passes before Jacob's large frame blocks my view of Emily's photo. I was too busy staring at her beautiful face to keep track of the time. It feels like we've been at the church for around an hour, but don't quote me on it.

"Do you still want to be a pallbearer?"

Nodding, I wipe my sweat-drenched hands down my trousers before standing. I'm shocked my heart can drum against my ribcage as wildly as it does when I take my spot at the front righthand side of Emily's casket. I thought it was too broken to respond to the pain roaring through it.

When Emily's brothers, Dominic and Aiden, lift Emily's casket in unison with Jacob and me, I recall how petite Emily was. Her coffin is as light as a feather.

As we walk out of the church packed to the brim with people wanting to say their final goodbyes to my beautiful Emily, I spot numerous familiar faces. Emily's mom, Patrice, and her dad, Mitchell, are in the row I just left. Lola is huddled close to her mother's side with tears streaming down her face and a ghost-white appearance. Jenni, Nick, and Nicole are in the pew behind them, and Slater and Marcus flank Maggie. All their eyes are rimmed with red circles, and many of the girls have tears cascading down their cheeks.

Once we exit the church's double doors, camera lights hinder my vision. I grit my teeth, annoyed by the paparazzi's intrusion. The police barrier is keeping them at a reasonable distance, but can't the vultures give me one day of peace so I can bury my fiancée?

My lips quiver when we take the final steps between the church and the waiting hearse, then moisture fills my eyes when we place Emily's casket inside so she can be taken to her final resting place at the Erkinsvale Lawn Cemetery.

After pressing my lips to her casket, I step back so the funeral director can close the hearse's door. My hand shakes when I flatten my palm on the cold glass window. "I love you, Beautiful."

As I divert my gaze away from her coffin in an effort to hold in my tears, my eyes lock onto a figure leaning against an old oak tree next to the church. I adjust my vision, confident the person I'm seeing is a figment of my imagination.

It's been years since I've seen him, but I'm certain I recognize the face staring back at me. His hair now has more strands of gray in it, and his face is more wrinkled, but there's no denying the dark, soulless eyes staring back at me.

They belong to my dad.

CHAPTER 45

NOAH

$\mathcal{M}$y dad spans the distance between us, his steps shaky and unsure. "It's good to see you, son."

Emily's graveside service at Erkinsvale Lawn Cemetery has just finished, so we're preparing to go to her parents' house for the wake. When I learned my dad had followed us to the cemetery, I asked Jacob to give me a minute. Today isn't about me, but I'm too curious about my dad's sudden arrival and can't harness my curiosity for a second longer.

With my hands stuffed in my pocket, I scan my dad's face. He looks as he did the day of his sentencing, but his eyes are darker than I remember. He has my wild hair and broad shoulders, but he's a couple of inches shorter than me.

I'm taken aback when he unexpectedly bands his arms around my shoulders. "I'm so sorry, son—"

"How are you here?" I ask groggily, still stunned by his arrival. *How does he even know about Emily, let alone that her funeral was today?*

My dad draws back before raising his soulless eyes to mine. Glancing into his makes it seem as if I'm looking into a mirror. The same shattered soul stares back at me. He has lost everyone important to him as well; there's just one difference: his losses were a result of

284

his recklessness. Mine weren't. I'd give anything to have Emily still here with me now.

"I was granted parole earlier this week..." My dad's words trail off when he detects the same snooping watch as me. Jacob is standing at our right, eyeballing our exchange with the focus of a hawk.

"Jacob."

Realizing he's been busted, Jacob spans the distance between us to return my dad's greeting. "Trevor."

After they shake hands, Jacob asks, "Are you ready to go? Emily's parents are waiting."

I jerk up my chin before returning my eyes to my dad to give him a wordless sendoff. If he thinks I appreciate him turning up uninvited like this, he's wrong. Today is not the day for us to hash things out. Tomorrow isn't either.

I honestly don't know if I'll ever be ready.

<hr>

Although I appreciate that Emily's family is holding her wake in a private location, far from the public eye, entering their home without Emily is more painful than I ever imagined. Her presence is felt in every room. Her photos adorn the walls; her vanilla scent is embedded in the furniture, and even strands of her straight, dark locks are knotted in a brush on the mantel.

Needing something to take the edge off, I head for the caterers serving attendees in the kitchen. When a pimple-faced teen hands me a glass of whiskey with a teeny drop in the bottom, I snatch the almost full bottle out of his hand, unscrew the lid, then swallow numerous mouth-filling gulps. My throat sets on fire, but the burn settles the wave sloshing in my stomach.

Clutching a half-empty bottle in my hand, I stumble into the living room. Well, I think it's the living room. My head is so woozy, I'm having a hard time recognizing anything. I flop onto a hideous floral sofa so I can gather my bearings. It's the same ugly couch Lola and Jacob were making out on over two years ago.

Over the rim of the bottle I'm guzzling, I notice Emily's best friend Jenni entering the room. Her cheeks are wet, her eyes, red. Fresh tears mark new stains when she spots me looking at her.

After a quiet word with Nick, she hesitantly paces toward me. She doesn't offer me the same consolatory words everyone else has been giving me today; she just slumps into the chair next to me before resting her head on my shoulder.

Her breaths flutter against my neck when she murmurs a short time later, "She'd want you to fight, Noah. You can't give up. You have to fight for her." Her tears dampen my dress shirt when they dribble down her cheek. "If you truly love her, you'll live *for* her."

She steals my chance to reply by snatching the whiskey out of my hand and strolling into the kitchen. She empties the rest into the sink before dumping the bottle into the bin underneath. She wants me to heed her advice, but she doesn't understand how much this hurts. I couldn't have loved Emily any more if I tried. She was the love of my life, so how can I be expected to live without her?

I receive the answer I'm seeking when I hear a baby crying in the distance. Jasper is nestled against his daddy's chest, his fist shoved in his mouth as he sucks frantically, announcing to the world that he's hungry.

I'm sure his stomach is gurgling as severely as mine is as it struggles to keep down the liquid I guzzled too quickly. I swallow numerous times in a row, hoping it will keep my stomach contents inside, but when its churning ramps up, I race for the bathroom. Since I haven't eaten the past four days, the only thing expelled is alcohol.

After swishing some water around my mouth and throwing some over my face, I exit the bathroom. Memories of the first time I met Emily filter into my mind when I glide down the hallway, stopping to admire the picture she busted me laughing at that night. Emily later told me she was ten years old in this portrait. She had already lived half her life when it was taken.

That's fucked. She didn't deserve to die any more than Michael did.

While clenching and unclenching my fists, I peer into Emily's childhood bedroom, which looks the same. Her pink floral bedspread is perfectly in place on her white cast iron bed, and her bedside table still holds the vanilla oil responsible for her sweet scent. It's as if she never left.

With my heart beating in an unnatural rhythm, I proceed into her room. I asked Emily to be my wife in here. She thought I only proposed because she found her ring in my wallet, but that wasn't true. I knew after our first month of dating that she'd be my wife one day, but since I wanted her to have a nicer ring than what I could afford, I waited.

What I wouldn't give to go back and fix the mistakes I made. If we had followed through with our original plans, we would have been married by now. Instead, Emily will be forever remembered as Emily McIntosh instead of her rightful title of Emily Taylor.

Strangers often argued that we were too young to get married, but those closest to us understood that age doesn't matter when you're marrying someone you're destined to be with. We loved each other with everything we had, so why should we wait years just to follow the norm?

After swirling Emily's bottle of perfume enough to leave her fragrance in the air, I exit her room. I'm so glad I didn't wait to crack the seal until I got home, or we may have never met.

"It's the last door on the left," I recall Lola stating when I asked her if I could use the bathroom before heading out.

"On the left," I repeat to myself. *The left.*

My heart freezes as my eyes flick between the bathroom door and Emily's room. Emily's bedroom is on the left; the bathroom is on the right. But Lola said it was on the left...

My bewilderment tapers off when the truth smacks into me.

That fucking bitch!

I storm out of the hallway, my legs moving surprisingly fast considering how much I was stumbling earlier. "Lola!" Numerous people stop what they're doing to stare at me, but none of them have the light brown eyes I'm seeking. "Lola!"

I move through Emily's house, seeking her older sister in a sea of hundreds. I spot Lola a few seconds later in the backyard, talking to friends. Jacob bolts for her when he sees the fury on my face, but I beat him to her.

"You said the door on the left."

Lola's eyes widen in fear when I fling her around to face me. The tears streaming down her face dampen some of the fury burning me alive, but they don't completely erase it.

"You said the door on the left," I repeat as my watering eyes dance between hers.

When she nods, my teeth grit. "Why would you do that?" My voice cracks with emotion as my grip on her arm tightens. "Why would you do that to your own sister? If she had never met me, she'd still be here!"

Before she can answer, Jacob appears at her side. "Noah, let her go."

I release Lola from my grip before my burning gaze drifts to Jacob. "Did you know? Did you know she sent me straight to Emily's fucking room?!" I point to Lola during the "she" part of my question.

Jacob steps closer to me while tugging Lola behind him. "Yes. I knew."

His urge to protect Lola surprises me more than his words. I'd never put my hands on a woman. Him, though, he might not come out of this unscathed. He kept things from me. Vital things. Things that could have saved Emily.

"Why, Jake? If we had never met, she'd still be here, but no, you had to force her into my fucked-up life, and now she's gone..."

My words trail off when someone places their hand on my shoulder, encouraging me to calm down. It has the opposite effect. I'm too angry to settle down. All of this could have been avoided if people just left me the fuck alone. They knew Emily wasn't a girl you'd forget meeting. She imprinted herself on everyone she met; you couldn't help but fall in love with her, but that wasn't their choice. They shouldn't have fiddled with fate—then she would still be here.

Asphyxiated with bitter anger, I grab the scruff of Jacob's shirt and drag him to within an inch of my face. More emotions than I've ever handled slam into me at once. Regret, sorrow, heartache, anger. They all have my fist rising to the occasion without a negative thought crossing my mind.

I'm seconds from dispelling some of my anger on Jacob's face when Lola's faint voice stops me. "What would you rather have? Two years with Emily, or none at all?" She places herself between Jacob and me, reminding me that her eyes aren't the only thing identical to her sister's. She's just as strong. "Because Emily would have picked to have two years with you than to have never met you."

I stare into her eyes, seeing nothing but Emily's reflecting back at me. They give me the same pleading look they did any time my anger got the better of me. They soothe me as only she can, except they're not really soothing me at all. They're tearing my heart straight out of my chest, because as much as I wish it were true, Lola's eyes aren't Emily's. They're similar, yet unique, because nothing could ever replicate the love Emily's eyes held when she looked at me.

That look is gone now. Forever. Never to be replaced.

As I take a step back, a sob tears at my throat, begging to be released. I shut it down. This is more than I can handle, but I'm done looking like a fool.

After shrugging off the person holding my shoulder, I storm through Emily's house until I reach the front yard. Jacob yells for me to stop, but I can't see sense through the madness surrounding me. It's too much—it *hurts* too much. I need to go home, back to the one place I've always felt at peace.

I need to be with Emily.

Upon spotting Nick's truck at the end of the driveway, I run over and jump into the cab. I search for the spare key he always keeps. I throw open the glove compartment, heave down the visor, then check under the seat before finally locating his key in the sunglasses compartment beneath his rearview mirror.

Nick's black beast fires to life on the first turn of the ignition. It's more alive than I've felt the past four days. When I rev the engine, Jacob yells for me to wait, but I pretend I can't hear him. He doesn't take my ignorance in stride. He bolts for Nick's truck, his speed remarkably quick for someone his size. He gets within an inch of Nick's bed when I flatten the gas pedal. I'm so busy watching his large frame shrink in the rearview mirror, I almost collide into a shadowed figure standing at the end of the driveway.

Dust kicks up around me when I lock up the truck's brakes. I skid along the loose gravel for several terrifying seconds before jolting to a stop, narrowly missing the person I was trying to avoid.

My nostrils flare when I realize I shouldn't have bothered. His life is as worthless as mine. "Move!"

Instead of moving, my dad plants his feet before folding his arms in front of his chest. If it were any other day but today, I would have appreciated his determination. That's not happening this week.

With the roar of a deranged man, I throw open the truck's door before jumping down from the cab. Anger surges past my heartache as I storm toward my dad. His sorrowful eyes follow my every move, but he doesn't object to my pathetic display of remorse.

"Get out of the way, or I'll move you out of my way. I'm not the little kid you left behind anymore."

"No, Noah," he answers, not the least bit concerned about the fury in my tone.

He doesn't even flinch when I raise my arm to take a swing at him. He won't shelter himself from the abuse he's suspects I've dealt with the past eight years. He knows all too well about the witch he left me with, what I suffered because of it—because he was once married to *her*.

Just before my fist connects with my dad's jaw, I'm walloped from the side. We hit the ground so forcefully, my lungs fight for air as violently as Jacob struggles to pin me to the ground with his weight.

"Stop, Noah! Please stop."

He tackled me so hard, he's knocked me back the twelve or so feet I stormed to confront my dad. Although impressed by his stamina, nothing stops my onslaught. I scream at him to get off me while throwing fists into his body on repeat, but no matter how hard I fight, our difference in size will always have me at a disadvantage.

"I'll let you go once you calm down."

He keeps his word when I give up a few minutes later. I'm exhausted, sweating like a pig, and on the verge of crying instead of fighting.

Under Jacob's watchful eye, I scamper across the gravel to brace my back on Nick's truck. My heart is beating fitfully, and my eyes are brimming with moisture, but I give it everything I have to keep my tears at bay. It's only been four days, but I'm already sick of feeling weak.

When Jacob plants his backside next to mine, my watering eyes stray to anything but him. I'm not angry at him; I just don't want him to see my tears—again.

He mistakes my request for privacy as anger. "You can hate me all you want, but I'm not giving up on you." He throws his arm around my shoulder and pulls me into his body as only he can. "You aren't the only one grieving, Noah. I'm lost; they're lost. We're all struggling."

When he nudges his chin to the door I stormed out of nearly twenty minutes ago, remorse clutches my heart. Patrice, Lola, and Jenni are standing on the front porch staring at me with worry lining their usually smooth faces.

I feel terrible that I've created more pain for Patrice. She nurtured me more the past two years than my mother did my entire life. She accepted me into her family as if I were her son, and when Emily was roofied, she thanked me for defending her daughter.

I would have thought busting me ravishing her daughter's mouth the following morning would have changed her opinion of me. I was wrong. Instead of being angry about what she'd walked in on, she told me I was the best thing that had ever happened to Emily, and that she would be incredibly proud to call me her son-in-law one day.

I was shocked. Excluding Emily and Jacob, I had never made anyone proud before. I honestly didn't know how to reply. I was left speechless. But in true mothering style, Patrice kept her word. I was included in every family event since that day and was treated with the same respect as her other four children.

As memories hold my emotions hostage, I slump down low against Nick's truck before cradling my head in my hands. It's the battle of my life to keep my emotions in check, but I give it my best shot. If I don't start getting a grip of reality, Jacob will continue nagging me about going to see a shrink.

I hate talking about my feelings. Talking won't change anything. It won't make things better, and it won't bring Emily back, so why bother? One day, I'll climb out of the bottomless pit I'm sitting in. It won't be today; it certainly won't be tomorrow, but I'm sure it will arrive eventually.

When gravel crunches underfoot, I raise my eyes, taking in polished black shoes, stocking-covered legs, a modest black dress, and the tear-filled eyes of Emily's mom on the way. Patrice has the same dark hair as Emily, but she has Lola's beige skin. She gave them both their turned-up noses, but her eyes are hazel—and reflect her pain.

"I'm sorry," I choke out via a sob. "I'm sorry for pulling your daughter into my miserable life by falling in love with her. I'm sorry for not being there to protect her this time. And I'm sorry you lost your baby girl."

After lowering my head to my knees, I cry over everything I'm sorry for. It's a long and painful twenty minutes spent wrapped up in Patrice's arms as she tells me repeatedly that I have nothing to be sorry for.

"Isn't it better to have loved for only a minute than not to have loved at all?"

CHAPTER 46

NOAH

The next morning, I wake up lying flat on my stomach, drooling on my pillow. When I lift my head, I have to shelter my eyes from the blinding light streaming through my curtains. It's so bright, I feel like I'm at heaven's gates, waiting for them to open.

My brow cocks when I peer at the alarm clock on my bedside table. It's 1:53 in the afternoon. Confusion engulfs me. Today is the first day Jacob hasn't thrown my drunk ass into the shower to sober me up.

Did I drink last night?

After my brain struggles to sort through the facts, I study my body for clues. My head is thumping, and I feel like I've swallowed a dozen razor blades, but other than that, I feel relatively normal.

Hope overtakes my confusion when I scamper up my bed.

Was it all a dream?

Is Emily still here?

After scrubbing the sleep from my eyes, they drift over my room. Excluding the odd sterile smell, it looks like it did before Emily left. My bed is in the same spot, my drawers still covered with random musical knickknacks Emily collected over the years. It's only after stumbling upon a crumpled suit in the corner does my hope vanish into thin air.

My beautiful Emily is still gone.

I sit for a few moments, reflecting on everything that has happened. When that fails to settle the unease in my gut, I throw on a pair of jeans and a shirt, then head out of my room in search for Jacob. He hasn't left my side the past five days, so I'm somewhat concerned about what changed his routine today.

When I reach the end of the hallway, I overhear part of a conversation.

"Not in a million years would anyone expect him to do that." I recognize the deep twang. It belongs to Marcus.

"It was written in the contract," retaliates another male voice, which may belong to Cormack. "We can't just ignore it."

When I round the corner, my eyes stumble upon Nick, Marcus, Slater, and Cormack conducting a meeting on Jacob's dining room table. Marcus is glaring at Cormack like he's on his hit list. Cormack is unaware of his fury; he's too busy scrutinizing a document in front of him to pay him any attention, and Slater and Nick are watching the charade unfold with slanted heads and folded arms. That's not unusual; when they're not creating tension, they're spectators.

Slater is the first one to jump back into the ring when the tension between Marcus and Cormack grows too great to ignore. "Enough semantics. Can you get us out of it?"

When Marcus swivels his torso to face Slater, he spots my stalking stance. He ribs Cormack with his elbow before jerking his head my way. In less than a second, all eyes in the room are on me. Usually, that wouldn't bother me, but today is different. Their panicked expressions have my nerves sitting on the edge of a very steep cliff.

They're heard in my voice when I ask, "What do they want you to get them out of?"

Glancing down, I discover the contract we signed to do a six-week tour with the O'Reilly Brothers is scattered across the table.

"It's nothing." Marcus gathers the loose papers in a stack. His neatness isn't surprising, but his inability to maintain eye contact is. That's not like him at all.

With my suspicions high, I flick my gaze to Slater. My curiosity piques even more when his eyes dart down to the table. He is as cocky as fuck, meaning he maintains eye contact even when he's lying. Although Nick has no issues keeping his eyes planted on mine, he's always been a little hard to read, so I still can't tell what they're discussing.

My bandmates might be skilled at keeping things from me, but I bet Cormack doesn't have the same set of talents. I walk around the table until I'm standing across from him. "What do they want you to get them out of?"

Cormack returns my stare for several heart-clutching seconds before shifting his eyes to Nick. From the corner of my eye, I watch Nick shake his head to Cormack's silent question. When Cormack's eyes float back to mine, I arch a brow, goading him to man up and make his own choices. He's a big boy. He doesn't need to run with the bullshit excuse the guys are giving.

Furthermore, if the boys' faces are anything to go by, this meeting is about the band. If it affects the band, it affects me, because I created it!

Just when I think Cormack will never answer me, he finally grows some balls. "You signed a contract agreeing to do a six-week tour with the O'Reilly Brothers."

"Yeah, then my fiancée died. That didn't just stop the tour; it upended my entire life." I flatten my palms on the table, prepared to launch over it if he says the tour is more important than Emily.

"It did, and that's why you need to let us handle this." Jacob enters the room from the kitchen. "You don't need to be a part of this—"

"A part of what? There is nothing to discuss. We can't do the tour; it's not that fucking hard to explain."

"It doesn't work that way—" Marcus's backhand stuffs more than Cormack's words into his throat. It comes with a heap of a spit, and a stern warning from Slater.

"Shut the fuck up, man." He adds to his threat by directing a stern finger point at him. Confident he has Cormack on a short leash, his eyes stray to mine. "We've got this."

"Got *what* exactly?"

When my question is met with silence, I turn to face Jacob. He has the worst poker face. Even a little lie, I'll know about its arrival before he can deliver it.

"What's going on?" When he scratches his brow, my anger gets the better of me. "Don't fucking lie to me, Jake. I'm at the end of my rope."

His hand drops from his face. "The contract had a financial clause attached to it. The promoters wanted to ensure they weren't liable for any loss of revenue in the event of another accident, like what happened to Redemption's lead guitarist."

Redemption's lead guitarist broke his leg in three places, meaning his band was unable to finalize the last half of their tour on the East Coast. That's why Rise Up was brought in as the opening act, but this is the first I'm hearing about added stipulations to our contract.

I thought our agreement was the same as Redemption's; that's why I didn't read it when the promoters gave it to me. I was so excited about securing our first tour, I signed anything they requested without asking questions. It was stupid of me to do, but at the time, I thought I was invincible.

How fucking wrong was I?

"What does that mean?" I ask Jacob, whose face seems gaunter today than it was five days ago.

Cormack answers on his behalf, "It means if you fail to meet your obligations as stated, you'll be required to compensate them for any loss in revenue for your contract period."

"So we have to pay to leave the tour?"

That can be arranged. Our album went to number one on the Billboard charts two weeks ago, so the checks from that should cover the concert costs, shouldn't it? "How much of a loss do they expect?"

My heart pounds into my ribs when Cormack rifles through the papers Marcus just stacked. Once he finds the document he's seeking, he peers back at me. The worry in his eyes has my gut paying careful attention to everything he says, and although they're only three little words, they hit me like a ton of bricks. "Two million dollars."

My stomach lurches. "Two million dollars?! How the fuck are the costs so high?" I slump into the chair in front of me before my legs give out. I must have heard him wrong. There's no way their loss could be two million dollars for a six-week tour.

Cormack double-checks his figures before nodding. "It's right."

"How? When we signed up, we were offered two hundred thousand dollars as the *total* payment for the entire six weeks, so how can two hundred thousand dollars blow out to two *million* dollars?"

"After your press conference last week, ticket sales rose by over 30%. Your acoustic performance on MTV created quite a buzz in the industry; your fans flocked to get tickets to your very first concert." Cormack glances down at the piece of paper in his hand. "You were scheduled for nineteen concerts over six weeks. Ticket sales alone were over one point four million dollars. Then they requested compensation for finding a replacement band, and full payment for the canceled concert in San Francisco that was supposed to be held yesterday."

He curses under his breath when he realizes his error. We didn't perform yesterday because it was Emily's funeral.

After squeezing my shoulder in support, Nick continues chipping at the shit storm raining down on us. "How much have we made from the album so far?"

"You don't make as much from the first album as you'd expect. Your contract is based more on the number of hits than actual sales—"

"How much?" My irritation rises right along with my snapped tone.

I hate that we're discussing band shit the day after burying my fiancée. It was my obsession with the band that saw me wasting away the last months I had with Emily.

"You're just shy of one point two million dollars."

My teeth grit when my quick calculation goes against us. We still owe a little over eight hundred thousand dollars.

"How the hell are we supposed to come up with eight hundred

thousand dollars? I just had a baby, for fuck's sake." Nick pushes back from the table so he can pace back and forth. He weaves his fingers through his hair so violently, he tugs a few strands from his scalp. Usually, Slater would laugh at his dramatics, but even he's too shocked to respond.

My disbelieving eyes shift to Jacob when he sits in the chair Nick just exited. "You don't need to worry about this. We'll work out something."

"Did you read the contract?"

He's good with legal jargon, so if anyone has a clue if Cormack's facts are accurate, it will be him.

"Yeah, I did." His pause isn't good. "It's as Cormack stated: if you fail to comply, you'll have to pay the compensation they're claiming."

I inwardly curse. Neither me nor the men surrounding me can afford this. Slater gave up his job in construction when the band signed a contract with Destiny Records. Nick used his first lot of royalty checks as a deposit on the house he lives in with Jenni, and she just gave birth to Jasper a couple of weeks ago.

Emily fell in love with Jasper on sight. When she was asked to be his godmother, she cried happy tears while whispering, "Yes," on repeat. She'd never forgive me if I'm the reason he becomes homeless. I don't want to disappoint her again. I disappointed her enough, but can I do this? Can I go on the road to help my friends who are more like brothers to me?

I can for her.

"I'll do the tour."

Nick freezes with his hands hanging mid-air. "No, Noah, we'll work this out. I'll sell the house, then we'll get a loan to fund the rest." His wide eyes stray to Cormack, "Can the studio give us an advance on a second album?"

Cormack shakes his head. "With everything going on... We're... Ah—"

"He knows I'm not recording another album."

Cormack knows I can't come back from losing Emily because he discovered firsthand how much I loved her when I begged him to let me perform "Surrender Me" on MTV. The TV execs wouldn't let me change the schedule without permission from someone in our record company. Delilah would have never agreed, so I called Cormack. After I explained what happened, he gave me permission without hesitation. He even called the producer of MTV directly to inform him of his decision.

When silence falls around me, I raise my eyes from the tabletop. Slater, Marcus, and Nick are staring at me with their brows furrowed. It's just dawned on them that they didn't only lose Emily five days ago; they lost me as well. After this tour, I'm done. I'll no longer be the lead singer of Rise Up.

"On one condition, though." Cormack watches me with wary eyes. "I will *not* perform 'Surrender Me' on any stage." Before a rebuttal can seep from his mouth, I shut down any ideas of a negotiation. "It's not negotiable. If you don't agree to this, I'll walk tonight."

CHAPTER 47

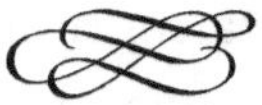

NOAH

I never thought I'd be the one convincing the band to do the tour as stated in our contract, but that's precisely what I've been doing the past forty-five minutes. As much as it shames me to admit, they'd never survive an eight-hundred-thousand-dollar debt. We've just started receiving royalty checks after twelve months of hard work, and before we were signed to a label, none of us were financially stable, so I can't burden them with this.

Emily would want me to do this; she'd want me to help our friends, so after a heated discussion, it's been agreed that we'll finish our tour. We won't be paid a cent since the two-hundred-thousand-dollar payment we negotiated with our contract will compensate for the loss in revenue of the San Francisco gig, but we won't be in debt either.

So, just five short days after losing my fiancée, and a day after burying her, I'm packing to go back on the road—back to the very thing that took me away from her for months. To say I feel guilty would be a major understatement, but how much worse would it be if I watched everything the guys worked so hard for go down the toilet? I can do this for them... then I won't feel so guilty when I leave them.

Music has pumped through my veins since the day I was born.

My dad lived his life through music, and I was following in his foot-steps, but my passion was extinguished when I lost Emily. She was the reason I worked so tirelessly the past year. I wanted to give her the world. Now, I'd give anything to have another day with her. I'd give it all away in an instant if I could see her beautiful face one more time.

I scrub at my cheeks to make sure they're dry when I detect I'm being watched. Happy I've kept my emotions at bay, my eyes float to the door. Jacob is standing watch—as he always is. After taking in my suitcase splayed across my bed, he steps into my domain.

"You know you don't have to do this, right?" He stops next to me with his arms folded and chest heaving. "Everyone will understand if you change your mind." He commands my eyes to his with a bob of his chin. When he gets them, he asks, "Do you want to do this?"

No. No, I fuckin' don't. I can't breathe without Emily, let alone perform, but since I can't tell him that, I pretend to consider his question before nodding. "Yes."

He exhales a big breath. "Alright, then I guess we're doing this."

We?

I follow him out of my room and down the hall. "We?"

"Yep, we."

He pulls down a suitcase from his closet before grabbing a handful of clothes out of his drawers. "I said I'd be at your side through this, Noah. I wasn't kidding. If you're going on tour, I'm going on tour."

He can't pack everything up and come on the road with me. He has a life here. A life he should be living—and I don't need a babysitter.

"What about Lola?"

He stops shoving his clothes into his suitcase as turmoil about his decision drains his face of color. After taking a few seconds to think of a comeback, he looks me straight in the eyes while declaring, "I know why you're doing this." His Adam's apple bobs up and down as his throat works hard to swallow. "You think this is your final penance to the band. Your last kind act before you can go be with Emily."

I nearly shake my head until I remember how well he knows me.

Taking my silence as confirmation, he continues packing. "I told you I'd fight with you, Noah, and that's what I'm going to do."

With my anger close to boiling point, I sit on his bed to rest my head in my shaky hands. I need a few seconds to calm down before I do or say another stupid thing.

I've barely got a grip on reality when Jacob crouches down in front of me. "I promised Emily I'd always be there for you. Don't make me break my promise."

The shake of my hands jumps to his when he places a white envelope on my thigh. It's unmarked and feels as light as a feather. When I shake it to check if there's anything inside, Jacob's face pales even more. He looks genuinely panicked, even worse than he did when I nicked my thumb on the razor yesterday morning.

When I tear open the envelope and upend the contents into my hand, a jabbing pain hits my chest. There's a wooden guitar pendant nestled in my palm. The lines of grain throughout the wood and the varnish coating it matches the guitar Emily gave me for my birthday last year.

If that doesn't already start an avalanche of emotions, I'm seconds from being shoved under a mountain load of snow when Jacob flips the pendant over. Emily's name is written on the back. It's her handwriting with a cursive Y and an elaborate E. It's scrawled in the same thick black ink she used when she signed my guitar. It may not be the whole inscription, but it's the most vital part.

Emily xx

"How?"

"It was found in the remains of your guitar. I wish I could have gotten the whole inscription." Jacob runs his thumb over Emily's name. Just like last year, the ink doesn't budge. "They sanded and lacquered the original shard onto this pendant."

The craftmanship of the pendant is undeniable. It's made out of solid wood and handcrafted into the same shape as my 1957 J-45 Gibson guitar. It's even varnished in its original sunburst color. The necklace holding the pendant is made of woven guitar strings, pieced together by a silver clasp.

I get a little choked up when Jacob removes the necklace from my grasp so he can place it around my neck. "Happy Birthday, Noah."

I balk. I had completely forgotten that today is my twenty-third birthday.

As I struggle to find something to say, I glance down at a gift I wish I could return but am so grateful to have. It sits so low on my chest, it rests right near my heart.

Now I have Emily back where she belongs: right beside my heart.

CHAPTER 48

NOAH

As we depart the San Francisco domestic terminal, we're inundated by the paparazzi. This is the first time the band has been seen together since our album reached the number one spot on the Billboard charts. The paparazzi could never be accused of being reasonable, but today is an entirely new type of hysteria. I feel like I'm about to be trampled as they push against the security personnel the concert promoters supplied for us.

As usual, they yell a range of questions at me, hoping to spark a response. I learned early on in my career that ignoring them is best for all involved. Today will be no different.

"Noah, do you wish to comment on your relationship with Hope Bennett?"

"Noah, where have you been hiding the past week?"

"Why did you cancel your first San Francisco concert?"

"Noah, this way, Noah."

With my head down low, I scan the area, seeking out the black limousine the studio sent for us. It's not an easy feat with how bright the paps' cameras are, but I find it a few seconds later.

"This way." I jerk up my chin, requesting for the boys to follow me.

We're halfway to our car when one question completely stops me in my tracks. "Noah, whose funeral were you attending last week?"

My heart sinks into my gut as my fists clench. I noticed the paparazzi at Emily's funeral, but because we kept our relationship a secret, no one knew how important she was to me. She was my everything, but it's being reported that I attended the funeral of a "family friend" last weekend.

Family friend, written in ink, as clear as day for the world to see. Not fiancée, not soulmate, not even girlfriend, just a family friend. I'll never forgive myself for not fighting harder for our relationship, so you can sure as hell be assured I won't take their disrespect sitting down today.

Marcus stops me from whipping back around by curling his arm around my shoulders. "Keep walking. By responding, you're giving them exactly what they want."

"They need to know she meant more to me than they realize."

"Why?" Marcus asks as his remorseful eyes dart between mine. "Emily knows what she meant to you, so why does it matter what they think?"

Stealing my chance to reply, the boys huddle in close before pushing through the swarm of hungry rodents surrounding us. I don't know whether to be relieved or pissed when we land in the back of the limo a short time later.

"Holy fuck, those fuckers are crazy." Slater braces his middle finger against the window the paparazzi have their camera lenses pushed up against. If they can see past the tint, all they'll see is him flipping the bird.

I've noticed a massive increase in the number of followers I've gained the past few months, but the rest of the band remained relatively unnoticed while going about their day-to-day lives in Los Angeles. I don't see that occurring anymore.

I jackknife to the left when a snarky voice says, "Good afternoon, boys."

From the craziness going on outside, I failed to notice the Ice Queen had joined us. Delilah is sitting on the bench across from us.

"What the fuck are you doing here?"

This woman is the *sole* reason Emily and I kept our relationship a secret, which means she's also responsible for the public being none the wiser to the fact I buried my fiancée only two days ago. I never thought I would despise someone as much as my mother, but Delilah is a close second.

I handled my mother's attempt at making the public believe I had abandoned her by throwing money at her. A cool one hundred thousand dollars was all it took for her to shut her mouth. When she accepted the check, she agreed to never discuss the band or me in public ever again. If she breaks the agreement, she'll be slapped with a lawsuit faster than she can blink.

If only I could throw money at Delilah to get her to disappear as well.

Delilah's bitch façade falters from my angry outburst. After swallowing harshly, she rolls her shoulders high before slipping a professional mask over her face. "It's nice to see you too, Noah."

She gets straight down to business by handing me a sheet of paper, our tour schedule for the next two weeks. We have three days to finalize preparations before our first concert at AT&T Park in San Francisco on Thursday night.

While scrubbing my tired eyes, I spot a crystal decanter in the wooden cabinet under the window of the limousine. After sliding across the dark leather seat, I pour myself a generous nip of the whiskey. Jacob eyeballs me but remains quiet. He knows as well as I do that this is the only way I will cope. If I don't drown my sorrows, I won't survive the next five weeks.

The rest of the trip to the hotel is a blur. The guys discuss concert dates, whereas my focus remains on the remarkable blue sky as the sweet numbness of alcohol dulls my feelings.

I spend the next three days of practice heavily intoxicated. The songs we're rehearsing I've sung hundreds of times before. I can sing no matter how wasted I am, but even when I miss the occasional line in a song, the guys don't say anything. They just continue playing like I'd never made a mistake.

Tonight we're playing at AT&T Stadium. It's supposed to be our third concert in San Francisco, but it will be our one and only show due to delays. AT&T is a massive outdoor stadium usually used for baseball games with incredible views of the San Francisco Bay behind the stage. Marcus stated earlier today that they're expecting over thirty thousand fans at tonight's concert. That is pretty impressive considering it's a Thursday.

When I met the O'Reilly Brothers earlier today, I remembered how Emily gushed over them when I told her Rise Up was their opening act. She said they were one of her favorite bands. If everything had gone according to plan, she would have seen them perform straight after us. Instead, I fucked everything up. I put the band before her. I made her feel less important.

When grief gets the better of me, I throw a glass of scotch across the room. Dangerous shards spray the dressing room, narrowly missing Nick, whom I didn't realize was sitting on the sofa until my glass collided with the wall. He gawks at me, but once again, he puts up with my appalling behavior. What could he possibly say? He's aware I'm only doing this for them, so he has no choice but to put up with my shit.

If only Jacob would follow suit. "You alright?"

He stands from his post in the corner of the room to clean up the mess I made. I should have known he'd be standing there, watching me like a fucking shadow. Usually, he stands in the doorway, so his big frame blocks the fans milling past our dressing room, hoping for a sneak peek.

I'm about to nod to his question when I spot Delilah heading my way. I need more than a bottle of scotch to drown her out. She spreads her hands across her cocked hip when she stops to stand in front of me. "I've been informed that you're refusing to sing 'Surrender Me.' Is that correct?"

I jerk up my chin.

"Would you please reconsider?"

I nearly fall off my chair, shocked she knows the word "please."

Although stunned, there's no chance in hell I'll perform *that* song. I penned those lyrics the night I made love to Emily, so if I were to sing it now, it may fucking kill me.

"Not a chance." My tone is calm even with my aggravation rising.

"It's the number one song in the country, Noah. Your fans will expect you to perform it—"

"I don't give a fuck what they want. I said no."

Pretending I can't feel her wrathful eyes boring into my head, I finish tying the laces on my boots, stand from my chair, then follow the sound engineer out of the dressing room. We're five minutes from showtime, so I don't have time to deal with Delilah and her unreal expectations.

While waiting in the wings of the stage for my cue to go on, I exhale some big breaths. I'm wearing my regular clothes I always perform in: black jeans, a white shirt, and my black stomping boots, but today I have the added accessory of the guitar pendant with Emily's name curled around my neck. Knowing she is here with me adds to the energy electrifying the air.

The crowd's cheer is near deafening when the lights dim, signaling it's almost time for us to go on stage. This is it, right here, right now: the beginning of the end for Rise Up.

After squeezing my pendant, I raise my eyes to heaven, where my angel now lives. "I love you, Beautiful."

In the roar of the crowd, I swear I hear Emily whisper back, "I love you, Noah."

Her voice is so crystal clear, I'm tempted to let my eyes dart across the stage seeking her, but with my heart not up for more disappointment, I keep them planted on the eerily starless night.

Not even a second later, I jump out of my skin when a warm hand slips into mine. It caresses my hand like Emily always did, the contrast in size making my heart rate rise as quickly as my hope.

The disappointment I was trying to avoid slams into me when I glance down. The hand slipped into mine is as tiny as Emily's, but the flawless red varnish on her nails reveals it isn't her.

Emily liked glamor but didn't wear vibrant, bright colors. Jenni, on the other hand, she loves the old school classic of pale skin with bright red lipstick and polish. "Emily is so proud of you, Noah."

After squeezing my hand, she shoves me into the blinding stage lights ready to swallow me whole.

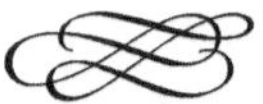

CHAPTER 49

NOAH

"Rise Up kicked off their first night of a five-week concert schedule at AT&T Park last night. Lead Singer, Noah Taylor, oozed sex appeal as he strutted across the stage. When you first see the band, you assume they're a bit of eye candy who can hold a tune. Only once they perform do you realize they have talent hidden under layers of sexiness. The raw edge projected by Noah while performing 'Hollow' caused goosebumps to break out amongst the tearful crowd last night. Their set was considerably short, only lasting thirty minutes, and noticeably absent from their playlist was their number one hit song 'Surrender Me,' but they still have the devotion of their fans. 'That was incredible, the best band I've seen live in years,' gushed one fan as she departed the concert. If you like a performance that's gritty, sexy and slightly haunting, Rise Up is the ideal band for you. I give them four out of five stars."

Cormack closes his laptop before his eyes drift between me and my bandmates. "All the reviews are similar to this one. They loved the performance, but they complain it was too short and that 'Surrender Me' was missing from the line-up."

My jaw ticks when his eyes land on me. The shortness of our show isn't my fault. I explicitly stated I would *not* perform "Surrender Me," yet what was the song the sound engineer announced we were to play next thirty minutes into our set? "Surrender Me."

I was fairly intoxicated, so I wasn't sure I had heard him right, but one glance at my bandmates told me everything I needed to know. Delilah had gone against my wishes—again.

She thought I wouldn't notice an alteration in our playlist since I was drunk. She was dead wrong. I finished the song we were performing without skipping a lyric, swung my mic into the crowd, raised two fingers in the air, then stumbled off the stage. Rage burned on Delilah's cheeks, revealing she knew who my two-finger salute was for, and she was even more ropeable when the remaining members of Rise Up followed me off the stage.

"That fucking bitch." Nick kicked a bin during the walk to our dressing room.

"Let's pack our shit and go home. I'm sick of her and her goddamn power plays." Marcus was the most pissed I had ever seen. Generally, nothing affects his cool, calm composure.

He wasn't the only one pissed. Slater was so stunned, the only comeback he could gather was about Delilah's nonexistent lady bits. "She's got bigger balls than me."

The roadies were left scampering when we left the stage thirty minutes before the O'Reilly Brothers were due, but they never once approached us to convince us to finish our set. Our standoffish demeanor revealed we weren't returning to the stage that night, if ever.

Well, I thought that was the case.

I don't remember much after storming off stage. I was ushered away from the stadium by Jacob. It's probably no surprise to learn I got rip-roaring drunk. I only woke up an hour ago after being thrown into a freezing cold shower by my asshat of a best friend. A decision to continue the tour must have been decided without me because my bandmates are ready to head out again this morning. I don't know what caused their change of heart, but I'll follow through with the promise I made to them. I don't make a promise I have no intention of keeping, just like I expect anyone who gives me their word to follow through.

Cormack isn't doing that.

"You agreed that I didn't have to sing that song." My words weaken when my stomach churns. I feel seconds from barfing. I don't know if my flipping stomach is because I've been drinking so much, or because every time I think about "Surrender Me," I see Emily's beautiful face. Then, not long after she smiles at me, the movie in my head jumps to her coffin being lowered into the ground.

Recalling my dad's trick for settling a queasy stomach, I stuff my thumbs into my fists and hum out a tune. I fight with all my might to hold down the contents of my stomach, but it's a pointless effort. With images of Emily's casket flashing before my eyes, I bolt from my chair and run to the restrooms located in the hotel foyer.

After emptying my stomach, I scrub at the spew on my chin with a square of toilet paper before moving to the sink to wash my hands. I've barely cleaned away half the despair when Cormack enters. He takes in my disheveled reflection in the vanity mirror before bridging the gap between us. The dark circles under his eyes reveal the past few days have been tough on him as well.

"You don't have to perform 'Surrender Me.' I spoke to the concert promoters this morning, and they've agreed to our stipulations." The shakes hampering me are more noticeable when he places his hand on my shoulder. "Delilah overstepped the boundaries last night, and she's been advised her behavior is not acceptable." He pauses to absorb my head bob before continuing, "But you have to finish the *entire* set, or we'll have another lawsuit on our hands."

He waits for me to nod for the second time before leaving the bathroom.

The next five weeks pass in a blur, which is not surprising. I barely remember what happened yesterday, much less weeks ago. Delilah has been noticeably absent a majority of our tour. *Thank fuck.* Jacob still shadows me everywhere I go, but gratitude for his support is surpassing my anger. He's stuck by my side like I wish Chris had when Michael died.

Rise Up is still receiving rave reviews, and our album has held its number one spot for the past five weeks, although "Hollow" overtook "Surrender Me" as the number one single on the Billboard charts. "Hollow" is doing so well because it's the one song I can perform without thinking. It's about devastation and grief—all things I'm currently feeling.

Three concerts remain in Los Angeles, then our tour will be complete. I want to say as the weeks ticked by, my devastation from losing Emily has diminished, but that would be a lie. It hurts every single minute of every single day. I miss her more than I could ever explain.

With our trip from San Diego to Los Angeles delayed due to a traffic accident, I keep myself busy with a bottle of whiskey, causing my footing to be unsteady as I make my way to the check-in counter at the hotel the record company booked for us. Although I'm intoxicated, my body is slowly getting a handle on the liquor seeping through its veins 24/7.

I barely slur when I greet the pretty blonde girl behind the desk with a friendly "Good evening."

"Welcome to the Boulevard Hotel. How can I help you?" Her greeting comes with a prolonged glance down my body, unaware she's gawking at an empty, hollow shell.

"Noah Taylor, checking in for three nights."

My voice only holds one-tenth of my usual anger when I'm propositioned. I've not visited one bar the past five weeks without having a hotel room key or number handed to me. I've even had groupies offer sexual favors in exchange for tickets backstage. Some didn't even have stipulations attached to their offers. They just wanted to be bedded by a rock star. At the start, it pissed me off. I couldn't believe how disrespectful they were being to Emily; then I realized they didn't know I had lost my fiancée only weeks earlier. No one knew.

I never accepted any of their advances, no matter how fucking drunk I was. I couldn't betray Emily like that.

The check-in clerk, whose nametag says "Mindy," lets her fingers fly over the keyboard before her brows scrunch together. "Oh..."

She glances over her shoulder to a man stationed behind her. When he notices her two-finger request for assistance, he struts over. Their shoulders touch when Mindy points out something to him on the monitor.

He huffs, his sigh as pompous as the ridiculous 70s porn mustache on his top lip. "We seem to have a problem with your reservation, Mr. Taylor." He sneers my name as if it isn't a formal salutation. "The last time you stayed at our hotel, you did considerable damage to your room."

I inch back, certain I heard him wrong. I realize the error of my ways when I peer around the hotel lobby. This is the hotel Jacob took me to after Ryan told me about Emily. I remember smashing the vanity mirror, but I don't recall any other damage.

"Sorry...?" I'm not sure what else to say. My entire world shattered that night. I was not thinking rationally.

"We have stringent policies at our hotel, Mr. Taylor, and behavior like yours is not acceptable—rock star or not."

My jaw muscle tenses as my fists clench. It's taking everything in me not to wipe the arrogant gleam off his face with my fists. "My fiancée died that night, so I'm sorry I broke your fucking mirror, but I wasn't exactly in the right frame of mind at the time."

Needing to get away from the bad memories in this hotel, I pivot on my heels and sprint for the glass revolving doors.

"Noah?" Jacob mumbles when I bolt past him. His long strides help him catch me before I hit the sidewalk. "Where are you going?"

I run my fingers through my hair, tugging it violently in hopes the pain will keep my emotions in check. "I can't stay here."

Jacob's gaze follows mine to the hotel sign swinging in the entranceway. "Fuck, Noah, I didn't realize."

He yanks out his phone to call us a taxi, but it's too late. I'm too far gone. Memories are crushing into me hard and fast. No matter how much alcohol I consume, nothing will stop the events of that evening from replaying in my head. Except today they're fresher—more disturbing.

I remember how surprised I was when I saw Ryan in LA, but I'd never stopped to wonder why Jacob was there that day too. He was standing on the other side of the glass door when Ryan broke both my soul and my heart with three little words: *Emily is gone.*

"Why were you in Los Angeles that day, Jake?"

We're a six-hour flight from LA, and it was a Tuesday afternoon, so there was no reason for him to be there.

Jacob stops scrolling through the contacts in his phone before his eyes stray to mine. He scratches his brow while exhaling a long, sharp breath. He's either preparing to lie to me, or to tiptoe around the truth.

Peeved as fuck, I step closer to him, only slightly fumbling before asking him the same question again. "Why were you in LA that day?"

Realizing we aren't leaving this sidewalk until I get answers, he murmurs, "I was there as part of a surprise from Emily."

"Surprise? What surprise?"

His chest rises and falls with each breath he takes. "Emily planned it the weekend she visited Jenni in Ravenshoe."

I move to a bench seat in a bus stop so I can bury my head in my hands, certain I'm not strong enough to hear what Jacob is about to say.

My intuition is proven on point when he says, "You asked her to marry you the night before you went back on the road. She filed for a marriage license that same week, so you could get married in Vegas like planned."

Pain cripples my heart as memories of that night filter through my head. When I asked Emily to marry me, I wasn't meaning a date months or years away. I wanted us wed immediately—that night. If I could have gotten her on a plane, I would have married her the instant we landed in Vegas. That's how much I loved her.

I had made so many mistakes the prior two months, and I was only partway through fixing the damage I did when I lost the chance to make things right.

Jacob crouches down in front of me before his gaze seeks mine. "The marriage license was approved. She was coming to LA to keep the promise she made."

My hand covers the sob tearing at my chest. It's my fault. The reason she's no longer here is my fault. I try to hold in my anger. I try to simmer it down by guzzling the last bit of whiskey in the flask I keep in my jacket, but I can't control the fury building so rapidly, it's tearing me apart from the inside out. I'm the reason Emily is gone. It's my fucking fault! She was coming to keep a promise she made to me.

I kick my leg out hard against the billboard flanking the bus stop. It warps under my boot, but the bulletproof casing keeps it from shattering. Unhappy it's intact when my heart isn't, I stand before walloping it with my fists. As I unleash my anger in a violent, ugly way, blood surges through my veins so fast, they feel as if they're about to burst.

"Noah." Jacob arches a brow, warning me he'll once again use his size against me if need be.

My fists suspend mid-strike. "Fuck you, Jacob!" I spit out venomously. "Three days. That's all I have to make it through—three more miserable motherfucking days—then, when the concert is done, I'm done. I can't handle this shit life anymore."

I make a beeline for the sidewalk to hail a cab. One stops in front of me a few short seconds later. Jacob barely clambers into the backseat before the taxi rockets into the bustling traffic, my offer of a hundred if he gets me to the closest bar too good for the driver to pass up.

Drowning my sorrows hasn't worked the past five weeks, but I'm not giving up hope.

The next morning, my head is thumping ten times worse than usual, but my prayer to choke on vomit while sleeping hasn't been answered. I'm alive and breathing—unfortunately.

I blink to lubricate my eye sockets when I hear a door creaking open. "It's all over the media." Jacob leans over me to grab the remote off my bedside table.

"What is?" Not that I care what he is talking about.

"Emily is."

I jackknife up so fast, my stomach lurches into my throat. "Why?"

"Someone leaked your engagement."

He dumps the *Los Angeles Times* next to my thigh. The headline on the front page reads: *"Noah Taylor, Lead Singer of Rise Up's Fiancée Killed in Tragic Accident."*

"It's all over the morning news as well." He jerks his chin to the muted TV across the room. There's a picture of Emily on the screen, the one they used for her funeral. I shake my head in anger. Only after she's gone does Emily finally get recognition for being the love of my life.

After Jacob fumbles his thumb over the remote, sound comes out of the TV. "Reports confirm Noah Taylor's fiancée was killed in a tragic accident six weeks ago. We believe this is why Rise Up's hit song 'Surrender Me' was noticeably absent from their recent concert tours along the West Coast. Previous speculations were that the song was removed due to plagiarism concerns, but this morning, Rise Up's publicist, Delilah Winterbottom, advised it was withdrawn out of respect for Noah's fiancée, Emily McIntosh."

Jacob pushes the standby button before dumping it on the bed. "Why are they reporting it now?"

I shrug. "No fucking clue..."

My words trail off when reality dawns. In my anger yesterday, I'd told the check-in clerk and her supervisor that my fiancée died. They must have leaked it to the press the instant I walked out of the hotel lobby. *Fucking assholes.*

I crank my neck to my bedside table when my phone vibrates. The anger I'm struggling to contain ramps up a notch when I peer down at the screen to discover it's Delilah.

Certain I can't deal with her and her antics right now, I send her call to voicemail. It does little to deter her. My phone blows up again and again and again until I'm seconds from strangling it. Or better yet, giving a piece of my mind to the person on the other end.

After a big breath, I hit the connect button then press my phone to my ear. Delilah doesn't wait for me to issue a greeting. "Did you know about the marriage license?"

"I was informed it was approved last night—"

"Why would you apply for a marriage license when part of your contract was to stay attainable to your fans? They're a public record, Noah. Anyone who does a quick search of your name will find it."

Fury scorches my veins. "Attainable to our fans! Are you fucking kidding me, Delilah? Emily is gone, and all you're worried about is the fans!"

I jump out of bed so I can pace back and forth. Neither pacing or Jacob's watchful eyes can make my rage simmer down. "Do you know what, Delilah? Fuck. You! I'm done!"

I peg my phone onto the bed, sending it bouncing off the mattress and onto the floor, where it remains in one piece. While pacing, I rake my fingers over my scalp, striving to calm down. I'm about halfway there when someone knocks on my door. It better not be Delilah, because if it is, I won't be held accountable for my actions.

I storm over to yank it open, ready to unleash a tirade of verbal abuse on Delilah. My words stuff into the back of my throat when I'm greeted by Cormack's remorseful face.

His lips twitch as he prepares to speak, but I beat him to the punch, "You need to fire Delilah—today!" I move back from the door to give him the chance to enter. "Our album has been number one for weeks now. Your record company is making millions off us. If you don't fire her, I'll quit. I'll walk away this very instant!"

CHAPTER 50

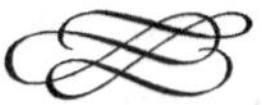

NOAH

While standing in the wings backstage at tonight's concert, I take a moment to reflect. The mood is more subdued than previously. The crowd is still roaring its chants, but their shouts of the band's name are interspersed between quiet moments. The crowd's pacified response is understandable. With the media broadcasting Emily's accident on repeat, the world is now aware of how much I've lost.

Fans lined up outside my hotel room windows the past two days, holding up signs of support for both Emily and me. Their tears flowed as freely as mine have the past six weeks, and I saw their heartbreak all over their faces. Those are the fans I love, the dedicated ones who support us throughout thick and thin. Not the ones who live in the fantasy land of lies and deception where Delilah resides.

I don't know whether Delilah was fired from the record company or not, but she's no longer in charge of Rise Up's publicity. I want to say victory has heated my blood the past two days, but the triumph doesn't feel so sweet. I should have stood up to her months ago; then maybe my life would be starkly different than the miserable existence I'm living now.

When the lights dim, announcing it's nearly time for us to go on, I follow the routine I've done at each concert. After grabbing ahold of my necklace, I raise my eyes to the sky. "I love you, Beautiful."

Once the sound engineer gives me the green light, I make my way to the taped X behind my mic stand. Tonight's first song we've prepared to perform is "Tastefully Despised." It has a long solo guitar riff Nick performs under the spotlight before the lyrics flow in, so I can't see the hundreds of posterboard messages of support throughout the crowd until my spotlight illuminates, but when I do, I take a step back. The messages are overwhelming. Many of them have photos of Emily, and the ones that don't are filled with supportive words.

I'm so taken aback by their support, I miss the introduction of the song. While tugging my earpiece out of my ear, I inch back from my mic. The crowd gobbles up every emotion crossing my face. They know I'm struggling, but they're not going to push me. I love that about them. Emily was the same way. She supported me without ever making it seem like I wasn't doing the best I could. Only I felt that burden.

She told me time and time again that I was all she wanted, yet I never believed her.

I do now.

"We need to play 'Surrender Me.'"

Nick pushes his earpiece in closer to his ear, confident he misheard me. "What was that?"

"We need to play 'Surrender Me.' It's the only song that will show them how much I loved and adored her."

I hear his throat work hard to swallow, then, "Are you sure?"

With my lips quivering, I jerk up my chin. "I'm sure. It's time."

Marcus, Nick, and Slater seem hesitant, but they count in the beat all the same.

I close my eyes in preparation to perform a song I know will cut me wide open before pressing my lips to my mic. "I dedicate this next song to my angel in heaven, Emily."

I keep my eyes shut the entire performance, imagining Emily's beautiful face and dazzling smile. She loved this song, and I'm singing it directly to her.

I was broken beyond repair,
shackled by my miserable existence
Like a prisoner in a cage,
I was disturbed and twisted.
You broke all my walls,
and fought through my resistance
Because you believed my life
deserved a better existence.

I surrender myself to you,
please look after my broken heart.
I surrender myself to you,
and promise we'll never part.

You mended my shattered heart
as if it had never been apart
and healed my blackened soul
by making my life whole.
Now I can live my life without despair
because I know you'll always be there.
I promise to cherish you in every way.
You are my girl, and I'll fight for you every day.

I surrender myself to you,
please look after my broken heart.
I surrender myself to you,

and promise we'll never part.

You're my best friend, my lover,
and one day you'll be my wife.
I promise to cherish and
love you every day of my life.

I surrender myself to you,
please look after my broken heart.
I surrender myself to you,
and promise we'll never part.

When the song finishes, the promises I'd made to Emily in the lyrics hit me full force. I promised we'd never part. I didn't keep my promise. I ruined them—*I ruined her.*

Marcus, Slater, and Nick's eyes track me when I run off the stage to empty my stomach's contents into a waste bin at the side. The pain is so intense, the only way I can get rid of it is by purging it out of my mouth. It isn't pretty, but neither is grief.

Once my stomach stops churning, I raise my eyes, swiping vomit from my bottom lip in the process. Although sure my stomach is empty, I'm close to barfing a second time when my eyes lock in on Cormack's troubled gaze. He's disappointed I've left the stage, but I'm not up for an argument.

"I can't do this anymore."

I lean my back on the stage walls before cradling my head in my hands. I knew singing "Surrender Me" would cut me raw, but I wanted everyone to know how much Emily meant to me, except now I feel like I'm being torn in two.

I expect Cormack to request that we finish our set, so you can imagine my surprise when he nods instead. He doesn't speak a word. He doesn't need to because his eyes reveal everything he wants to say. He's giving me permission to leave.

I'm done. I'm finally free.

And I don't waste any time sprinting to my freedom. I race to the back entrance of the stadium faster than my legs can carry me. I'm wheezing by the time I break through the double doors, but I feel the most alive I've felt in months.

The area surrounding the stadium is dark. Not even the paparazzi are on guard yet. No one expects the performers to exit the building at showtime. Upon spotting a taxi dropping off a late concertgoer, I rush over and dive through the door she's holding open.

After giggling at my eagerness, her face turns to stone. "Noah...?"

I flash her a quick smirk before throwing money at the driver, encouraging him to leave. I don't care where he goes, he just needs to move—now!

He does precisely that a nanosecond before Jacob bursts through the doors. When he spots me sitting in the back of the cab, he pushes off his feet and chases me down. He follows us all the way out the parking lot and halfway down the street before he finally realizes he can't chase down a moving vehicle on foot.

With his hands resting on his head, he stands in the middle of the busy street to suck in some ragged breaths. He will always be my brother, and I love him for that, but my love for Emily is greater, and it is time for me to go home.

When my taxi arrives at the Los Angeles Domestic Terminal, I hand the driver a one hundred dollar bill. Just like every day the past few weeks, my trip was a total blur. Traffic must have been light because we made it here in record-breaking time.

Not waiting for my change, I crank open the door and step onto the sidewalk. Just as I'm about to enter the sliding doors of the terminal, my vision is blinded by a bright light.

"Noah, where are you heading?" A paparazzi member with a chubby frame and a vicious sneer blocks my entrance to the terminal. "Aren't you performing tonight? Did the concert get canceled?"

When he shoves the camera right up into my face, I push it to the side. With my blood still thick with adrenaline, I'm stronger than I realize. The pap's camera smashes into his nose, adding a scratch to the bend at the top.

"I could sue you for that." After tossing his camera under his arm, he grabs a handkerchief from his pocket. He wipes it under his nose to make sure it isn't bleeding before tapping it over the cut. Now that his face is exposed, I realize he's one of the regulars who harassed me relentlessly the past six months. Not even the prospect of a broken nose slows him down. He gets straight up in my business again, blocking each attempt to skirt by him.

I bite on the inside of my cheek, battling to keep my anger at bay, but the smug grin on his face makes it impossible. With my annoyance now at a boiling point, I snatch his camera out of his hand, slam it against the concrete, then stomp on it with my boot.

As he bends down to pick up the broken pieces of his camera, he mumbles, "Come on, Noah, fuckin' hell, I'm just doing my job. I've got college tuitions to pay for."

His grumble reminds me of the time Emily and I were caught at Bronte's Peak. She defended them the same way. She said they were only doing their job. I laughed at how she saw the good in anyone— even the vultures of the paparazzi.

With guilt weighing heavily on my chest, I bend down to help the man. "I'm sorry; I'll arrange to buy you a replacement camera."

Not appreciating my offer, he snatches the piece I'm holding out of my hand before nudging his head to the right, giving me my marching orders. Happy to leave, I stand, step by him, then break through the double glass doors as I attempted many times only minutes ago.

I'm almost free from controversy when three little words stop me. "Tragic accident, eh?"

I clench my fists so tightly, my nails dig into my palms. I remind myself time and time again that he isn't worth it. He's algae on the bottom of the ocean, scum on a shower door, but he isn't worth my time.

I'll be the better man by walking away.

He doesn't follow suit. "She probably offed herself to get away from you."

Blood roars through my ears as rage overwhelms me. Anger about everything that has happened the past six weeks rolls into me like a freight train. I storm toward him with my head in lockdown and my anger at an all-time high.

Rearing my leg up, I kick him in the chest with my boot. He flies backward, his head impacting with the concrete when he lands with a thud. I could let that be the end of it, but I could never be accused of being rational when I'm losing control.

I force him onto his feet by clutching his hair in a tight fist. "Say it again, but this time, say it to my face like a real man, you fuckin' piece of shit!"

He doesn't flinch or protect himself. All he does is smirk, loving that he forced a reaction out of me—even more so when he realizes how many of his peers have cameras pointed our way.

Blood dribbles out of his mouth when he taunts, "Smile for the cameras, Noah."

He's a foolish man. Only someone with a death wish would taunt a man who has nothing left to lose. Not thinking, my fist adds to the ugliness of his face. As his head flings to the side with a sickening crunch, I'm tackled to the ground. My body doesn't register the pain of being sandwiched between a police officer and the rigid concrete sidewalk. The pain tearing through my chest is too intense to feel something as weak as pain.

Two police officers use their bulky frame to pin me to the ground. "Stay down; if you move, I'll pepper spray you." One smashes my cheek against the sidewalk while the other removes his cuffs from his belt. "Put your hands behind your back. You're under arrest."

Officer number one circles his cuffs around my wrists before locking them into place, unaware my arrest is most likely being streamed live around the world. After dragging me onto my feet by yanking on the cuffs, a third officer walks me to his police cruiser.

"You have the right to remain silent. Anything you say can and will be held against you in a court of law. You have the right to an attorney. If you cannot afford one, one will be appointed to you. Do you understand these rights as I've said them to you?"

He pushes down on my head, assuring I don't whack it against his cruiser's door before shoving me into the back seat. When I nod, he slams the door shut. Just like they do every time I'm engulfed by silence, my thoughts stray to Emily.

When things are really quiet, I swear I can hear her whispering in my ear. I want to say it's an experience I seek often. Unfortunately, that would be a lie. I can't think about her without it tearing me up inside. That's why I drink so much. Being able to hear her but not touch her is killing me.

I'm not strong enough for this.

<hr>

Several hours later, Jacob picks up a visitor's phone before taking a seat behind the thick glass wall lodged between us. "How are you holding up?"

I'm being held in custody awaiting trial since I was refused bail at my arraignment this morning. Jail is everything I expected it to be: three concrete walls and a steel cage door. I can't stay in a place like this. My memories are haunting enough when I'm drunk, but they're ten times worse when I'm sober and staring at white walls.

"Can you get me out of here? They don't even let me have shoelaces, for fuck's sake." I don't give a fuck about my shoes. I'm just saying anything to get me out of here. I'm going stir-crazy.

When Jacob scratches his brow, my jaw clenches. Now I know why everyone is looking at me with sympathy. Jacob had me put on suicide watch. I'm not fucking happy, but I'll deal with him once I'm freed from hell.

Jacob gets a stay of execution when he discloses, "Nick reached out to Jenni's parents. Michael is trying to get the charges downgraded if you agree to plead guilty to lesser charges, but they're saying you'll still do time, Noah. You knocked the guy out cold on live TV. He's suing you for damages."

He can take me to the cleaners. I'll give him every penny I have just to get out of this hellhole. When I say that to Jacob, he promises to do everything in his power to have my charges dismissed.

Three days later, I'm nervously tapping my foot as the judge hands down my sentence. I accepted a plea offered by the district attorney's office, but the judge has the final say on what my punishment will be.

"You should consider yourself very fortunate, young man." The judge peers down at me. Even with me crapping my pants, I can't believe how similar he looks to world-famous actor Morgan Freeman. "You will escape a jail sentence this time around, but if there is a next time, you'll not be as lucky. I'm only giving you this chance after your lawyer informed me about the circumstances regarding your behavior as of late."

Relief washes over me, pleased I'm not going to jail, but the gleam in his eyes warns me to hold my relief for a few more seconds.

I understand why when he bangs down his gavel while saying, "I sentence Noah Taylor to alcohol and anger management counseling for three months. If he fails to complete the necessary requirements of his rehabilitation, he will complete the remainder of his sentence in a state correctional facility." He stands before peering down at me. "This is a chance to get your life back on track. Listen to the people trying to help you."

When he steps down from the podium, the bailiff's loud voice booms into my ears, "All rise."

Once he exits the chambers, I slump back into my seat before my eyes stray to my lawyer. He appears pleased with the judge's verdict. I have no idea why. For three months, I'll be continuously monitored. If that isn't bad enough, I have to participate in counseling sessions. Just the thought has me rethinking my plea. Maybe I should just go to jail.

Spotting the disdain on my face, Michael leans into my side. "You're lucky he only gave you three months. Judge Jackson isn't known for clemency. I was praying for anything under a year. You only got three months."

He can say that because he's forgotten about the life sentence I'm already serving.

CHAPTER 51

NOAH

"This will be good for you, Noah."

I stop watching the scenery rolling by my window when Jacob directs his car down the driveway of Hope Hills Center for Drug and Alcohol Rehabilitation. It's set on a large hill overlooking the City of Los Angeles. The manicured grounds are crowded with patients participating in several programs. One group is doing Tai Chi, whereas another is painting.

"Yeah, *real* good."

How will Tai Chi ease my grief from losing the love of my life?

The judge granted me three days of reprieve to finalize my affairs before my forced stay at Hope Hills. Jacob once again became my shadow, but he ramped up his efforts by not even allowing me to use the bathroom in privacy. It's lucky he's like a brother to me.

After parking in a space right at the front, Jacob removes my bag from the trunk. My eyes shoot in all directions as we walk up the stark white stairs in silence. Hope Hills Center is built around an old-style 1950s Hollywood mansion. The walls are white; the tiles are white, and the uniforms of the staff members are white. If it weren't for the green vines creeping up the concrete pillars, there'd be no color whatsoever.

My heart races as we stroll to a glass desk in the middle of the foyer. A well-built middle-aged woman peers up from her computer screen to greet us.

"Name?"

Jacob's voice shakes when he begins to speak. "Noah Taylor, he is here for—"

"This is as far as you can go."

Jacob's lips quirk at her snapped tone, but he doesn't respond. Instead, he dumps my bag on the desk before giving me a brief man hug. "I'll come back and see you when I can."

He turns on his heels and bolts out of the foyer like his backside is on fire, leaving me to fend off the dragon alone.

The receptionist stands from her leather chair to rummage through my bag. "Do you have any alcohol on you? We'll search you either way, but you should come clean now. Her eyes wander over my body. "It's more complicated when it's found during the strip search."

Unsure if she's being serious or not, I pull out the flask of whiskey in my leather jacket and hand it to her.

She *tsks* me. "I was joking about the strip search, but I'll jot this down for future reference." She points to a set of double doors on my right before handing me a sheet of paper. "Go through there, then take a left. The second door on the right is Dr. Miller. She's your counselor."

With a click of her fingers, two orderlies take my bag to a bench near stained glass windows to rifle through it.

"They'll drop it off in your room once they're done." She once again points to the door. "Get your skedaddle on. Dr. Miller doesn't appreciate tardiness."

While pacing to the large white double doors, I suck in some deep breaths, praying they will settle my nerves. I don't know if I can do this. Three months I'm stuck here. Three... long... motherfucking... months!

Just as I break through the double doors, the receptionist shouts, "Make sure you knock before entering."

The horrible sanitary smell every hospital and dentist's office has smacks me in the face when I merge into a long white corridor with several doors on each side, each with a plaque with the doctor's name and the rehabilitation service they specialize in.

I take a left and walk four paces before stopping at the door with "Dr. R. Miller, Anger Management Counselor" on the front. I saunter into the office, only remembering once I'm halfway in that I'm supposed to knock. With a grimace, I pivot back around.

"You're already in, so you may as well keep entering," murmurs a female voice from a red leather seat butted up against a wooden desk covered with papers.

My brow cocks when Dr. Miller swivels her chair to face me. She's a lot younger than anticipated. I've never been overly good at guessing ages; Emily was living proof of that, but I'd say Dr. Miller is in her late twenties, maybe early thirties. Her straight light brown hair is pulled back in a low ponytail, and she has wispy side bangs. Her skin is flawlessly white, contrasting with her thick-rimmed glasses, and she has a V-shaped groove between her green eyes.

The reason for the sickly smell in her office is revealed when she squirts a sterile solution into her hands. Once she has finished rubbing it in, she does a one-handed clap, requesting the piece of paper I'm holding. When I hand it to her, she gestures for me to take a seat in the chair opposite her, which I do, albeit disgruntledly.

"Noah Taylor, singer, twenty-three years old, anger management and alcohol rehabilitation." She peers at me over the paper, unable to miss her disdain. "Aggravated assault on a cameraman, three-month conviction, yada, yada, yada."

She drops the paper onto the desk before sinking into her chair. "Why don't you tell me why you're here..." She checks the document to ensure she calls me by my correct name before finishing, "...Noah?"

I shrug. "The footage the judge saw didn't show what actually happened."

The footage streamed live around the world didn't capture what the cameraman said before I kicked him. To the public, it appeared as if I attacked him without being provoked, which only I know isn't true. It probably didn't help that I knocked him out cold on live TV, but that fucker got what he deserved.

Dr. Miller balances her elbows on her desk before clasping her hands together. "So you don't have any problems with anger?"

I shake my head. If you don't piss me off, I'm as soft as a teddy bear.

"Of course you don't." She peers down at an open day planner on her desk. "Your first counseling session will commence at 3 PM in Room 32. Don't be late."

I drop my eyes to my watch. It's a little after 2 PM.

She doesn't mess around, does she?

Standing up, I push back from her desk before realizing I don't have a clue where I'm going.

Like she can read my mind, Dr. Miller says, "The orderly will show you to your room."

When I exit her office, one of the orderlies who searched my bag jerks his chin up. I follow his anal march down one of many corridors. They appear to sprout in all directions from the one I was originally in. For its size, this compound should be busier than it is. Its eerie quietness has me more than panicked. I can't stand silence.

This side of the building has patients' names on the doors instead of doctors. I nearly crash into the orderly when he stops in front of one that has my name scrawled across it. "Your clothes are in the closet. You'll be expected to wear them during your stay. I need you to remove your boots; they'll be returned once your rehabilitation period is over."

He waves his hand across his body, signaling for me to enter my new living quarters for the next three months. My room is pretty bland. There's no surprise that the walls are white. A twin bed is pressed against one wall, and a desk and set of drawers are opposite it. There are two doors on the far wall. I assume one is a closet, and another may be a bathroom?

After dumping my bag on my bed, the orderly glares at my boots. Gritting my teeth, I undo my laces, remove my beloved black stomping boots, then shove them into his chest. My toes wiggle when

I peer down at my sock-covered feet. *Who knew you could feel naked while fully clothed?*

As he exits my room, the orderly shocks me one final time. "There are slippers in the closet."

Slippers? He can't be serious, can he?

Curious, I stride over and open one of the doors. The one on the left is the bathroom. It's finished with white tiles, a standard vanity, an upright shower, and a toilet. The door next to the bathroom is a closet, and just as advised, three pairs of hard-soled slippers still in their protective plastic are nestled beneath three pairs of light gray cargo pants and three plain white v-neck shirts.

After yanking down a pair of cargo pants and a shirt with more force than needed, I head into the bathroom to get changed. As I slip my shirt over my head, my eyes stray to the man in the vanity mirror. The thick, scraggly beard on my chin and my dark, sunken eyes make me barely recognizable. I haven't shaved since Emily's funeral, and I've lost pounds of muscle the past two months, making me not only look gaunt, but sick as well.

When I step out of the bathroom, the orderly who brought me to my room marches over to yank on the drawstring in my pants.

"What the fuck are you doing?"

I step away from him. The elastic in my pants keep them in place even without their drawstring, but I don't like him touching me.

"I forgot you're on suicide watch, so no cords, strings, shoelaces, belts, razors or any other device you could use to harm yourself are allowed."

Drawstrings? Does he seriously believe I could kill myself with drawstrings?

While removing the drawstrings from the pants hanging in my closet, he arches his brow. "Yes, it's happened before." He stuffs them into his pocket for safekeeping before turning around to face me. "You better get a wiggle on. You don't want to be late for an appointment with Dr. Miller."

"I've got plenty of time. It's barely past two..." My words stop when my eyes drop to my watch. I've got two minutes to get over to the other side of the compound. "Shit!"

My socks fail to gain traction when I skid out of my room. I have no clue where the past hour went, but it disappeared faster than groupies' morals when invited backstage at a concert.

"You're late!" Dr. Miller chides when I enter the counseling room five minutes later.

She's pissed, but I'm impressed I'm only a few minutes late. My room is located in the west wing; the counseling sessions take place in the east wing. You can't get more impressive than that. When Dr. Miller glares at me, I mumble an apology under my breath.

"Tardiness is not acceptable. I have a hectic schedule. If all my patients arrived five minutes late, I'd lose precious hours every day."

When she yanks off her glasses to get her point across, I wonder if she is as old as I first thought. She may be closer to mid-twenties than late. She's attractive, if you like the dorky schoolteacher look. Her white blouse tucked into her pencil skirt shows off her curvy body, and she has long, lean legs.

My throat works hard to swallow when I return my eyes to her face. She noticed my perusal of her body. Her brows are pulled together, and her eyes are narrowed into thin slits. Although she's uncomfortable with my stare, she keeps things professional.

"You may *wrongly* believe rehab is a waste of time, but this is my job, so the least you can do is be respectful enough not to waste *my* time." She paces around her desk to pick up a form on the edge. "If you can't do that, you'll leave me no choice but to sign this form stating you do not wish to participate in the rehabilitation program I've designed for you. If I do that, you'll be incarcerated in a medium-security prison for the next three months. Is that what you want, Noah?"

I shake my head without thought. Rehab will be hard, but I'd rather be here than left rotting in a four by four cell with nothing but memories to occupy my time.

Gratitude flares through her eyes as her shoulders slacken. "Okay.

Good. Then don't be late again. Do as instructed, and the next three months will be over before you know it."

She sits in a recliner before motioning for me to sit opposite her. When I do, she pulls a yellow notepad and pen out of a briefcase resting next to her chair. "Now, how about you tell me about yourself? There has to be more to you than what's on your admission forms."

I cross my right ankle over my left as I scrub at my beard. This is as uncomfortable for me as it gets. If there's one thing I hate more than sitting down and talking, it's being forced to talk about myself.

Dr. Miller gnaws on the end of her pen as she impatiently waits for me to answer. "Anything?"

When I remain quiet, she chomps down on her pen so firmly, it looks seconds from snapping. "Alright, if you don't want to talk, I guess we'll just read what they have down here." Her exhale flutters her hair out of her eyes. "You're the twenty-three-year-old singer of a band called Rise Up. You're unmarried, have no kids, an issue with alcohol, and need to learn how to control your anger issues." She does a little chuckle that makes my spine bristle with anger. "Nothing out of the ordinary here, is there?"

"You don't fucking know me."

"No, I don't. That was the point in me asking you to tell me about yourself. All I know is what is written on this form." She hands the document to me. It's the standard admission form every hospital has stating my name, address, occupation, age, marital status, and the reason I'm being forced into rehab: aggravated assault.

My eyes lift from the paper when Dr. Miller says, "Tell me you don't read that in the exact manner I just did. Another spoiled, rich, little rock star who thinks he can do whatever he wants, and once the law finally catches up with him, he'll say how sorry he is before he goes running off to rehab."

I throw the admission form back at her side of the desk before leaping to my feet. "Fuck you! I don't need to put up with this shit."

My long strides to the door slow when she shouts, "If you leave, I'll be forced to sign the document stating you're refusing to follow your rehabilitation program."

Sweat slicks my body when I stomp back to stand in front of her. She's no longer sitting in her seat; she's facing me eye to eye. "You don't know a thing about me. You don't know the fucking hell I've been through, yet you feel you have the right to judge me."

"And there's that uncontrollable anger you say you don't have a problem with," she replies, not once backing down on her firm stance. "You can't beat people up because they say something you don't like."

"You don't know what he fucking said!" I point to the door like the man I assaulted is standing behind it. "You don't know what he said about her!"

"Then tell me. I can't help you if you don't tell me what's going on!"

"She was my everything."

The sternness in Dr. Miller's eyes softens. "Who was your everything?"

"No one knew how much she meant to me. She didn't even know how much she meant to me."

Not willing to let the tears brimming in my eyes fall in front of a witness, I spin on my heels and stalk down the long, isolated hallway, where I spend the next two hours lying on my lumpy mattress in my cold rehabilitation room.

I stop running my thumb over my favorite photo of Emily when a cough breaks through the silence surrounding me. When I lift my gaze, Dr. Miller hesitantly strolls into my room. She waits for me to sit up before dropping her eyes to Emily's photo.

"She's very beautiful."

Beautiful is too simple of a word to describe Emily. She was beyond perfect.

My head slants to the side when Dr. Miller starts our conversation in a way I wasn't anticipating. "I'm sorry for the way I judged you earlier. I've just returned to my position after having twelve months off. With social media not being my thing, I was unaware of what had happened."

When she takes a second glance at Emily's photo, the real reason for her visit is exposed. She must have researched me the last two hours, and if my intuition is anything to go by, I'm sure the first thing that pops up when you type my name into the search engine is Emily. She's everywhere at the moment.

After squeezing my hand, Dr. Miller makes her way out of my room. "I want to start your counseling again tomorrow morning. Meet me in Room 32 at 10 AM." When she enters the hallway, she cranks her neck back to peer at me. "Please don't be late. Our sessions are more vital to you than you realize."

CHAPTER 52

NOAH

"Say anything that makes you comfortable, anything at all."

Dr. Miller pushes her bangs out of her eyes before biting down on her pen. We're currently halfway through my sixth counseling session on day three of my three-month sentence. I won't lie. The past three days have been the longest days of my life. I have two one-hour counseling sessions per day, and every day Dr. Miller asks me the exact question she just did. It's getting really tiring really fast.

Wanting to keep the focus off me, I shift it to Dr. Miller. "How long have you been married?"

She smiles warily while lowering her gaze to the rings on her wedding finger. I take note of the way her eyes sparkle when she smiles. Emily's did the same thing. "A little over three years."

"You must have gotten married young?"

Her smile grows before she nods. "Yes, we did. I was just shy of turning twenty-five; he was twenty-six."

Her answer reveals my original guess of her age was right. She's twenty-eight.

After spinning the diamond ring around her finger to ensure it's correctly aligned, she returns the ball to my side of the court.

"Although I'm glad you're speaking up, our sessions are supposed to be about you, Noah, not me." An understanding glint brightens her eyes when she asks, "Would you like to talk about Emily?"

Just hearing her name spikes my heart rate. I'd give anything to talk about her, but sometimes, no matter how hard you pray, not all your dreams come true.

When I shake my head, Dr. Miller's shoulders slump. The words we exchanged today are the first we've shared since our initial altercation. Clearly, she was hoping it was the start of a confession avalanche.

She's across the room, but her voice projects so well, it feels like her lips are pressed against my ear when she assures me, "Talking helps. It won't take away your pain, but it will help you heal."

"I'll never get over losing Emily."

"I won't pretend it's easy, but your pain will lessen over time," Dr. Miller replies, making me realize I said my last statement out loud instead of in my thoughts. "How did you meet Emily?"

While scraping my hand along my unshaven jaw, memories of the night Emily busted me laughing at her family portrait filter through my mind. Her leaning against her bedroom doorframe. The jersey she wore. Her beautiful smile. I see it all in crystal clear detail.

"The instant my eyes landed on her, I knew my life would never be the same again."

She was so under my skin, I begged Jacob for her number during our drive home. Jacob, forever being an ass, pretended he didn't feel right giving her personal information to a stranger. Only a few months ago, I found out he and Lola were conspiring to get us together all along.

"I tried hard to stay away from her."

I even went out with Nick a few weekends to try and forget her sparkling brown eyes and sexy tanned legs. It did me no good. When I was making out with a girl in my truck, Emily's beautiful face kept interrupting my thoughts. Because the girl I was occupying my time with had long brown hair similar to Emily's, I pretended it was her kissing a trail from my chest to the crotch of my jeans. I was so fucking hard, I nearly made a mess of my jeans when she slid down my zipper. It was only when she lifted her eyes did my excitement crash and burn. Her eyes were blue, and her face was nothing like Emily's.

I felt like an ass, but I yanked up my zipper, planted her backside in the passenger seat, then drove her home. I'd only met Emily once, but it felt wrong occupying my time with another girl. Furthermore, no one could compete with her, so why settle for second best?

"Emily deserved better than me."

I was a broken man, but even I knew burdening her with the task of mending my shattered heart and blackened soul was wrong. I hadn't gotten over losing Michael when Chris's grief became too much to bear.

To this day, I still don't understand what happened with Chris; he seemed to be doing well. He was helping me rebuild my truck and had picked up some work at a garage in town. He wasn't living the best life, but he was doing okay... then he overdosed in his bathtub on the fourth anniversary of Michael's death.

I sink low before folding my arms in front of my chest. I've done enough talking for one day. When the sleeve of my sweater tugs up high, I notice we still have fifteen minutes left in our session.

I put the time to good use. "How did you meet your husband?"

"Oh...umm..." Dr. Miller chuckles. She was so caught up listening, she didn't anticipate my return serve back to her side of the court. "It was at a college party." Her hand clamps over her mouth when she smiles a full-toothed grin. "We were freshmen with no interests in dating, so what happens...? *Boom*—here it is! Love straight out of the gates."

I laugh at her description of insta-love. I always thought it was something people made up to excuse acting on lust outside of the norm. Emily proved me wrong. She knocked me on my ass in under a second.

"It wasn't roses and sunshine, but we got there—eventually." Her smile falters at the end of her confession. She twirls her engagement ring before returning to the court we've been playing on the past fifty minutes. "What about you? Have you ever been married?"

Ignoring the clawing pain hitting my chest, I shake my head. "Emily and I were engaged, but we never made it down the aisle."

Our second anniversary was the day before Emily's birthday. We had planned to get hitched that day but postponed so I could remain attainable to my fans. How stupid was I to agree to that? If I hadn't, we would have continued planning our wedding, and Emily wouldn't have been killed traveling to surprise me.

I take a few seconds to settle myself before the tightness around my neck turns into a sob. Just thinking back has me all torn up. I was in San Diego on Emily's birthday. I arranged for a florist to take the biggest bouquet of white lilies to her gravesite. I should have visited her myself, but I can't bring myself to do it. Just the thought of her being buried under all that dirt fucking kills me.

Although I was a coward that day, I manned up and called Emily's mom. It was the first time we had spoken since Emily's funeral. She had left several messages inviting me home for the holidays, but I never replied.

She sounded happy to hear from me and made me promise I'd keep in contact more regularly. I was shocked. I thought she'd blame me for Emily's death like my mother blamed me for Michael's, but I heard nothing but genuine concern in her voice during our ten-minute conversation.

I stop reminiscing when Dr. Miller leans over to squeeze my knee. "You did well today. Let's pack it up and try again tomorrow."

With Patrice still on my mind after my counseling session, I head to the payphone in the lobby to keep the promise I made to her the last time we spoke. Patrice answers on the very first ring.

"Noah, I've missed you so much."

CHAPTER 53

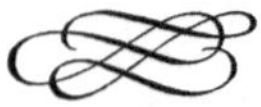

NOAH

"Today we're going to try something different." Dr. Miller lowers the privacy blind on the two-way glass in the counseling room before nudging her head to a daybed. "Lie down."

My brows stitch when the room plunges into darkness from her switching off the lights.

"Are you fucking serious—?"

"Language, Noah; I will *not* tell you again," Dr. Miller growls as her shadowed outline heads my way. "Swearing indicates a lack of intelligence, which we both know isn't the case for you."

I roll my eyes before lying on the daybed as requested. Today is day thirty-five of my three-month stay in rehab. Dr. Miller, or Rachel as she's permitted me to call her, has been using me as a guinea pig while striving to "open my lines of communication."

As required by law, I've attended my twice-daily sessions without fail. I miraculously shared the story about Michael's death without breaking down, and Dr. Miller was aware of Chris's suicide, hence me being on suicide watch, but any time Dr. Miller switches the focus to Emily, my throat closes up.

After waiting for me to get comfortable in her incredibly uncomfortable daybed, Dr. Miller sits in the chair next to me. "Close your eyes and listen carefully to me speaking. Take in slow, deliberate breaths as you feel yourself relax. Relax your toes, your legs, your chest, and your shoulders until all the muscles in your body relax."

As I slowly drift into a calm state of awareness, memories of Emily bombard me. They don't haunt me as they usually do. She seems happy, almost peaceful. She's even smiling.

"Em... "

"Good job, Noah, keep breathing in and out, in and out. Can you see Emily?"

I nod. She's standing in front of me, as beautiful as ever.

"Is she happy?" Dr. Miller's question concludes with Emily breaking out her breathtakingly beautiful smile.

"Yes, she is."

I'd reach out to touch her, but I'm too scared she'll vanish. Instead, I ball my hands into fists and keep them planted at my side.

"Keep breathing, Noah, in and out; suck in a nice big breath, hold it in, then breathe it out." Once Dr. Miller has my heart rate under control, she asks, "What do you want to tell Emily?"

"I'm sorry." My whisper is barely audible over the hammering of my heart. "I'm so sorry for everything I did, for all the time I wasted."

"Breathe, Noah, keep breathing, in and out; try and stay calm."

When Dr. Miller curls her hand over my clenched fist, I lurch up from the daybed. "I can't do this."

The pain is so unbearable, I feel like I'm drowning. I can't breathe. I can't sleep. I can't live another day without Emily in it.

"It's okay, Noah; continue breathing. You did well. I'm so proud of you."

Dr. Miller praises me over and over again until the heaviness on my chest lessens enough, I can suck in my first breath in what feels like minutes. Confident I have a handle on things, she raises the blinds, illuminating the room with artificial light again before crouching down in front of me.

When her lips twitch, like she's preparing to speak, I cut her off. "I fucked everything up."

I wait to be reprimanded for cursing again. It never comes. She just watches me cautiously, her face marred with both confusion and concern.

"I let jealousy waste our last two months together."

I let a man unworthy of Emily steal her away from me...

"Come on, Noah, stop being a pussy and come out with us." Slater slaps Nick on the shoulder before messing up his hair. "Even Nick is coming out."

Nick's lips straighten, but he keeps the peace by not retaliating to Slater's tease. It's the least he can do after everything he put Slater through.

Although I wouldn't mind watching them make fools out of themselves at a new karaoke bar that opened a few blocks down from our hotel, my day has been so hectic, I haven't had time to call Emily tonight. I'm dying to hear her voice, so there's no chance I'll skip calling her just to get proof I'm the only singer in my group. I've called Emily every night since the day we became a couple. Tonight will be no different.

"I have to call Em."

Slater whips me with an invisible whip. "Pussy-whipped."

I give him the finger before digging my cell out of my pocket and dialing Emily's number. I'm dying to see her face, so I FaceTime her instead of calling her.

"Hi, baby." Emily adds to her greeting with a blinding smile, nearly blocking out the dozen or more people surrounding her. She must be out and about.

"Hey, Beautiful. Sorry I'm calling so late. Things were hectic in the studio today."

"When aren't things hectic for you?"

I smile at the laughter in her tone. She's forever optimistic, never letting a lack of face to face time dampen any conversations we have. Things are taking off for the band. I'm stoked, but it sucks I no longer have weekends off. It kills me not seeing Emily as regularly as we did at the start of our relationship, but technology has made it more tolerable.

"I miss you, baby, so fucking much."

Her face breaks into a traffic-stopping smile. "I miss you too."

My heart thrums against my ribs when Emily all of a sudden moves out of frame. Not even two seconds later, a male voice shouts, "Emily, baby, I've missed you so much!"

I don't know if he's mocking me or not, but just the fact someone other than me is making Emily giggle while caressing her has my anger reaching its boiling point.

"Em..." I tilt my head since her phone is being held upside down. "Are you there?

Put off by the unease in my voice, Marcus joins me at the side of the living room. When he glances down at my screen, he curses under his breath.

"What?"

He points to a man whose smug grin is filling the screen of my phone. "That's Zander."

"Zander? As in, Emily's ex?" When he nods, I sneer, "Are you fucking kidding me?"

Out of all the guys in the world, why does the one who took Emily's virginity get to smirk in the background like a smug prick?

Marcus's lips purse. "He's aged since I last saw him, but that's Zander. No doubt."

I try to keep my anger under control. I tell myself time and time again that I trust Emily, and that she wouldn't break my trust like this, but the more she giggles under the hooded eyes of her ex, the more my resistance slips.

When I hit the end call button with enough aggression, I almost crack the screen of my phone, Marcus removes it from my hand. "It doesn't mean anything—"

"Then what the fuck does it mean? Why is he there with her? She said he went to school in another state."

Marcus shrugs, his anxiety palpable. "I thought he did too. Maybe he switched schools—?"

"Or maybe Emily lied."

"Noah..."

Marcus's reply is cut short by Slater exiting the bathroom. "Ready?"

"Let's go," I answer on Marcus and Nick's behalf.

While gathering my leather jacket, I dump my ringing cell phone into the fruit bowl on the dining table.

"Yee-ha! Pussy-whipped Noah is coming out for a drink." Slater stops

whipping me with his invisible whip when I throw open our hotel room door with enough force the door handle smacks through the drywall.

"Noah, wait up!" Marcus catches up with me at the elevator banks. "Don't do anything you'll regret tomorrow. Things may not be as they seem."

I consider what he's saying during our short walk to Mr. Mix's karaoke bar. It doesn't weaken my anger in the slightest—especially not when I see a couple getting friendly in the alley.

Is that what Emily and Zander are doing right now? Are they sucking face?

I stop watching the couple getting hot and heavy when Slater says, "It's packed; do you think we can get in?"

I take charge of the situation like I wish I had my phone call. "Come on." When I saunter past the hundreds of people lined up to go inside, the boys follow me. The bouncer on the door is a huge son of a bitch, but his size has nothing on the chip on my shoulder.

"Noah Taylor, lead singer of Rise Up." We've been working our asses off, so shouldn't we start getting some benefits for our hard work?

"I know you," The bouncer's white teeth gleam in the moonlight. "Come on in."

Numerous patrons stuck in the line let out a loud, angry gasp when he opens the red velvet rope for us to enter.

"Fuck yes." Slater's tongue peeks between his teeth when he struts into the VIP entrance. "About time we got some pull in this industry."

As I follow his peacock strut, my eyes drink in the surroundings. A karaoke stage takes up a majority of the back wall; a glass bar is on our left, and stacks of tables and chairs take up the right. A handful of plush booths flank the bar, revealing why the line outside is so long. There are several well-known actresses, actors, and musicians sitting in the roped-off VIP section.

We lift our jaws from the floor when a short, tubby man stops in front of us. "Good evening, gentlemen, I'm Tony, owner of Mr. Mix's. It's a pleasure to have you in my bar this evening."

Tony is so short, the top of his head doesn't even reach my chin, and his shoulders are as wide as he is tall. His inky black hair is slicked into place with hair gel, and his eyebrows are penciled on.

"Noah Taylor, nice to meet you." I accept the hand he's holding out. Shockingly, his handshake is firm.

"Would you like to sit at the booths or in the regular seating?" His nose screws up during the last half of his question.

I do a quick flyover of the people in the VIP section before returning my attention back to Tony. "Regular seating will be great, thank you."

Just because you're famous, doesn't mean you need to be a snob. Without fans, you're nothing. Most of the people in the VIP booths need a reminder of that.

Once we take our seats, Slater buys a round of shots. I'm not usually a fan of hard liquor—beer is my drink of choice—but with my blood still thick with jealousy thinking about Emily and Zander, I need something more potent than beer.

"To success and getting Noah smashed!" Slater clicks his shot glass against mine before downing his shot in one hit.

I follow suit with that one and the many that follow.

Once I've lost track of time, I've also lost count of the number of shots I've downed. Alcohol is dousing the rage burning me from the inside out, but it does sweet fuck all for the jealousy heating my blood. Even if Emily and Zander are just friends, I hate that he gets to see her when I can't.

The more we enjoy the endless bar tab Tony supplied for us, the more crowded our table becomes. Eager fans hover close, loving the opportunity to party with someone famous. We sign a few autographs, and I even sign one girl's cleavage as per her request.

I've just returned her permanent marker when Nick yanks me back into my seat. "What the fuck, man?"

Marcus adds to Nick's disappointment. "You're better than this."

Anyone would swear I'm getting a blowjob from the way they're acting.

"You should sing, Noah." A pretty blonde whose breasts are dangerously close to escaping her tight tank top flutters her eyelashes at me.

"You want me to sing?"

As her tongue darts out to lick her top lip, she nods.

I bring my face to within an inch of hers. "What do you wanna hear?"

"Umm... I don't know. Something sexy? Like you."

"Sexy, hey?" When she nods again, I nudge my head to the stage. "Alright, *go pick something for me to sing, and I'll sing it to you." I tap her nose. Well, I think I'm tapping her nose. I'm so fucking drunk, I could be poking her in the eye for all I know.*

While she makes a beeline for the DJ, I slump low in my seat before shooting my hand out for my drink. Slater removes it before it gets within an inch of my mouth. "I think you've have had enough."

He's pissed. For what? I don't know.

When I seek assistance from Marcus and Nick, I notice they're giving me the same filthy look Slater is. I can read Marcus better than both Nick and Slater combined, so it doesn't take me long to realize what has him so worked up.

"It's a song! I'm not fucking her."

Hating their babying, I stumble out of my seat and head for the stage. When I accept the microphone the fan is holding out for me, I attempt to curtsy. I say attempt because I trip over my feet, which has me crashing into the screen I'm supposed to read the lyrics from. Fingers crossed she picked a song I know, or I'm screwed.

After gathering my footing, I take my spot at the front of the stage. I begin to wonder how many wrinkles the fan is hiding with makeup when the intro to the song she selected booms out of the speakers. She's gone for an old classic with Bon Jovi's "Always."

It's the perfect song to reflect how I'm feeling, so I have no troubles belting out the first few lines, but when I reach the chorus, all I hear are the promises I made to Emily. How I'll love her forever, and that I'll never let anyone come between us. How she'll be my wife one day.

The microphone drops to the stage with a donk when I stagger back to my table to search my jacket for my phone, forgetting I left it at the hotel.

"Here." Marcus shoves his cell into my hand.

While dialing Emily's number I know by heart, I seek privacy outside.

Emily answers just as I break through the line still waiting to get inside. "Is he okay, Marcus? I'm panicked out of my mind. I've been calling him nonstop—"

"It's me."

She sucks in a relieved breath. "Oh my god, thank goodness. I've been calling you for hours. Where are you? Are you okay?"

"Why did you lie to me?"

The panic in her tone switches to suspicion when my question comes out with a slur. "Are you drunk?"

"Yes! But answer the goddamn question! Why did you lie to me?"

She exhales before replying, "I haven't lied to you."

My anger takes a step back. When she breathes like that, it means she's about to cry. Even though I'm mad at her, it still kills me knowing she's upset.

"Where are you?" she questions between sniffles when the bass from the karaoke bar is distinguishable in our silence.

I drag my hand across my tired eyes. "I just left a bar." Too drunk to stay upright, I sit in the gutter. "Why him, Em? Out of everyone in the world, why him? You deserve so much better."

"Who are you talking about—?"

"Fucking Zander!"

My slurred words gain me attention I don't want. People leave the line when recognition dawns on why I appear so familiar. Regrettably, they're the only ones focused on me. Emily is as quiet as a church mouse. If it weren't for her tiny inhalations of air, I'd assume she had hung up.

When I spot Marcus heading my way, I prompt Emily to answer me. "Em—"

"You have no *right questioning me about my past—no right at all! I live knowing the countless women you slept with before me, but you can't handle me having* one *man in my life before you!"*

"The past?!"

Zander was so much in the past, he was standing behind her, smiling at the fucking camera like he had the world at his feet. I guess he did since he had Emily in his sights.

"Yes, Noah—the past! You're being an immature, jealous, insensitive jerk." Her huff rumbles down the line. "Call me when you're sober. If I've forgiven you by then, I might answer."

When she hangs up, I scream my frustration into the street, startling those brave enough to approach me, but not brave enough to interrupt my heated conversation.

"You know Emily, Noah. She'd never break your trust like this."

Marcus helps me out of the gutter before walking me back to our hotel. Because I'm so intoxicated, I go to bed angry.

That never ends well...

What Marcus said that night was true, I trusted Emily, but Zander's presence played on my insecurities that Emily would one day leave me for someone better. It reminded me that she deserved more than I was giving her, and it was the reason I worked so tirelessly the two months after our fight. I wrongly believed money would bind us together, where all it did was divide us more.

If I knew now what I did back then, I would have told her what I saw that night. I came close when we were confessing our secrets in the cave at Bronte's Peak, but Emily's hungry tummy stole my chance, then it never presented again, leaving me with another burden on my already heavy shoulders.

CHAPTER 54

NOAH

Over the next few weeks, I talk about Emily more regularly. It still hurts, but Dr. Miller has me convinced that my two-month absence didn't make Emily feel less loved. Although we've worked through a lot of my guilt during our twice-daily sessions, nothing Dr. Miller can say will convince me I wasn't in the wrong.

Our time apart began because of a misunderstanding, but I should have manned up and asked Emily about Zander instead of letting my insecurities fester for weeks on end. If I had done that, I wouldn't have to live with the fact it was Zander who proved Emily had never lied to me...

Cormack's executive assistant taps on the conference room door. "Noah, there's someone here to see you."

Since we've just finalized our meeting about our upcoming tour with the O'Reilly Brothers, I shadow Peta into the foyer. I'm excited about who could be visiting me... until an arrogant smirk becomes recognizable halfway through Peta's introduction.

"What the fuck are you doing here?" I tug Peta behind me like it's my job to protect every woman on the planet from scum like Zander Louisa—Emily's ex-boyfriend.

"I just want to talk..." He glances past my shoulder. "Alone."

When I follow his gaze, I spot Delilah watching our exchange with evil, beady eyes.

I return my focus to Zander. "Five minutes."

A cool breeze blowing in from the west does little to calm my anger when I break through the glass door of Destiny Record's temporary office. Zander's feet barely hit the sidewalk when I begin our "talk" with a warning. "If I find out you touched her, I'll—"

"I haven't touched her," Zander interrupts. "She doesn't even know I exist."

He drags his fingers through his long, dark hair, making me realize he's still a surfer boy who has no clue how to treat a lady. Age hasn't matured him. If anything, it has him striving to maintain his youth, which means he's even less worthy of Emily now than he was when he took her virginity with fake promises and a bunch of lies.

"I don't know why I'm here. I thought... I wanted..." He exhales while shooting his eyes up to the cloud-filled sky. I don't know what he sees, but it has him singing his confessions like a canary. "I transferred to Parkwood State a few months ago. I noticed Emily in my first class of the day, economics. I couldn't believe out of all the colleges in the country, I trans-ferred to the same one she attends. Guilt has plagued my dreams for years, so I thought fate had played its hand, and this was my chance to make things right with her."

He laughs a pained chuckle. "I waited for her outside of her building later that afternoon. It took me all day to work up the courage to speak to her. I nearly chickened out when I saw her galloping down the stairs, but her smile stopped me." He nervously shifts from foot to foot. "It was her *smile; you know, the one that makes time stand still?" Although he's asking a question, he continues speaking, "The one you'd give up everything you have to see time and time again."*

His eyes return to me. "She only gave me that smile once. It was the day I fucked everything up, so to see it again... I was ecstatic." He rubs his hands together, either striving to warm them up or rid them of sweat. I'm not sure which. "It was only when she leaped into your arms did I realize her smile wasn't for me. It was for you. The gleam in her eyes, the extra spring in her step as she raced down the sidewalk, they were all for you."

I can't tell if he's pissed or pleased. It may be a combination of both.

"I should have been happy that what I did didn't irreparably scar her, but that was the last emotion I felt. I was angry, sad, and for some fucked-up reason, jealous."

Although aware of how quickly Emily imprints herself on people, I hate that she causes that neurosis from men like Zander—even more so with what he says next, "Instead of being happy for her, I waited in the wings, seeking an opportunity to swoop in and win her back." His throat works hard to swallow. "The perfect ruse was unearthed when I overheard her talking to you. I asked my friend Matt to grab her in a bear hug, hoping a little jealousy would have you fucking up. It was only when Emily dropped her phone did the brilliance of my plan truly shine. Even the most confident man hates the idea of his girl in the same room with the man who popped her cherry."

I fist his shirt before pulling him to within an inch of my face. Even though his tone is crammed with remorse, that night was the start of the worst two months in my relationship with Emily. And for what? For him to hurt Emily all over again.

"She never gave me a second look; no one had a chance with her." He could be trying to weasel himself out of a fucked-up situation, but his next set of words shows a different motive. "She took extra classes and hid in her room, waiting for you to call." He laughs again, more troubled than his first. "She didn't even notice me when I was right in front of her last week. Her shoulders were hanging as low as her head. She seemed miserable. When I saw your performance on MTV, I realized why. I had hurt her again." His remorse-filled eyes bounce between mine. "That's why I'm here. I fucked things up, so I'm here trying to make them right."

"You love her?"

I don't know where my question came from. It could be the gleam in his eyes, or the fact he's confronting me instead of Emily, but I'm so confident in my assumption, I don't need to see his nod to know of his confirmation.

I push him away from me before I make matters worse. I stand in the street clenching and unclenching my fists as I strive to think of a solution that doesn't include violence. It's a goddamn long five minutes. He caused Emily months of torment. She was ridiculed and bullied to the point those around her grew worried about her mental state. How can I walk away from that without forcing him to endure one-tenth of the pain she experienced? Wouldn't that make me as bad as him?

It's only when our eyes meet for the quickest second do I get my answer. He's in love with a woman he'll never have. I'm not any better than the pathetic man standing in front of me, but I still have Emily's love. So, as much as I want Zander to pay for what he did, he's already being punished.

With that in mind, I leave him standing in the middle of the street while I go and call the love of my life to ensure she knows how much she means to me...

CHAPTER 55

NOAH

"You're in the final stretch now, Noah, your very last week."

I grin at the eccentrics in Dr. Miller's voice. I never thought I'd survive three months of rehab, yet here I am in the final week. I won't lie. It's been an eye-opening few months. After heavily detoxing my first four nights, I was concerned I'd never play the guitar again. Thankfully, once all the gunk I had pumped into my veins the prior three months was out, my hands stopped shaking, and normal finger functions returned.

Although he appears extremely uncomfortable during his visits, Jacob has visited me every weekend of my stay. I told him he didn't need to come every weekend, but he's always here bright and early every Saturday morning. His visits added a touch of amusement to my week. Not just because he's a funny fucker, but because his face stays as white as a ghost from the second he enters until he's in the safety of his car. I've never seen him more petrified in my life. I shouldn't get comfort in the fact rehab freaks him out, but I do.

My grin slackens when Dr. Miller fills the seat across from me. "Today, we'll discuss what life will be like once you leave Hope Hills. When you arrived here, I misjudged you. I apologize for that, but you need to understand your life will be starkly different when you walk out these doors." She points to the doors of her office like they're a gateway to heaven. "The temptation to drink will be unyielding, especially for someone in your profession. You'll have the paparazzi nipping at your feet, begging you to take the bait they're throwing out, and fans will want more than you're willing to give."

She scoots closer to me. "You can't let *any* of them get to you. If you're feeling tempted, remember the steps you've been taught. Stop and assess the situation, breathe deeply, consider what other actions you could take, analyze the situation, and act in a responsible, calm manner."

When she leans over to curl her hand over mine that is balled, I know she's about to hit me with something big. My intuition is spot on when she murmurs, "I also think it's vital in your recovery to visit Emily. Denying what happened isn't helping anyone. It's time for you to face reality head on. Can you do that, Noah? Can you take a step forward instead of back?"

I never knew a nod could take so much effort until now.

The remaining week is spent preparing for me to enter the real world again. My boots, clothes, and toiletries were returned yesterday, and the cargo pants hanging in my closet still have their drawstrings. I'm one step closer to going home; I just have one final matter to take care of.

While peering at my reflection in the mirror, I scrub my hand over the messy facial hair covering my jaw. I give the scruff one final tug before splashing water on my face. Once I have a thick lather of shaving cream covering my jaw, I glide a razor down the wiry hair.

A smile tugs my lips higher when I recall Emily shaving me the weekend of her nineteenth birthday. When I picked her up from school, she thought we were heading to Rise Up's final show at Mavs. She had no idea the band and I had planned a surprise birthday party for her.

Ollie was hesitant when we asked to host the event at his pub, but he was quick to change his mind when we agreed to perform an impromptu gig at Mavs any time we were in town. It wasn't a hard offer for us to make. Mavericks was and always will be our stomping grounds.

Although, I'm not sure I'll ever see it in the same light now. Even with parts of the old Noah reappearing, my life will never be as it once was. Nothing is the same without Emily.

Dr. Miller pops her head into my room. "Ready?"

"As ready as I'll ever be."

I place a photo of Emily on top of the clothes folded in my suitcase before grabbing the last of my things from the bathroom. While I shove my toothbrush, razor, and deodorant into a waterproof bag, Dr. Miller peruses my photo.

"She is really beautiful, Noah." When she runs her index finger down Emily's face, the gleam usually projecting from her ring finger is missing. She's not wearing her engagement and wedding rings.

"Is everything okay, Rachel?"

I don't often call her by her first name because it seems too informal, but her mannerisms are off today, so they have me acting differently as well.

Her eyes turn to mine. They're sadder than I've seen them before. "Yes, I'm okay."

Tears glisten when a bare finger stops her attempt to twirl her engagement ring. She stares down at her hand, her breathing labored. "I figured it was time to take them off."

I watch her curiously, unsure what she means.

"My husband was a wonderful man, Noah. He was the love of my life, as Emily is yours." She wipes at her cheeks, removing the tears rolling down her ashen skin like she's embarrassed about their arrival. "He died last year. That's why I had just returned to my job when you started your rehabilitation here."

"I'm so sorry."

I try to think of something more to say, but I'm at a loss. Everything I've been battling the past few months, Dr. Miller has been going through as well.

"He fought hard to stay with me, but he wasn't strong enough. He had thyroid cancer. We tried every treatment recommended by his doctors. Nothing worked. I was his nurse the last few months of his treatment. The pain of watching the man I love fade into one I no longer recognized was harder than I ever anticipated." The determination in her eyes can't be missed when she murmurs, "Be the man Emily wants you to be, Noah. Fight for her; make yourself the man she deserves."

As I stare at her in shocked silence, she struggles to regain her composure. She drags her hands across her cheeks multiple times and pinches her thigh, but when her tears continue to fall, she moves for the door, only stopping for the briefest second to whisper, "I'm sorry about the baby, Noah."

Baby? What baby?

Oh god no.

With my knees as shaky as my hands, I sprint into the hallway to catch up to Dr. Miller. I reach the corridor in record-breaking time, but Dr. Miller is nowhere to be seen. After gathering my bag from the door, I gallop down the stairs of the Hope Hills Rehabilitation Center. Jacob is picking me up today, so if anyone knows what baby Dr. Miller was referring to, it will be him.

I find my truck in the parking lot a few seconds later with Jacob leaning against the passenger side door.

"What baby, Jacob?"

His eyes widen as his throat works hard to swallow. When he scratches his brow, I yell, "No more fucking secrets; I made her promise there'd be no more secrets!"

"We didn't tell you because we didn't want it to hinder your recovery—"

"Was Emily pregnant?" I already know the answer, but I need him to spell it out for me.

My heart shatters when he murmurs, "Yes, Noah."

I stumble backward, my head swirling as the realization of how much I've lost rains down on me.

Why did our baby have to die too?

Haven't I been through enough?

Why must I continue living this miserable, painful life?

With my heart in lockdown, I jump into the driver's seat and fire up the motor. My engine roars to life on the first turn of the key. When I flatten my foot on the accelerator, my truck flies out of the rehabilitation center, leaving a cloud of dust in its wake. The hazy midmorning fog conjures up visions of Emily sitting cross-legged on the floor, eating pizza while asking me if I want kids.

Did she know then she was pregnant? If so, why didn't she tell me? She had no reason to lie to me. I said I wanted kids. I would have had her knocked up the instant she gave me permission. She didn't need to keep this from me, so why did she?

As I dangerously weave my truck down the rolling hills of LA, recollections of Dr. Miller's anger management training filter through my brain.

"Stop and assess the situation, breathe deeply, consider what other actions you could take, analyze the situation, and act in a responsible, calm manner."

In the hope of settling my anger, I suck in many lung-filling gulps of air. They calm me enough to remember Emily's smile when she asked me if I wanted children. She must not have known she was pregnant then, or she would have told me. She knew how much I hated secrets and would have never kept anything so important from me.

As I continue sucking in big breaths, the anger raging inside of me fades. I need to act responsibly, like the man Emily deserved. I also need to turn around and pick Jacob up, who's most likely standing in the dust cloud striving to work out what the fuck just happened.

Since I'm peering in my rearview mirror, checking if it is safe to turn around, my sharp veer around a tight corner has me almost colliding with a small child in the middle of the road. He holds his hand out in front of his body, begging for me to stop, but I'm going too fast to evade the inevitable. Instead, I slam on my brakes before yanking my steering wheel to the right. My tires skid across the road's surface a mere two seconds before they lift from the pavement.

As I sail through the air like a paraglider, I shift my eyes back to the little boy. He's watching me closely, his brown eyes oddly familiar. He smiles in a way that burns my soul before he vanishes behind a cluster of trees. Knowing he is safe makes me smile.

I'm seconds from death, but instead of feeling fear, I finally feel free. I'm soaring freely through the air like an angel would—like Emily would every day in heaven. When my truck glides toward a massive tree trunk, I don't shield my body from the impact. I just close my eyes and surrender, no longer having the strength to fight.

I think about Emily: her beautiful light brown eyes, her breathtaking smile, and her flawless face. It's time to go home, back to Emily —the only place I've ever belonged.

When my truck collides with the tree trunk, my body jerks forward. Blood splatters my chin when my ribs slamming into my steering wheel splinters my lungs with shards of bone. A sticky warmth slides down my face when a sheet of red clouds my vision. My headbutt with the dashboard leaves a wound from my hairline to my left brow.

In the distance, I hear Jacob calling my name, his shouts closely followed by his fists frantically banging on my window. Within seconds, he shatters the glass next to my head.

"Hold on; help is coming. I need you to fight, Noah. You have to fight!"

I want to tell Jacob it's okay; I'm at peace, but I can't talk through the blood gargling in my windpipe. It's for the best. He needs to let me go; I can't fight anymore. I'm too tired, and it hurts too much. I can't take the pain anymore.

Jacob grips my hand, his eyes begging me to fight as blackness slowly rolls in.

His pleas come too late.

I am finally at peace.

"Charging, fully charged, stand back, clear," is shouted before a surge of electricity courses through my broken body.

As my back bends in response to the zap attempting to revive me, Emily's beautiful face flashes before my eyes. The movie rolling through my head is a slideshow of our two years together. In every image, Emily is either smiling or laughing. She looks so peaceful —happy.

Toward the end of the reel, I have to shield my eyes from a bright white light shining into my room. It's so bright, it's almost blinding. My hand lowers from my face when I hear Emily's singsong voice. She sounds close, like she's just outside my room, waiting for me.

"Em..." I whisper huskily when I think I see her darting past the open door. I swing my legs off the bed, then stand, my strength admirable considering how badly my body is damaged.

Halfway to the door, I hear someone yell, "Fight, Noah, fight!"

When I crank my neck back, the air sucks from my lungs. I'm still lying on the hospital bed, and a handful of doctors and nurses are working hard to save me.

"No. Let me be."

As much as what I'm seeing is shocking, I want them to let me go. My time has come. It's time for me to go. I want to be with Emily.

I just have to find her. *Where did she go?*

When I enter the long white hallway outside my room, Emily's vanilla scent streams through my nostrils. I breathe in deeply, relishing her delicious smell.

The breath I've just sucked in is forced out in a hurry when I spot her standing at the end of the corridor. She isn't wearing her regular skinny jeans and vintage rock shirts I'm used to seeing her in, but she's as beautiful as I remember. Her dark locks hang loosely down her back, and her face is as flawless as an angel's.

I knew she'd be waiting for me. I just wish I hadn't made her wait so long.

CHAPTER 56

NOAH

My heart rate quickens when Emily stops gazing at something in her hand to spin around and face me. As she stares at me, a concerned mask slips over her face. She's as stunned to see me standing before her as I am her.

I prepare myself for a new type of impact when she breaks into a brisk jog. Her vanilla scent intensifies with every step she takes, making my heart rate climb, and my arms stretch out to catch her like I did every Friday for most of our relationship.

I'm finally home, back with Emily, the only place I've ever belonged.

When she gets within touching distance, I close my eyes to enhance her scent while murmuring, "Fuck, I've missed you, Beautiful."

I'm braced, waiting for her final leap.

It never comes.

My eyes pop back open as air fans my cheeks. Confusion thickens my blood when an empty corridor presents before me. Emily is no longer running toward me; she's nowhere to be seen.

As panic curls around my throat, my eyes dart up and down the corridor, trying in vain to locate her. I find her a few seconds later when a code blue siren screams out of the room I just exited. She's standing at my bedside, grasping my frail hand in hers, begging me to hold on as tears roll down her cheeks unchecked.

What the fuck is going on?

I step into the room just as Jacob pulls Emily away from my withered body. She fights against him, lashing out violently.

"Let her go, Jake!"

Jacob doesn't flinch at my words. He just looks straight through me.

"Noah!" Emily kicks and wails against Jacob so fiercely, her tears splash on his arm curled around her waist. "Please, Noah, fight!"

I want to caress her beautiful face, but I'm scared to touch her, petrified she'll disappear again. Instead, I use words. "It's okay, Em. I'm here. I'm right here."

I stare into her glistening light brown eyes, begging her to acknowledge my presence, to see me as I'm seeing her.

It never happens.

Just like Jacob, all she can see is the frail, tired man lying on the hospital bed behind me.

"Charging, fully charged, stand back, clear!"

I crank my neck in just enough time to see a doctor zap my body with a defibrillator. His hit is so fierce, it forces me onto my knees and flashes up memories I don't recall living. Painful, tormented memories that are more nightmares than dreams.

After shaking my head to rid it of the confusion clustering there, I devote my attention back to Emily. I'm not the only one who suffered from the zap of the defibrillator. Emily collapses into Jacob's arms, the stress of seeing me fade away too much for her to bear.

"Still no cardiac output," advises a nurse standing next to the monitors at my bedside.

"Charge again," the doctor instructs a second nurse.

While they do that, my room illuminates with a bright light streaming in from the hallway. It's so intense, I need to shelter my eyes with my hand. I do that in just enough time to see two dark figures moving into the entrance of my room. They stand at vastly different heights. One is as tall as me, but the other is only a boy.

"Michael?" I mumble when I recognize the inquisitive brown eyes staring back at me.

He's older now than he was when he passed, but I'd never mistake his unique, inquisitive eyes. They're the same pair that stared at me in awe when I taught him to play the guitar, and the same pair that peered at me in fear when my truck veered off the road earlier today. I'm certain of it.

As my brain struggles to work out what the fuck is going on, I'm hit with the defibrillator for the third time. It brings up memories I'd rather forget than remember. They're of the past four months. They're playing in reverse, but they're as crystal clear as the image of my brothers before me.

My rehab with Dr. Miller, the paparazzi attack, the concert tour, Emily's wake and her funeral. It all flickers through my head at the speed of light, only stopping when I enter the idling taxi outside of Emily's dormitory the day I lost her...

After sliding into the back seat of the taxi, I brace my J-45 Guitar on my knees before instructing my driver to take me to the airport. I don't travel without my pride and joy; having it means I carry a piece of Emily with me everywhere I go.

When the driver stubs his half-smoked cigarette into the ashtray, I notice it is 4:55 AM. I have an hour to drive the forty-five minutes to the airport, check in, and board my flight. I'm cutting it close.

Not wanting to deal with Delilah if I'm late, I tap the driver's shoulder. "If you can get me there in thirty-five minutes, I'll tip you two hundred dollars."

His brow cocks, assuming my ripped jeans and grungy shirt means I won't be able to keep my side of the bargain. Smirking, I snag my wallet out of my back pocket so I can throw a Benjamin Franklin over the seat at him. Upon spotting the crisp new bill, he slams his foot on the accelerator, lurching his taxi forward at a lightning-fast speed.

"I'll get you there in thirty."

His efforts are aided by the early hour. The roads aren't as busy as usual since rush hour hasn't started. While he weaves through the occasional car, I scroll my Facebook feed. A grin tugs on my lips when I see Jacob has been tagged in a few photos with the guys from my band. Although he's always been a key player in our success, I'm confused as to why he's in Los Angeles... on a Tuesday.

Gratitude fills me when I scroll through the rest of Slater's pictures. If the amount of glitter, tassels, and cleavage are anything to go by, they hit a couple of strip clubs last night. I'm glad I was visiting Emily, because there's no way I'd be dragged to a place like that. Strippers on tap, no thanks! Who wants a cheap and nasty chop, when you have a premium steak at home?

Jacob looks reasonably intoxicated in most of the photos. He's grinning while tucking dollar bills into a stripper's sparkling panties. Happy to stir the pot, I tag him in the images Slater missed. Let's see if he's still smiling when Lola discovers his Monday night escapades. I don't know how they label their relationship. I've asked Jacob a handful of times, but he is just as in the dark as me. Lola is a feisty little temptress who'll never be tamed, but Jacob isn't ready to throw in the towel just yet.

My eyes lift to the rearview mirror when the driver asks, "What make is your guitar?"

"A 1957 J-45 Gibson." I lift it so he can get a better look.

"That's a sweet guitar."

I can't help but smile at his description of my pride and joy. It's more than sweet. It's a fucking masterpiece.

"Yeah, it was a..." My reply is cut short by a blinding light heading straight our way. "Watch out!"

The rumbling of a semi's horn sounds through the eerily quiet winter morning. As its tires bounce across the asphalt, my thoughts stray to Emily. I recall how beautiful she looked when I left her sleeping in her bed only minutes ago. She was as beautiful and as peaceful as an angel.

When the truck's grill inches closer to my side of the cab, I brace myself for impact. I cradle my guitar close to my chest a mere second before metal crunching against metal deafens me. Glass filters into the taxi like stars sparkling in a blackened sky.

My body lurches forward at a rate too fast to stop, only ending when my head smashes against the crumbled doorframe.

Then all I see is blackness.

As my eyes jerk open, agony rockets down my spine. The pain radiating down my face is intense. It feels like I'm being torn in two. When my lungs battle to fill with air, blood splatters the headrest in front of me. I attempt to move my legs, but they don't budge an inch. I'm trapped, my legs crushed by the driver's seat.

I blink to clear my hazy vision when a quiet female voice says, "He's gone."

A female paramedic is leaning through the window of the cab. She's being held by her ankles by a male paramedic outside.

After placing a white sheet over the driver's still body, she crawls over shards of glass to reach me. I try to voice my thanks for her assistance, but the blood gurgling in my throat thwarts my words.

Goosebumps prickle my nape when she places her fingers on my neck. "He has a pulse; it's faint, but it's there." When a male paramedic hands her a neck brace, she carefully places it around my neck. "Just hold on, okay? Keep fighting; help is on the way."

I blink, acknowledging I heard her. She doesn't notice my efforts.

A blanket is thrown over my head seconds before a machine crunches through the metal holding me hostage. Since I'm drifting in and out of consciousness, I don't know how much time passes before the roof of the taxi is curled back like a sardine can lid, but I do know one thing. It fuckin' kills when they attempt to drag me out of the crumbling taxi.

The reason for my pain comes to light when the fireman advises my foot is crushed under the front seat, and that there's a bone sticking out of my thigh. After using the jaws of life to free my foot, they lift me onto a back-board without any hindrance.

As I'm stretchered across the asphalt, my gaze strays to the deathtrap I've just been freed from. The taxi is precariously perched on its side. It looks seconds from toppling. Once I'm lowered to the ground, paramedics rush around me. Although they're speaking, I can't understand a word they're saying. I'm woozy and sick, and my head is thumping so much, it feels like my brain is about to explode.

"Em..." I try to say.

I need Emily with me. She'll take away my pain. She makes everything better.

My head lolls to the side when a shadowed figure blocks the low-hanging morning sun. Ryan is standing at my side, and even though my eyesight is poor, I can't miss the tears threatening to spill from his eyes. I stare at him in shock. He doesn't cry—ever. Not even when he told me Chris had killed himself.

"Noah..." Ryan chokes on his spit as a single tear rolls down his ashen face.

Before I can tell him I'll be okay, someone yells in the distance, "You need to move now; the taxi won't hold much longer."

Bile rushes up my throat when I'm moved to the grass shoulder bordering the roadside. Although I'm in an immense amount of pain, I'm grateful for the additional jab of a needle in my arm. It eases the ache overwhelming every inch of me, but also increases the blurriness inflicting my head.

As I lie on the ground, struggling to breathe through the pain, I peer up at the fluffy clouds floating in the brilliant blue sky. Memories of Emily and me doing the same thing during our multiple trips to Bronte's Peak parts my lips. I don't know whether to cry or smile at the memory. If I don't fight, we may never have a day like that ever again. I can't let that happen. As much as this kills me to admit, Emily needs me as much as I need her. We complete each other, so I can't leave her no matter how much I'm hurting.

Just as I gain the courage to fight, I hear, "Noah," shouted in the distance. Even with my pulse shrilling in my ears, I recognize the voice. It belongs to Emily.

I try to move; I try to go to her, but I can't. My body is so damaged, I can't even wiggle my pinkie.

"Noah," Emily calls out again a mere second before she falls to her knees in front of me.

"Em..." I breathe out slowly, my words strained through the pain clutching my throat.

She curls her hand around mine before resting it in her lap. "I'm here, baby; I'm right here."

Her words are swallowed by a massive groan rolling up my chest. The pain ripping through me feels like it's crippling me. My head pounds profusely as my body thrashes against the ground. I shake without control, my body surrendering to the pain tearing it in two.

I return my focus to Emily, needing her beautiful eyes to ease the pain. She has a way of comforting me like no one else can. She'll ease my pain.

My heart stutters when I see Ryan dragging her away from me. "No!" I attempt to yell, but nothing comes out.

When Emily kicks and thrashes against Ryan, I stretch out my arm, trying to reach her. My efforts are pointless. Ryan is too quick. He's taking her away like he has everyone in my life.

"Let her go!" I want to scream, but the pain radiating down my face paralyzes my words.

I try to get up, to move, but I'm too weak to protect Emily like I promised. Ryan is taking her away from me. He can't do that. He was present at every terrible event that has happened in my life. He was first on scene when my little brother Michael died in a traffic accident, and he found Chris overdosed in his bathtub. He was there when I lost two of the most influential people in my life, and now he's taking Emily away from me too.

Just as Ryan darts behind a police patrol car, my vision locks on a pile of wood scattered on the middle of the ground. After adjusting my eyes, the final crack to break my heart beyond repair hits me. The guitar Emily bought me for my birthday sits to the left of the taxi. It's shattered, as unfixable and damaged as my heart.

With Emily stripped away from me, and my body crippled with pain, I allow the blackness engulfing me to take over...

My eyes bulge as my memories flood back in. Emily didn't leave me. I'm leaving her.

"No!" I drop to my knees in front of Emily. I want to touch her, to wipe her tears away because I hate when she cries, but she looks straight through me, not seeing me kneeling before her. "I'm sorry,

Beautiful. I'm so fucking sorry. I wanted to come back to you. My brain just got confused. I thought I had lost you. I made a mistake. I'm so sorry."

I apologize over and over again until the whiteness of the room becomes so blinding, I no longer see Emily standing in front of me.

CHAPTER 57

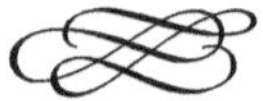

NOAH

It's so fucking bright, my eyes strain to adjust to the rays making my eyelids red. I blink on repeat, lubricating my eye sockets before slowly fluttering them open. My vision is so hazy, I can't make out anything in front of me. It's all foggy, like a windy gust floating over a frozen pond in winter. It's worse than I've experienced the past four months, which is shocking considering I haven't touched a drop of alcohol in weeks.

With my vision shut down, my other senses pick up its slack. The bed I'm resting on is as hard as a rock, and there's an annoying beep of a hospital monitor, but my side and chest are nice and toasty, and a familiar scent is lingering in the air. It's rich and sweet, almost sugary.

My heart beats madly when I realize why it's so memorable. It's the vanilla oil Emily dabbed onto her wrist and neck every morning since she was fourteen. She smells close, like she could be the cause of the hairs tickling my neck.

Desperate to have my theories confirmed, I open and shut my eyes for the next several seconds, clearing my vision enough I see Jacob's grinning face standing over my bed. His ugly mug wasn't the first I expected to see, but with my mind a little fucked up, I'll take anything I can get.

When Jacob presses his index finger to his lips, telling me to be quiet, I attempt to give him the finger. The reason for Emily smelling close is revealed when I move my arm. She's snuggled at my side, sleeping peacefully with her head on my chest and her arm draped over my midsection.

Oh my fucking god, she came back to me!

With my eyes close to bursting, I dip my chin so I can take a huge, undignified whiff of her hair. More tears burn my eyes when her smell carries through my body. She smells as good as I remember, and it has me going back for whiff after whiff after whiff.

When Jacob tells me he'll be back in a minute, I jerk up my chin, but my eyes remain arrested on Emily. I'm not taking them off her for a hundred years. I glide them over the thick lashes touching her olive cheeks, down the little curve in her nose, then across her plump, inviting lips that are slightly parted as she takes in shallow, heart-fixing breaths. She's so fucking beautiful, perfect in every way.

I'm about to take her in for the sixth time when I feel something move under the hand resting on her waist. I yank my hand away, frightened by the alien-like movement. "What the fuck?"

A sound so perfect it convinces me I'm in heaven echoes around the room when Emily giggles. It is so faultlessly perfect, it's lyrical gold to my ears. After enclosing her hand over mine, she guides it back to the slight curve in the bottom of her stomach before raising her eyes to mine. They're dampened with tears, but more than anything, they show her pride.

"You came back to me." When her stomach ripples under my hand, she corrects, "You came back to us."

"Us?" I strangle out, my confusion at an all-time high.

"Yes. *Us.*" She presses her lips to mine, her kiss innocent yet earth-moving. "You're going to be a daddy," she whispers over my mouth.

I yank back, fucking my head up with more dizziness. "You didn't lose our baby?"

Emily's brows furl before she shakes her head. "We had a bit of a scare, but everything is okay." As her stunned eyes bounce between mine, her teeth graze her bottom lip. "How do you know about that?"

I shrug, unsure how to explain anything. I'm so fucking confused right now, I'm not yet convinced any of this is happening. I feel like I'm in a trance, which isn't far from how I've felt the past four months.

Like the sun rising over the horizon, it dawns on me that our baby moved in her stomach. Doesn't that only happen once they're a few months along? "How far are you?"

My heart skips a beat when Emily smiles. Dream or not, I don't want to ever leave this room. I want to stay here forever, with her, for eternity.

"Twenty-three weeks."

My brows jump up my face. "How long does a standard pregnancy last?"

Emily giggles again. It's just as magical the second time around. "Normally forty weeks."

"So in a matter of months, I'm going to be a dad?"

My heart races when Emily nods. "In around seventeen weeks—"

"I'll be a dad—to a baby I created with you in seventeen weeks?!" *Fuck yes!*

When I scoot across the bed, my stomach launches into my throat. In my excitement, I failed to register my leg is being held together by a stupid splint.

"Are you okay?"

I scrub at the worried groove between Emily's brows with my thumb before nodding. "But I need you to lie down."

She glances at me with curious eyes before doing as requested. Once she's flat on her back, a small curve protrudes from her midsection. Ignoring the shake of my hand, panicked she's about to vanish, I place it on her stomach. It doesn't take long to feel the tiny flutters.

"He's showing off for his daddy."

My eyes rocket to Emily's. "It's a boy?"

She shakes her head. "Not officially. I'm just guessing."

My lips quirk. "Hmm, we'll see."

I don't know why, but the image of a little girl with dark curly hair and light brown eyes flashed before my eyes when I put my hand on Emily's stomach.

I stop tracking my thumb over the little person wiggling in Emily's stomach when a female voice shrills into my room. "He's *finally* awake."

Turning my gaze, I see a blonde lady with a medium build who appears to be in her late twenties. I recognize her voice, but I can't place her face.

"I knew you'd eventually come back."

The mirth in her tone is usual, but the snarky way she delivers her sassiness has me more than curious. I swear we've bickered numerous times the past few months, but if that's true, why does she look so different than the image in my head?

It can't be her, can it?

Too confused to hold back, I stammer, "Dr. Miller?"

She smiles a full-toothed grin before winking. "Bingo."

Emily takes in a sharp breath as she scoots up the bed. The more her eyes bounce between Dr. Miller and me, the lower her jaw hangs.

"I told you the cochlear nerve was the last to go," Dr. Miller advises Emily as she paces to my bedside. "How are you feeling? Any cramps, muscle spasms, pain, etc.?"

When I shake my head, too shocked to form a verbal reply, Emily's eyes narrow. I hate hospitals, so I'll lie through my teeth if it will have me discharged.

Refusing to disappoint Emily any more than I already have, I murmur, "I'm a little achy."

"That's expected. You've been in a coma for three months. It will take extensive physical therapy to get your body back to its original condition, but I have no doubt you will make a full recovery. You're a fighter."

I stare into Dr. Miller's hazel eyes, dazed and confused. She did just say I've been in a coma for three months, didn't she? How can that be right? I just completed three months of rehabilitation with her, didn't I?

My bewilderment is heard in my tone when I ask, "Sorry, but who are you—*exactly?*"

"I'm the specialist your record label brought in to assist you with your comatose state—"

"So you're not a therapist for people with anger and alcohol issues?"

Her smile enlarges before she shakes her head. "No, I'm not that type of therapist."

My eyes drift to Jacob, who has his shoulder propped against the doorframe of my room. If anyone will help me see sense through the madness, it will be him.

Regrettably, he appears as confused as me. Everyone in the room is looking at me weirdly, like nothing I'm saying is making any sense. They're not the only ones reeling. I'd pinch myself to check if I'm alive if I wasn't panicked it would steal Emily back away from me.

My eyes stray back to Dr. Miller when she places her hand over mine. "Studies have proven the cochlear nerve is the last thing to be affected in patients in a comatose state. That means, while you appear unconscious, your brain still picks up events and things happening around you and formulates its own response to them. Although the thoughts in your head may appear real, more times than not, they're a result of your subconscious activity."

I stare at her, certain I misheard her explanation. Everything I've been through for the past few months, believing I'd lost Emily, her funeral, the band tours, and my time in rehab couldn't have been a part of my subconscious. It felt so real, and it hurt so much. You don't dream shit like that. It was a nightmare... a real-life motherfucking nightmare.

Dr. Miller breaks the silence teeming between Emily, Jacob, herself, and me. "Do you want to talk about what happened while you were unconscious?"

"No," I force out without a second thought.

They're not memories I want to rehash. They were the worst months of my life, so I'd rather forget they happened than explain them to people I'm not sure aren't figments of my imagination.

I pull Emily into my chest. Hallucination or not, she's here, with me. That's all that matters.

When Emily peers up at me with wide, panicked eyes, I murmur, "I'll tell you one day, just not today. Okay?"

She nods, acknowledging she heard me before burrowing her face into my chest. I tighten my grip around her torso before closing my eyes to relish having her in my arms again.

"*Psst.*" I peg a rolled-up tissue at Jacob, snarling when it misses its mark. It floats to the ground instead of smacking him in the chops. I give it a second shot to gain his attention, except this time, I use a pen. "*Psst.*"

When he grumbles a curse word, unappreciative of the pen smacking him in the nose, I press my finger to my lips. Emily is asleep in my arms, my early morning awakening tiring on her pregnant body. Apparently, her favorite sleeping position didn't alter while I was in a coma. She just had to wait for the nurses to do their final checks before slipping into my bed. Her favorite side changed, though. With my left leg fucked up, she now snuggles into my right.

Upon spotting my signal, Jacob jerks up his chin before leaning close to my bedside. He's the same Jacob I remember from the past few months, just not as hazy.

"Can I ask you something?"

When he notches his chin up for the second time, I swivel my tongue around my mouth to loosen it up before speaking words I never want to speak again. "Did Emily die?"

"Huh?" Jacob's brows furrow. "Emily? As in *your* Emily?" He sounds as confused as I still feel. Although I "woke" hours ago, I still feel like I'm dreaming.

When I nod, he murmurs, "No. Why would you think that?"

"We went to her funeral." Confusion blasts through his eyes when I wave my hand between us. "We carried her coffin out of the church. You stood at my side."

"I stood at your side at Chris's funeral—"

"This wasn't Chris's funeral. It was Emily's. There were lilies on her casket, and a photo of us on top."

Jacob urges me to calm down when the heart monitor next to my bed reveals the spike of my pulse. Once it is settled, he asks, "That photo?"

He points to the window ledge in the far right corner of my room. There's a photo of Emily and me in a frame next to a large bouquet of white lilies, the same photo from her funeral.

"I brought the photo because I knew it was your favorite. We don't know who the lilies are from. They've been coming in every week for the past three months."

I lick my dry lips as I try to break through the fog in my head. Now that I'm thinking back, Emily's funeral was held at the same church Chris's was. Jacob watched over me that day as he did at Emily's funeral, there was just one difference: my dad didn't crash the event.

"My dad was there."

"Here?" Jacob corrects, assuming I worded my statement wrong.

I didn't.

"No, he was at Emily's funeral."

He gives me a look, one that reveals he's worried about my mental well-being. I understand his worry. I'm feeling a little unhinged right now. "Your dad was granted parole the day of your accident. He's been floating in and out of your hospital room the past three months."

"Okay." I'm not convinced, but who am I to argue? I think one thing happened, when everyone around me believes another.

As a timeline of the past few months roll through my head, my hand darts up to my neck. I'm still wearing the guitar pendant Jacob gave me the day after Emily's funeral.

Before I can ask Jacob about it, he confesses, "Ryan found a shard of your guitar in the wreckage. With Jenni's help, I had it placed onto the pendant for you. I knew how much your guitar meant to you; I'm just sorry I couldn't get the whole inscription."

"You've said that to me before, haven't you?"

Jacob peers at me in utter shock. "Yes. The day I put it around your neck in the very bed you're sitting in. You heard what I said that day?"

"No... not exactly. I don't know what the fuck I heard or didn't hear. I'm so confused."

When I lean back to run a shaky hand over my head, Emily murmurs in her sleep. My panic switches from soothing me to comforting her. I run my hand up and down her arm until the rapid movements of her eyes settle. Comforting her eases the turmoil in my gut. I can feel her, smell her, and touch her, but I'm afraid I'm seconds from waking up to discover I'm once again dreaming. That's why I can't sleep. I don't want to risk losing her again.

Jacob aims to settle my confusion. "What else happened in that head of yours while you were asleep? By the sounds of it, none of it was pleasant."

While Emily rests, I go through every event I believe occurred the prior four months. My attempt to end my life, the band's tour, my run-in with the paparazzi, and my months in rehab. For every event I recall, Jacob offsets my claims with an activity my muddled brain may have misconstrued.

The words Jacob yelled at me after my suicide attempt were the words he screamed when I tried to end my life after Chris took his. The band did owe two million dollars for failing to fulfill our contract, but instead of going on tour, Nick's older brother Isaac loaned us the money. I didn't beat a member of the paparazzi; Jacob did after he snuck into my room to get an exclusive picture of me on my death bed, and although my months of rehab were true, they weren't as I remember them.

Dr. Miller specializes in rehabilitating patients in comas. Our twice-daily conversations occurred without fail, but they were as one-sided as I wish they had been when I experienced them.

Jacob even has plausible explanations for the most minute things, such as Emily traveling to me so we could get married. He said they were discussing it in my room. He even mentioned the suit he left hanging on my closet door. His description matched the suit I thought I wore to Emily's funeral.

An uneasy grin stretches across Jacob's face as he scratches his brow. "How long did you think it was before you went on the road?"

Although unsure where he's going, I reply, "Six days."

His grin enlarges. "And you performed, right?"

"Yeah. Why?"

Air whistles between his teeth as he shakes his head in disbelief. "Day six of your coma was the first day we registered movement from you. You tapped your fingers on the bedsheets." He sinks into his chair, his hand shooting up to scrub the messy beard on his chin. "It was to the beat of 'Hollow.'"

I stare at him in bewilderment, shocked beyond words. Over the past thirty minutes, he has proved without doubt that every event I thought occurred was based on things I overheard while in a coma. My fucked-up brain just didn't register them as good snippets of information. It flipped them on their head, making what should have been pleasant dreams terrifying nightmares.

"This type of thing isn't unusual, Noah." Jacob scoots closer to my bed, ensuring I can hear his whispered words over Emily's faint snores. "From the research Rachel showed me, nightmares occur more often in comatose patients than people realize. Some patients take longer recovering mentally from their injuries than physically when they wake — especially ones with circumstances like yours. Emily was with you before Ryan pulled her away. With your history, it's understandable that you got a little muddled up."

"So I'm not dreaming? Emily is here? Alive and well?" I hate that my voice cracks, but when it's a choice between crack or sob, I'd rather it be the former.

Jacob stands from his chair to mess my hair before pulling my head into his chest. I don't feel like such a soft-cock when I hear how hard his heart is raging. He's struggling too, his reasons are just different than mine.

"Yes, Noah. She's here. With you. Alive and well. She's not going anywhere. I promise you that."

CHAPTER 58

NOAH

To say the past month has been a fun, exciting time would be a major fucking understatement. The grueling twice-daily sessions I had with Dr. Miller the past three months still occur, except we no longer sit around and chat. She rides my ass with painful physical therapy sessions and a workout routine not designed for a man who spent the last three months in a coma.

Dr. Kirkpatrick, the doctor who refused to give up on me when I went into cardiac arrest the night my head thought I was in a car accident, denied my request to discharge myself from the hospital against medical advice. When Jacob threatened to pin me to my bed until I abided by his terms, I glared at him. He returned my stare, but his was brimming with confusion, unsure why I grumbled my frustration about him using his size against me.

That was the first but, unfortunately, not the last time I've fucked up when striving to separate fact from fiction the past month.

Adjusting back to the reality of life is hard, but as the days roll on, I have more understanding on how events that transpired during my coma played havoc with my subconscious.

Just the fact Ryan was the one who dragged Emily away from me at the accident scene made me believe she was dead. He told me about my brother dying, so when I meshed those days with the morning of my accident, the worst nightmare of my life commenced.

Thank god Emily's death was nothing more than the inner workings of a fucked-up, disturbed mind.

Although the past month has been grueling, there's also been many wonderful moments. The most gratifying was seeing my baby kicking inside Emily's stomach. Dr. Kirkpatrick arranged for Emily to have an ultrasound at the hospital clinic so I could be wheeled down to attend. They have the coolest 3D ultrasound machine. We saw our baby's ten little fingers and ten little toes in crystal clear detail. It was so defined, I'm convinced our baby will have Emily's little turned-up nose.

When they asked if we wanted to find out the baby's gender, Emily's gaze turned to mine, wordlessly seeking permission. I shook my head. After everything we have been through, I wanted it to be a surprise. I thought Emily would be upset because she seemed so excited when the ultrasound technician asked, but her smile didn't falter. It was as blistering as it was the day I woke and the thirty-seven days that have followed.

Emily hasn't left my side. I use her for motivation. Her standing at the end of the walking bars is all the incentive I need to get to the other end. Her smile inches higher on her face with every step I take toward her. Her smile is nearly as large as her belly has grown the past month. She can still get away without looking pregnant if she wears a loose shirt, but if it's fitted, she can't hide her little bump. I'm glad, because I can't wait to share the news of our baby with our fans.

They've been so dedicated the past five months, our album continues to hold its number one spot. It's the longest number one selling album Destiny Records has ever produced, and its royalties meant the debt the band had with Isaac was repaid in full within the first week I came out of the coma.

I'll be honest, I was surprised Isaac could lend us that much money. His dance club is very popular, but I didn't think he had millions of dollars in the bank to borrow on a whim. However, I'm beyond grateful he eased the pressure placed on Emily's shoulders when she found out I was being sued.

At Emily's request, the two million dollars the acoustic version of "Surrender Me" has raised was donated to a brain injury research fund. I'm incredibly grateful I didn't sustain any permanent damage from my accident, but others aren't as lucky as me. I survived, but the driver of my taxi did not. Part of the profits from our current album will go to the driver's family. I know firsthand what they're going through, so I want to lessen their grief in any way possible. Money won't do that, but it will give them time to grieve.

I haven't seen or heard from Delilah the past month. To be honest, I don't give a fuck what's going on with her, as long as she's kept away from Emily. When Jacob let slip about some run-ins Emily had with Delilah, I was furious. Jacob swore he took care of it, and I trust he did. He protects the people he cares about just as fiercely as I do. For that alone, I'll be forever in his debt.

So here I am, four months after my accident, and one month after waking up, I'm finally allowed to go home. I'm not walking out the same Noah I once was. My leg was severely broken, leaving me with a slight limp, which Dr. Miller guarantees will vanish over time, and I have a scar running down my forehead from where I headbutted the doorframe. I'm scarred both mentally and physically, but Emily still looks at me like I'm the only star in the sky, so that's all that matters. Nothing but her and our baby matter. The rest is just white noise.

"Ready?" Cormack joins us at the double glass exit doors of the hospital.

I smile before dipping my chin. "As ready as we'll ever be."

With Emily cradled under my arm and my hand hovering over her stomach, we walk headfirst into a tsunami of reporters and fans.

CHAPTER 59

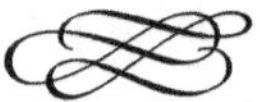

EMILY

*N*oah's eyes pop out of his head. "How much?"

After grinning a beaming smile, Cormack repeats his estimate. "Ninety-eight million dollars."

Feeling woozy, I take a seat at the dining table Cormack and the band are seated around. Cormack has been updating the band on how well their album has been selling since Noah woke from his coma. Never one to tiptoe around the obvious, Slater asked Cormack straight-up what type of royalties the band would see from "all those sales."

We were aware their album held the number one spot for months, but we had no clue what that meant money-wise. Now we do. In not even six weeks, the band has earned themselves ninety-eight million dollars.

When silence descends around me, I peer at Noah. His mouth is open wide, and he's frozen in place. It's only when Nick and Slater bound out of their seats to scream in jubilation does he finally snap out of his trance.

"Can you believe it?" He drops to his knees in front of me before placing his hands on each side of my belly. "We did it." My heart melts when he kisses my rapidly growing bump.

"I knew you would."

Not wanting the baby to steal all the glory of his excitement, I pull his handsome face to mine to give him a long, tantalizing kiss. I don't care who's watching. I have months of missed kisses to make up for, so I get them in at every available opportunity.

Noah and I only stop sucking face when Jacob slaps Noah's shoulder. "You did it!"

Noah's lips rise against mine before he stands to return Jacob's excitement. "*We* did it, Jake; *we* fucking did it."

When Noah slings his arms around Jacob's shoulders, Jacob's face goes deadpan. Noah has never been overly affectionate, but I've noticed an uptick in man hugs and bro cuddles with Jacob and his bandmates since his accident. I hate that it took a near-death scare for him to realize how many people love and adore him, but at least it happened before it was too late.

My hand darts up to stifle my giggles when Jacob spins Noah around the room like he usually does me. "You love my big teddy hugs."

"Put me the fuck down, Jacob!"

Noah's anger only makes Jacob spin him more. He twirls and twirls and twirls him until Noah's stomach curdles as violently as mine did the first three months of my pregnancy.

Can you imagine the shock? Discovering you are pregnant by reading a note your fiancé left to say he arranged his transportation to the airport.

Noah signed the bottom of his note, "*I can't wait for you to be my wife and the mother of my children.*" I read his message over a dozen times before it finally dawned as to why my eyes wouldn't stop watering, and I was extra emotional from his note. My period was late.

That's how I stumbled upon Noah's accident. I was racing to tell him about our baby.

But instead of it being the most glorious day of our life, it was the most tragic.

Seeing Noah like that... I can't put it into words. It was horrific, an image I'd give anything to remove from my mind. The three months he spent in a coma were the hardest months of my life. I endured vicious run-ins with Delilah and members of the paparazzi who don't understand the word respect, but those exchanges were nothing compared to the pain I encountered when I woke up one morning with my underwear covered with bright red blood.

Unless you're a woman in the glow of pregnancy, you'll never understand the terror that shreds through you when you think you're having a miscarriage. You blame yourself. You think you did something wrong. When in reality, nothing you did or could have done would change the outcome. Some babies are born to live. Others aren't.

I thank my lucky stars every single day that our baby was a fighter like his daddy. Noah fought to find his way back to me, just like his son or daughter fought to hold on. They're both strong-willed individuals I'll worship until the day I take my final breath.

I check my cheeks for wetness when Jacob finally relents to Noah's threats of disembowelment. Noah stops in front of me, his wobbly legs barely keeping him upright. "Stop looking for a house. I know the perfect one for us to buy."

"Okay. Where...?" I leave my question open, hoping he'll fill in the gaps. He does no such thing. He just presses his lips to mine before bolting into our bedroom.

When he was discharged from the hospital, we headed straight for Jacob's. Jacob is family, and he welcomed us with open arms, but with a baby on the way, the sooner we find a place of our own, the better. I'm not nesting—*yet*—I'm just dying for a little bit of privacy.

I'll forever love Rise Up, but with Noah not itching to get back to the industry he adores any time soon, Jacob's house is constantly overrun with rowdy bandmates and associates of theirs. Excluding the times we're snuggling in bed, I barely get Noah by myself.

Noah and I talked a lot about the band the past two weeks. Although he's planning to go back to music at some point, he won't make any definite plans until after our baby is born. A couple of months won't hurt anyone. It will give Noah time to recover, and will have him going back refreshed and eager to entertain his fans. Even Cormack agrees a few months will be good for all involved.

After showing Cormack out, I head to our room to see what Noah is up to. He's taking a call, but he notices me in an instant. He summons me to his side with the wiggle of two fingers. When I reach him, he pulls me down until I'm straddled on his lap. Air hisses between my teeth when I feel how hard he is. I was afraid he wouldn't find me attractive once he woke from his coma—I did look like I had swallowed a cantaloupe.

But I had no reason to fret.

Within days, I realized Noah couldn't get enough. He's always been an attentive and affectionate lover, but it grew tenfold since his accident—even more so since we don't need to keep watch for nurses like we did when he convinced me to get freaky with him at the hospital.

Dr. Miller hasn't looked me in the eyes since she walked in on us after a physical therapy session one afternoon. She was polite and quickly diverted her eyes, but her cheeks were the color of beets when she darted out of the room.

I haven't been the only one a little sensitive the past two weeks. Noah will never say anything, but I know he's worried his limp ruins his appeal. But the exercises Dr. Miller has him doing twice daily means you hardly notice it anymore, and the scar on his forehead is a great conversation-starter.

For someone who hates talking, Noah loves making up stories to tell strangers about the gash on his head. You wouldn't believe the stories he makes up. They range from being bitten by a shark to being eaten by a grizzly bear. They believe him too! It's only when he can't stop shaking at the end of his story do they realize they've been punked.

"Four weeks?"

I graze my teeth along Noah's earlobe, feeling his cock twitch, before dropping my lips to his neck. I'm doing my best to pretend I'm not paying any attention to his conversation, where in reality, I'm eavesdropping like he's about to spill next week's Powerball numbers.

"If you offer them more, can they shave it down to one?" He pauses a beat before continuing. "I don't care how much, as long as it's ASAP."

I stare at a speckle of dust on the windowsill when Noah detects my snooping eye. With a grin of a man who makes my pussy tingle, he stands, taking me with him. He carefully deposits me onto our bed and mouths for me to *stop being a snoop*, before tapping my backside and exiting his room with a strut that leaves no doubt his sexy rock star swagger is back full force.

Approximately two weeks later, Noah requests for me to go for a drive with him. During our twenty-minute trip, I try to pry out of him where we're going. He's better at keeping secrets than me. He only smiles before telling me to be patient.

When his truck pulls into a familiar-looking driveway, excitement bubbles in my veins. "You rented the cabin again?"

My insides tap dance. I fell in love with this cabin the first time we came here, but we didn't get much chance to enjoy it with everything that happened between Nick and Jenni.

"Is it just us staying? Or are the rest of the guys coming too?" I peer past my shoulder, praying there isn't a lineup of cars behind us.

There isn't. It's just us. *Yes!*

After parking his truck at the front of a four-car garage, Noah throws open his door before running around to assist me down from his truck. "Careful," he murmurs when I hop down the last step.

He's such a worrywart, forever panicked me or the baby might get hurt. I don't know why. We weren't the ones who spent three months in the hospital. I did have that one scare a few weeks ago, but other than that, things have been relatively smooth.

As we walk hand in hand toward the cabin, I take in its beauty. It's not a rustic cabin by any means. It has two stories, six bedrooms, large wrap-around porches, and a kitchen a gourmet chef would jizz in his pants to cook in. It sits on nearly an acre of land, and the neighbors are far enough away that it's quiet, but it doesn't have that isolated, country feel you get when you live in the middle of nowhere.

Noah's quick strides stop when we reach the front door. "I have to do this right."

A girly squeal rips through my lips when he bends down to hoist me off the ground. He cradles me in his arms like a husband would a wife while carrying her over the threshold.

I realize that's exactly what he's doing when he enters the foyer. "Welcome home, Beautiful."

My eyes snap to his as my pulse spikes. "You bought the cabin?"

My heart beats triple time when he nods. "Really?" When he nods again, I throw my arms around his neck and hug him tight. "I love you, I love you, I love you." I place a kiss on his face with every declaration of love I make.

"So you're not angry?"

"Why would I be angry? I love this cabin! It's private too, so the annoying paparazzi will be less likely to get a picture of us here."

Noah's jaw tightens. On his way out of the hospital, at Noah's request, Cormack arranged a press conference at the front. There were thousands of fans in attendance, excited to see Noah walk out of the hospital. Noah began the junket by announcing that we're engaged and expecting our first child at the end of June. Although there was a handful of disgruntled faces, for the most part, fans have been supportive of us and our relationship.

The paparazzi though...not a day has gone by without me hearing the click of a camera. Even the most mundane tasks don't scare them away. I was hanging clothes on the line the other day when Jacob's dad, Tom, watered out a pesky reporter with a garden hose. He complained he would sue us for damages, but he calmed down when Tom said next time he'll shoot him for trespassing. Tom wasn't joking.

After hearing what had happened, Cormack hired a bodyguard to stay with us. Because Noah is forever concerned about my safety, he sided with Cormack. I wasn't worried. Who in their right mind would break into a house that has both a previous fighting champion and an overprotective father-to-be inside? You'd have to be certifiably mad.

My thoughts return to the present when Noah sweeps me back into his arms. "Time to christen the master suite."

"We already have."

I'm not joking, every surface of that room was thoroughly christened our first visit here.

I grow wet when Noah presses his lips to my ear. "Yeah, but that was when we were guests. We get to do it as owners this time around."

CHAPTER 60

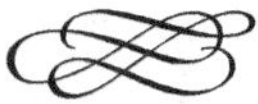

NOAH

"Dr. Morgan kept saying, 'he,' during the scan?"

My gaze drifts from the road to Emily, who is sitting in the passenger seat of my truck. She looks the same as she did when I woke from my coma, except now it appears as if she shoved a basketball down her shirt.

"That doesn't mean anything."

"Yes, it does! He didn't just say it once he said it three times—I was counting."

Fuck, she's beautiful when she's playful like this. If I weren't driving down the freeway, I'd pull her luscious lips to mine to ravish her beautiful mouth. Instead, I continue our banter. "He called the baby a 'he' so he wouldn't have to call it an 'it.' He was being professional."

Emily rolls her eyes. "In just a few short weeks, you'll be eating your words, Noah-*Stubborn*-Taylor."

My cock braces against my zipper when she giggles. Fuck, I love her laugh. Her smile. Her face. I love everything about her.

"Uh-huh, we'll see who's wrong."

Ten minutes later, I pull my truck into the driveway of the cabin we now call home. It's been an amazing few months. I get Emily to myself for twenty-four hours of every day. We cook together; we talk; we make love, then we laze around just enjoying each other's company. I had no clue how vital downtime was until I thought I lost everything important to me.

I'm still struggling to remember I never lost Emily, that my mind was just playing tricks on me, but it's becoming easier with each day that passes. It's amazing how much comfort I get from never letting her out of my sight. I'd keep it this way forever if I could.

"Can you pull in close to the stairs? I'm about to burst."

I laugh before doing as instructed. We're returning from Emily's fourth ultrasound with her obstetrician, Dr. Morgan. Although my mother works as a receptionist at Dr. Morgan's clinic, Emily really wanted Dr. Morgan to be her obstetrician. She had a bond with him after he assured her a low-lying placenta was the cause of her scare the day I woke from my coma, and I hated that my mother was stopping her from having what she wanted. I had promised her the world, and I intended to keep my promise.

It took some negotiating, but Dr. Morgan now oversees Emily's care, and instead of her going to his office, he visits Emily at our house. It's costing me a pretty penny, but the look on Emily's face when Dr. Morgan came for her first appointment was worth a million.

Emily is now thirty-six weeks pregnant. We found out today that the placenta has moved out of the way so she can have a natural birth. I'm ecstatic, because the idea of Emily going under the knife freaks me the fuck out. Her being injured in any way is one of the neuroses I'm still working through. Just like all my recoveries, it will happen —*eventually.*

Emily snickers when I dart around from my truck to help her down. She thinks I'm a worrywart, but she doesn't know what I went through. I still have nightmares about losing her and our baby. They feel as real as the months I was in a coma. I wake up screaming with drenched clothes and vomit sitting at the base of my throat. One glance at Emily's face while she sleeps calms me down in an instant, but that's also the reason I can't let her out of my sight. I don't know how I'll respond if I wake up like that and she's not there.

As Emily waddles toward our house, my cell rings. Pulling it out of my jeans pocket, I notice it's a call from Jacob. "I'll be a minute, Em."

She raises her arm, acknowledging she heard me, but she's in too much of a hurry to reply.

After swiping my hand over my screen, I press my phone to my ear. "Hey, Jake."

"Hey, is Em with you?"

A grin curls on my lips. "Nah, she just waddled into the house."

Jacob's laughter joins mine. "About to pee her pants again?"

"Something like that."

He takes a moment to settle his chuckles before advising why he's calling. "Sparks can do the aisle as you're requesting, but their quote made my eyes water."

Jacob could have a million dollars in his account, yet a $100 bill makes him want to cry. He's not cheap. He's just...*cheap.*

"I don't care how much it costs. I'm happy to pay if the aisle will be like I envision."

He whistles like I'm made out of money. With how well our album is doing, I'm beginning to wonder if I am.

"Alright, I was just checking. I'll call you later."

After christening the cabin for a second time, I asked Emily to be my wife—*again.* I balked when she responded by jumping out of bed to get dressed. When I asked her what she was doing, she said we were going to get the first flight to Vegas and marry the instant we land. I was stoked she was as eager to get hitched as I was, but I wanted us to have something more memorable than a Vegas quickie.

When I told her that, tears welled in her eyes, but she agreed we deserved something special after everything we had been through. She seemed a little apprehensive when I said I wanted us to wed before our baby was born. It was selfish of me to want her to have my last name before our child enters the world, but that wasn't the only reason I wanted to marry her so quickly. I know just how fast the rug can be pulled out from beneath your feet, so I didn't want to waste a single moment.

With that in mind, I began planning our wedding. In just two short weeks, Emily will *finally* be my wife. If it weren't for Jacob, we'd most likely be getting married with our guests' butts planted on bales of hay. Well, not quite that bad, but it wouldn't have flowed as easily without Jacob's help.

He's always been great like this, so I wish he'd give my offer to be my assistant more thought. He didn't have to shoot me down as rudely as he did. He told me he'd rather fuck himself than become my assistant.

He thinks his refusal was the end of it. He has no clue I've been transferring money into his account every month since the week before my accident. He can be my assistant, even without an official title.

That's what best friends are for, right?

CHAPTER 61

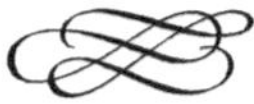

EMILY

"*B*reathe, Emily."

I clutch Jenni's wrist as my lungs fight for air. I'm not in labor; I'm just panicked out of my mind. I guess nerves are common for brides on their wedding day. It isn't that I have cold feet; it's the fact I'm thirty-eight weeks pregnant and about to walk down the aisle in front of our family and friends. Please don't let today be the day my water breaks, or if it is, can it be after I've seen what Noah planned?

I don't know any details of our wedding, except that the ceremony and reception are being held in the gardens at our cabin. Noah banned me from going outside the past week. He's lucky my heavily pregnant body hates the heat, so I've been more than happy to veg out in the air conditioning, watching my favorite movies.

"Here you go."

I can't help the smile that curves on my lips when Nicole hands me my bridal bouquet. The stems of the white lilies are wrapped in bright fluorescent yellow ribbon. It matches the fluorescent yellow dress I wore the night we became an official couple. I love all the little details Noah has included in our day. It shows how truly romantic he is.

A wolf whistle parts my lips when my dad joins Jenni, Nicole, and me in the foyer. I've never seen him in a suit, much less scrubbed up as nice as he is now. His shaggy dark hair is combed out of his eyes, showing off his murky green irises to perfection, and the long sleeves of his suit cover the tattoos on his arms. He looks handsome and put-together, which is a rarity for him.

"Ready?"

Smiling broadly, I nod. I'm more than ready. The day I've often dreamed about is finally here. I'm about to become Mrs. Noah Taylor. When Jenni and Nicole take their place in front of me, butter-flies tap dance in my stomach. I'm not the only one shaking. I swear I can hear Nicole's knees clanging together.

I was fine with Noah planning our wedding, but I requested permission to choose the bridesmaids' dresses because I wanted to force Nicole out of her comfort zone. Nicole is so shy, if Jenni and I don't give her the occasional push, she'll live a boring, sheltered life. We don't need her to go bungy jumping or swimming with sharks, we just want her to feel comfortable in her own skin.

When she sees everyone's reaction to the daring dress she's wearing tonight, I'm confident that will happen. It's a spaghetti strap design with a fitted bodice. The back drapes drastically, stopping just before the two dimples in her lower back. She'd never wear a dress so daring, but not even she could deny how beautiful she looked in it. I'm glad she's an accommodating bridesmaid, or things would have gotten extremely awkward.

When I exit the wooden double doors of the cabin on the elbow of my dad, I'm blinded by the flash of a camera. Thankfully, this time around, it isn't the annoying paparazzi. It's the cameraman Noah hired to capture our day.

The gasps of our family and friends as I walk down the steps of our cabin prick my eyes with tears. They stare at me with the same wonder Noah's eyes hold when he looks at me. I feel loved, protected, and beautiful all thanks to their admiring glances.

After following the white-carpeted aisle around the corner, I spot Noah. He's standing on a glass platform in the middle of our infinity pool. With lights flickering through the sturdy glass material, it's a truly magnificent visual, although it can't compete with the sight of Noah in a suit.

The darkness of his pin-striped suit matches the intensity of his eyes. Pair that with the midnight black dress shirt underneath, and the single white lily pinned to his chest, and you've got an incredibly alluring visual that wipes away the image of him lying lifeless on the pavement months ago from my memory bank.

Noah's gaze never wavers from mine as I make my way down the aisle to him. He mouths for the entire world to see that he loves me before accepting the hand my dad is holding out for him.

Once they shake hands, he assists me onto the glass platform while whispering, "Because we have the whole world at our feet."

Tears gather in my eyes. "Yes, we do."

He rubs away my tears with his thumbs. "No crying, Beautiful, not today."

Nodding, I hand my bouquet to Jenni before joining Noah in front of our celebrant. She gets straight down to business.

"Family and friends, we've joined here today to share with Noah Gibson Taylor and Emily Faye McIntosh an important moment in their lives. In their time together, they have seen their love and understanding for each other grow and blossom, and now they have decided to live out the rest of their lives as one. If any person can show just cause why they may not be joined together—let them speak now or forever hold their peace."

Noah's face pales when a cough sounds from behind his shoulder. With his jaw ticking, he cranks his neck back to the person interrupting.

Jacob gives him a playful wink before dropping his eyes to mine. "Are you sure you want to marry him, Em? I'm still available."

I laugh along with our two hundred guests. "Thanks for the offer, Jake, but I'll stick with Noah."

Jacob shrugs like he can't possibly understand why I won't run away with him before shifting on his feet to face the celebrant. "Okay, I guess you can continue."

Everyone laughs again, except Noah. He appears seconds from strangling him.

I run my thumb along his hand clasped around mine, striving to get his focus back on me. When his dark, intense eyes land on me, I whisper, "I love you."

"I love you too, Beautiful." He doesn't whisper his words like me. He declares his love for the world to hear, not the least bit embarrassed. I love that about him. That he's not ashamed to show he's in love. A lot of people could learn a thing or two from him.

Overwhelmed by how much I love him, I lean forward to press my lips to Noah's. Our guests laugh again when the celebrant says, "We're supposed to save *that* for after the vows, but whatever floats your boat."

My cheeks flame with heat as I pull back. "Sorry."

"At least we know you're not here against your wishes." She waits for the guests to stop laughing before starting our ceremony. "Who gives this woman to be wed?"

"We do," declare my mom and dad from the front row.

After admiring my mom's stunning peach-colored lace dress, I shift my eyes to Noah's dad, who is seated next to my dad. Noah made contact with him a few weeks ago. It's a slow process, but it feels right having him here to celebrate our day.

"Repeat after me." The celebrant tilts her microphone toward Noah's mouth.

An adorable gleam brightens Noah's eyes as he confesses, "I have my own vows I want to recite to Emily."

My lips curve into a smile. I've also written my own vows.

Once the celebrant gives him the go-ahead, Noah recites his vows straight from his heart. "Emily, I knew the day you were leaning against your bedroom door in a football jersey that you'd be my wife one day. I thought I could fight the inevitable, that I could resist your charm. I was wrong. You are more than I've ever hoped for, and more than I deserve, but I will love you until the end of time. Your face will never be marked with tears again unless they're from happiness radiating from deep inside you. Your smile will never be washed away, not with me by your side. You're my best friend, my lover, and now you're my wife. I promise to cherish you and love you every day of my life."

Heat spreads across my chest, loving that he used part of the lyrics from "Surrender Me" in his vows.

"I also have my own vows," I inform the celebrant when she angles the microphone to me. After a nerve-clearing breath, I say my memorized vows. "Noah, I loved you from the first moment I saw you, although it took you a little longer to notice than I would have liked." I stop to admire Noah's dimpled grin. "You're the beat to my rhythm, the step to my dance, and the lyrics to my song. I promise to continue helping you heal, to take care of you, and to stand by your side for the rest of my life. I promise to love, honor, and cherish you every day of my life."

"Now, we'll exchange the rings."

When the officiant directs Jacob to hand her our rings, I wait with bated breath for him to joke about forgetting them, so you can imagine my surprise when he simply gives them to her.

"Noah, repeat after me..." The celebrant's words taper off when her voice is drowned out by a helicopter hovering above us.

Noah shakes his head, disgusted at the lengths the paparazzi will go for an exclusive photo of our wedding. He has no clue how close they came to broadcasting images of him in his hospital bed to the world. If it weren't for Jacob smashing the pap's camera before knocking out his teeth, who knows how much the media would have profited from Noah's accident?

I've grown so much disdain for the media the past six months, I choked on my spit when Noah asked me to agree to an exclusive spread in a worldwide, well-known gossip magazine. I was shocked. I never thought he'd sell our wedding photos. It was only when he explained the money from the sale would be donated to a suicide prevention campaign did the reason behind his decision make sense. We both struggled with our own form of depression in our teens, so I was more than happy to support such a worthwhile cause. Noah made the donation in Chris's honor, and that, ladies and gentlemen, is another reason I fall in love with him more every single day.

Ignoring the interruption, Noah peers into my eyes as if I'm the only person in the world. "I, Noah, take you, Emily, to be my wife. I promise you love, honor and respect, and to be faithful to you, forsaking all others, until death do us part."

After swallowing harshly, he places my wedding ring on my finger, his hand trembling.

"I, Emily, take you, Noah, to be my husband. I promise you love, honor, and respect, and to be faithful to you, forsaking all others, until death do us part."

Once the platinum band is slipped on his finger, the celebrant says, "By the authority vested in me, it's my pleasure to pronounce Noah and Emily husband and wife. Noah, you may kiss your bride."

Smiling his panty-dropping grin, Noah tilts closer to me. While giving me a torturously slow and teasing kiss, our family and friends wolf whistle and cheer around us. They have no clue how much I wish they weren't here right now—even more so when Noah murmurs, "I can't wait to see what you're wearing under your dress."

I placed Noah on a two-week sex ban to make our wedding night more special. He thought it would only be hard on him, but since I'm pregnant, my appetite is tenfold. I'm struggling not to ravish him in front of our family and friends. I wouldn't hold back if my mom wasn't in the front row.

When I catch the gleam in Noah's eyes, I return his tease. "In another five to six hours you might find out."

Noah groans, just realizing we have the entire reception to get through before he discovers the strapless bustier and garter I'm wearing under my dress. The garter has blue guitars across it. Jenni gifted it to me this morning, citing it was perfect for something new and something blue.

After gathering my bouquet from Jenni, Noah and I walk down the aisle side by side. Our guests throw white rose petals at us while our photographer takes a million shots.

Several hours later when I walk into the reception tent at the back of our cabin, I gasp. The burgundy tulle draped down the white canvas ceiling matches Jenni and Nicole's dresses to perfection. The two dozen round tables scattered around a dance floor have burgundy table runners, and the plates and cutlery covering them are gold-dipped. On top of the table runners are glass vases filled with burgundy long-stemmed roses and white lilies, and there are millions of tiny fairy lights scattered throughout the room. It's truly breathtaking, the stuff of fairytales.

I spin to face Noah, my eyes once again watering. "How did you know the color of the girls' dresses?"

When we picked them, I swore Jenni and Nicole to secrecy, but the color of the burgundy in our reception tent is an exact match.

With a broad grin, he taps his nose with his index finger. "A little birdie told me." He bands his arms around my waist to tug me in as close as he can without squishing my thirty-eight-week pregnant stomach. "Do you like it?"

"I love it." I raise my chin up high so our eyes align. "I love you."

"I love you too, Beautiful." He presses a kiss to my lips before dropping to his knees. "And I love you too."

We spend the rest of the night celebrating with family and friends. Jacob and Jenni deliver heartfelt speeches before toasting to Noah and me having a long and happy marriage. We dance our first dance as husband and wife to the acoustic version of "Surrender Me" before my dad cuts in to ask for a dance, and Jacob and the guys from the band get heavily intoxicated.

Although our guests are loving the endless bar tab, Noah is stone-cold sober. He refuses to drink one drop of alcohol, believing the day he drinks will be the day I'll go into labor, and since he refuses to drive after consuming a drop of alcohol, his veins are filled with nothing but blood.

I jump out of my skin when I'm suddenly grabbed from behind. "Emily, baby! You love my big hugs, don't you?"

Noah laughs, finally catching on to Jacob's antics. With Noah not biting as he usually does, Jacob ups the ante. His kiss is only a peck, but it's sloppy and wet, launching Noah into action. "Fuck off, Jacob!"

Jacob laughs when Noah yanks me away from him. "There's still time, Em. The ink isn't dry yet." The bad slur of his words reveals he's drunker than I thought. I barely understood a thing he said.

Before I can assure Jacob not even a voided marriage certificate could steer me away from Noah, a soft voice pops up. "Congratulations, Noah and Emily."

Heat tracks across my cheeks when my eyes collide with Dr. Miller's. This is the first time we've locked eyes since she busted Noah and me getting hot and heavy in her physical therapy room. "Thank you."

Jacob stands straighter when Dr. Miller's eyes stray to him. "Hello, Jacob."

"Rachel," he greets her, no longer slurring.

My gaze shifts to Noah, wondering if he too can feel the tension in the air. He's watching Dr. Miller and Jacob with as much interest as me.

If I'm reading things right, Lola has competition, and considering she's seductively prancing toward Jacob as I speak, I'd say I'm not the only one aware of this.

When Lola leaps into Jacob's arms, his first response is shock. That's soon set aside for pleasure when Lola mashes their lips together, not caring when she's subjected to the wrathful glare of Dr. Miller.

"What did we miss?" Noah asks when Jacob and Lola veer off in one direction while Dr. Miller stomps in another.

As confusion gurgles in my stomach, I shrug. "I have no idea."

Jacob rarely left my side the three months Noah was in a coma, but even I'm shocked by the tension his interaction with Dr. Miller left hanging in the air.

CHAPTER 62

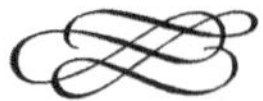

NOAH

Finally, our guests are gone and I have my beautiful wife all to myself. She's sitting on our bed, wearing nothing but a lace bustier and a garter with blue guitars around the elastic. She's fucking ravishing, and I'm dying to taste her again, but she stretches out her arm, halting my tiger-like prance.

"Stop right there."

I cock a brow, wordlessly warning her my patience is stretched thin. I haven't touched her sexually in two weeks. I can't wait any longer.

As her teeth rake her bottom lip, her eyes drift over my suit. "Strip... *slowly*."

The zipper in my trousers bites my cock when her tongue delves out to lick her top lip. Her confidence is at an all-time high today, and I'm loving every minute of it.

As I unbutton my suit jacket, her lust-crammed eyes watch me like a hawk. She's panting so hard, her tits thrust high with every breath she takes, and the scent of her arousal intensifies the longer we stand across from each other fighting the tension, but loving it at the same time.

Once I have my coat removed, I drop it to the floor then yank my dress shirt out of my trousers. Emily's lips part when I fiddle with the gold cufflinks on my sleeves. They're engraved with our initials: N & E. When I walk to the dresser to place my cufflinks on the top, Emily's eyes track my walk. Her eyes are full. I've never seen them as needy as they are now.

As my hands dart up to the top button of my dress shirt, I keep my eyes fixed on her. I go purposely slow, un-popping one button at a time, following her command to the T.

From the way she keeps fidgeting, I'm confident she's regretting her decision. She's so eager for me to hurry up, I haven't even gotten the third button undone before she races across the room, grips the lapels of my dress shirt in her hands and rips them open. "

"Oops," she murmurs when pearl buttons ping around the room.

She's not sorry. Not in the slightest. Her eyes are smoldering more now than they were when she stripped for me.

My belt is the next article of clothing she removes. She drops it to the ground with a clatter before her index finger treks down the ridges in my stomach. Once she has my muscles bunched up, she unclasps the button in my trousers then lowers the zipper. My cock twitches when her needy eyes drop to watch it be freed from my boxer shorts. It springs out with a *boing*, its buoyancy compliments of the vivaciousness in her eyes.

Precum beads on my knob when her French-tipped nails scratch my thighs as she guides my trousers down my legs. She huffs when my polished dress shoes foil her endeavor to strip me naked, but she doesn't let it dampen her eagerness. With the hunger of a woman who has never eaten, she falls to her knees, curls her hand around my cock then lowers her luscious lips down my twitching shaft.

My hips jerk forward, ramming in another two inches her hard suck missed. I mumble out an apology when she gags from swallowing too much of my cock in one go, but I don't think she hears it. I fist her hair to slow her pace. It isn't that I don't appreciate her eagerness, I just don't want her hurting herself. Just the thought of her in pain softens my hardest erection.

Any hope of slowing her down sails out the window when her

beautiful eyes lock with mine over the newly reforming bumps in my stomach. They relay her every want, need, and desire while also revealing that she wants this as much as I do.

Trusting that she would never do anything to harm herself or our baby, I loosen my grip on her hair and let myself go. My head flops back as my lips part to suck in much-needed air. The visual of her on her knees, sucking my cock slicks my body with sweat. She gives it her all, deepthroating me like she's been sucking my dick for years.

Although she was inexperienced when we first got together, it didn't take her long to learn the ropes. She didn't think I noticed, but I saw the way she paid attention to every moan tearing from my throat when we fooled around in my truck. Within weeks, she knew my body better than I did.

A gruff groan escapes my mouth when her tongue skids over the crest of my cock. Her moans over the drop of precum she gathered tickle my shaft. After moving her hair to the side to improve my view, I rock my hips faster. I feed my cock in and out of her mouth, smug as fuck that a woman as beautiful as Emily is on her knees, sucking my dick with my ring on her finger.

How the fuck did I ever get so lucky?

I just married the girl of my dreams, and now she's kneeling before me, answering every one of my wet dreams in the most fantastic way. Life can't get better than this.

No longer capable of reining in my desire to taste her again, I band my arms around Emily's waist and lift her from the ground. A disgruntled groan rolls up her chest when my cock pops out of her mouth. I steal every whimper by sealing my mouth over hers.

While our tongues dance a fire-sparking tango, my hand slithers down her lace bustier to unfasten the clasps. Our lips only part when the last hook is undone and her bustier falls to the floor without a noise.

I place Emily onto our bed before inching back to marvel at the view. Precum drips from my cock when my eyes absorb the raw beauty in front of me: inches of luxurious skin, generous curves that make my mouth water, and the most alluring face I've ever seen.

I can't breathe, think, or blink as I take her all in. My lips will touch every inch of her, but I don't know where to start first. At her glorious tits that have grown even more ravishing as our child grows inside her, or at the wetness between her scissoring legs that's begging for my attention?

How about both?

Emily licks her lips when I lean over her body to take her pert nipple into my mouth. As my tongue swirls around the hardened bud, I drop my hand to her pussy. She thrusts her hips forward when my thumb finds her clit. I circle it before sinking two of my fingers inside her.

I watch her over the bouncing globes of flesh on her chest, ensuring nothing but pleasure crosses her features as I pump in and out of her at the same tempo she sucked my cock. Her face is red with ecstasy, her lips are parted, and she's hot all over.

"You're not just a rock star on stage, are you?" She pushes away her bangs getting in front of her eyes. "You're also a rock star between the sheets."

The sexiness of her words has me working even harder to unravel her beneath me. I want her calling my name as she quivers in the aftermath of an orgasm. Needing to taste her as she comes, I release her nipple from my mouth with a pop before trailing my lips down her stomach.

"Leg up, Beautiful. Let me see you." My last four words come out with a groan when she places her leg on my shoulder before sweeping open her thighs. Although it's only my fingers pumping in and out of her, the visual is as enticing as when it's my cock.

I watch her for a few more minutes, relishing her pussy sucking at my fingers as if it is my dick, before I lower my mouth to suck on her clit. I eat her expertly, gobbling up every drop of goodness she's awarding me.

"Noah..." Her back arches as her juices dribble down my fingers. "I... I..."

She finalizes her statement in the most glorious way. She shakes so violently, her vibrations rattle all the way to my cock. I give him a tug, telling him to calm down. His turn is coming; he just needs to be patient.

After bringing Emily down from climax with slow, precise licks to her clit and pussy, I climb up her body, roll her onto her side, then enter her from behind. She shudders for the second time when I feed my cock in as far as it can go before sliding it back out.

She braces her foot on our bedside table, allowing me to get the last two inches of my cock in before cranking her neck back to peer at me. I swear to god I nearly come like a virgin when her eyes lock on mine. I've never seen anything more beautiful than what I'm seeing right now. Her eyes are filled with nothing but happiness and love, and I plan to spend the rest of my life assuring they stay that way.

CHAPTER 63

NOAH

*S*everal orgasms later, Emily and I are lying in our bed. She's in the crook of my arm, tracing my tattoo with her finger. I can tell she's deep in thought, but I don't realize how deep until she asks, "Why did you look frightened when you said, 'till death do us part'?"

I huff, not surprised she noticed my reaction, more annoyed I reacted at all. The subconscious dreams I had while in a coma are still playing havoc with my emotions. Even now, with Emily safely in my arms, I can't help but feel as if I still lost her. I know she's here, but I'm waiting for the other shoe to drop.

When Emily sighs, disappointed I've skirted her interrogation as I have many times the past few months, I lower my forehead to rest against hers. We're further apart than usual, her pregnant tummy keeping a decent gap between us.

After lowering my hand to her belly, I confess the secret I've been keeping. "I thought I lost you both."

Emily's brows stitch, but she remains quiet, waiting for me to elaborate. I don't keep her waiting long. Just that one small truth lifted a ton of weight from my shoulders, so I can't wait to see how much more it eases when I confess to everything.

"The months I was in a coma were the worst months of my life. My biggest fear had become a reality. When Ryan took you away from me, my muddled brain thought you had died."

"Noah..." Emily breathes heavily as she struggles not to cry. "I was there every day, baby; I never left your side."

"I know that now, but at the time, I thought I had lost everything. My entire life was upended..." I stop when the first lot of tears splash down her cheeks. "No tears, remember? I promised only tears of happiness mere hours ago. You don't want me to break my promise, do you?"

When Emily shakes her head, fresh tears spring down her face. She's quick to wipe them away, but not quick enough for me not to notice them.

"I'm sorry. I'm not crying because of what you're saying. It's having something Dr. Miller said months ago confirmed."

Once her cheeks are dry, she exhales a big breath before breaking into a painful script. "Dr. Miller and I didn't see eye to eye at the start. She said some not very nice things about you that pissed me off—"

"That I'm a spoiled rock star who says he's sorry before running off to rehab?"

Emily's pupils dilate to the size of saucers. "How do you know that?" I lose the chance to answer her when she swipes her hand through the air. "Never mind. That's my point. After we settled our differences..." —I smirk when she pulls a face that reveals she defended me as I'll forever defend her— "...Dr. Miller included me in some of the exercises she did with you." Her throat works hard to swallow before she continues. "It didn't take long for us to realize any time my name was mentioned, you reacted in a negative way."

My heart breaks from the devastation in her tone. "Em—"

"It's okay. I understand now. Just at the time, it hurt."

I scoot even closer to her until our tummies touch. "I thought I had lost you. I hated everyone. I was mean and violent and didn't want to live." My eyes dance between hers that are watering. "But not once did I hate you. I would *never* hate you. It just hurt talking about you. Do you understand?"

It's the fight of her life to nod without freeing any of the tears rising in her eyes, but she does it. She keeps them at bay.

"You just need to be patient with me. I thought I'd lost you, so I'll spend the rest of my life loving you as if I did. I'll cherish every single moment we have because I know how quickly things can change. The pain I felt when I thought I had lost you..." I stop when I choke on my words. "It hurt, Em." I bang my chest, shocked it doesn't sound hollow. "It broke me here. It broke me everywhere."

"Baby..."

She cradles my head in her hands before scooting up the bed so she can rest my head on her chest. Her heart is raging as fast as mine, but the comfort it brings is immense. There's no denying its thump. It's robust and healthy, the ultimate proof that she is here, with me, forever.

CHAPTER 64

NOAH

The pounds of Emily's heart alone could lull me to sleep, but add them to the soothing way she's raking her nails over my scalp, and you've got me faintly snoring within a matter of minutes. She's taking care of me as only she can, ensuring my mental health is as robust as my physical health. Without her, I wouldn't be half the man I am.

Emily peers down at me with clear, dry eyes when I murmur, "I love you, Mrs. Taylor,"

"I love you too..." Her words are pushed aside for a groan as pain etches onto her face.

"Em..." I scoot up the bed. "Are you okay?"

She holds her index finger in the air, wordlessly requesting a minute. Instead of speaking, I watch her cautiously. My heart is racing a million miles an hour, my mind blurred with stupid memories I need to let go of, but like a missile coming out of nowhere, the truth smacks into me hard and fast: our baby is coming.

"Is it the baby?" Not waiting for her to reply, I jump out of bed to throw on some clothes.

"I think so."

When she attempts to sit up in the bed, she looks like a turtle stuck on its back. I can't help but chuckle before assisting her into an upright position.

"Thank you." She brushes away the hairs stuck to her temples before raising her eyes to mine. "I think that was my very first contraction."

The joy in her tone surprises me. Don't get me wrong, I'm glad she's excited because I am too, but I'm also crapping my fucking pants.

"What do you want to wear?"

I'm halfway to our walk-in closet when Emily replies, "A nightie."

"A nightie?"

Does she really want to wear pajamas while driving to the hospital?

I shrug. *If a nightie is what she wants, that's what she'll get.*

I rush to Emily's section of our closet. Her clothing options are still as limited as the day we moved in. My side is crammed with designer jeans, leather jackets, and shirts that stretch the entire wall. Emily's handful of vintage rock shirts, skinny jeans, and dresses don't even take up one hanging rack.

The only charges I've seen on our joint credit card are for a one-time purchase at a maternity clothing store in town, and even that purchase was made under duress. Up until last week, she could still fit into her favorite skinny jeans. She couldn't do up the button or fly, but she was adamant wasting money on a maternity wardrobe wasn't necessary. No matter how many times I tell her what's mine is hers, she won't spend a penny she hasn't earned herself.

Although most of Emily's time the past four months has been focused on my recovery, she's snuck in some studying as well. She still has goals and aspirations she's pursuing, and I'm more than happy to help her achieve her dreams. I just wish she had chosen a career not filled with nasty, ruthless people.

Do you know what Emily wants to be when she grows up? A publicist. No, I'm not joking. After everything Delilah put us through, Emily wants to ensure the same thing doesn't happen to new, upcoming stars. She wants them represented with integrity and honor.

Once she's qualified, I have no doubt she'll be inundated with people wanting her to be their publicist. I just hope she doesn't get too popular, because I'd love for Rise Up to remain her number one client.

When Emily told Cormack of her plans, he hired her as an intern at Destiny Records, confident she was the perfect fit for my band. Her internship will be part of her university studies, but unlike many interns, she'll be paid for her services.

Once I got over my shock, I realized it was the perfect solution, because once our baby is born, Rise Up will embark on our first concert tour only a few short months later. Because Emily is Rise Up's publicist, she and our baby will travel everywhere we go.

Isn't it perfect? It's everything I've ever wanted.

After snagging one of Emily's nighties out of her drawers, I race out of our closet. My hurried pace slows when I spot Emily standing next to our bed, gripping the wooden bedpost as she fights through another contraction.

"Breathe like they taught you." While she does that, I rub her back the way the Lamaze instructor showed me.

The panic on her face lessens with each breath she takes. Within a few seconds, her grip on the bedpost loosens. "They *really* hurt."

"Then why are you smiling?"

I already know her answer, but I want her to spell it out for me.

"Because without pain, I'll never deserve the reward at the end."

While smiling at the beautifully smart woman I married, I slip a white cotton nightie over her head before pulling her dark locks out of the neckline.

"Thank you."

My brows stitch when she removes the scatter pillows from our bed. "What are you doing?"

She's in labor. We need to get to the hospital—like now!

When I tell her that, she laughs. "We have hours until we have to leave, so I'm going to get some sleep while I can." She pulls back the covers before slipping between the light blue sheets.

My heart rate triples. "Sleep? You can't sleep. We have to go to the hospital. You can sleep after you've had the baby."

With a roll of her eyes, she scoots across the mattress until there is enough room for me. She pats the bed, inviting me to join her. If she thinks I'll sleep, she has another thing coming. There's no chance in hell I can sleep.

"We have to go, Em."

My voice is laced with a disgusting amount of fear, but she brushes off my concern with a smile. "Babies take ages to come—"

"Uh, no they don't. Jenni had Jasper in under an hour. Nick is lucky he didn't have to deliver him in the parking lot of the hospital. I'm not delivering our baby, Em. I'm not trained for that."

"Come here."

I want to deny her request, but the happiness dazzling in her light brown eyes is too great for me to ignore. When I sit on the edge of our bed, she pulls me back by my shoulders until I'm lying next to her. Her beautiful scent infusing the air soothes some of the irritation prickling my spine. I scoot closer to her, hoping a second bout will take care of any lingering worries.

"You won't have to deliver the baby. I promise." She stares straight into my eyes so I can see the truth beaming from them.

After gathering her into my arms, I squash my lips against her temple. "You better not be making a promise you can't keep."

CHAPTER 65

EMILY

ir hisses through my clenched teeth as I breathe through another contraction. This is one of the most painful things I've ever endured. My stomach tightens so much, I feel like someone has lassoed a rope around my waist, and they're tightening it to the point of strangling me. The pain is intense, much worse than my worst period.

Noah begged me hours ago to go to the hospital, but all the books I read said first babies take hours to come. Jenni was just an exception to that rule. Now I wish I had listened to him sooner. We're two miles from the hospital, which means we're two miles from the people who can make my pain more bearable. Two miles doesn't seem like much in laymen's terms, but when you're in an immense amount of pain, it feels as slow as crossing the Arctic in a recreational fishing boat.

I should have stayed in the shower Noah and I shared the past hour. The hot water rolling down my back was a godsend. It was so sweet, I would have never left if Noah hadn't advised my contractions were five minutes apart. Five minutes was his cut-off point. He refused to let me stay home once my contractions were that close together.

In protest, he gathered me into his arms, carried me down the stairs, placed me in the passenger seat of his truck before making sure my seatbelt was firmly in place, and this is where I've stayed the past ten minutes.

"Is it another one?" Noah questions when he hears my teeth grinding together mere seconds after they unclenched.

Nodding, I snap my eyes shut while struggling to remember the breathing techniques taught in Lamaze class. It does me no good. The pain is too much.

When a scream shreds from my throat, Noah pulls his truck to the side of the road and clasps my hand within his. "Breathe, baby, keep breathing." He rubs his thumb along mine while mimicking the noises I'm supposed to be making.

I attempt to copy him. It somewhat helps.

"That's it. Just like that. You're doing great."

Once the contraction eases, which feels like a good ten or more minutes, even though it's more like thirty seconds, I open my eyes. The first thing I notice is Noah's alarmed gaze staring back at me. "They're three minutes apart now."

I smile. Three minutes is good. It means we're getting closer to meeting our baby.

"Are you okay? Should I keep going?"

When I nod, he pulls his truck back onto the asphalt.

"You don't have to pull over for every contraction. It's sweet, but it will make our trip to the hospital twice as long."

Noah's eyes shift from the road to me. His brows are furrowed, his mouth ajar. "Yes, I do. There's no way I can concentrate on the road and help you through the pain."

I'm about to tell him I can handle it when another contraction rips through my body without notice. As I scream through the pain tearing me in two, Noah yanks his truck back off the road.

"Breathe, Emily."

I hear the command in his snapped tone, but nothing can take away the pain. I'm screaming without mercy as tears stream down my face and snot bubbles in my nostrils. I'm certain I'm seconds from dying when Noah unclasps his seatbelt before sliding across the bench seat to cradle me into his chest, assuring me I'm not.

"It's okay, Beautiful, you're okay, just keep breathing," he whispers in my ear as he soothingly rubs my back. "You're doing great; you've just got to remember to breathe."

"It fuckin' hurts," I cry into his chest. "I can't do this; it hurts too much. I'm not strong enough."

"Yes, you can. You can do this. I know you can." He removes the sweaty hairs sticking to my temples before raising my eyes to his via my chin. "You are so strong and brave, so if anyone can do this, it will be you."

Our eyes dart down in sync when a small pop sounds through our ears at the same time my nightie soaks through. My water just broke all over his red leather interior. With my eyes bugged, I return them to Noah. He appears as if he's going to be sick at any moment.

"Is the contraction gone?"

When I nod, he dives into his seat, shifts into gear, then takes off down the road like a maniac. "You better not have made a promise you can't keep, Em!" He flattens his accelerator to the floor. "Close your legs!"

I can't help but laugh at his request. "Closing my legs won't stop our baby from coming."

"Don't say that. It's not funny."

His face is as white as a ghost when he weaves his truck in and out of the traffic. I giggle even louder. I've never seen him so nervous. He usually oozes cockiness, but now, he just looks shocked and scared—nearly as panicked as he was when he told me what he dreamed about while in his coma. My heart broke for him during his confession.

Dr. Miller had theories on why he always clenched his fists when she mentioned me. Now I know her theories were accurate. Excluding the day I went to my appointment to ensure our baby was safe, I never left Noah's side. Not once. I often whispered in his ear and snuggled into his side, but I thought the heavy sedation he was under was why he never acknowledged my presence like he did

Jacob's. I had no clue it was because he was trying to block out his pain because he thought he had lost me.

I wish I could block out my pain like he did when another contraction hits me full force. While my nails dig into the dashboard, I scream in pain.

"Hold on, Em; we're nearly there."

Noah's truck pulls into the emergency bay just as my contraction eases. It's the same hospital where he recovered. I haven't been back here since he left a little over fifteen weeks ago. Seems more like a lifetime. His strength still amazes me. The fact he overcame his injuries and is living his life to the fullest makes tears spring to my eyes.

As painful memories flood into me, Noah helps me down from his truck. "Careful."

When he scoops me into his arms, my eyes drift to the no parking sign next to his truck. "You have to move your truck, or they'll tow it."

"Let them tow it. You're more important."

Once we're outside the locked double doors of the delivery suite, he places me on my feet before hitting the intercom button.

"Hello," greets a voice over the intercom. "How can we help you?"

"My wife, Emily, is in labor."

I'm in an immense amount of pain, but a smile still stretches across my face. This is the first time he's called me his wife in public. When a loud buzz declares the door has been unlocked, Noah pushes it open before attempting to scoop me back into his arms. I assure him I can walk, but I barely make it three steps when another contraction buckles my knees.

Noah gathers me off the floor before running to the nurse's desk in the middle of the delivery suite. One look at his panicked face tells the midwives everything they need to know. They usher us into a private room before directing Noah to place me on the bed.

He does so before spinning around to face them. "You need to give her something for the pain."

A midwife with gray hair brings over a cart filled with scary-looking instruments. "After we've assessed her, we'll discuss pain relief."

"No, now. She's hurting bad. *Please* help her."

The plea in Noah's tone is too much for her to bear, so she peers at me past his shoulder. "Do you need pain relief?"

Noah stares at me in shock when I shake my head. "Let them give you something," he insists after pacing to my bedside.

I shake my head again. "No, I don't want anything. I can do this. You said so yourself."

He has overcome so much pain and heartache in his life. If he can survive that, I can handle the pain of bringing our child into the world. I'm strong too, and I want him to see that.

"Are you sure, Em?"

"Yes, I'm sure," I reply just as a blinding contraction has me regretting every decision I've ever made.

CHAPTER 66

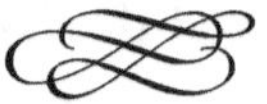

NOAH

Emily rolls into a ball as she screams through the pain ripping through her body. I try to offer her comfort and support, but I don't know what the fuck I'm doing. I can't take her pain away, and she's refusing pain relief, so I'm at a loss on how I can help her.

When her cries become too painful for me to bear, I hold her hand before reminding her about how strong she is.

The midwife who brought us into the room adds to my encouraging words. "Good girl, Emily. Just remember to keep breathing. Big breaths through your nose and out your mouth."

As the midwife glances down at a silver watch attached to her chest, Emily's wide, scared eyes lift to mine. "I… need… to… push." She pants between each word, the pain in her voice unmissable.

With my panic at never-before-reached levels, my gaze snaps to the midwife. She's rapidly gathering equipment from around the room. "Hit the buzzer."

I glance at all the buttons on the wall. There are several different ones, so which one does she want me to push?

She rolls Emily onto her back before answering my silent question, "The call nurse one."

While my finger jabs the button on repeat, Emily releases a long, penetrating scream. I've never heard a noise come out of her like that before. She sounds like she's possessed.

As a pager announces assistance is needed in Room 22, I devote my attention back to the midwife strapping Emily's legs into stirrups.

"Where's her doctor?"

Emily has seen Dr. Morgan weekly for the past six weeks. He advised he'd meet us at the hospital when I called him before I forced Emily into my truck. Thank fuck I didn't let her stubbornness deter me from getting her to the hospital.

"There isn't enough time." After tightening a strap to Emily's leg, the midwife peers at Emily. "Your baby's head is crowning, Emily, so when you feel a contraction, I need you to push."

A second young blonde-haired midwife joins us. "You need to calm down and breathe, Emily. You're in good hands; you've done so well." She scans paperwork coming out of a machine next to Emily's bed before her blue eyes drift to mine. "Help her calm down. Your baby's heart rate is very high; he's stressed, so we need everyone to take in some big breaths."

I nod, aware Emily needs me now more than ever. After placing my arm around her shoulders, I press my lips to her ear. "You can do this, Beautiful; you're strong and brave. I'm so proud of you. You just need to breathe like the Lamaze instructor showed you."

I feel like a fucking idiot breathing as if I'm in labor, but I'd do it in front of millions if it has the same results. Emily's screams diminish the more she pants.

"Good girl. You're doing it."

Her fingernails pierce my skin when she fights through another contraction.

"Okay, Emily, pull your chin in close to your chest, and push right down deep into your bottom."

I repeat the midwife's instructions to Emily. She nods before balancing her chin on her chest and pushing with all her might. Her torso raises off the bed as she squeezes my hand so firmly my bones creak. I endure the pain, certain it is nothing on the suffering Emily is currently experiencing. She bites her lip so hard during each push, she's probably close to drawing blood.

She suffers through several contractions in the same manner before the midwife announces one last push should see our baby delivered. "Good girl, Emily. When you feel another contraction, push with all your might."

While sucking in long, ragged breaths, Emily's tired eyes lift to mine.

"You're doing it," I beam. I'm so fucking proud of her, my heart is beating out a tune I've never heard.

"You're about to become a daddy..." Her words are pushed aside for a grunt.

"Okay, Emily, push again, right down low into your bottom. Take a big breath then push."

Emily sucks in a huge breath before she bears down again. Just as her lips are freed from her teeth, she lets out a long, ragged scream.

"Stop pushing and pant," the midwife instructs Emily.

"Pant, Emily, pant," I whisper into her ear, recalling how imperative the Lamaze instructor said this part was.

Emily pants as requested, and not long later, we hear the tiny cries of our baby. Emily flops back onto the bed, relieved the pain is finally over, while our midwife lifts up our baby to show Emily her reward for all the pain she endured.

"It's a girl," announces the midwife as she moves our screaming bundle to the humidicrib located at the side of the room.

"A girl?" Emily mutters in disbelief. She was so convinced we were having a little boy, she only packed blue sleepers in her hospital bag.

"I told you it was a girl!" I press a kiss to her sweat-drenched head. "I'm so proud of you."

My eyes float between hers when she drags her hands across my wet cheeks. I was so caught up in the miracle of childbirth, I hadn't noticed the sneaky tears that fell down my cheeks. I quickly scrub my hand across my face, not wanting to look like a pussy, but in all honesty, seeing our baby girl being born was the most exhilarating thing I've ever experienced. She is proof that insta-love exists, because the moment I laid my eyes on her, I knew I'd love her for the rest of my life—just like her mother.

My heart beats in an unnatural rhythm when the midwife heads our way with a bundle of pink in her arms. When she hands our daughter to Emily, fresh tears burn my eyes. I wear these tears with pride.

"She has your dimples," Emily gushes as she loosens the blanket wrapped around our daughter.

I smile when I spot two perfectly placed dimples in her cheeks. Her sprouts of hair are as dark as her mother's, but her eyes are currently blue. She has her mother's turned-up nose, but the shape of my face. She is the perfect mix of us both.

I run my index finger down her chubby cheek before tracking it across her tiny hand, which has poked out from the blanket. When she snags my finger in her hand, my heart flips.

Emily sighs before teasing me, "Daddy will be wrapped around your little finger, won't he?"

I don't care what anyone says; anything my baby girl wants, she'll have. I'm planning to spoil her and her mother for the rest of my life.

"What shall we name her?"

We never discussed baby names. Emily was so adamant we were having a boy, she picked the name Maddox. I liked the name, so we had no reason to discuss the matter any further.

"I don't think Maddox will work for a girl."

Emily ribs me with her elbow before lowering her eyes to our little girl. I do the same while striving to think of a name to match her adorable face. She is as beautiful as her mother; her cheeks are just ten times chubbier.

"What about Maddie? It's strong but cute, just like her mommy."

Emily's eyes snap to mine. "Maddie," she murmurs, testing out the name on her lips. "I like it."

"Maddison Grace Taylor?"

Emily's mom's middle name is Grace, so I think it's fitting for her granddaughter to follow the tradition of having her grandmother's middle name. Emily has her grandmother's middle name, even though she hates it.

"It's perfect." Emily uses my shirt to pull my lips to hers. "You're perfect."

And just like that, our duo becomes a trio, and I have another little person I'm terrified to lose.

EPILOGUE

NOAH

Two years later...

The waistband of my jeans absorbs the sweat gliding down my back. I'm not joking this time when I say I need to remove my shirt because the stage lights are roasting my skin. The spotlight following my every move makes it seem as if I'm standing on the sun.

When I lift the hem of my shirt to rub away the sweat descending from my temples to my chin, the crowd catches a glimpse of the tattoos I've collected the past two years. They let out a roar, closely followed by numerous requests to remove my shirt.

As I continue belting out the lyrics to "Hollow," I glance over at my wife who is standing in the wings of the stage. She's wrangling a feisty Maddie, who doesn't want to wear the baby pink earmuffs required to ensure her hearing doesn't get damaged while listening to her daddy's band play. Maddie has attended every concert I've performed at; she's never missed a show, and neither has her mother.

Once Emily wins the earmuff battle, she nods, encouraging me to remove my shirt. She's not stupid; her job as the publicist for Rise Up is to get the band exposure money can't buy. Sex sells, so she's willing to let others "ogle my assets," as long as she gets full access to those so-called assets after each concert. There's nothing I love more than watching my wife's eyes fill with lust from watching me perform, so I'm more than happy to fulfill her side of our agreement.

After whipping off my shirt, I throw it into the crowd. Several women in the front row fight over it, proving they haven't become any less vicious in their attempts to capture my attention. Delilah's concerns about me needing to remain attainable to our fans was nothing more than a crock of shit. My wedding photos were splashed on the front cover of every gossip magazine in the country, and I bear my wife and daughter's names on my chest, yet I'm still propositioned at the end of every concert.

It's lucky Emily trusts me, but there's been a handful of times I've had to step between her and overeager fans. Most fans are respectful, but I've been caught unaware by groupies trying to ram their tongues down my throat when I think they're coming in for an innocent peck on the cheek.

Emily was on to them fast, telling them they're disrespectful pieces of shit for attempting to steal a married man away from his family. She has said multiple times she can't understand why groupies act the way they do. I personally don't think they'll ever be understood, but they are, unfortunately, a part of our industry.

Although I shouldn't love Emily's jealous streak, I do.

I can't say the same for my annoying neurosis. I don't just have to be cautious about the roadies hitting on my wife. I have to deal with the likes of men like Isaac. It became apparent after his debt was repaid that Isaac didn't help the band for his brother. He did it for Emily.

An hour of dancing, and he was hooked. He'd never admit it, but I think he was hoping I'd succumb to my injuries, so he could fly in and sweep Emily off her feet. I fucked with his plan when I came back to her.

You should have seen the expression on his face when he learned Emily was pregnant. He looked like he was going to be sick. Isaac is a great guy, but he needed to keep his gray eyes on someone other than my wife. I told him exactly that when Emily went to fetch him a drink. He swore he wasn't looking at her like I thought, but I didn't believe him. There was something more than friendship behind his fascination with Emily. I just have no clue what it was.

My thoughts shift back to the present when Slater counts in our next song. Tonight, we're performing at AT&T Park in San Francisco. It's just as I dreamed it would be, although we're no longer the opening act. We are the main event. We have over sixty thousand attendees at our show, and the vibe is electric.

Our second album, *Next Coming,* skyrocketed up the charts even quicker than our first. It didn't stay in the number one spot as long as our first, but our single, "Eyes like Her Mother's" went straight to number one upon its release. It's the song I wrote for our daughter, Maddison. She's the spitting image of her mother, except for her dimples and her attitude. She loves being in the spotlight and craves attention. Even when we're getting hassled by the paparazzi, Maddie grins at them before giving them the peace sign like Jacob taught her. Everyone falls in love with her.

I'd initially wanted to keep her out of the spotlight, but she thinks she's the rock star of the family, so I can't stop her from doing something she loves. She just turned two and has more spunk than her mother and me combined.

As I reach the end of our set, Emily places Maddie down on the ground. With a squeal, she runs over to leap into my arms. Her curly brown hair bounces as she waves at the crowd with excitement. We finish every concert the same way each time we perform.

"Say hello to our fans, Maddie."

"Wello!"

The crowd coos at her cuteness, adoring that she hasn't worked out her H sound yet.

She gives the crowd a peace sign before sprinting to Jasper, who is hiding behind his daddy's leg. Jasper's personality is the complete opposite of Maddie's. He's shy, and she's dominant.

The poor kid doesn't have a clue what he's in for. I would warn him, but that would be like Emily cautioning Jenni to stay away from Nick. You can tell them until you're blue in the face that it isn't a good idea, but they'll never listen. You can't help who you fall in love with, and I think Jasper is already madly, deeply in love with Maddie.

I salute our fans before making my way off stage to give Emily a long, scorching kiss. Our kiss lasts as long as our fans' shouted requests for an encore, but it's nowhere near long enough to appease the hunger I have for my wife. I'll never get enough of her.

After pulling back from her plump lips, I glide my finger down Emily's flushed cheek. "Have you heard from Jacob?"

Her smile switches to a frown. "No. Not yet."

I exhale a big breath as panic makes itself known in my gut. Everything in my life has finally worked out like I had hoped, so now I need to stand at Jacob's side, supporting him until he too gets the life he deserves.

Part two in the Perception Series is *Jacob's* book. It is available now.
<u>Fighting Jacob</u>

Do you know there's a novella that fills in the three months Noah was in his coma from *Emily's POV*. You can find out how he stumbled into that dark and tormented place by what occurred around him. You can find the book under: <u>Saving Emily</u>

Join my Facebook page:
www.facebook.com/authorshandi

Join my READER's group:
https://www.facebook.com/groups/1740600836169853/

Join my Newsletter:
Subscribepage.com/AuthorShandi

If you enjoyed this book - please leave a review.

Lady In Waiting

Man in Queue

Couple on Hold

Enigma: The Wedding

Silent Vigilante

Hushed Guardian

Quiet Protector

Enigma: An Isaac Retelling

Twisted Lies *

Bound Series

Chains

Links

Bound

Restrain

The Misfits *

Nanny Dispute *

Russian Mob Chronicles

Nikolai: A Mafia Prince Romance

Nikolai: Taking Back What's Mine

Nikolai: What's Left of Me

Nikolai: Mine to Protect

Asher: My Russian Revenge *

Nikolai: Through the Devil's Eyes

Trey *

The Italian Cartel

Dimitri